A Rainbow Book

Praise for *21 Aldgate*—

"I read it with the greatest interest . . . a fascinating and absorbing look into the past."

—Sir Martin Gilbert, Churchill biographer and bestselling author of *Churchill and the Jews: A Lifelong Friendship*

". . . while some of the thoughts and actions in *21 Aldgate* are indeed fiction, there is a strong element of reality present throughout. That and the integrity of all the main characters makes *21 Aldgate* a standout. Alas, for me, *The Oriental Wife* simply paled in comparison to *21 Aldgate*. . . ."

—Donna Bird, SleepingHedgehog.com

"Anyone with a tie to London's East End is likely to enjoy Patricia Friedberg's latest novel."

—Candace Kreiger, *London Jewish Chronicle*

"Patricia Friedberg's *21 Aldgate* is a book for the movie-goers who sat in Memphis theaters recently and applauded at the end of *The King's Speech* and *Sarah's Key*."

—Rosemary Nelms, editor of the "Author, Author" column, *The Commercial Appeal* (Memphis, TN)

"Patricia Friedberg's *21 Aldgate* has been a very popular pick with our area book clubs. Combining all the best elements of historical fiction with an illicit affair make it the must-read novel of early 2011."

—Ashley Dacus, manager, Davis-Kidd Booksellers (Memphis, TN)

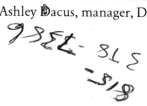

continued

"The vicissitudes of World War II are splendidly delineated in this intriguing novel."

—*Jewish Book World*

"In *21 Aldgate* Patricia Friedberg — a wonderfully compelling writer— brings the reader into a pre-war and WWII London that had been unknown to many of us Americans, certainly to me. She gives a clear picture of the hardships German bombings brought to London's citizens while telling the story of a strong young woman and her resilient family. We follow the main character, Clara, through her love affair with a famous artist and through her adventures as a spy during the war. But the hero(es) of the book are the British people and the bravery with which they faced the threat of an enemy near at hand. This one is well worth reading."

—Georgia Court, owner, Bookstore 1 (Sarasota, FL)

21 Aldgate

PATRICIA FRIEDBERG

Rainbow Books, Inc.
FLORIDA

The Library of Congress has cataloged the hardcover edition as follows:

Friedberg, Patricia, 1934-
    21 Aldgate / Patricia Friedberg. — 1st ed.
        p. cm.
    ISBN 978-1-56825-124-0 (alk. paper)
    1. Jewish families—England—London—Fiction. 2. World War, 1939-1945—England—
Fiction. 3. London (England)—History—Bombardment, 1940-1945—Fiction. 4. East
End (London, England)—Fiction. I. Title. II. Title: Twenty-one Aldgate.
    PS3606.R553A613 2010
    813'.6—dc22

                                        2009051062

21 Aldgate Copyright © 2010 Patricia Friedberg
softcover ISBN: 978-1-56825-142-4

Published by

Rainbow Books, Inc., P. O. Box 430, Highland City, FL 33846-0430
www.RainbowBooksInc.com, rbibooks@aol.com

Editorial Offices and Wholesale/Distributor Orders

Telephone (863) 648-4420

Individuals' Orders

Toll-free Telephone (800) 431-1579
www.BookCH.com, www.AllBookStores.com, www.Amazon.com

Winston Churchill's speeches are reproduced with permission of
Curtis Brown Ltd, London on behalf of The Estate of Winston Churchill.
Copyright © Winston S. Churchill

The author acknowledges she has researched and used the internet for information
with reference to Paul Maze and has in her possession his book, *A Frenchman in
Khaki*, with a preface by the Rt. Hon. Winston Churchill, London, Toronto, W.
Heinemann, Ltd. 1934 and an inscription by the author. All references to Paul Maze
are either fictional or drawn from his own account of his experiences in the First
World War.

The paper used in this publication meets the minimum requirements of the American
National Standard for Information Sciences — Permanence of Paper for Printed
Library Materials, ANSI Z39.48-1984.

First softcover edition 2012

15 14 13 12   5 4 3 2 1

Printed in the United States of America.

For Mandy, Adrienne, Richard and Adam

Acknowledgments

To MaryAnn Amato, my friend and producer of the feature film based on *21 Aldgate*, I owe more than I can say. Her patience, her determination and her loyalty are far beyond anything I could ever have hoped for. Without her neither the book nor the film would have survived.

I wish to thank those who read the early version of *21 Aldgate*. Virginia Riebe, Richard and Barbara Steinfirst, Martin and Barbara Yamnicky, William and Barbara Rizer, Lewis Cross, Cindy Everhart, Thomas D. Lee, Marjorie "Bunny" Tabatznik. Together they gave me the confidence to go on, write and rewrite until my publisher's editor said, "You're done!"

To Roy Howard who traipsed through London looking for maps and old documents in all weathers; Michael and Sandra Sawyer who searched out books on the East End of London; Leslie and Leila Dubow and Michael and Maria Howard who gave me shelter on my many visits back to London, Anne Young for her French translation, George Akers for his help with the German chapters, and to Rudi and Joan Schnuerch for the German translation and who, over the years of our friendship have reinforced what I've always believed, that it's politicians who create war and not those who are summoned to fight them. True friendship knows no geographic boundaries.

And finally in memory of my mother Clara, who lived *21 Aldgate*. At the age of ninety-nine she said, "Living is easy, but dying is hard." She knew when it was time to depart this world, and she left reminding us she would be looking down from Cloud Nine, watching over all those who'd impacted her life and, by so doing, helped her become the remarkable woman she was. I miss her and will always miss her.

Prologue

Prologue

THE SEPTEMBER SUN shone brightly through the French doors leading to Clara Simon's well cared for English garden as she sat down in a comfortable arm chair, a light lunch before her, ready to watch the one o' clock news. She'd had her shower, studied her naked image reflected in the full length mirror, and said to herself, as she had so many times before, "Not bad for ninety-five."

Pleased with her own approval, she'd decided on the day's apparel. Linen slacks and the blue knit top recently purchased from Marks and Spencer. Clara wasn't about to wear old lady clothes. Not for her widow's weeds. Her late husband objected when she wore black, so muted colors were never part of her wardrobe. He had liked her in blue — matched the color of her eyes. Always a bit of a romantic, he was.

Age was of no consequence to Clara, apart from wanting to receive the Queen's telegram for achieving the grand age of one hundred. After that she'd decide whether to stay around for another year. "When it's time to go, I'll go," she informed her daughter Victoria. "I know Daddy's up there waiting for me; he'll just have to wait a little longer."

Clara picked up the TV remote and clicked on to the BBC. No news there. Just some movie she didn't want to watch. She tried other channels. The same movie appeared each time. She clicked on CNN. There it was again — the same movie. The news should be on. Then the awful realization began to dawn as she read the tape running below the picture. It was morning in New York, five hours behind London's time; and this was a live broadcast.

Something dreadful had happened in New York City, and every channel was covering it. The Twin Towers, internationally familiar

3

landmarks in Manhattan, were disappearing in a cloud of concrete dust and shattered glass. She'd gone to the top of one of them when she was last in America. Those monstrous, indestructible monoliths were imploding, collapsing, falling with thousands of people inside, unable to get out, trapped or jumping from windows, all annihilated before her eyes.

Clara had lived through two world wars and close to a century in London, and never in all her life had she seen or experienced anything to compare with what was playing out now on the television screen.

Earlier that morning her daughter, Victoria, had called from her hotel to say goodbye. She was to catch a late afternoon plane back to the States. There was no way of getting hold of her. Surely she will phone again, Clara thought. Then she wondered frantically: Where is she?

As VICTORIA WAITED in the lobby of the Langham Hotel for a taxi, a television in the bar area was attracting attention, people rushing to it. "To see what?" she asked the concierge.

"Two planes. One crashed into one of the Twin Towers in New York, another flew into the second one. First they said it was an accident, now the story's changed. It's a terrorist attack. All airports across the globe have been shut down. I suggest you forgo your drive to Heathrow, madam."

Victoria pushed her way into the crowd around the television. Was this really happening? What to do first? Call her children, her mother? She hurried back to the desk where she had just checked out and tried to book in for another night, maybe two. The clerks were bewildered, unable to function, glued to television sets and computer screens. Eventually she managed to attract a clerk's attention. "I just checked out. I want to book my room for another night, maybe two. And I need to make a phone call."

"You can do that from your room, madam; it hasn't been reallocated yet." He spoke like an automaton, his mind not on anything other than what was happening on the TV screen.

"Just give me the key," Victoria impatiently demanded.

Back in the room she turned on the television and sat glued to it. She tried to call her family in New York. No calls were going through; the lines were jammed. She phoned her mother.

Clara ran to pick up the phone. "Oh, thank God. I thought you'd left already. What's happening? What am I looking at? Is it real? What about my grandchildren — Emma and Peter? They live in New York; are they all right?"

More questions. No answers.

"I can't get through to the children right now. I will try again later," Victoria said. "I'm staying at the hotel until flights are resumed; it's total confusion. I'll just have to wait until they let me know. Turn off the television, Mother. It will only upset you more."

"No, I have to watch. Renee, my neighbor, just came in. She'll stay with me. We're both crying. I'm beside myself with worry. Keep phoning the children. I won't rest until I know they are safe. What is this world coming to, my darling?"

"I don't know, Mummy; whatever it is, it isn't good. I'll ring you when I can get through to New York — I love you."

EVENTUALLY THE TELEPHONE lines cleared, and Victoria made contact with her children in New York. They were in shock like everyone else.

"It's awful, Mom, clouds of debris, dirt and only God-knows-what everywhere — on the pavements, on the window ledges, thick clouds of it rolling in on Broadway. Joan's husband works in one of the Towers. She doesn't know if he managed to escape. She's frantic. People are walking around with photos asking strangers in the street if they've seen this or that person. It started out a beautiful morning; it's actually dark now. The pollution has reached the west side of town right where we live. I've closed all the windows. I can't go out. None of us can go out. The air is thick with dust and dirt. Nothing we can do but wait. Call again, Mom; we don't know any more than you do right now. Can you give Grandma Clara a call? Tell her we're safe, bewildered but all right. When I get a dial tone I'll try to call her. It's a miracle you got through."

The conversation ended, and the television droned on. Every aircraft in the United States of America was on the ground. The entire country was locked down. There was no way she was going to leave London today.

Suddenly Victoria felt like a voyeur watching death take life indiscriminately. She had to get out of the room, go somewhere, take a walk in the park, anything other than see the same scenes repeated over and over again. It was shameful, heartbreaking and unbearable. In a split second of time, life on earth, not just on her little piece of earth, but on the entire planet, had taken a different course, a tragic, evil, dangerous course. Terrorists had shut down the world's airways, closed airports and held all travel in their grasp. Al-Qaeda proudly took responsibility for the assault on the Twin Towers while America counted its dead.

Victoria phoned her mother again. Clara answered on the third ring. "Victoria! Oh, tell me, please tell me — the family is safe."

"Everyone's safe, Mummy. They're all safe. Peter is close to the Twin Towers, well, what *was* the Twin Towers. He's up on the roof of his building taking photographs — "

"He shouldn't be breathing that polluted air; tell him I said to get down to his flat immediately."

"Mother." Victoria called Clara *mother* when she wanted to get Clara's attention. "Make a cup of tea, turn off the television and sit in the garden."

"No. I will not. I cannot. Who did this? What maniacs did this? Can you come over?"

"Later — when I have some idea of when the planes will be flying again."

"I have to see you before you leave."

"I'll be there. I'm staying over night. Heathrow is closed. Emma will phone you. She promised."

Victoria replaced the phone in its cradle and began to pace like a caged animal in her hotel room. She thought about turning off the TV, but it seemed sacrilegious to do so. Then she remembered. She'd planned to visit the London art galleries before leaving for the States, but time had run away from her; theatre and family had taken precedence. Why not go now? Watching television wasn't going to help anyone in New York. She rummaged in her suitcase for a clean blouse, put on a comfortable pair of shoes, applied lipstick and closed the door behind her, leaving the TV on. She took the lift to the ground floor.

The lobby was teeming with people, demanding rooms, asking questions, wanting answers. French, German, Hungarians, every nationality. And Americans, a woman sobbing, sitting on her suitcase. A New Yorker on his cell phone, a family from San Francisco wanting to get back home, it was all too much. Victoria walked out of the hotel into the late afternoon sunshine to the taxi rank. The concierge was nowhere to be seen. She beckoned a driver. He drove up; she got in.

Londoners were going about their business, still in shock, still in disbelief and probably thinking if it happened in New York, it could happen there.

"Bond Street, please," The driver looked foreign. Dark skinned. She wondered whether he was a Muslim. He couldn't be drawn into conversation. Better to stay quiet, perhaps.

She stared out of the window; everything seemed to be happening in slow motion. Piccadilly Circus was uncannily quiet. In Hyde Park the deck chairs stood empty. The driver turned into Oxford Street and was held up in a traffic jam outside Selfridges.

"I'll get out here," she told the driver.

"Four pounds." He held out his hand for the money.

She gave him four pounds and an extra fifty pence, and he drove off. Not even a thank you. Perhaps he was ashamed. Perhaps he was scared. She looked at her watch. She had about two hours to wander and a five minute walk to get to where she wanted to be.

The Bond Street galleries were open. She went into a few of them, saw the Tissot collection, and an R. L. Lowrie exhibition several doors down. Sotheby's had some interesting paintings on view for an upcoming auction, medieval art, not her favorite. She didn't stay long. Out on the street she walked up to the bronze sculpture of Churchill and Roosevelt sitting on a bench, so lifelike, as if in person, talking to each other. If only you were both here now, she thought.

She wanted to get to Cork Street, where contemporary art was more likely to be shown.

It was in a Cork Street gallery window that she came upon a watercolor by Paul Maze, a name she recalled from her childhood. Her mother had worked with him many years ago, helped write a book called, *A Frenchman in Khaki*. The door was locked. She knocked, hoping she'd be allowed in. A young man came to the door and opened up. "We keep our doors locked now; can't be too careful."

"I understand."

"Terrible news today."

"Yes, awful."

He didn't seem to know what to say next. Then, gathering his thoughts, he said, "We're showing a retrospective of the work of Mr. Maze. Are you familiar with his paintings?"

"Oh, yes, yes, I know him," Victoria answered as she tried to recollect the past, and her memory failed her.

"Did you know he was also a writer?" He picked up a book from his desk and handed it to her. "*A Frenchman in Khaki*. It's just been reissued."

The cover wasn't familiar; otherwise it was exactly the same as the one on the bookshelves of her parents' home. It had been there for as long as she could remember.

"I know this book," she said, returning it to him.

He took it and stepped away to allow her to view the exhibition.

One particular piece caught her attention, a painting of a young woman surrounded by a field of sunflowers. Victoria stood before the painting for a long interval. There was something familiar here. Still, she couldn't put her finger on it. Finally she moved on to view the remainder of the show. But in the end she returned to the sunflower painting to become lost in its simplicity. Yes, there was something special here, something haunting. She didn't know what it was. Perhaps it was the shy smile on the young woman's lovely face; it was almost as if that shy smile held a secret. Or perhaps it was nothing more than the sea of sunflowers. The terror of the day faded, the serenity of sunflowers, just for the moment, allowed her to let go of the image of disaster awaiting her in New York.

The young man came to stand beside her. "Mr. Maze did a series of sunflower paintings." He pointed out the one she happened to like. "This is from his private collection, part of his estate. Mr. Maze passed away in 1979. He was ninety-two." He waited a few moments. "Lovely, isn't it?"

"Yes, it is." Victoria examined the painting closely; there was something about it that drew her to it. Was it because she remembered knowing him slightly when she was a very small child? She shrugged off lost memories. "I would like to buy it," she said, as surprised at herself as was the young attendant selling it.

The 1930s

CHAPTER 1

Clara

IT WAS A Friday, nearing Clara Simon's lunch hour, and she had finally made up her mind to take the plunge. No longer could she tolerate Ernest Maxwell Abbott's slurs and outbursts.

Abbott had come sputtering into the outer office and at the top of his voice announced to the entire office staff, "Jews requiring my assistance are to be put on a very long waiting list; better still, advise them our quota is filled." He proceeded to throw a folder onto Clara's desk, directing her to file it or destroy it, he didn't mind which. He topped his outburst with what would be his final insult:

"In the future my regular gentile clients will take precedence over every off-the-boat immigrant!"

Abbott, who prided himself on his grammar school education, had often responded negatively when having to deal with foreigners, though up to now it hadn't prevented him accepting Jewish clients. He disguised his inferiority complex by blustering his way through most of his cases. Not having attended university, as the more distinguished of his profession were privileged to do, he'd received his legal training the old fashioned way, being articled to a law firm for five years. Dealing with foreigners demeaned his reputation — or so he said

Carruthers, the solicitor's clerk, knew a thing or two about Abbott, not the least of them being his delight in avoiding income tax. Said Carruthers, "Cash on the table, don't have to send bills, takes their money, gives them a few words of advice, then sends them packing. No skin off his nose — next month, maybe next week, when he needs a few extra bob, he'll ask why they've gone missing — that's why he puts up with them." So, Abbott had good reason to remain in Whitechapel, not too far from where Clara lived, seemingly indifferent to his posh partners in the city.

Clara knew Carruthers was right. If Abbott sluffed off a few Jews, what did it matter? He could always rely on her to find him a few more.

Clara couldn't fault Carruthers. He earned his weekly wage, never spoke out of turn and kept his mouth shut. He was Abbott's lackey; it just didn't occur to him that she might be offended.

She'd made up her mind. She was moving on. She would no longer be a sounding board for Abbott's constant remarks on "a bunch of filthy foreigners unable to speak the English language and apparently unwilling to learn it." In his pompous, mercenary way, there was no covering up for his irrational behavior.

"Immigrants," he'd told her repeatedly in the past, and now said again, "should respect the law, stay out of sight or go back where they came from." He was an ungrateful, insensitive, anti-Semitic hypocrite who took advantage of the poor and never stopped complaining. He had money in his pocket, and what his partners in the city weren't aware of, he wasn't about to tell them. The cash was his — no need to share it with the tax man or his partners, and he wasn't expecting Clara to pull the carpet out from under him.

Clara followed Abbott back into his office. She slammed the folder he had just thrown on her desk on to his, and with that she announced, "Find someone else, Mr. Abbott. I'm leaving. Under no circumstances will I be back."

"Now come, come, Mrs. Simon, I didn't mean you. You are different from those demanding Jews who venture into this establishment. You have poise. You are an intelligent young woman. You could even pass for one of us."

Clara looked directly at Abbott, her face red with anger, and speaking in a voice she struggled to control said, "I wouldn't want to pass for one of your lot if they were the last survivors on the planet. I have no need to disguise or deny my heritage because of the likes of you. In case it has slipped your observation, we are all members of the human race, and we all deserve to be treated with respect and dignity. You can post my paycheck to my home address." With this final parting remark Clara left the employ of Ernest Maxwell Abbott.

The feeling of satisfaction didn't last long; in fact, it was gone the moment she stepped into the rickety lift and pushed the ground floor button. The realization of what she had done hit her. She had given up a perfectly good, well-paying job because of a prejudiced boss whom she should have had the guts to confront earlier. You have to stand up to bullies, that's what Mum had told her when she was a kid in school, not run away from them and let them believe their behavior is acceptable. That's what she had done, and it was obvious to her that Abbott wouldn't change his attitude. He'd just go through a series of employees until he retired.

So, what now?

Far more people were looking for jobs than having them; she would soon be replaced, and she'd be the one looking for work. At the same time she tried to think how to explain her hasty retreat to her husband Sidney and the family. Sidney wouldn't be that difficult; it was the rest of them. They would all have an opinion, and they'd express it, asked for or not. No use going home in mid-afternoon; it would immediately send up a red flag. She couldn't face any of them without a fully thought-out explanation, and what was more to the point, a plan for the future — not that she had one.

She buttoned her coat as she hurried along the street. It was cold and miserable, though no one appeared particularly concerned about the weather as they went about their business. Good day for the sale of wooly scarves and fur hats nicely displayed on stalls outside the fashion establishments on the Mile End Road. These were the fellows starting up in business and not yet ready or able to afford a real shop. Hard working lads, all of them, out in the heat of summer or the cold of winter, selling their goods to suit the season. Always had umbrellas on hand, one of their best sellers, the English weather being what it was. April showers may have brought forth May flowers; nothing stopped it teeming down throughout the rest of the year.

"Furs for your 'eads and scarves for yer necks; what more could a pretty girl like you need to make your life complete?" a bloke in a balaclava shouted.

"'Ow about an 'usband? I'm available," his mate suggested.

She thought about answering, "A job might help," but when one engaged them in conversation it wasn't easy to get away without making a purchase. She could have sold them just as fine a collection; she had drawers full of hats and scarves back where she lived at Twenty-One. Instead she gave them a smile and walked on, as if in a hurry.

She needed to think — a cup of tea might do the trick, give her time to work things out. The teashops in the East End were noisy and smoky, and someone she knew was bound to be sitting at one of the tables. The last thing she needed now was to explain to some nosey parker why she wasn't at work. No, having told Abbott she would not be back and still feeling a bit anxious, she had to get farther away. The only place she could think of where the solitude she sought was readily available and the price affordable was Lyons Corner House in the Strand. She crossed the Mile End Road and waited for the next bus heading for the West End. She didn't have to wait long; one pulled up at her stop.

Under normal circumstances she'd have gone upstairs but not today; only the foolhardy would choose to weather the winds up there. Her friend Johnnie once told her that if you go upstairs in cold weather the conductor never came near you, so you'd probably not have to pay the fare. Still it wasn't worth it to save a penny h'apenny and catch your death of cold when there were plenty of seats available downstairs.

"All fares, please, all fares . . ." the conductor shouted as he walked through his bus. "Where you going, lady?"

"The Strand. Lyons Corner House, actually."

"Then have a cream cake on me," he said. "Use your pennies to buy something really nice," and he gave her a free ticket.

Things were looking up; she hadn't had to go upstairs to get a free ticket. Perhaps this was a good omen and she'd done the right thing walking out on Abbott. On the other hand, a free ticket wasn't really the answer to getting a job when so many were out of work. What did Londoners do when they were in a quandary? They have a cup of tea, she told herself, and that's where she was heading — to have a cup of tea and try to come up with a solution to the hasty decision she had just made.

Chapter 2

Ronan

IT WAS CUSTOMARY for the maître d' to seat a single woman away from the main area of a restaurant and often close to the kitchen. Lyons Corner House in the Strand was no exception. Clara was not in the mood for the comings and goings of waitresses pushing their way through swinging doors. From past experiences she knew if she said she was expecting someone to join her and flirted a little, she'd be given a better table. It worked. She was shown to an alcove with a window view, table number seven.

Five musicians were playing a selection of Ivor Novello songs as she settled into a comfortable velvet armchair. She would have preferred a Cole Porter selection, but never mind; the next set might well include more of her favorite tunes. She thought the violinist was overdoing it a bit, fiddling dramatically while perched on the edge of a small platform, upstaging his colleagues. One false step, and he'd land on the dance floor.

The conductor kept one eye on his ensemble and the other on the violinist, occasionally raising the palm of his hand in the violinist's direction, warning him to slow down. After all, they were supposed to finish at the same time, and this was intended to be background music to quiet conversation.

The pastry waiter, silver tongs at the ready, his outfit spotless — black trousers impeccably creased and white shirt collar dressed with a black bow tie — silently glided his pastry cart to her alcove, "I 'ave *pastrie* for ze *madame, oui?*"

Waiters came from Europe to learn the language, and Clara thought it kinder to let him struggle on. He really didn't have to say

15

anything; the selection of cakes and desserts spoke for themselves. What an assortment — mille feuilles and rum babas, Black Forest cake, strawberry flans, custard tarts and chocolate éclairs, all under a glass dome and waiting to be set free!

"Zee flan is zee best. I give it to you."

"I'd prefer something not so rich." Clara wasn't about to be rushed.

A waitress came to Clara's table. She too was immaculate — black dress, a whiter-than-white pinny and the usual fan-shaped head piece that reminded Clara of a nun's half wimple. The female Corner House staff was helpful and efficient; their job was to serve and not to get involved in conversation. Clara studied the menu, examined the cart, and though the pastries were tempting, she settled for a pot of tea and a Bath bun. "I'd like the stickiest one you have."

The pastry waiter captured the bun with his silver tongs, placed it on a china plate and handed it to the waitress who served it on the table.

"Pot's hot, madam, be careful," she said. "Would you like me to pour?"

Clara opted to allow the tea to steep a little longer.

"And the Bath bun, is it to your liking, madam?"

Clara nodded, it was just fine, and the staff drifted away to wait on other customers.

All very well sitting there staring at a Bath bun, as if there was not a thing wrong in her life. Monday morning she'd have to go to the Labor Exchange to see if they had anything to offer in the way of work. She'd put up with Abbott for one reason only — she and Sidney wanted to save enough money to buy a home of their own. They'd lived with her parents and siblings in a crowded flat for a year since their marriage. Not that it was unpleasant or even uncomfortable, it was just that they desperately needed a space they could call their own. And what had she done? Thrown caution to the wind and walked out on a steady job. What's more, an explanation would have to be made — she glanced at her watch, "Oh, my God," in less than three hours!

The musicians took a tea break. Strange, she thought, considering they were there as entertainment. She wondered where they went — probably in the kitchen, annoying the waitresses, having a cigarette, maybe sorting out what they were going to perform next.

She couldn't help thinking of her cousin Sonny who played bass in the Hippodrome pit — had done so for years, routine repetitive songs, he knew them all by heart, could have played it blindfolded. The only way he managed to keep the job was by reading a book or magazine attached to his music stand. This kept him awake, alleviated the boredom of having to play the same old stuff over and over again, he'd told her.

His participation consisted of a few low boom-booms, and as long as he came in at the right place, it didn't take much concentration. He did, however, have one party piece, called "The Bull Frog," which required numerous boom-booms in different keys, a virtuoso piece for him and a cacophony of unmelodic notes for everyone else. Sonny's most challenging task was to transport his instrument from one gig to the next — impossible to take it on a bus, not easy on a train and too expensive in a taxi. His mum suggested he turn it in for a piccolo!

Clara set aside thoughts of Sonny and his bass and settled down to her cup of tea, enjoying this moment of leisure while it lasted. Real life would happen soon enough.

"Would you mind if I join you?" said a voice from out of nowhere.

It was Ronan standing at her table, a colleague from Abbott's office who'd been an articled clerk there. He'd left over a year ago. He leaned over and gave her a kiss on the cheek. "How are you? So good to see you."

"Ronan Nelson!" she exclaimed. She'd always liked him, a good looking fellow with a fine sense of humor.

Ronan pulled out the chair opposite Clara and sat down with her. "Still with Abbott? Must have turned a new leaf, if he gave you time off. And how is the old fart?"

"He's an impossible, ranting lunatic."

"Hasn't changed then?"

They both laughed.

"Just popped in to think, actually," she said. "Glad I did. You're the last person I expected to see."

"Serendipity, my dear Clara. Tell me all that's happening in that den of iniquity."

"I handed my notice in this morning," she heard herself saying.

Ronan gave Clara a look of approval. "I knew you were too savvy for him. Good for you."

"And so I came up here to work out whether I should commit suicide before or after I tell my family."

"A little drastic, don't you think?" Ronan laughed.

"They're from the old school. Make a commitment, and you stick to it. Doesn't matter if the stress eventually kills you."

"If they knew what it was like to work there, they'd understand," Ronan assured her. "Anyway, you've probably broken the Abbott employee record. He must have been beside himself."

"He was gobsmacked. He didn't believe me, told me to take the day off and come back rested."

"Didn't *want* to believe it, more likely."

"Either way it's his problem — not mine. I feel a bit guilty leaving Carruthers. He's a faithful old boy, harmless enough, still, he's deaf as a door post — so it really doesn't matter what Abbott says to him."

Clara was grateful for Ronan's company. "What harm did that monster do to you?" she joked.

Ronan thought for a moment. "Not much. Mostly I learned how not to run a practice. When you're articled to a firm, and you have a goal in sight, you stick it out. I had no choice, really. Finally, five years of doing his scut work paid off. I can deal with all sorts now."

"I often wondered what happened to you," Clara admitted. "After you left, it was just day to day misery."

Ronan took a long look at Clara. "Doesn't seem to have done you any harm; you're as lovely as ever. He'll never get anyone to take your place, that's for sure."

The waitress came to the table. "Bath bun, sir?"

"Just tea, please," Ronan returned his attention to Clara. "Any prospects for another job?"

The conversation took a rest while the tea was served.

Finally Clara admitted how dim her prospects were. "None. This all happened two hours ago. It's a bit frightening, really. Still something will eventually turn up. One thing's for sure, I won't go back there. I can always do temporary work I suppose."

"Well, now — it just so happens . . ."

"Please, Ronan, no more law. I admire you, and I'm sure you're very successful, but I think I'd like to try something new, something not quite as grueling and perhaps a bit more challenging."

He took a sip of tea and leaned forward with an air of excitement. "Hear me out. It's nothing to do with the law; it's as far from the law as one could get. It will be assisting my stepfather. He's French and quite a well known artist, really a very nice man. He's writing a book about his experiences in the Great War. Some publisher commissioned him, and he accepted. The only problem is that his written English is appalling. He's looking for someone to help him. I think you'd be just the right person."

"Sounds interesting, but my French isn't all that good, Ronan."

"It's your English he needs. Remember how you used to correct Abbott's atrocious grammar? Probably have to do the same with Mr. Maze. Paul Maze, he's who you'll be working for — at his home in Chelsea. Lovely surroundings; nothing like those dingy East End rooms we slaved in with Abbott."

"Chelsea? That's miles away from where I live. How am I supposed to get to Chelsea every day?"

"The same way you got here to the Strand, I should imagine, by bus." Ronan removed a gold pen and a small notebook from his inside suit pocket. He opened the notebook and began to write. "This is the address, Fourteen Cheyne Walk. I'll tell him you'll be there at eleven this coming Monday." He ripped the page from the notebook and slipped it across the white tablecloth to Clara.

Talk about challenging? Clara had never in her life thought of a job like that. A law office had not prepared her for assisting in the writing of a book. "It's a . . . well, I'm not quite sure what to say. I mean, Chelsea's not really my bailiwick. He might not want someone like me."

"Nonsense. I don't want to hear any excuses."

Clara eyed the notebook page with the address written on it. Sidney, the family, all of them, might think, at the very least, it showed she hadn't altogether lost her marbles, and it was a lead to another job.

"Nothing ventured, nothing gained, Clara. He's a great chap. Bit of an extrovert, a charmer, knows everyone who's anyone and all in all a delightful man. He walks every morning, usually back by tenish, doesn't rush, and he won't be on you all the time. He's the complete opposite to that Scrooge Abbott."

Clara picked up the piece of paper and held it in her hand. "Do you really think I'm right for the job?"

"Yes, I do. I wouldn't have suggested it if I had any doubts."

"Then I'll take you up on it. Thanks, really, you've given me the wherewithal to face the family — the chance of a job. You have no idea how much I'm in your debt, Ronan."

"No thanks needed. Now let's change the subject. Tell me something more about yourself, and finish your tea before it gets cold."

"Cold tea makes you beautiful, so my Aunt Lizzie always said."

"You tell your Aunt Lizzie you don't need it, Clara. You're beautiful enough."

"I can't. My Aunt Lizzie married a German and lives in Munich."

"Well, with or without cold tea, you're still beautiful."

CHAPTER 3

The Family

THE BUS CLARA rode back to Aldgate was taking forever. A horse had broken loose from its coal-carrying cart and refused to budge from the center of Theobolds Street. The driver pulled the reluctant creature by the reins while a scrawny lad pushed it from behind. Neither could make it move. Cars and buses were lined up on either side of the street, and the honking of horns frightened the horse even more.

Eventually the conductor came upstairs, sat down beside Clara, propped his feet up on the shelf by the window and resigned himself to the fact that they would be there for some time. "These blokes 'aven't a clue what to do with their 'orses; if you ask me, they should put 'em all out to pasture. Animals and locomotives, the two just don't go to'gever, never 'ave and never will." He took a Woodbine cigarette out of his pocket and lit it. "We've got to get ourselves up to date — 'orses wot work belong in the last century or on the race track, that's where I likes to see them. If I were you, young lady, I'd get off the bus and take a train to wherever you're goin'."

Clara took his advice. She walked to Holborn Underground Station, leaving behind irate motorists, an unruly horse and two coalmen swearing their heads off.

"ALDGATE EAST. ALDGATE Out, Aldgate Orf," the guard holding a megaphone announced as Clara alighted from the train and headed for her home at number Twenty-One, Aldgate High Street.

Thousands of Jewish immigrants from Eastern Europe had settled in Aldgate, and there was no mistaking their presence. Even a nearsighted Litvak could make out the signs: RECOGNIZED BY THE

BETH DIN. EVERYTHING IN HERE IS KOSHER, written in thick white Hebrew script on every shop window.

Yiddish wasn't spoken or understood in the Levy family. Nelly, Clara's mother, insisted she could trace her roots back to William the Conqueror, although there were no records to prove it. She considered herself British through and through, and let no man question her loyalty to King and Queen. The fact that most of her neighbors were recent arrivals from Eastern Europe only made her more aware of the fact that she and her family spoke cockney English, and proud of it, too.

Nelly said the immigrants, who secretly in her mind weren't really up to snuff, didn't have to learn English; they had their own clubs and shops, stayed separate and seemed to enjoy each other. She referred to them as, "Those foreign Jews." In this respect she wasn't much better than Abbott, except challenge her on her Jewishness, and you'd be sorry you ever opened your mouth.

The Levy clan chose to live in the East End. It was where their families had lived for more years than they cared to remember, and whether they fraternized with their neighbors or not, they took some comfort in knowing they were among their own. They were a stone's throw from Petticoat Lane where they could buy everything from a herring to a dining room table, and there were at least five synagogues to attend, if the necessity arose. Clara's dad Henry, of Sephardic background, occasionally attended High Holy Day services at Bevis Marks, while Nelly showed up at the Great Garden Street Shul for weddings, funerals and bar mitzvahs. The Levy's were traditional, secular Jews — Jews who observed the holidays, lit the candles on Friday night, never ate pork and agreed Nelly made the best chicken soup in the whole of the East End. They were Jews who married each other and later on — they hoped much later on — were buried alongside each other in the Jewish cemetery in Edmonton.

And perhaps the real reason why they stayed was Nelly, who would have to be taken out kicking and screaming if anyone tried to move her. She was born in Aldgate, and she had every intention of taking her last breath in Aldgate. Never would she willingly relinquish her seat at her front room window, one story up above the Half Moon Pub. It was her window on the world below. She was mistress of all she surveyed.

When Milly Garfinkle, all dressed up, had a date with Harry Shapiro, Nelly was there to report. When her children crossed the High Street on school days, Nelly with her watchful eye was there to make sure they got safely over to Old Castle Street on the other side.

And what was even more important, she knew when Henry, her husband, was waiting for the bookie on the corner of Goulston Street because she could see the *Racing Gazette* in one hand and sense his betting money in the other. He'd move the coins around like worry beads being counted and recounted to make sure the amount was sufficient for the bookie when he turned up. On would go Nelly's hat and coat and out she would trot to drag Henry back home before the coppers on their beat got hold of him. So far, he'd been lucky. "The day will come," she told him "when you'll be up before a magistrate for loitering with intent, and if you think I'll be there to bail you out, you have another think coming!"

"What intent?" Henry asked all innocent-like.

"Intent on spending our grocery money on horses that haven't a hope in hell of ever leaving the starting post, let alone winning. That intent!"

Still, Henry was nobody's fool; he knew she'd be up at the front room watching out for him, and occasionally, just for a lark, he'd gather a few of his cronies around him, all studying the *Racing Gazette*, and stand where she could see them. Mostly, though, they'd keep out of sight, knowing they were no match for Nelly when she was on the warpath.

CLARA APPROACHED HOME with some trepidation. It was nearly six o' clock. She knew Sidney wouldn't be back from work until much later, Anna would be helping Mum prepare dinner, Dad would be doing the football pools, and the rest of them would be discussing the day's activities with Mannie, her sister Sula's husband — an amputee and a radical Commie — interrupting everything they said. When Mannie spoke it was usually a diatribe on the incompetence of the government and the shortage of jobs. He never tired of politics, whether the subject be unemployment, the 'haves' versus the 'have nots' or the futility of war.

Clara had decided to tell Sidney privately that she'd left Abbott and let the family know later. Fat chance of that happening — the moment she entered Nelly's parlor, any hope evaporated. She hadn't removed her coat before Anna, her older sister, spilled the beans.

"So I go to Abbott's office in my lunch hour thinking you and I could have a sandwich together at Blooms, only to be informed by Carruthers that you'd walked out in a huff and were not coming back! What's all that about?"

Seeing no way out, Clara gave a short explanation, knowing her announcement would take precedence over all other information, yet every one of them would have an opinion, asked for or not.

Nelly looked at Henry. Henry looked back at Nelly. Nelly gave Henry a get-on-with-it stare, and the inquisition began.

"Are you out of your mind, young lady? Have you any idea how hard it is to find a decent job? Only last week Wuffie Rosenblume told me his daughter's been searching for a secretarial position for a month. She finally found a job in a cigarette factory. She could have found you something, if you'd let on what you were planning."

"It wasn't planned, Dad. I just had enough, and you can forget about a cigarette factory. You won't get me working there. I didn't go to night school to learn how to stuff a cigarette. I'm a qualified secretary. Don't compare me with Fanny Rosenblume's daughter, who hasn't got a brain in her head, smokes and stinks of tobacco!"

Nelly made sure Henry hadn't just stopped to take a breath. "That's it. Is that's all you have to say?" she asked Henry.

"Yes, your turn." Henry handed it over to Nelly.

"All right, then. I have the solution. Clara will go back to Abbott in the morning, say she acted hastily and apologize."

"I will not. He can shove his job. I'm not going cap in hand to anyone, Mum. In fact, I won't need to; I've already been offered another one."

"And there are fairies at the bottom of my garden, too," Mannie muttered.

"Leave her alone. She doesn't need our advice," Sula said as she came to her sister's defense.

Clara thanked Sula and waited for the next attack. There wasn't one. Mannie refrained from his usual pontificating. He'd heard enough.

No one knew better than he did how difficult it was to find work. Why else would he be out on the streets, holding placards high with slogans demanding jobs for the people and help for the poor? Henry was right; work was hard to get; not that Henry would know. He'd never been to an Employment Exchange in his life. A man of many trades and master of none, Henry made a living in the markets, selling toiletries. "Self-employed," he'd say, if anyone asked.

"And just to let you know, and I'm not making it up, I have an interview in Chelsea on Monday. If successful, I'll be working for an artist."

"Chelsea!" Mannie exploded. "Chelsea — where the high and mighty hang out, the sods who sent us into the trenches while they sipped their brandy at their gentlemen clubs, working out how many more they could dispatch to win a war none of us were equipped to fight? My God, even the enemy didn't know why they were there!"

Henry took the floor again. "Would you mind telling us why an artist needs a secretary? What you supposed to do — hold his brushes and mix his paints? Pose for him in the altogether?"

"Shut up, the lot of you. Give the girl a chance," Nelly shouted, eager to hear more from Clara.

"When I know, you'll know. I happened to meet an old friend who used to work at Abbott's. If I get the job, his stepfather will be my employer. The man is an artist, and he needs a secretary because he's writing his memoirs. It sounds a really interesting and challenging position, and I hope I get it. In the meantime, I'm dying to go to the loo."

Clara left them arguing among themselves.

"Left a respectable job to work for an artist — never heard of such a thing." Nelly was beside herself. "Don't know what's going to become of her."

"Her boss was an anti-Semitic, deceitful, unpleasant bastard. I hardly think you can refer to his practice as respectable," Sula again defended Clara. "Come, I'll lay the table. Anna, get the tablecloth, Mannie, fill the jug with water, and, Dad, help Mum get the plates down."

A parrot, with the improbable name of Boadicea had taken up residence near to the phonograph. Every time they played a record it joined in. If it recognized a word, it would repeat it over and over again until someone shut it up. This time it heard "dinner," and it screamed, "Dinner, dinner, bloody dinner," until Nelly threw a rag over its cage.

"I rue the day I allowed that sailor to leave it with me," she said. "Comes up here with one of Anna's friends and tells me he'll collect it in a week — it's been six months, for gawd's sake."

"And its vocabulary leaves a lot to be desired. It would make a porter in Billingsgate blush," Henry remarked. He was an unusually proper man.

"One more week, and you're going." Nelly lifted the rag to let Boadicea know her days were numbered.

Anna protested vehemently; she'd made a promise to look after it until the sailor came back from sea.

Henry exploded. "Parrots live forever! Nothing does-in a parrot! If you think we'll ever see that sailor again, you're wishing up a monkey tree. It will still be here after we're all dead and gone if we don't do something about it."

Their concern for Clara and her upcoming interview was put aside. Boadicea and her uncertain future now took center stage.

Nelly disagreed with Henry. There must be a method by which to remove an unwanted bird. "I'm taking it up on the roof," she declared, "opening the cage door and letting it free. It can find its way back to Africa!"

"It didn't come from Africa," Mannie informed her. "Parrots come from South America."

"I don't care where it bloody well comes from or where it's bloody well going! I've even tried offering it to the cat, and she won't take it," Nelly kept up her diatribe.

Mannie wanted to close down the parrot discussion. "Come off it, Mum."

But, of course, it wasn't over; they'd had this argument on numerous occasions, and Boadicea stayed exactly where she was, in her cage next to the phonograph and, more often than not, covered with the rag. Take that rag off and Boadicea performed a recital of the sailor's expletives and a few "Good morning, darlings," whether it was in the afternoon or after midnight. Why, that parrot even had the audacity to sing along with Chaliapin when the family sat down to listen to an evening of music, and, what's more, matched voices with Gracie Fields on the morning radio shows. Chaliapin was too fine a singer to perform a duet with Boadicea, and Gracie Fields would have gone straight back to Rochdale had she known a parrot in Aldgate was accompanying her in a sing-along.

Clara came back right in the middle of the Boadicea argument. Her patience for family arguments had grown thin over the years; finally she managed to put an end to Boadicea's uncertain future by taking Sidney by the hand the moment he came home and heading him back out the door.

"You can carry on without us. We're going for a walk," Clara said, and they departed, leaving Anna to plead for the life of Boadicea, while Nelly was plainly resolute on its demise.

CHAPTER 4

Chelsea

CLARA WASN'T SURE whether the numbers went up or down on Cheyne Walk, and neither did the bus conductor know when she inquired.

"Not my neck of the woods, luv," he admitted. "I suggest you get off half way down the road and work it out from there."

Cheyne Walk stretched out in front of her, lined with immaculate, tall, red brick Georgian houses looking out over the River Thames. Chelsea was the yacht-sailing, posh part of the Thames, nothing like the industrial dock area five miles down river where Clara played as a child at the Tower of London under the bridge and in sight of Traitor's Gate.

At the time she was in mortal fear of Bill Stickers, whom she believed was a wanted man. Notices imprinted with his name were in windows and on lamp posts, reading, "BILL STICKERS WILL BE PROSECUTED." An imaginative youngster, not knowing the difference between prosecuted and executed, Clara was constantly on the lookout for a suspicious character for whom the police might be searching. She knew for sure one day she would see Bill Stickers brought through Traitor's Gate, tried for treason, and, thence, beheaded on Tower Hill for a most heinous crime.

Along the Cheyne Walk, nannies, two by two, held spotless toddlers on reins as they tried to keep up with their energetic charges, straining to get away. Chauffeur driven cars passed silently on a well maintained road. Men in morning dress and ladies wearing white gloves strolled leisurely, not seeming to want to get anywhere in particular. She wouldn't have been surprised if she'd bump into Noel Coward walking by with Gertrude Lawrence on his arm.

She looked around for someone to ask. They all seemed unapproachable. Better to work it out for herself. Talk about a fish out of water. She couldn't be more removed from Abbott's office if she'd applied for a job on Mars.

CLARA STOOD AT the bus stop, wondering whether to turn left or right. On the right the numbers went up; on the left they went down. She turned left and soon found the address Ronan had given her — Number Fourteen, engraved in ebony letters on a recently polished brass plate. There were two entrances. One down the steps to a very ordinary looking door, maybe a tradesman's entrance, the other, up five steps, led to an imposing wooden door with a cast iron knocker molded in the image of a naked woman. Good thing her dad hadn't accompanied her; she'd be dragged away, his voice ringing in her ear, "If a naked woman's on the outside, gawd knows what might be inside." Maybe the flat downstairs belonged to someone else, she decided. From Ronan's description it didn't appear to be where Mr. Maze lived. Up the steps she went, not knowing what to expect.

Clara tried to lift the handle; she couldn't get it high enough to bring it down with a loud enough noise. Above the knocker on the right hand side was a bell that she could reach. One light push, and it boomed out in a very loud, Big Ben-sounding peal.

A formidable man in pin-striped trousers and black jacket opened the door. He alone was enough to frighten the life out of her. He stood there. She stood there. Someone had to say something.

Clara finally gave in and tried, "Is this the residence of Mr. Paul Maze?"

"It is, madam."

"I have an appointment to see Mr. Maze."

"Ah, yes, then you must be Miss Simon. I am Rogers, the Maze family butler."

"*Mrs.* Simon, actually." Up to this moment Clara had only read about people who employed butlers. So this is what a butler looks like, she thought.

Rogers was over six foot, sported a greying mustache. Must have been a sergeant major at one time. He ushered her in. "Mr. Maze is aware of your intended arrival. He is known to have a small problem with punctuality and could be a little late. Do not fear, he turns up eventually."

Clara followed Rogers through a marble foyer into a resplendent sitting room — a room filled with antique furniture and leather couches, all significantly placed on vivid Persian rugs. Lining one wall a library of books were stacked on shelves from ceiling to floor. To get to the higher shelves there was a sliding ladder; she'd seen something similar at the British Museum when her teacher took the class on an outing. Never had she been in such a beautifully appointed room — paintings and antiques and ornaments, hard to know where to look first. It was impossible to take it all in at one glance.

"Make yourself comfortable, Mrs. Simon. Can I offer you some tea?"

"No, thank you."

"Then I will leave you to enjoy the art work of Mr. Maze and some of his friends. That one over there, a Pissarro, quite exquisite don't you think? Many of the pieces are Mr. Maze's own work. He is a much sought after artist, a most prolific painter."

Clara walked around the room examining each painting. Mazes' work was decidedly Impressonist. She and Sidney often went up to the National Gallery or the Tate on a Saturday afternoon. They'd seen some memorable exhibitions together. He preferred the Old Masters; plenty of those in the National. She favored the Turners at the Tate, the sunsets and the seascapes. The Pissarro, Rogers pointed out, was an oil, "Chaff Pickers in the Field". It had to be worth a fortune. There was another — looked like a dead chicken, certainly didn't seem alive — signed by a Heinrich Luftmann. Maze's paintings were quite lovely, landscape and still life — also, two nudes, one on a couch, the other sitting in a chair.

A tall, stand-alone glass cabinet caught her attention. In it were hundreds of brilliantly colored tin soldiers, battalions of them, all in identical uniform, an amazing collection. She didn't recognize the regiment. She walked over to take a closer look and soon became completely engrossed until the door was flung open. In came a tall, handsome man, wearing a black cape and a soft felt hat with a broad brim. Rogers followed no more than three feet behind him, catching the man's hat in midair and taking his coat from him.

Maze sat down in one of the overstuffed chairs, picked up a newspaper and started to read. He hadn't noticed Clara in the room.

"I don't know why I bother to get *The Times*, Rogers. Don't like it and don't trust it. Where's my *Figaro*? Bring me a paper I can appreciate."

"I will, sir, when it is delivered."

"Then I will wait until it arrives."

"Sir, there is a Mrs. Simon here to see you, the young lady Ronan recommended to assist you with your book."

"Then show her in, Rogers. What are we waiting for?"

"We're not waiting, sir. She is in, over there by the glass cabinet."

Maze put down his paper and looked over to where Clara was standing. "Well, my dear, I never thought a young lady like yourself would be interested in tin soldiers." Maze had a slight French accent, noticeable, not difficult to understand.

"They are quite spectacular. There's a shop in the Haymarket that has regiments of tin soldiers in the window. That's the only place I've seen such an array," Clara replied.

"My father started the collection many years ago. I inherited them and add to them when I can. I love the pageantry of the British military." Maze invited her to sit down; she wasn't sure quite where. "Rogers, did you offer the young lady a cup of tea? You know the English have to have their tea."

"I did, sir. She declined."

"Oh." Maze looked as if he'd been reprimanded. "When you get to know us better, Miss Simon, you will realize Rogers is always right, and I am often wrong — which is why he stays my butler, and I remain his servant!"

"It's *Mrs.* Simon," Rogers corrected Maze and directed Clara to a seat close to Maze.

"You see, he just proved what I said."

"Is there anything else you might like, sir?"

"No, I am complete — a lovely young lady and time to find out whether we will suit each other."

"I would like to remind you, you have a lunch date with Mr. Churchill at noon. It would not be polite to keep him waiting. He's a busy man."

"I know, I know, Rogers. I haven't forgotten. Mrs. Simon and I have to get to know each other, and we can't do that with you hovering in the background."

"Quite right, sir."

Maze waited for Rogers to close the door and turned his attention to Clara. "I adore Rogers. He can be, as you English say, a bit of a pain in the neck, yet I have little doubt about his usefulness. I cannot imagine what my life would be like without him."

He broke into French. "*Alors, Ronan m'a dit que votre ancien patron aura des difficultés à vous remplacer.* Ronan said you are lovely to look at, *une jolie jeune femme,* and you are your own person. I'm not exactly sure what that means, *je crois bientôt l'apprendre,* and if I can persuade you to help me, I'd be a very lucky man."

Clara was a little embarrassed. "Ronan is too kind. When he left the law firm, I had to deal with the awful Mr. Abbott by myself, and it wasn't pleasant. No one to share a laugh or a complaint, just me and Old Carruthers; Carruthers had been there for centuries, well, so it seemed."

"Lawyers can be a strange breed; some take it up just for the money and others, like Ronan, actually love the law and practice it with integrity. I sent him there to learn about life from a different perspective; rich or poor, the law must represent us all."

Maze removed a small sketchbook from his pocket and chose one of the many pencils from a carved wooden open box on the table beside him. He began to sketch.

Clara waited for the interview to begin. Maze kept on sketching. After what seemed an age he looked up. "Oh, please move closer." He continued sketching.

Clara sat demurely, taking in more of the grandeur of the room. A lovely arrangement of lilies and roses in a cut glass vase stood majestically on a rosewood table. A musical instrument, she thought perhaps a harpsichord, was off in a corner. There was so much to digest, it was hard to focus on anything in particular. Paintings, books, sculpture, lamps, embroidered cushions, velvet flocked wallpaper; she'd seen that before in the window of the elite Sanderson's store on Berners Street — Purveyors of Wallpapers to the King, no less.

As for Maze, himself, he was a handsome man with straight blondish hair falling over his brow, deeply set blue eyes, a prominent nose and an air of nobility, perhaps; a foreigner, yes, but seemingly at ease with himself and his surroundings, a man whom she hoped she would get to know.

"Ah, my apologies. I just had to get the image in my head down on paper." Maze was ready to talk. "I see so much when I take my morning stroll. Just have to capture it before it fades from my memory. Now tell me about you."

Where should she start? She decided the best way was to be straight-forward and not to hide her background. Ronan had probably told him why she left Abbott. "To be honest my family was not keen on my taking a position so far from home, working for someone totally removed from my experience and theirs. My father doesn't trust art-ists, not that he's ever known any, and my husband wanted me to find a job closer to home." She hesitated. "I'm babbling. Excuse me, please."

"Continue."

"I was not going to be persuaded by them. It was my decision, not theirs. Perhaps that's what Ronan meant by my being my own person."

"Now I understand!" Maze, though sketching again, appeared to be listening.

"I studied French in school and took evening classes, too. I would say my French is adequate, not perfect, a bit rusty, but I'm sure it will improve with use. I take down shorthand at sixty words a minute, and I can type." Her credentials given, she waited for Maze to respond.

Maze put his pencil down and placed his sketch pad on the side table and looked straight at her. It was obvious that he was admiring her honesty — and he liked her looks. "My English is not good enough, and my French, well, I suppose, having spoken it all my life is prob-ably sufficient! What I need is someone to help me write my book — I know what I want to say, it just doesn't sound right when I write it down. I hear French in my head, but when I put it on paper in En-glish it is, well, not good enough. I have never been to the East End of London, so in that way we have something in common — one of us has not ventured east and the other west of this great city. I do not think it matters where one comes from, though not many from these parts would agree with me. They are what we French call snob. I am not. You will have to suffer them as I do."

Clara smiled. She liked his attitude. He had a sense of humor, didn't seem at all pompous, his English was perfectly understandable, and she understood him when he lapsed into French. So far, so good. He was talking again. She had to stop daydreaming. She wanted this job.

"If you can do what I cannot — that is, make sense of my story and help me write it down — *nous serons partenaires*. Oh, just one other thing you must know about me. Rogers is my timekeeper. I do not own a watch. You will find you might have to work late or some days not work at all. *Je peins et maintenant j'écris*. I prefer painting. When the writing is over I will once again be a full time painter."

"*Voulez-vous m'aider à écrire en anglais?*"

"*Je ferai de mon mieux.*" Clara's answer delighted him. Could he want more than that?

Strange, she didn't feel out of place; it all felt perfectly natural except for the grandeur of it all. Maze had nothing to do with the law, thank God, and he'd be a challenge. Should she chance it? Of course she should. He was unlike anyone she'd known before. He seemed, well, normal wasn't the word. Normal wasn't a description one could apply to him. Anyway, who wanted normal? She didn't. She'd be an idiot not to accept. She answered him in French, wanting to let him know she could speak it well enough for him to take her on. "*J'aimerais beaucoup travailler pour vous. Je vous aiderai à écrire.*"

"*Pour moi?* For me? No. With me would be better," Maze corrected her.

"When would you like me to start?"

Rogers entered before Maze could answer. "You do remember your luncheon appointment at the Ritz with Mr. Churchill?"

"I have not forgotten, Rogers."

Rogers disappeared, and Maze turned back to Clara. "See what I mean? How about Monday? Will that be all right?"

Clara nodded. It appeared she'd been hired. "I will find the fastest way to get here — haven't got that worked out yet."

"Can't help you there, but, not to worry, you will be welcome whenever you arrive. And salary? Do you have a figure in mind?"

A surprising question! She was supposed to suggest her wage? She thought for a moment. "Well, I was earning two pound a week with Abbott."

"Then I will offer you three pounds. Would that be sufficient?"

Clara was stunned by the amount offered. All she could think to say was, "Thank you."

Rogers entered. "I have your winter coat in the foyer together with your gloves and a more acceptable hat."

"What's wrong with my felt hat?'

"It's old and worn," Rogers answered.

"And very comfortable," Maze added.

"But not what you should wear to take lunch at the Ritz, sir."

Maze let Rogers win the hat discussion.

"I will be waiting for you, Mrs. Simon. We will start work on our book on Monday then. *C'est merveilleux.* Am I not the luckiest man alive?"

"Most of the time you are, sir," Rogers replied, then quietly warned Clara as he led the way into the foyer, "You will need stamina and patience, Mrs. Simon. If you have these qualities, your time with Mr. Maze will be well rewarded."

"Where are my gloves, Rogers?"

"In your right-hand coat pocket, sir."

"And my hat?"

"In *my* hand, sir." Rogers continued his conversation with Clara, "He knows where every paint brush, canvas, crayon and other art utensil is, but he cannot dress himself unless I put his clothes out."

"Come, Mrs. Simon." Maze ushered her out of the foyer. "We both have to leave. You to find your way back to the other side of London and me to try to behave respectably at the Ritz. Meanwhile, don't believe a word Rogers says. He is a perfectionist, *et moi, l'artiste, je ne peux pas être parfait.*"

"Pardon me, sir, I was only giving the young lady a word of advice."

Maze walked briskly down the steps to where a shiny black limousine was waiting. A chauffeur stood holding open the car's back door.

Clara, closely following Maze and now on street level, spotted Winston Churchill inside the limo, smoking a cigar and waiting for Maze to join him.

As the car drove off Clara hurried to the bus stop with one thought in mind:

Wait 'til I tell the family who I saw today. Bet they won't believe me!

CHAPTER 5

Sidney

THE ARSENAL FOOTBALL Club was Sidney's other love. Clara, much to Sidney's dismay, couldn't tell one team from another and wasn't interested in finding out. Come hell or high water, however, Sidney could be found at the Arsenal grounds, shouting his head off for the team he'd supported from the moment someone gave him a ball. Never in the posh seats, not even in the cheap ones, he had to be right on the field, living for one day a week what he always wanted to be — a professional footballer. Jews, his brothers informed him, had to work for a living, and hitting a ball or kicking it wasn't considered work. Sidney, a born athlete stuck in a factory all week, needed the Arsenal more than the Arsenal needed him.

Sidney's father had died six months before Sidney was born. His mother, left with five children, had neither the strength to rear him nor the money to feed him, so he was raised by his illiterate grandmother, whom he adored. Theirs was a religious Jewish family, Polish immigrants who understood the meaning of hard work with a wage packet at the end of the week. Football as a profession was out of the question; but it didn't stop Sidney playing amateur club football, and in the long summer evenings he couldn't get out of the factory quick enough to rush home, throw off his working clothes and run over to Clissold Park to kick a ball around.

The fur factory he worked in was in a dismal Victorian building, one of many in the East End, cold in winter, too hot in summer, cheap labor, dingy surroundings and long working days. It was in this environment Sidney learned the fur trade. He started when he was only a boy by sweeping the floor and eventually became a master cutter. He wasn't ambitious or a risk taker, and with no one to advise him otherwise, he remained in the safety of his grandfather's business. The machinists, all young girls looking for a husband, found him attractive, flirted, brought him mugs of tea, trying to get his attention, but he wasn't interested. Sidney was there to work, to take the sewn skins, wet them, stretch them and nail them onto large wooden boards ready for him to cut into fashionable garments. One week he worked on mink, another on ocelot — when Persian lamb came into fashion he worked on that; there wasn't an animal skin Sidney couldn't make into a beautiful, expensive coat.

Julius, the oldest brother, who never dirtied his hands, never did any of the actual manufacturing, took control of the business after their grandfather died. He soon came to realize the business depended heavily on Sidney's expertise. Two of Sidney's brothers had already given up the trade, which left Sidney to do all the work — and Julius wasn't about to let him go. While Julius took charge of the glamorous side of the fur trade, attending fashion shows in Europe and America and selling to buyers from exclusive London stores, Sidney stayed in the factory. He knew he wasn't cut out to be in sales, so he had little alternative other than to let Julius do what he did best, while he slogged away supplying what Julius sold.

At the end of the day it was only a job. He wouldn't let it interfere with his personal life. A bit of a loner, he took himself to the theatre and the pictures, and when he wasn't rushing off to the Arsenal Football Ground, he took lessons in ballroom dancing, the latter suggested by his friend Ralph who told him he'd never get a girl if he couldn't do the foxtrot!

Sidney was a young man in fine physical shape and good looking in a Semitic way. He spotted Clara Levy at the Hammersmith Palais Dance Hall on a Saturday night in August 1928. "I didn't actually get to meet her then," he said, when he related the story of how they met to one of Clara's admirers who was jealous as all get out that Sidney had a date with her — he'd been turned down.

"I watched her dancing with another fellow," Sidney told him. "I'd seen her with him on a number of occasions. Didn't seem like they were a romantic couple, and anyway the men were like flies around her, and I didn't think I'd have a chance in hell of even getting a dance with her."

For Sidney, Clara was his idea of the perfect woman, blond, slim and lovely; she was his Carol Lombard, the movie star she so closely resembled. Even from a distance he could see her smile drew all the young men to her. From that moment on there was no other woman for Sidney Simon. It was love at first sight; she was all he ever dreamed of.

Every Saturday night Sidney would go to the Palais, hoping Clara would be there. Most Saturday nights she was there wearing a pretty dress, having fun and very often dancing with the same man. Later he found out the man was her cousin, a chaperone, sent to keep an eye on her. Eventually, through the help of a friend, he was introduced to her, asked her to dance, and finally he gathered up the courage to ask her out.

"You could have knocked me down with a feather when she agreed," he told his friend.

"So, why you and not me?" one of the regulars at the dance hall asked.

"Don't know," Sidney answered sheepishly.

THE FOLLOWING SATURDAY Sidney called for Clara up at Twenty-One.

Nelly opened the downstairs door. There stood Sidney, dressed very smartly in his striped Hackney Boys Club jacket, grey flannels and white shirt, holding a bouquet of flowers in one hand and a large box of chocolates in the other.

"So you're Sidney," she said and gave him the once over. "Heard a lot about you." She led him up the stairs to the parlor, leaving him to wonder what she could possibly have heard and making him even more nervous than he already was.

"This is Clara's friend, Sidney," Nelly introduced him to Henry, who sat at the table figuring out which horse to bet on in the upcoming Grand National. Henry stood up to shake Sidney's hand. "Clara tells me you're not from around here."

Sidney looking like Charlie Chaplin waiting for a date, flowers now drooping and chocolates clutched tightly, replied, "I live in Hackney, only a couple of miles down the road."

"Not the East End, though," Henry said as if every Jew in the world had to live where he lived. "Still, I hear Hackney's very nice." Henry hesitated, not sure what to say next.

Nelly took over. "What you do for a livin', son?"

"Furs, I work on furs."

"I knew a bloke in the fur trade once — can't think of his name right off the top of me head." Henry had a puzzled look on his face. "You remember, Nelly?"

"Don't matter who it was, Sidney's here for our Clara, who ought to be ready by now. Get a move on, girl," she called up to Clara, "Sidney's here. Can't leave the poor fellow waiting forever." Then to Sidney, "Here, give me the flowers. Aren't they lovely! I'll put them in a vase."

Sidney handed over the flowers but still held on to the chocolates. He'd never felt more awkward and couldn't wait for Clara to appear.

"Here I am!" Clara came into the parlor looking as pretty as a picture. She twirled around to show how well her silk print dress flowed.

"Save that for the dance floor, Clara," said Nelly.

Sidney's eyes were glued to Clara; there was no one else in the room as far as he was concerned. Nelly could see he was obviously smitten, and Clara knew it, played it up for all it was worth.

"Those for me?" Clara asked, looking at the chocolate box in Sidney's hand and knowing full well they were.

Sidney handed over the chocolate box, awkward to the end.

"Black Magic, my favorite. Here, Mum, and don't eat them all before I get back."

"Wouldn't dream of it," Nelly replied, a smile on the lips that would open to test the contents of the box the moment Sidney and Clara departed her parlor.

"You have her home by midnight, young man," Henry warned. "Don't want to stay up half the night waiting for her."

"Oh, Dad, I'm not a kid, go to bed. I'm safe with Sidney."

FROM THAT MOMENT on and for the next six months Sidney was a Saturday night fixture up at Twenty-One, always with a bunch of flowers and always waiting for Clara to get ready. After the first few Saturdays Nelly confided in Clara. "I've run out of vases and the parlor is beginning to resemble a funeral home, so tell him nicely, if he has to bring something, it should be chocolates."

Sidney took Clara dancing, to the theatre, out to dinner and for walks in Regent's Park. He wanted her with him all the time. He was so proud of her, so in love with her. She was all he ever wanted and was devastated when a few months later Clara said she needed more time to herself and thought perhaps they should separate for a while. She had other friends she wanted to be with. She had a full time job; she was enrolled in a French course at Toynbee Hall two nights a week; she belonged to a poetry group; and, there were books she wanted to read. Though he was a really nice young fellow, she couldn't devote herself purely to him. She suggested, in a letter, he take out other women, find someone who wanted to settle down.

Sidney had no intention of letting go and had no interest in other girls. He'd found the girl he wanted, and he'd find a way to hold on to her somehow.

"WHY YOU SO miserable, Sid?" Ralph inquired as they kicked a football to each other in Clissold Park.

"It's Clara. She wants a break. Doesn't go to the Palais anymore. Got a letter from her this morning out of the blue, says we should give it a rest for a while."

"Want to know what I think?" Ralph said, and didn't wait for a yes or a no. "Write to her. Tell her how you feel."

That night Sidney sat down in the quiet of his grandmother's house and wrote to Clara. He was a man of few words and what he had to say wasn't easy to put down, but he had to clear the air, and if it took him all night, he'd stick to it until he got it right.

June 6, 1929

My dear Clara,

> *When I received your letter I was unprepared. I did not know exactly what to say to you. It's useless going on with each other time after time just for more friendship without any definite purpose. I see you home, say good night and so it goes on. We enjoy each other's company as friends, and that's about all there is. There is no feeling attached to it on your part, something is lacking. Things can't go on like this. It must come to a crisis some day. In your last letter there was nothing definite. In the meantime I suggest we see each other occasionally where possible or correspond when we feel inclined, perhaps when we meet again our feelings may be different towards each other and our minds may be more*

settled. I hope when you write to me again, you will include your photograph. I would very much like to have one. It will bring back happy memories. This is all I have to say. Goodbye till we meet again.

Yours sincerely,

Sidney

Clara showed the letter to Sula. "Poor thing, you're cruel, Clara. He's obviously in love with you. At least write back."

"I have to take a break, Sula. Not sure he's the man for me."

Two months went by before Clara received another letter from Sidney. It was short and to the point.

August 12, 1929

Dear Clara,

I have been going through my things, as I am about to move out of my grandmother's home. I came across a book I borrowed from you some time ago. I would like to return it personally. Please let me know when it might be convenient for me to visit.

Yours sincerely,

Sidney

As it turned out, Clara had a bad case of chicken pox when Sidney's letter arrived. She immediately wrote back to say it would be better if he posted it.

On receiving her note Sidney made a most uncharacteristic decision: he ignored her request and delivered the book in person.

CLARA SAT IN bed studying her French homework. She'd missed two classes at Toynbee Hall, and it looked like she'd miss the next one too. She'd caught chicken pox from one of her young cousins. She looked awful and felt dreadful. Nelly's old-fashioned cure to dab the spots with gentian violet left Clara looking like a Dalmatian with purple spots. She refused to see anyone and felt sorry for herself. She'd even pinned a notice on the bedroom door that read: NO VISITORS.

Thinking her sister Sula, of all people, would respect her wishes, she was surprised when the door opened, and Sula announced, "Sidney's in the parlor with Mum and Dad, and he wants to see you."

"Tell him to go away. Look at me. I'm a freak; he'll run a mile if he sees me like this."

"I can't do that. Come down. You're not infectious anymore. He's returning a book you lent him."

"I told him to post it. Come to think of it, looking like this might do the trick; he'll leave me alone. It's sure to put him off."

"Don't know about that. Now brush your hair, put on your dressing gown and come down."

Nelly shouted from downstairs. "Are you coming or not?"

Sula, back in the parlor and sensing this was not just an ordinary visit, invited Sidney into the front room. "You'll have some privacy there, more than any of us get around here."

Finally Clara came down in her dressing gown, hair combed forward to hide some of the spots and otherwise covered from head to toe. "Where is he?"

"In the front room — and be nice," Sula instructed.

Gingerly Clara entered the front room where she found Sidney standing, clutching the book and looking out of Nelly's window. He turned to greet her. "Clara, I wanted to see you again. You never answered my letter."

"Sorry. I thought it better for us to take time off — didn't want to start it up again. I apologize for my appearance, Mum said gentian violet would stop spots from pitting my face."

"Well, you are a bit purple," but then he rushed on to say, "otherwise no different. You feeling better?"

"Yes. Just wish these spots would go."

He handed her the book. Sidney made no further comment on her appearance but went on to say, "I've missed you terribly. I think of you all the time. I can't get you out of my mind." He leaned over and gave her a kiss on the cheek, undaunted by the spots. "I had to see you."

"You chose the right time," Clara said with a hint of sarcasm. "If you can stand to look at me like this, then — "

"Then what, Clara?"

Clara was caught in her own flippancy. "Doctor Shapiro says another week, and I'll be back to normal . . . Well, all right, you know the telephone number; we'll arrange something."

"I've waited this long, Clara. Another week or so won't make much difference."

After he departed, Clara thought about what he'd said. He'd proved himself to be an entirely genuine chap. He loved her; even purple chicken pox spots hadn't put him off.

"What you think, Mum?" she asked Nelly.

"About what, luv?"

"About Sidney."

"Well, he's kind, he's insistent, and a blind man could see he loves you. If I were you, I would certainly give him another chance, Clara. You're twenty-seven, you've had your fling, and it's time to settle down. All this gallivanting about is all right while you're young — "

"I'm not exactly on the shelf, Mum."

"That's not what I mean. There comes a time when you say to yourself, I'd like a family, my own home — that sort of thing. For that you need someone like Sidney. Free spirits need an anchor, not the type that holds you in one place, but an anchor with a long rope that can be pulled in when the waters get a bit choppy."

The spots faded. Clara went back to work and, having given it much thought, she wrote a note to Sidney.

November 18, 1929

Dear Sidney,

I see Joe Loss is playing at the Palais this Saturday. Shall I meet you there?

Sincerely,
Clara

Sidney wrote back:

November 20, 1929

Dear Clara,

I will be there. So looking forward to seeing you.

Faithfully yours,
Sidney

CHAPTER 6

Aldgate to Chelsea

CLARA HAD RETURNED from Chelsea to Aldgate overwhelmed by the success of her interview with Paul Maze. She had a job, not just any job; she'd be working in quiet, serene surroundings in Chelsea. It was beyond all her expectations.

Could anything be more removed from Chelsea than Aldgate? she asked herself as she glanced around. The chaos, the noise, even the smell, none of it had struck her as anything other than normal — until now.

Every day the same confusion played out. Stray dogs and feral cats under foot; tired horses tethered to milk carts; trams clattering along the deep steel tracks embedded in cobbled road; overhead wires swaying dangerously above; women standing in doorways chatting with one another; men in shirt sleeves standing outside the pubs and waiting for them to open; and, not a sign of a Rolls Royce anywhere. Clara laughed, giddy with her good fortune.

Aldgate was known for its factories and shops, one after the other packed into small spaces — holes in the wall, they called them. Living space upstairs, shops at street level, where, if two people were being served, other customers had to hover outside for their turn. No one minded the wait; it was all part of a day out. Meeting a friend or relative in the same queue gave them the chance for catching up on the daily gossip.

"Apples, toffee apples, one-a-day keeps the doctor away, two-a-day makes yer dentist 'appy — if you can afford the bastard!" Harry Marcus chanted as he maneuvered his barrow to his usual spot in Wentworth Street.

Benny, a blind man, sat on the pavement rattling a few coins in a tin plate — not enough to buy a cup of tea. It was a cold day; he needed a hot drink to warm him up.

Clara knew him. She stopped for a moment and spoke to him. "Got a rise in pay today, Benny," she told him and dropped a threepenny bit in his plate.

"Good for you, Clara." He knew her voice.

"More for me, more for you," she replied, then continued on her way.

And there was Fat Zelda, the enormously large bagel lady. Clara, as a child, thought Fat was Zelda's first unspoken name. She'd been there forever, always in the same spot, always on the same low stool, selling bagels so delicious one was never enough. Clara stopped and said, "I'll take a dozen, Zelda."

"You got the butter to go with 'em?" Zelda asked, dropping them into a brown paper bag. "No good without a thick coat of butter, Clara."

Finally Clara arrived at the archway set back a little from the High Street. On the other side of the arch were Half Moon Passage and the back of the pub over which the Levy clan lived.

NUMBER TWENTY-ONE stood in the middle of a row of narrow soot-covered brick structures joined together and facing the High Street. Hard to distinguish one from the other, some with a back entrance like Twenty-One, others with a front door squeezed between shops. Number Twenty-One's steps stood out like a beacon of light in a stormy sea. Whiter than white they were. "Front step tells you what's inside," Nelly believed and told her visitors to wipe their feet on the mat or leave their shoes outside. Henry didn't approve of leaving anything outside, let alone his shoes. "I'll be lucky if they're still there when I need 'em," he told his wife, "This ain't a mosque, for gawd's sake."

And it wasn't only Nelly who took pride in the whiteness of the front step. It was Edie's task too. Edie, Nelly had recently revealed, became their maid when she gave birth to Mary. Until then no one could fathom how the Levy family afforded a maid, a red-headed one at that. The truth came out when Anna, Clara's sister, innocently asked, "How come Mary has ginger hair, and none of us do?"

It was then that Nelly owned up to the truth. Henry's Uncle Joe had put a bun in Edie's oven — in other words, had got Edie in the family way. They knew it was him because he had ginger hair, and Mary, the child he sired, came out of the womb with the same flaming ginger mop! Up to the time of Edie's delivery Joe denied it vehemently, said they were just friends, but after that there was no mistaking who the father was. Nelly, not usually a pushover, took pity on Edie, adopted Mary and gave Edie and her daughter a room in the attic of Twenty-One. Joe started a new life in Australia but not before siring a couple more ginger-mop kids.

"One's enough," said Nelly. "I'm not taking in any more of his mistakes. Nevertheless, one of those mishaps must have found a home close by, for the boy who delivered the morning paper up at Twenty-One was the spitting image of Mary.

IT WAS MONDAY, Edie's day off, and sweeping the step was Nelly's chore. Clara crept up when Nelly's back was turned and gave her a big hug.

Nelly, taken by surprise, let out a yell, "Don't do that! You'll give me a heart attack."

Clara apologized and kept on hugging.

"What's all this about, then?"

"I got the job, Mum!"

Nelly stood her broom against the wall and wiped her hands on her apron. "The Chelsea one, I presume?"

"Yes, Mum."

"Well, then we'd better go up and get it over with. You're in for a bit of a ribbing, you know."

"I'm ready for them. They can say what they like. I'm employed, and I start on Monday."

"I hope you know what you're doing. Might have been wiser to stick with what you know. Chelsea's not for the likes of us. Don't even know where it is."

"If you follow the river, you'd find it."

"You mean you got to go by boat?"

"No, silly. Just giving you an idea of the direction. It's west."

"So how'd you get there?"

"Train and a bus. Or I can walk the last bit, if it's not raining."

"Abbott was just around the corner, no fares to pay, much more convenient." Nelly couldn't imagine anyone leaving the East End to find a job.

"Forget Abbott. I refuse to spend the rest of my life frightened to leave Aldgate, Mum."

Nelly got the message. "I suppose you're right, luv. Not partial to change me self. Stuck in the rut we made for ourselves; too late to get out of it now. But don't you get highfalutin' ideas. Always remember where you come from, and who you are. We're Jews, and the gentiles don't like us whether we stay here in the East End, move to Stamford Hill or emigrate to Palestine. Look what happened when Aunt Lizzie married that German fellow. The Jews wouldn't speak to her, and the Germans didn't accept her. Moved for the better and landed up the worse!"

Clara wasn't about to defend her decision on the front step with the neighbors looking on. She'd been given a chance to get away from the East End — the ghetto, as many called it. She'd get to know a different class of person; wouldn't hurt them either if they met a Jew instead of imagining what they were like and listening to others who stereotyped them.

"Come, no use putting off the inevitable." Nelly retrieved her broom and up to the parlor they went.

THEY FOUND HENRY chewing on the end of his pencil and engrossed in the back page of the *Evening Star*. "Caught in the act," he said, red faced. "Big race tomorrow, give me a minute." After much deliberation he put pen to paper, absolutely certain his horse was a winner, though he did have one more important decision to make: how much should he stake? Half a crown each way or go for broke and put in five shillings. One look at Nelly, and he decided on the lower amount. It was the end of the week, and the rent was due.

Henry turned his attention to the front page; he'd learned long ago not to give Nelly an opportunity to pounce on his gambling entertainment. "This Hitler bloke ain't 'arf got a mouth on him." Better to discuss the news than let on he'd been wasting his time "studying." Theirs was a loving marriage with an obvious flaw — Henry's weakness for the horses. He wasn't about to give them up, and she wasn't going to cease nagging him for wasting what little money they had.

"Dangerous sod, this Hitler bloke. Can't understand why the government has anything to do with him," Sula said. She was sitting with Henry and reading over his shoulder.

"Lot of fear mongers, if you ask me," Nelly noted, shooing a cat off her chair. "My turn, Esmerelda. You go off and feed them kittens of yours."

Nelly's chair stood next to the stove, a big black cast iron contraption that cooked the food and warmed the room at the same time. From where she sat she could reach out to stir the soup and settle back for her well-earned forty winks — but not this time.

Boadicea had decided otherwise. "Lovely lady, lovely lady, bloody nuisance, bloody nuisance . . ."

Henry got up and threw the rag over Boadicea's cage.

"That's it." Nelly had been on about the parrot for weeks. "I mean it this time — if that creature is still here . . ."

Anna was a bit concerned; but so far nothing drastic had happened. In fact, she was beginning to suspect Nelly actually didn't mind the bird. She'd caught her teaching it new words, probably hoping against hope it would forget some of the embarrassing phrases its sailor friend had taught it.

Clara wished they'd stop the parrot talk.

"Parrot soup, that's what you'll get for dinner next week. Mark my words." Nelly had had her say.

"Come, Clara, at least give us a hint," Mannie urged.

"Better than I expected," Clara gave Mannie a clue. "If you don't mind, I'd like to discuss it with Sidney first."

"What's the mystery? Either you have the job or you haven't." Mannie wouldn't be left out.

Nelly answered for her. "She's got the job, now leave her be."

"It's all right, Mum," Clara conceded. There were too many of them to placate. They were all there: Mannie and Sula, Henry, Anna and her mother. She'd better get it over with. She told them just a little of what occurred at the interview, and they were enthralled, all, that is, except Mannie, who had no time for anything living or breathing outside the boundaries of London's one square mile. "It's such a beautiful home with servant quarters downstairs."

"You with them, then?" Mannie despised the class system.

"No, of course not. I imagine I'll have to be where Mr. Maze is. He's not likely to be stuck in the basement now, is he? Anyway, he's a really nice man, and he offered me a good wage, too."

Henry wanted to know how much.

"Not telling. But I will tell you one thing: it's a darn sight more than Abbott coughed up, and there's no comparison when it comes to working conditions. And, by the way, guess who I saw as I was leaving Mr. Maze's home?"

Dead silence.

"Mr. Winston Churchill, sitting as large as life at the back of a smashing shiny black chauffeur driven limousine, waiting for Mr. Maze to go to lunch with him."

"Now I know she's been down the pub having a few," Mannie asserted.

"My sister does not drink." Sula poked her head up from behind the newspaper. "If she said she saw Mr. Churchill, then she saw him. Good for her; we should be patting her on the back and telling her how proud we are of her instead of sitting here like members of the Spanish Inquisition. Well done, Clara."

Henry pulled himself up from his chair, stretched to his full five foot six inch height and gave his opinion. "Number one: I don't like the idea of your working in a bloke's home. Number two: I don't think it wise working with a foreigner. Number three: It's too far away . . ."

Nelly took up the count. "Number four: It isn't any of our business, and it should be left up to Clara and Sidney to work it out. On the other hand, she's already accepted the position, so what we're all going on about, I don't know."

Henry, shot down for the umpteenth time, tucked the newspaper under his arm, ready to remove himself from the conversation.

"Looks like you're really worried about that Hitler bloke, Henry, or is it the back page what concerns you more?" Nelly was on to Henry's shenanigans.

"When nature calls, a man has to go, and if he needs a bit of help to pass the time, he takes something to read with him."

"How about the *Jewish Chronicle*, Henry? That not good enough? Your dad thinks I was born yesterday." Nelly addressed her remark to no one in particular. "Never any peace for the wicked; here I was hoping to have a few minutes of shut eye, and I may as well forget all about it 'cos dinner's ready. Who's going to lay the table?"

Sula offered, and Mannie helped her get the dishes out of the cupboard when Sidney walked in. Sidney greeted Clara warmly, "How'd it go?"

"Lots to tell you, but not in front of everyone."

Clara, taking Sidney's hand, waited for the commotion to die down. They'd have their time together a bit later. She knew he wouldn't be altogether thrilled. If he had his druthers, she suspected, he'd much prefer her to find a job nearer home.

Mannie, taller than all of them, reached up for the dinner plates. Why Nelly insisted on putting them on the highest shelf was a mystery to him — maybe just to make sure he was included in the dinner ritual. He handed the plates one at a time to Sula, who placed them on the table.

"Don't forget to lay a place for Bernie," Nelly called out. "He should be here any minute — wouldn't miss my chicken soup and matzo balls."

"His favorite," Anna responded wistfully. She'd recently become engaged to Bernie, met him through Henry. A nice enough bloke, not exactly what Nelly wanted as her son-in-law, though. Bernie had the dubious occupation of being a bookie's runner, and he soon became Henry's personal connection to the illegal side of horse racing.

"Look at it this way," Henry had explained to Nelly, "you've got your Edie, and I have Anna's Bernie — helpers, that's all they are; you got someone to help in the house, and I've got Bernie to work on the street. What's the difference?"

"I'll tell you the difference, Henry. Edie's legal. You and Bernie could land up in prison!"

"Nonsense! I give a few bob to the copper on duty, he turns a blind eye, and we carry on with our business. Everyone makes a profit."

Nelly refrained from saying, "If the horse wins." She'd said it so many times, she was tired of repeating herself.

Mannie handed the extra plate to Sula. She attempted to raise her right hand, but it wouldn't budge, she couldn't lift her arm. Same thing happened with her other hand; she could not grasp the plate, her arms dropped limp at her side, and the plate fell to the floor. She stood there, transfixed, not able to move.

Mannie, realizing this was more than a slip up, helped her to a chair and sat with her. She seemed to be in a daze, not comprehending what had happened. It took a few moments for her to recover.

"Just another episode," Sula managed. "Don't know what causes them."

Clara rushed over to Sula and spoke gently to her. "I'm going with you to the hospital, Sula. You must see a doctor. You can't go on like this."

"Doesn't need a doctor; drop of chicken soup will do the trick." Chicken soup was Nelly's cure-all for everything. "It's only a broken plate — never matched anything anyway. Anna, sweep up. Mannie, don't just stand there, get another plate. Clara, lay the table."

Sula was not taking the incident well. She knew something was wrong, had been for a while. She'd confided in Clara a few days before: she tried to pick up a pencil to jot something down, and she couldn't grip it properly. Her hand refused to take it; her fingers stiffened. "I must be coming down with something — can't hold on to a blooming thing." They decided to give it a week to see if what she thought might be the beginning of some strange condition that would become worse. This wasn't just an accident.

Henry came back, closely followed by Bernie, unaware of the drama that had just taken place.

"Smells good, Nelly," Henry said as he sat in his usual place and waited to be served. "Come on, you lot. Don't want to sit here all on me lonesome."

Bernie came in, shivering. "Perishing cold out there," he said, rubbing his hands together. "Need your mum's soup to warm me up."

Anna moved a place over and beckoned him to sit next to her.

"Always room for one more," Nelly said as she dished up from the stove, and they all tucked in.

Bernie savored every mouthful; no one made a better soup than Nelly. He wasn't much of a talker, probably just as well, for to get a word in when the Levy mob sat down at the table was well nigh impossible. He made up for it by being a most appreciative eater, finishing long before the rest of them and always going for seconds.

"Who's doing the washing up? Don't all rush at once!" Nelly wasn't moving from her place at the table.

Worried about Sula, Clara stayed with her. Anna offered to clear the table and wash the dishes. Sidney wiped up. But Sula was in no condition to help.

LATER, ALONE IN their bedroom, Clara told Sidney about her new job. "It's a pound more than I was getting with Abbott, Sidney. The extra money will help to get us a place of our own. I'll put it away in the Building Society, and we'll get interest on it."

Sidney had to agree it was an excellent opportunity, and, of course, the extra money wasn't to be sneezed at. They both wanted a nice little house in one of the new suburbs; the one they'd liked turned out to be more than they could afford. This new job would be a way to save up for the down payment — Clara bringing in a bigger pay check, adding it to what he earned, they could finally say goodbye to Aldgate and hello to a modern three bedroom jewel sooner than planned.

CHAPTER 7

Paul Maze

H ENRY WAS RIGHT; there was no direct route from Aldgate to Chelsea.
"How many people do you know from here who'd ever want
to go there?" he asked Clara. "The bus companies aren't in the
'airy fairy business; they're in it to make a few quid, and they'd
lose their shirts if they depended on the likes of you to keep them
going." Henry had his London transport map stretched out in
front of him. One of his early jobs was as a conductor on the
buses. He stuck it out for a couple of years before giving it up, or,
truth be known, it gave him up.

"Don't worry, Dad. I've worked it out," Clara said, appreciating
her dad's concern. "The number six seventeen passes all the Nursery
Rhyme Churches and gets me to Charing Cross Road, where I catch a
thirty-nine to Cheyne Walk."

"That's right, I sang 'Oranges and Lemons' to you when you were
a little girl. " 'Oranges and Lemons, say the bells of St. Clements, I
owe you five farthings, said the Bells of St. Martins.' "

Clara joined in, " 'Pray when will that be, said the old bells of
Stepney, When I grow rich, say the bells of Shoreditch.' "

And there were still a few more verses neither of them could
remember.

"Now, you be careful. Give yourself enough time and don't
talk to strangers." Henry folded his map. "You know your mum
and me don't approve, but if that's what you want, then, well," he
looked around to make sure Nelly wasn't in earshot, "then good
on yer! Mind you, I still don't understand why an artist has to
write a book."

PAUL MAZE REFUSED to wear a watch; he relied on Rogers to tell him where he had to be and at what time. If his appointments were away from the house, Rogers would drive him. Maze had never been on a bus. Clara, always a conscientious worker, made a point of getting to work on time. Rogers, fully aware of her starting off point, thought it remarkable she managed to get there at all.

CLARA HAD BEEN in her new job for a week and hadn't accomplished very much; in fact, as far as the book was concerned, she'd done nothing. Maze said he needed time to collect his thoughts. He suggested she get to know the staff and set up a working area for herself. She liked Mrs. Smithers the cook, a jolly, roly-poly woman from West Yorkshire. Mrs. Smithers insisted she sit with the rest of the staff at lunch. She made friends with Maggie, the parlor maid, a pretty girl recently arrived from the Scottish Highlands and unaccustomed to city life. And then there was Eddie, the general dog's body, a cheeky young cockney whippersnapper who Rogers kept admonishing for one thing or another.

Fourteen Cheyne Walk seemed to be divided in two parts: a hive of industry downstairs and a meeting place upstairs. With so many visitors she wondered how Maze would ever find time to write. She confided in Rogers, "How on earth does he get anything done?"

"Oh, he does. And you'll get used to him and his ways. Don't be surprised if the Duke of Kent knocks on the door, or some Sir or Lord turns up for tea, all close friends. A number of — I suppose you would call them dignitaries — come in and out of this establishment, from penniless artists to royalty; it's quite a mixture, and when you've worked here as long as I have, they all, well, nearly all, seem to be much like the rest of us. You'll soon find out our Mr. Maze is a very social creature."

Rogers, showed her around, explained the way the Maze residence worked or, as he said, often didn't work. He was quite different on a personal level, unapproachable in his butler persona, warm and helpful when he was just himself.

"So, do I suggest we get down to working on the book?"

"If you don't, you'll be here till the cows come home." Rogers chuckled. "Give him a gentle hint, and you'll be off and running!"

"Is there a Mrs. Maze?" Clara inquired, having seen no sign of a wife since she'd been there.

"Mrs. Maze resides most of the year in Scotland. She visits occasionally. She prefers Scotland while Mr. Maze's preference is London."

"So, they live apart?"

"Not for me to comment on, Mrs. Simon."

Clara was quick to apologize. "Sorry, shouldn't have asked."

Rogers continued. "Mr. Maze might seem at times eccentric; after all, he is an artist. He's known to have the odd tantrum, and my advice to you is to ignore them if and when they occur. He is what can only be described as a colorful character, not the run of the mill in any way. He treats us better than others I know who work in service. Oh, and he gave me this envelope. If there is anything else you need to know, just ask."

"Thanks, Rogers, I feel better now."

The envelope contained notes Maze had jotted down, mostly thoughts and remembered incidents written in a mixture of French and English. There were little pencil sketches on each piece of paper: a soldier sitting and reading a letter, a nurse pouring medicine into a spoon, a man on a motorbike that looked a bit like him. She really had no idea where to start, and the only way to find out was to ask. She walked up the stairs to the studio and knocked on the door.

"*Entrez.*" Maze was there, palette in one hand, brush in the other, finishing off a lovely watercolor. "Good morning. Isn't it a delightfully bright day, so rare for London?"

"Good morning, sir. We have too few days like this. It is quite warm outside."

"The English love to discuss the weather."

"That's because we never know what to expect," Clara replied.

"I am happy you found your way up here. I am sure this setting is not what you are used to, but I assure you I can paint and work on the book at the same time. I apologize for not being with you sooner."

"Are we to work in the studio?"

"There will be days we work here and others when we work in other rooms — or if the weather allows — outside, beside the river, in the garden, no set place; it will be as the mood takes me. What do you think of this?" he asked, standing back and admiring his work.

"It's lovely, really . . ."

"I can take criticism, young lady. What's wrong with it?"

"Nothing, sir, it's just — "

"No, no, not sir, don't call me sir. *Qu'en pensez-vous?* What do you think?"

"Of the painting? I told you it's lovely, but the book, you employed me to help you write your book. I've been here a week, and you haven't dictated anything. I've read your notes, and though they are very helpful, if you could just tell me where the story begins, I could get on with it."

Clara opened her notebook, ready to write and make corrections as he spoke. Maze picked out a new canvas, set it on an easel, dipped a brush in a bright blue oil blob on his palette and began once again to paint. He spoke as he applied his brush to the canvas. "I think, well, I know it had to do with being a field artist. There weren't many of us; fact is, I never met another one. I worked alone — not attached to any regiment and never had a uniform. Neither the enemy nor the allies could tell who I represented, and in that way I was, well, I suppose you would say I worked incognito. All I had was a motorbike and a sketch pad."

"You weren't given a gun?"

"No. I had nothing to defend myself. I gave my sketches to General Gough; he said he found them very useful. I made maps too; helped him to know where the enemy was encamped, how large an enemy contingent I had come across, what weapons they had, that sort of thing. So, though there have been many books written by better writers than me, the publishers considered my involvement was different. I was asked to give a personal account, to write, not from a soldier's point of view, but from a civilian one. You see, I lived with the villagers, I spoke their language and I worked with the British. It's where I met Churchill; he'd rejoined the army after his disastrous plan for the Dardanelles."

Clara wrote furiously. She had many questions, but they would come later. This was a beginning. It would need fuller explanation, but she let him go on without interruption.

"General Gough became a good friend. I believe it was he who made the suggestion to the publishers. When their editor first contacted me, I refused, but I was finally persuaded. He said my experience was unique. I believe that is the reason they asked me."

Clara looked up from her notebook. "I think it might be more interesting to the reader if we start in France. Isn't that where you were born?"

"Yes, a background. Just like a painting; you need my background. Don't worry, I can paint and talk at the same time. Painting is second nature to me; writing is why you are here."

Maze began with recollections of his early years in Le Havre, the relationship with his father, an avid art collector who introduced his young son to artists, many of whom later became famous — Pissarro, Braque, Dufy and Bonnard. They were known as Impressionists, which is why he considered himself a post-Impressionist, a younger artist influenced by their work. He continued his education in London, working for his father. Representing a textile company helped pay the rent while he learned the language and took art classes.

"*Voilà pourquoi je suis à l'aise en parlant, de temps en temps, pour trouver un mot, je reviens au français, comme maintenant.*"

"I am here to help you with your English, I understand. Please carry on."

Maze was impressed; he could see Clara wasn't intimidated when he broke into French. "Art has a language of its own," he went on. "It can be seen and interpreted any way the viewer wishes. I must say I was fortunate my father had another son, not artistic; he became an accountant. My arithmetic is far worse than my written English! Then the war began, and I had to return to France."

"Where you became a Frenchman in khaki?"

"Brilliant! You have given me my title! *A Frenchman in Khaki, merci.* Enough for one day; we end with the beginning!"

Clara, a little confused, said, "End? Beginning?"

"*Oui*, the title is my beginning, and we have come to an end of my writing for the day."

"Oh." Clara, pleased with herself, closed her notebook and looked around for somewhere to start transposing her shorthand.

"You can share my desk. Rogers will bring up the typewriter. Here we have a beautiful view, the river and the trees. I have to be beside water; if not the Seine then the Thames — both will suffice. When a man is born by the sea he has to live by the sea, and if the sea is not visible, then it must be a wide river." Maze pulled on a cord hanging near his desk. "When you need Rogers you just pull this," he said.

Rogers came in almost immediately.

"Coffee for me, and tea for Mrs. Simon, please."

"I will let Mrs. Smithers know," Rogers replied.

"Send Maggie up with it; Mrs. Smithers has enough to do."

"Quite right, sir; she's working on the menu for your dinner party tonight."

Rogers left, and ten minutes later Maggie arrived with a pot of tea and another of coffee. She set the silver tray down on a flat drawing board and asked if there might be anything else required.

Maze contemplated the tray. "I would like some of those shortbread biscuits my wife sent down from Scotland."

Maggie sped off to the kitchen to find them.

"She's a pretty little thing, isn't she?" It was a rhetorical question; he wasn't expecting an answer. "Came down from Scotland a few weeks ago, worked for my wife's family. Our last girl left, pregnant, I think. Had to be replaced, and along comes the *charmante* Maggie."

Pregnant? Clara wondered if it was one of the staff. None of her business, really. She turned her thoughts back to the book. "I really should begin transcribing, Mr. Maze."

"Plenty of time for that. You pour, please. I rarely drink tea, only coffee. Of course, I have to bring it back from France; the coffee here is abominable. At one time I thought I might have to change my habit and accept tea as a substitute. It is beyond my reasoning why the British are incapable of making a decent cup of coffee. I'm beginning to think it's because it is too European for them!"

Amused, Clara set out the cups.

Maze stopped painting, wiped his hands on a paint-stained cloth and walked over to where he stacked his completed works. "This one Winston calls my dead duck — actually it's my abstract — 'Black Bird One' of a series of three; you probably saw one in the room downstairs. Where he gets a duck from I don't know, and it isn't dying. I think it looks very much alive." Maze paused and then said, "Painted it years ago in my student days with a fellow student called Heinrich Luftmann. Winston became an artist before politics took hold of his life, and we sort of lost him to the government. He loves to paint. Finds it relaxing, lays bricks, too. Invited me to do bricks with him the other day. I flatly refused. 'To stand out in the cold covered in wet mortar *ce n'est pas pour moi,*' I told him."

"Cold wet mortar? I don't blame you. Can't he find a laborer to work for him?"

"It's another of his hobbies. He lays bricks and works on ideas for his speeches at the same time. It's a good thing he's a busy man. His wife would be walled in if he wasn't."

"Walled in?"

"*Absolument.* Winston has built a wall around his estate at Chartwell. His wife, Clemmie, once said to me she hopes he stops soon — or she'll be a prisoner, might never find her way out."

Clara could not get the image of Mr. Winston Churchill laying bricks out of her mind. It seemed so incongruous.

"Winston, you'll meet him, comes here quite often to complain about something going on or not going on in Parliament. I try to calm him, not had much success. He's constantly on about this Hitler fellow. Says we're not taking him seriously. I think he may be right." Maze changed the subject as he pounced upon a portfolio of his drawings, "As you can see, I appreciate the female form." He brought the art work over for her to take a closer look. "Better get used to naked bodies; you'll be seeing a lot of them."

Clara had to smile; it was just what Henry warned her about. Certainly wouldn't mention a word of it at home. At least they weren't male models.

Then, as if Maze had read her mind, "Oh, I do have male models, but I won't bore you with them now."

So much for that consolation. But now she wanted to get him back to the book. "We're at the part where you go back to France, the beginning of the war," she reminded him, glancing at her notes.

"I tried to enlist in the French army; they wouldn't have me. I wasn't healthy enough; I'd had asthma as a child. Hadn't been sick a day since puberty. Still they turned me down. I was determined to serve my country. I knew there was a British Battalion encamped not too far away, so I jumped on my motorbike and drove like *un maniaque* to find it. First, they said French men were not accepted in the British

Army. I said I might be French but I spent much time in England, and they hear I speak English."

" . . . heard I spoke English, Mr. Maze, not hear I speak English." Clara had summoned the courage to tell him and wrote as she had done from the beginning, correcting as she went along.

"See why I need you; writing it down for me is very bad. Where was I?"

"Speaking English."

'They must have been desperate. After much discussion about what I could do for them, they agreed to take me on as a field artist. I'm convinced it was the motorbike they coveted. They had very little transport, weren't really prepared to take on the Germans who were much better equipped. They gave me a makeshift uniform, a jacket from one regiment, a pair of trousers from another and an old leather satchel. I had to supply my own paper and pencils. The captain told me to report the next day. That was August nineteen fourteen. I served with them until the very end of the war. Four years later I was one of the few to get out alive."

Clara could sense his relief. It was obvious he'd been emotionally scarred by his experiences. Writing about it might help him. He seemed well adjusted on the outside but perhaps not as well on the inside.

MANNIE, CLARA'S BROTHER-IN-LAW, was another who had never fully recovered. He too marched off full of enthusiasm and determination to answer the call to help his country fight and win. He returned wounded, disillusioned, angry and crippled. Fourteen years on, and the country was still dealing with young widows, children without fathers and ex-soldiers who couldn't find a job.

It was because of neglect and indifference of government officials that Mannie became a spokesman for what he termed "the forgotten patriots," men willing to serve when their country needed them and ignored when they were no longer of use. Men who fought for their country, no rewards given, not even if they gave their lives — a few monuments, poppies at the Cenotaph, waffle in the House of Commons. Forget the Lords, the self-proclaimed high and mighty inheritors who did nothing to warrant their titles and for which Mannie had only disdain. They'd returned, many unscathed, and back to their country homes and their posh residences in Belgravia, back to what they did before, mostly nothing, finances intact. How could they relate? They didn't have to, nor did they want to. Foot soldiers came back to poverty, to their sweethearts and wives who'd suffered real hardships, to children who had no idea who they were and back to a load of unkept promises.

MAZE STOOD AT the window looking out at the river, at the tug boats chugging along carrying cargo to the docks farther down stream — and the beautiful yachts, no particular destination intended, drifting with the assistance of a slight breeze.

"It was a dreadful war," he told Clara. "I witnessed atrocities no man should come upon. I saw weak men die and brave men weep. I was a young, naive boy when I signed up; I returned after the fighting finally ceased a mature adult, wiser and fully aware of man's inhumanity to man. The images remain vivid in my mind. They stay; they torment me. I thought I could paint them out. I cannot. I have to speak them and write them."

Clara departed Chelsea at the end of that day with a little more insight into the man she was working for. His appearance, his surroundings, his art told her he was not just another reluctant warrior. There was something compelling about him; he made her want to know more about him. She began to understand why he was asked to write his memoir and now understood why he had to. If her dad asked her again why an artist needed to write a book, she had the answer.

"He had to write what he couldn't paint."

Chapter 8

Mannie and Sula

Oswald Mosley, a Fascist, a racist and a Jew hater, intent on targeting the East End, sought police protection for his intended march on the densely populated Jewish immigrant areas of Whitechapel and Aldgate.

The Jewish Board of Deputies denounced the march as Jew baiting. A leader of the East End Jews petitioned the British Home Office to stop Mosley only to be turned down without explanation.

If the Home Office wasn't going to stop it, then the Jews and their sympathizers would. They knew the route, and none of them were going to get past Aldgate Station or near St. Botolph's Church.

Organized rallies continued in the East End.

Mannie spoke in Hyde Park at Speaker's Corner and during the week at his old haunt St. Botolph's. He and the Aldgate boys went to listen to the many speakers who railed on about labor and unemployment. Yes, they needed work, but now there was another threat on their doorstep. The black-shirted Fascists were planning to march where they lived, past their homes and shops. What the speakers had to say was lost in the fray.

Mannie learned about the march a week before it was to take place. He called upon his Socialist partners and fellow Jews to rally outside St. Botolph's to prepare to face the Mosley marchers. They were to use whatever it took to stop the march. It was time to make their intentions known. This was not to be a peaceful demonstration; they were to take a stand and make sure Mosley would never set foot in their East End again.

"This is where we live! This is our terrain!" Mannie shouted above the noise of the every increasing crowd. "The police should be protecting us, not watching out for them, and seeing that the police won't do they're job, we'll just have to do it for ourselves."

Mannie stood on a bench in front of hundreds of people; the word had got around. The turnout was far better than expected, and more kept coming. All were tired of Mosley's attacks; they'd had enough. They were there to stop this happening, to show them in no uncertain terms Jews could and would fight back. The placards they carried said it loud and clear.

The crowd grew quiet as Mannie, goaded on by the response, lifted his bullhorn and demanded their attention. "How were they given permission, and we get turned down? How come they get police protection, and when we ask for it we're ignored? There's something very wrong here. Stop them in their tracks. Show them we're not going to sit back and let them walk all over us."

Mannie had accomplished what he'd set out to do; he'd whipped up the crowd. "Find whatever you can, dustbin lids, umbrellas, sticks, or use your fists if one of them attacks you. Defend yourselves. Put an end to Mosley and his thugs."

A roar of approval went up from the crowd; he had their attention.

"We, the workers — that is if we happen to have a job, of course — have fought for our country, have given our lives and are now expected to allow these dregs of humanity to march down our streets in Mussolini uniforms, uninvited and unstopped. Have we all gone soft? Are we not insane to allow this to happen? Has this country of ours completely lost touch with reality and common decency?"

"If they 'ad it in the first place!" one of them yelled.

Mannie pressed on: "We're right back to where we were before the war, the war they tell us we won. If this is the result of that win, I'd hate to see what it'd be like if we lost!"

"We won the war and lost the battle," a voice came from the crowd.

"Has anyone bothered to tell them they're the minority in this country?" Mannie threw the question out to the crowd. "We keep their factories and mines going, polish their floors and wash their clothes."

"And look after their kids while they sun themselves on the Riviera. Too bloody right." Response was coming from the left, the right and center.

"They don't give a cod's wallop what happens to us," Mannie kept on. "They don't hear us, and they don't care about us. It's about time we made ourselves heard, and if it means a bit more bruising, so be it. They've already done about as much harm as they could. They wiped out more than half of us in the trenches, thousands and thousands left behind dead on the battlefields. It wasn't our war; it was theirs. It's in memory of those lads who perished that we demand compensation, housing, pensions for their families and a decent living for ourselves. And Mosley, who is himself one of them bloody aristocrats, cannot, will not and shall not march in our streets. He will be stopped. He and his miserable men will never march our streets again, not as long as I have a voice to command you to stop this assault once and for all."

"Right! 'It 'em over the head with their cricket bats, that's what I says!"

"Pinch the copper's truncheon," another piped up.

"I've got me own; don't need no copper's truncheon!" a protester shouted, wielding it above his head.

Mannie wasn't to be sidetracked. "Listen, listen to me. We start first with the chief bastard, Mr. Oswald Mosley. A Fascist supreme, he does what he likes, says what he likes and marches where he likes, and we have to put an end to it. He wants the Jews out. We want him out. He wants the immigrants deported. We want him stifled. He wants the country ruled by Fascists. We want the country ruled by a responsible government. This is Great Britain, for God's sake, not some poverty stricken, corrupt island in the middle of nowhere. This is birthplace of Chaucer and Shakespeare, and if we add Dickens, we're up to date with men of conscience. I say to you today, we wipe out the Fascists and take back your country!"

"Bloody right!"

"'Oo gave them permission?"

The crowd responded, just as Mannie had hoped for. And his second in command whispered in his ear, "The police; they're circling. Don't like the look of it."

It didn't stop Mannie. "You've got a job to do. Get to it. Take a stand. Do whatever it takes to get those buggers out of our East End." Mannie wasn't going to stand down.

A policeman shoved his way up to Mannie and tore the bullhorn out of his hands. Another pulled him off the bench. "For your own good, mate."

"Mosley has the right to march. I have the right to speak. We fought for that right." Mannie struggled to be set free.

"Then do it in Hyde Park, Speakers Corner. Join the other 'nutters. Plenty of them there — just like you."

"I live here. I'll speak here."

"You'll do what you're bloody told, rights or no rights."

"What about the Black Shirts?" yelled Mannie at the top of his voice. "We're the criminals, and they're the good old boys. There's something very wrong in our society!"

SET FOR THE following Sunday, October the fourth, Mosley was granted permission and summoned his men, five thousand of them, to congregate at the Tower of London, where, in Fascist uniform, black shirts, jodhpurs and boots, he gave the order to begin the march. With police protection and led by a band of drummers, pipers and trumpet players, they paraded down Royal Mint Street toward their intended destination.

Six thousand police stood by, many on horseback, all there to hold back defiant Jews, Communists and Laborites intent on stopping the march. Six thousand mounted and foot police by actual count were armed with guns and batons. Not there to protect the Jews; they were there to insure Mosley's march went off without incident. Mannie's followers, loyal British citizens, and thousands of others, members and sympathizers from all parts of London, mobilized and vowed to put a stop to the Fascists. It was time someone did, since the police weren't on their side. Barriers were constructed, buses moved into horizontal positions and human chains across major roads as the East Enders awaited the approaching hoard.

Word travelled fast; the boys devised a plan. Mannie and his colleagues ran to all the toy shops in the East End, bought up every marble they could find, gathered up more of their followers and rushed to Cable Street where the Mosley marchers were headed from their starting point at the Tower of London.

The mounted police attempted to hold back the thousands of protesters lining the streets. Surreptitiously, Mannie and the Aldgate boys moved within the assembled crowd till they reached the curb. There they scattered handfuls of marbles onto the cobblestones in the path of the marchers causing police horses and the Fascists to slip and lose their balance. Foot police barged into the crowd, swearing, hitting and kicking.

Mannie's brigade fought back.

Wheelchairs swung into booted brutes. Fists bashed in Black Shirt's noses. Mannie held high his walking stick, using it as a weapon, swinging and landing it on Mosley's Fascist hooligans. He grabbed a young Fascist by the scruff of the neck, pushing him into an alley. "Who the hell do you think you are?" Mannie yelled, giving the Fascist no time to answer. "You want to be a Fascist. Buy a one-way ticket to Italy. Mr. Mussolini will welcome you with open arms. In fact, take the whole bloody lot of them with you. If Mussolini turns you down, go to fucking Germany and join the Nazi Party!"

Still holding the Fascist by his shirt collar, Mannie twisted him 'round. "See those blokes there, the ones in wheelchairs, the blind and the maimed; they fought for your freedom. Millions more of them are buried in Ypres, in Paschendale and under white crosses on Flanders Fields. You should be kneeling at their tombstones, not hounding us. You're a disgrace to your country." Mannie let go. "If ever I see you here or anyone else for that matter in that ridiculous uniform, I promise not even your mother will recognize you by the time you get home — that is, if you manage to get home." He gave him a final kick in the groin and left him, rolled over, clutching his genitals and crying out for help, until a copper cuffed Mannie and dragged him to the Black Maria, already packed with protestors, to be carted off to jail.

HENRY, NELLY AND Sula watched the remaining marchers from their front window facing onto the High Street.

"What's the use of barricades? Black Shirts, hundreds of them, all over the place. Mannie's right; the police aren't looking after our side. That's for sure, Nelly. I'm not 'avin it." Henry couldn't take it any more. He left the room.

"Where you goin'?" Nelly asked.

"You'll see when I get back." Henry returned with a bucket of water.

"What's that for?"

"Chuck it over them. Pity the chamber pot's empty; that would go, too." Henry let go of the contents of his bucket and was about to go for more.

Nelly held him back. "Won't do no good, luv."

"Don't care; makes me feel better." And off he went to fill his bucket again. "Bunch of bloody Nazis, that's what they are." Henry emptied another bucket. "How they get away with it is beyond me."

"They're not Nazis — they're Fascists," Sula corrected her dad.

"So? What's the difference? One lot wears black shirts, the other brown!" Henry snapped.

"I'm going to drag Mannie home before he gets into more trouble."

"Let him fight his own battles. You stay here," Nelly demanded.

"I've got to find him. He's not in the best of shape, you know. Won't be able to hold his own against this lot." Sula gave Henry a kiss on his bald head and took her leave.

"I don't know what's got into our girls, Nelly. One off with the toffs where she's no right to be, another married to a bloke without an ounce of common sense. Anna's about the only one not bouncing off the walls, and the way things are going, I can't see her being a pushover for much longer. Gawd, we got it wrong somewhere!"

"You listen to me, Henry Levy. Our girls are strong young women; they ain't prepared to take a back seat to no one. I'd say we did them proud!"

"You did, not me, luv; you made them who they are."

It was getting fierce out on the streets of the East End. Shots were heard. Ambulances arrived. Horses slipped on the cobblestones as protesters threw marbles under their hooves. The police were overwhelmed, never had to deal with anything like this before. Lorries blocked the smaller streets. Barrows upturned. Shop windows smashed. The Jews weren't giving up; neither were the Commies nor the Socialists.

And Nelly wasn't done with them, either; she shouted epithets out the window. "Bunch of bloody hypocrites, think you look so smart in those disgusting uniforms. When you take 'em off you'll still be the ugly buggers you always were underneath."

"Yeah, but for the first time we're fighting back, and it's about bloody time too." Henry hung out the window shouting and waving his fist. "Give it to 'em, comrades."

"You're not a Commie," Nelly reminded him.

"I don't care; at a time like this we can be what we like. They're fighting for what we believe in, and if I were a few years younger, I'd be down there with them."

Nelly let him be. He had every right to express his outrage. This was something she never thought she'd ever see in Aldgate, and it was happening before her very eyes.

SULA, AVOIDING THE High Street, took the side alleys to reach St. Botolph's in search of Mannie. The situation was out of control.

She pushed her way through the crowd, avoiding the horses, ducking under the areas the police had cordoned off before coming face to face with a couple of Black Shirts who'd broken ranks. She spat at one of them. He turned to attack, but by then she'd disappeared into the crowd. She was just nearing St. Botolph's when she lost her balance and fell, scraping her head against the stone steps.

Three young men in the crowd saw her go down and formed a protective area around her. One of the sturdier chaps lifted her gently as the others cleared a path for him to carry her into the church.

"Here, take this handkerchief. Try to stop the bleeding. That cut looks deep."

He applied the handkerchief to the bloody scrape on Sula's head.

"I can't feel my legs," Sula managed. "Everything's numb from my waist down."

"I'll go find someone. Here, hold on to this."

Sula pressed the hanky on the wound. "Please don't leave me here. I'm scared," Sula begged.

"You need a doctor. I'll try to find one."

A priest came to her. No, she didn't need the last rites, but she did agree she needed a doctor.

"I saw a St. John's Ambulance close by," Sula told the young man. "It was near Castle Street."

The priest stayed with her and the young man ran off toward Castle Street. The priest hovered. "What were you doing in the middle of all this?" he said, unable to understand why she was out among the crowds.

"Wanted to save my husband from himself," she answered.

"And did you?"

"Obviously not; only hoping he hasn't been taken by the police."

"He'll have a lot of company. They're taking them away by the dozen. Don't worry; nothing will happen to them. They're probably safer in custody. I'm more concerned about you."

An hour later Sula was on her way to the Royal London Hospital on the Mile End Road, while Mannie was being escorted to the local Police Station where he was charged with inciting a riot.

Mosley and his marches were finally disbanded, the rising had ended. The Socialists and Communists went back to their community halls and the Jews, proud of what they'd accomplished, began to clean up the debris. Glass and marbles, horse manure and broken barriers, bashed in dustbin lids and torn leaflets, fruit from the barrows rolled into the gutters while police cuffed looters and store keepers gazed upon the damage to their property. Traffic was beginning to move again. The announcer on the wireless called it the worst riot in living history as the walking wounded limped home.

WITH DINNER READY and only Henry, Anna and Bernie present, Nelly was frantic; neither Sula nor Mannie had come back. Clara was probably having a hard time getting home, and Sidney could be caught in a jam near the factory. Mannie, who had been known to stay in the pub longer than need be, would have been dragged out by now if Sula had found him.

"Mannie's probably been picked up," Anna said nonchalantly, as if it was something that happened every day.

"I'll go to the police station, see what I can find out there." Bernie put on his coat, ready to leave.

"It wouldn't be the first time," Anna carried on. "Mannie should stick to writing and give up politics. Can't see he's getting anywhere with it! And you, Bernie, you empty your pockets of all that horsey stuff; we don't need you in there, too."

Henry chimed in, "Mannie'll shut up when hell freezes over, and that ain't going to happen. I'm not waiting for them. Put the grub on the table, Nelly, your old man's starving."

"You 'aint got your priorities straight, Henry Levy."

"Yes, I have. No one listens to me. I told Sula not to go, and she went. I've said to Mannie on more than one occasion to give it up, and he hasn't. As for Clara, she's hopeless. So, what else can I do? No sense letting the food get cold. I'll have mine with you now; they can have theirs when they get back."

"I'll wait for Bernie." Anna wasn't in the mood to eat.

Bernie returned an hour later, having found Mannie where Anna said he would be — at the station with half a dozen down and outs, prostitutes and drunks, all waiting to be fingerprinted.

"They're keeping Mannie overnight, fined him two pounds. They'll release him in the morning."

"That's a lot of money," Nelly complained.

"Worth every penny, if you ask me," Henry stated with pride.

"Probably didn't trust him not to start it all over again," Nelly surmised. "What's more to the point, where do you think Sula is?"

"She's not at the station, I know that much," Bernie spoke up. "Maybe she's having trouble getting through the mess outside. It's really bad."

"She could be with her Toynbee friends, spouting poetry; you know she gets carried away when she's with them. She'll turn up sooner or later. She always does."

"No. I got a funny feeling. Something's not right."

"What's for dinner, Ma?" Bernie asked, hungry as usual.

"Cold soup, cold meat and cold potatoes," was all that Nelly had to say. She was putting on her coat to go out and look for Sula.

"Where you going?" Henry got up to stop her.

"I have to find Sula."

"You just sit down, have your supper and wait like the rest of us. Sula will come home when she's ready. No sense walking the streets looking for her. Not now. Not with what's been going on all day."

For one of the few times in Henry and Nelly's long marriage, Henry persuaded Nelly to listen to him. He was as worried as she was, but this time he refused to show it.

CHAPTER 9

Sula

NELLY AND HENRY sat up all night. Bernie collected Mannie from the police station. They went back to Twenty-One hoping to find Sula had come home. She hadn't. They were about to go search for Sula when a knock came on the door downstairs. Henry rushed to find out who it might be, hoping against hope it was Sula.

It wasn't.

Constable Higgins stood on Nelly's front step. He introduced himself, as if an introduction was really necessary. Higgins had been around for years, walked the neighborhood beat for so long he was part of the fixtures and fittings. Known as Flat Foot Charlie, his claim to fame was he'd helped apprehend a famous criminal early on in his career; nobody really knew if this might be true. Some said it was Jack the Ripper, others suggested it was a royal personage looking for a prostitute. As a young girl Clara was convinced it was Bill Stickers. When she grew older and wiser she dropped his name from her list. Whoever it was or was not, it had nothing to do with why he had rung the doorbell at Twenty-One this particular day.

"What is it? If you have something to say, then you better say it to all of us." Henry stood aside to let Higgins in, then led the way upstairs.

Higgins, facing the family all seated around the parlor table, spoke to them in his official voice. "I am 'ere to inform you that a female going by the name of Sula Lewis, who I am told lives 'ere, 'as been taken by ambulance to the Royal London 'ospital and 'as been admitted to the neurology ward. She will be 'eld there under medical supervision for further investigation."

"What happened? Is she injured? Is she ill?" Nelly begged for information.

"Spit it out, Higgins. What else do you know?" Mannie demanded.

"This is what I know, Mrs. Levy," said Higgins. He ignored Mannie completely. "Your daughter was one of many participants in an unruly crowd 'angin' out at St. Botolph's. In the confusion that ensued she was knocked down, and though not visibly injured except for an abrasion over her left eye, appeared in good condition, though 'er legs stopped working."

"What you talking about?" Nelly didn't comprehend.

"I gather she couldn't walk, ma'am."

"And don't describe her as being in good condition, Higgins; you make her sound like a stray animal shoved in the dog catcher's cage!" Henry wanted a bit of respect shown for his daughter.

"I was attempting to ease your mind, sir. Rest assured she is being well looked after."

"That's better," Anna spoke up.

Looking beyond Nelly and now directly at Mannie, Higgins couldn't resist a dig. "And I know all about you — you were the instigator of the incident at St. Botolph's."

Henry held on to Mannie as he got up to clobber Higgins.

"That being the case one would expect the 'usband of the injured to stop blowing 'is mouth 'orf and accompany 'is wife to the 'ospital," His voice dragged on. "On the other 'and, perhaps she isn't as important as your need to 'ear the sound of your own voice."

The color drained from Mannie's face; he'd no idea Sula attended the rally. "Why didn't somebody tell me?" he cried out. "Why didn't someone stop her? When did she leave? When did the accident happen? I specifically told her to stay away; I knew it could become violent when the Black Shirts turned up."

Nelly suggested Mannie take a deep breath and calm down. Anna was busy looking up Clara's work number to phone her, hoping to catch her before she left work.

Mannie had another go at Higgins. "I didn't bloody well know my wife was there. I expected a large turnout, and we got it. I told her to stay away. If you and your constabulary continue to allow Mosley to march down the streets of our neighborhood wearing Fascist uniforms, you can expect more outbreaks and more injuries. My wife is in the hospital because of you and your inability to stop them — or maybe it's just because you're on their side and don't give a shit about us. We stand up for ourselves — can't depend on your cooperation. You've got a lot to answer for, Constable Higgins; you and your mates caused this, not me."

Henry, anticipating what could happen next, stepped in again before Mannie got himself into more hot water. He shoved Mannie out of the way and thanked Higgins for coming over.

Higgins, giving Mannie a perishing look, removed his helmet from under his arm, placed it on his head and made ready to leave. "I wish to impress upon you," he said in a most formal manner, "I am only the messenger in this instance. I am an officer of the law doin' my duty, and in this case more than my duty. The 'ospital advised me to inform you, and that I've done. Visiting hours are from seven to nine each evening."

Mannie wasn't waiting for visiting hours. Amazingly active, considering his disability, he made it down the stairs alongside Higgins, causing the constable to hang on to the banister for dear life.

"Watch it, mate. I could 'ave you up for — "

Mannie wasn't there to hear the rest of Higgins prosecutorial utterances. He was out the door and limping his way to the hospital less than a mile from where they lived.

BACK IN THE parlor, Henry wasn't helping matters by repeating over and over again, "I should have stopped Sula, should have made her listen to me."

Nelly, not knowing what else to do, grabbed a duster and began polishing the furniture — first the piano, then the gramophone. That finished, she attacked the floor with a broom. She pulled the red chenille tablecloth off the table and gave it a good shake. Even Boadicea's cage got a good clean out.

"What you doing? That's Edie's job!" Anna exclaimed.

"Got to get the place ready for when we bring Sula home."

"I'm not waiting for the bloody matron's permission to see my daughter," Henry announced. He grabbed his jacket and struggled to pull it on as he hurried out of the parlor and followed in the footsteps of Higgins and Mannie.

Nelly knew it was a waste of time trying to stop him; he might even catch up with Mannie if he started off in the right direction. Still sweeping up invisible dirt, she shouted after him, "You'll be lucky if you get to sit in the waiting room. I've been through this before with Sula; when she had a chest infection they wouldn't let me in 'til visiting hours. We're better off staying here; can't see standing in a cold corridor, waiting for the doors to open — won't do nobody no good."

Henry was well out of ear shot now. He was on a mission; she was his daughter, and he was going to find out what happened to her. Nelly could wait for visiting hours. He wasn't waiting for anyone's permission!

THE ROYAL LONDON Hospital, founded in 1740, was run by a mixture of volunteers and paid professionals. It was there Edith Cavell, a nurse in the Great War and wrongly accused traitor, worked before going to Belgium to run an Army hospital unit. Cavell was later executed in 1915. The hospital building had not been renovated or improved since the early Victorian era.

For the Levy family, the Royal London was conveniently situated. Nelly didn't believe in doctors or hospitals and rarely needed to visit either. Her babies were delivered at home with a midwife and her handed-down remedies worked for most other ailments. If, on the rare occasion, a fever lingered too long or someone broke a leg or needed more than she could manage, Henry was dispatched with the patient to the hospital and given strict instructions — they were under no circumstances to be admitted. They were there to be seen, be plastered, bandaged, stitched and medicated and then returned home.

"The trouble with hospitals," Nelly's mantra began, "is you get more than you bargain for every time you set foot in one. My sister Lizzie went in with a cold and came out with pneumonia. Not to mention the kids who go to have their tonsils removed and leave bleeding like stuck pigs. Okay, if you're dying; otherwise, stay away." Nelly, determined to get Sula out of hospital as soon as possible, laid down the law. "I'll deal with her; I'm not leaving it to them."

SULA WAS IN a ward of twenty patients, ten on each side of a long row of beds. A matron, starched stiff and heavy jowled, sat at one end of the ward, a sister sat at the other. There was no way of getting past either of them until the bell for visiting hours rang. It would have been easier to steal the Crown Jewels from the Tower of London than get past those two dragons. Rules were rules, and they were not to be broken.

Matron kept her wards spotless, even the bed knobs had to be sparkling. The hospital help despised her, the doctors avoided her and the sisters, hoping to become matrons themselves one day, made excuses for her. There was a little more leeway allowed by the night shift staff; unfortunately for Mannie, the matron in Sula's ward had not yet been replaced by the night shift. She'd come on duty at six in the morning and, impervious to long hours served, remained immovable, inflexible and infuriating to all who visited.

Mannie paced the corridor. He'd tried cajoling, shouting and even bribing, but his efforts fell on deaf ears. Matron held fast; she wasn't about to let him in or anyone else until the visitor's bell rang to signal bona fide entry. The few intrepids who managed to get as far as the ward corridors were dispatched post haste to the waiting room, an uninviting, stark and uncomfortable area with no windows. It was smoky and full of visitors in various stages of emotional stress, and there weren't enough seats. Mannie had to stand.

"What do they think we're going to do, steal the bed pans!" Mannie exclaimed to no one in particular. "I can't see my wife because that dragon of a matron sits there like a guard at a prison camp and won't tell us anything."

A woman in her late fifties, who also had plenty to grumble about, said, "Buggered if I know. My 'arry's been in here for weeks, still can't find out what's wrong with 'im except 'ee's gone yellow and looks like a Chinaman."

"Bloody marvelous, isn't it?" another frustrated relative said. "If you see a doctor, you're lucky. Forget about a consultant. I mean, if you actually see one of them with your own eyes, I think you're supposed to genuflect. They're unapproachable. They walk around like Jesus Christ with his disciples, carrying a stethoscope in place of a cross. They won't speak directly to the family, they *convey*, that's their word, not mine — had to look it up in a dictionary. They *convey* through a lackey who tells us we have to go through the matron."

"And you land back exactly where you started," a tall fellow responded as he munched on a sandwich under a sign that read: NO FOOD, DRINK OR PIPES ALLOWED. "I suppose, like me, you've noticed how the matron suddenly gets very busy and has no time to speak to you the moment she sees you approaching. Charming, absolutely bloody charming."

One of them recognized Mannie. "You're the bloke who spoke at the rally. I got no answers from Matron 'eiver. I tried to ask the sister; she looked at me as if I'd crawled out of a piece of cheese, said wait for the doctor, and I'm still waiting. If you're lucky, you might get a smidgen of information from a first-rung-of-the-ladder nurse, and what does she know? Bugger all, she can tell you if your dad's eaten his breakfast or 'ad a bowel movement. That's about it. Add that to your list of grievances, comrade."

They were all clamoring to have their say.

"Wait till my lot get here," Mannie announced. "She'll have a hard time chucking them out!"

A messenger came into the waiting room. "Is there a Mr. Mannie Lewis present?"

Mannie identified himself.

"Come with me."

Mannie followed him to a small room off Sula's ward, where a man in a white coat sat at a desk reading. He looked up as Mannie entered. "Sit down, Mr. Lewis, I'm Dr. Shapiro. I have your wife's notes here; it is your wife, I presume, and you are the husband of Sula Lewis?"

Mannie nodded.

"Your wife had a minor accident, couple of grazes and no broken bones. That is the good news. On examining her I found she has some form of muscular degeneration; we will have to run some tests. Her condition may well be chronic; by that I mean, if it turns out to be one of the muscular degenerative diseases, then all we can do is treat her and hope she goes into remission. In other words, although the accident was not serious, it was in many ways a fortunate mishap, not that I approve of large crowds shoving young women to the ground, you understand."

"We were doing all right until the Black Shirts arrived, and she wasn't supposed to be there." Mannie, in shock, wasn't taking it all in.

"Right. I haven't got time to get into politics now. We have placed your wife in the neural diseases ward. I have spoken with her, more or less a repeat of what I've just told you. Under the circumstances, I am giving permission for you to see her now." He scribbled something on a piece of paper and gave it to Mannie. "Hand this to Matron, and you will gain entry." Shapiro smiled when he saw Mannie's reaction. "Matron's bark is far worse than her bite, believe me. I have experienced both."

"Thank you, Doctor. Thank you for taking the time to speak to me." Mannie made his way to Sula's ward and handed Matron the doctor's note; miracle of miracles, she read it and waved him through.

Sula saw Mannie making his way to her bedside. He looked okay, walking with his crutch, a plaster over his right cheek — must have got that in the Botolph's brawl. He gave her a kiss, and for a few seconds both were lost for words.

"Now see what you've gone and done," he said, trying to lighten the gloom.

"Me?"

"Yes, you. Sitting up in bed like the Queen of Sheba."

"Then you better get me a throne, 'cos I can't walk. Wish I knew what it was. Going for tests tomorrow; hope we find out soon. I feel so helpless. I hate being in hospital. I lost my balance — wasn't your fault, Mannie. You really got the crowd going. Just wanted to be there to support you. That'll teach me to mind my own business."

"Not you, Sula; my business has always been your business. I need you; you're my soul mate."

They spent time consoling one another. He told her about the rally and being taken off to the police station, said he'd had a talk with her doctor, liked and trusted him. She told him about the St. John's Ambulance men and how she had to wait on a stretcher until they found a bed for her. "Stuck in a church, I was. A Jewish girl looking up at Jesus Christ, priests hovering, the flower arrangement committee wafting perfumed hankies over my head. One of them even brought a lily; she thought I was dead. Have you any idea how strange that felt?"

"Got to hand it to them, though; they dealt with you well. Have to pop in and thank them one of these days." Mannie changed the subject. "Seems a nice chap, Dr. Shapiro."

"He is. A bit young, but then I prefer young to old and stodgy. Mum and Dad coming?"

"Yes, they'll be here for visiting hours. I wouldn't be surprised if your dad isn't somewhere in the hospital as we speak. He's probably lost, causing a ruckus on the wrong floor. Matron wouldn't let him in anyway."

"He's got no sense of direction. Should we put out an alert?"

They both laughed.

"At scheduled visiting hours, if he's here, he'll be shown to the right ward," Mannie said.

"What about, Clara? Does she know?"

"Anna phoned her at work; she'll come in on her way home, I'm sure." Mannie glanced around the ward. Every bed was filled.

"They said I was lucky to get a bed. Lucky? I hate it here," Sula moaned.

But Mannie pressed on, saying, "We'll get you out as soon as we can. Just need a diagnosis."

CLARA WAS ON her way to her desk in the studio when Rogers stopped her on the stairs.

"There was a telephone call for you a few moments ago. I took the message. Your sister Sula was found admitted to Royal London Hospital on the Mile End Road. I think the caller was your other sister; she said her name was Anna. She wanted to let you know — said perhaps you could go to hospital on your way home this evening. I would be more than willing to drive you now if you wish."

Concerned, Clara asked, "Did she say why she's in the hospital?"

"No, and I didn't think it was my place to ask."

Clara glanced at her watch. It was nearly time for her to leave. "Do you think Mr. Maze would mind if I leave a bit early?"

"Of course, not. You must go. I'll inform Mr. Maze. It's a family emergency; he wouldn't want you to stay under the circumstances."

Thank God I'm not with Abbott, she thought; the roof could fall in, and he'd keep me sitting there 'til knocking off time. "I'll be here tomorrow, I promise, and on time. My sister has had a couple of incidents recently. I have to believe it has something to do with that." Clara broke down and told Rogers about the riots in the East End.

Sula hadn't come home that night; and she and her family had been worried sick.

"I read about it in the *Evening Star*. Awful, just awful. You should not have come in to work at all. Mr. Maze would have understood, but wait before you leave," Rogers said. "Cook baked a batch of biscuits; she took them out of the oven just a few minutes ago. I'll ask her to put some in a bag for you to share with your family. Have them with a nice cup of tea." Rogers lifted the intercom phone and called down to the kitchen.

A few minutes later Maggie came up holding a bag of warm, freshly baked, wonderfully fragrant ginger biscuits.

"Thank you, and thank Cook for me," Clara said, completely overwhelmed by their kindness.

"Steady as you go, Mrs. Simon. If you need us, do not hesitate to phone."

ON THE DOT of seven Nelly arrived at the hospital. She went straight to the admitting area, asked where emergency cases came in and was directed from there to Sula's ward. Henry, on the other hand, was still searching. Eventually Mannie said he would go and look for him while Nelly stayed with Sula.

"Don't know what to do about your dad; if he was looking for a race track he'd find it in a minute! Not to worry; he'll turn up eventually. He always does. Now let's have a look at you. Told you not to rush out, didn't I? Never listen to your old mum — "

Sula interrupted, "It had nothing to do with the riot, Mum; it just happened there. Could have been anywhere, really. We'll know more after the tests come back."

CHAPTER 10

Challenges

THREE WEEKS LATER Sula learned about her condition. She was right; it had nothing to do with Mannie. Sula had disseminated sclerosis, and there would be lots more tests and experimental treatments, though no known cure. Remission possible — but she had little choice other than to accept the fact that she had a permanent lifelong condition.

That was all Nelly had to hear. Every day she arrived at the hospital with nourishing food in a wicker basket and a lecture to boot. "Home cooked food, not the mash they serve up. You'll eat what we eat, don't care where you are. If I have to come up the fire escape to deliver it, you'll have what's going to make you strong. Your legs are your slaves, Sula, not your masters: work them, control them and use them."

Henry, his heart breaking, unable to be upbeat like Nelly, wanted to do everything for his daughter; he reached for objects out of her reach, couldn't bear to see her try to walk when the pain got too much, would have taken the disease as his own if he could.

Nelly, on the other hand, was determined to overcome all obstacles. "It's no use skulking around with dreary faces. She mustn't let it get the better of her. Got a tribulation, face it, and do something about it. She don't give in, and neither do we. If she has to walk with a stick, it's not so terrible. Mannie has to — at least she didn't have to go to war to earn hers! The sooner we can get her out of here the better. A few more treatments — and that's that. No more experiments on my daughter. Plenty of rats around here. Let 'em experiment on them!"

Some days Sula was ready to throw in her hat, others her determination overcame her depression. It wasn't easy. But Nelly kept on at her; she had a devoted husband, a caring family, an inquisitive mind, all the positives she could come up with, and if she kept those in mind and eliminated the negatives, she would make a fool of the disease and become the ruler of her fate. Clara came in every evening after work. She kept Sula amused with stories of Paul Maze and the people who came to visit.

"You'll meet him one day. He's unusual in many ways. Has no side to him. Just the other day I found him having a long conversation with Tom, the chimney sweep. Lord knows what they were on about. He traipsed poor Tom up to the studio, dropping soot on every step, sat him down on the model's stool and sketched. Rogers was beside himself — called for Maggie to come immediately with brush and pan, and clean away the coal dust. Finally Maze let Tom go, and poor Maggie, having just got to the last step, had to start again at the top. That's what he was there for in the first place; when he'd finished the smoke went up the chimney instead of into the room, and Maze had done his portrait!"

"Tell me more," Sula said, laughing for the first time since she'd been admitted to hospital.

Clara bumped into Mannie on her way out of the ward that evening. "Two visitors at a time, Sister said."

Nelly was a fixture; she wasn't about to give up her place, and it was Mannie's turn. "Haven't seen too much of you lately, Clara," Mannie said, stopping to chat. "Guess you're too busy for the likes of us."

"Nonsense. Sometimes I think it's you avoiding me!"

"Never. Why would I do that? Anyway, I've got good news. I, Mannie Lewis, Socialist supreme, actually had an article published in *The Times* last week. Not bad, eh?"

"That's terrific." Clara was genuinely impressed. "Mr. Maze gets *The Times* delivered daily. Might still be a copy around."

"Didn't expect him to get *The Daily Worker!*" Mannie countered.

"*The Times*, eh? That's quite a feather in your cap." Clara wasn't about to give credence to his sarcasm.

"And you — what you up to?" Mannie inquired. "Is the grass any greener on the other side of the fence?"

"They're people just like us. Some nice, some a bit toffee nosed. I enjoy the work."

Mannie took her by the arm, steering her away from the hospital exit, down a long corridor to the military ward. "Want to see the real world, Clara? Take a look in there; all these years on, and they're still coming in, still suffering. Have they got jobs? I doubt it. See any officers? Don't bother to look; they're not in here. They got special treatment in private hospitals and convalescent homes. We lost over a million foot soldiers — kept feeding us in like cattle to the slaughter. Does your Chelsea bloke have nightmares every night, wake up in a cold sweat frightened and scared to close his eyes again? I do, and they do. Fighting a war with a pencil and paper isn't exactly a hardship."

Clara turned away, defending Maze. "I can only tell you what I know. Mr. Maze volunteered for the Army. He not only volunteered, he persevered until they accepted him. He carried out the orders he was given and did reconnaissance for both the French and the British armies, and if you think a gun makes you more of a patriot than an artist with a pencil who rode his motorbike through mortar fire to bring back information for the generals, you are wrong. Maybe he's writing a book because he can't get the pictures of war out of his mind. Mum says none of this goes into your boots. It has stayed with him as it has with you. You write what you feel, and so does he. Perhaps someone, some day, the people who start these wars will actually listen, will read and get the message before shedding the blood of innocents. That's my hope, Mannie."

"Come in with me; talk to these poor buggers."

"I will, but not tonight — over the weekend. I'm going home. Not much visiting time left."

"Here's a suggestion for your Mr. Maze," Mannie said in parting. "Tell him to add an epilogue to his book and call it, 'Not Over Yet.' He hasn't seen these blokes; his lot mourn their own fallen heroes and never come to visit ours. Well, tell him in this hospital these men, these soldiers, are our living dead, our everyday heroes. The only mistake they made was to stay alive."

Clara did not pursue the subject. Instead she said, "Better hurry now, Mannie. Visiting hours are fading."

He nodded and turned away — off to see his Sula.

CLARA HAD BEEN at the Cheyne Walk establishment for nearly a month. She was getting on well with Maze and settling into her new environment. Ronan had not exaggerated one iota when he said Maze needed help; Maze's command of the English language when spoken was near perfect, but when it came to the written word it was anything but.

On the days Maze had appointments in town, he left her notes scribbled in smudged pastels, usually on backs of envelopes, all in vivid colors and near impossible to decipher. His notes were amusing, often accompanied by a sketch of himself running or sitting or just thinking. Clara was getting to know this man; he could be entertaining and amusing one moment and completely serious the next.

Clara suggested very politely that it might be more advantageous and certainly easier for her if he used a pencil and a clean sheet of paper when he needed to record ideas. He promised he would. She left pencils and paper on his desk, in his studio, in the sitting room, anywhere he might be when an idea grabbed him. That's what he said — not what he did.

She continued to struggle with his scraps of information until Rogers came to her aid. Over a cup of tea in the kitchen he tried to explain the enigma that was Maze. "You have to learn to tame the beast, albeit a very nice beast, really not a beast at all. He's what I would term an eccentric original. You have to be firm. Insist he work on the book every day. Don't be afraid to gently reprimand him. Today is a good example. He's out on his *promenade*. He never calls a walk a walk; it's always his *promenade*. Before he leaves make sure he's left you sufficient work for the day; he could be out for hours."

"I haven't laid eyes on him today." Clara shrugged, not knowing what else to say.

"Mr. Maze meets people in the park or finds something to sketch, and we never know when he's coming back. By taking a few simple steps and applying them at the appropriate times, the book could be completed on schedule."

"It's a bit daunting, Rogers."

"You'll do all right, Mrs. Simon, once you've learned how to handle him! We've had parlor maids, chambermaids, cooks and even employed a gardener. Totally unnecessary, the latter. We haven't got a garden, just a couple of window boxes at the back of the house, and I

could have kept them up. You're the first secretary, Mrs. Simon. If I
can help you with anything, I am more than willing to do so. I have
learned to read his handwriting."

"You've got enough to do. I'll struggle on," Clara said.

Maze came back an hour later, invigorated by his walk. "Not too
many days like this in London, had to make the most of it."

This was Clara's opportunity. "Can we talk about the reason for
my being here, Mr. Maze?"

Maze looked at her, somewhat perplexed. "And what does that mean?"

"You employed me to help you write your book. So far we have
the start of a chapter, a lot of scribbled notes, a number of photos and
not much direction as to what I'm supposed to do with it all. I would
like to set up a schedule for us to work together on the book."

"No schedules. The very word frightens me. We'll start right now.
I'm ready, are you?"

Maze had an uncanny knack of taking the wind out of her sails.
Still, she had made her point.

"Take a seat, Clara."

"Here?"

"Why not?"

Clara opened her notebook and tried to keep up with the stream
of consciousness coming at her from Maze. She only hoped she would
be able to read her shorthand back when he'd run out of steam, and
in her estimation that would probably be well past dinner time up at
Twenty-One.

THE NEXT DAY Rogers entered the library, where Maze and Clara
were working, to announce the arrival of Winston Churchill, who
apparently wasn't about to wait to be announced. He and Maze knew
each other well enough, no need for formalities; he was in the room
before Rogers could say a word.

Clara looked up from her notebook, saw Churchill and didn't
know quite what to do. Should she stand, curtsy or follow Rogers out
of the room? She'd never been so close to a man of his importance in
her entire life.

Rogers helped Churchill off with his hat and coat, winked at
Clara, who was attempting to leave while Maze motioned her to stay.

"Rogers, before you go, a brandy for Mr. Churchill and one of those fine Cuban cigars, make it two, one for his pocket." Maze was in a bountiful mood. "Take a seat, Winston. Always good to see you. What's the news of the day?'

"The usual. I'm on the back benches of government these days. I talk, they appear to listen and no one does anything about the stuff going on in Germany. Mark my words, deaf ears cause blind trust."

Clara stayed put. She was back to the shoulds. Should she go over her notes and wait till she was spoken to? Should she excuse herself, saying she had work to do? Maze had indicated she should stay. She guessed she better stay.

"And who is this delightful young lady?"

"She's my gift from the gods. Ronan gave her to me to help write my book. Wouldn't know where to begin without her." He made her sound indispensable.

Churchill gave Clara the once over. "You're a very lucky man, Paul; my secretary's as old as Methuselah — been with me for years. Never was much to look at, but I still couldn't possibly let her go. She's part of the fixtures and fittings. Pleases Clemmie, though; no chance of hanky panky there."

He didn't look the flirtatious type. Clara wondered for a moment whether Maze had any idea what Churchill meant by hanky panky.

"How's the book coming along?" Churchill asked with a nod in Clara's direction, obviously expecting her to speak.

She cleared her throat. "We're making slow progress, sir."

"Got to keep his nose to the grindstone, young lady."

Clara, showing a little more confidence, answered, "I'm trying, sir."

"I see she's got your number, Paul. Get your head together, my friend; it's a story we need right now. Memories are short in certain parts of this land of ours, particularly in the House of Commons. Mind you, they don't forget the mistakes I've made. Like bloody elephants when it comes to throwing them up in my face. You'd think they're lily white. Well, they're not. Politicians make mistakes; we're all human — well, some of us are." Churchill smiled at his own joke. "Anyway, enough of that. If you require my help, Paul, I'll be only too glad to look over what you've written." He turned to Clara again.

"Send over a few pages every now and then; do me good to take a rest from my own writings."

A knock at the door and in came Maggie carrying a silver tray; it held a decanter of brandy, two cut glass snifters and a couple of cigars. She set the tray down on the sideboard.

Maze came over from where he was standing and poured a drink for his guest and one for himself. "To your good health."

"And to yours, too. Don't forget the cigars." Winston was eager to light up.

"Will there be anything else, sir?"

"No, Maggie. Thank you."

Clara realized dictation was over for the day.

"You certainly know how to winkle out pretty girls, Paul."

Maze took the compliment. "It's because I have the eye of a Frenchman."

Churchill remained loyal to his country. "There is absolutely nothing wrong with our English eyes, Paul. We're just more reserved, and perhaps a little intimidated, when it comes to the fairer sex."

"Aah, you are most probably right there, my dear friend."

The book became the topic of conversation. Churchill liked the title; he thought it had a good rhythm to it. Being a man of letters, he knew the importance of strong visual words. Clara could see Maze appreciated Churchill's approval.

Churchill took a puff of his cigar. "Nothing to beat a Cuban. Thanks. I'll keep one for later. Have to hide it from the doctors and Clemmie. Try not to smoke at home; those darn photographers always catch me with a cigar in my mouth. Can't hide from any of them. They are both a horror and a blessing. The horror is they don't leave me alone. The blessing is they're still interested!"

"They'll always be interested in you, Winston," Maze observed. "You go from being the bad boy to the golden boy and back again to the bad boy. Never know where you will turn up next or which government position you will get. That's why they're constantly on your tail."

"Looking back on it now, I question whether we actually won that war," Churchill reflected, sipping his brandy. "Perhaps we only won the peace. When you look at what's going on it seems we both lost. Mistakes were made, and I'm as guilty as the next one on that score. I know better now; before we get into another one, I intend to hammer Baldwin and his cronies until they see some sense. As I've said before, they haven't forgiven me for the Dardanelles. Must admit my judgment was off then. Terrible mistake; I'll carry the guilt forever. Have to make up for it in some way."

"Uneasy lies the head that wears the crown," Maze responded.

"Shakespeare always managed the right phrase." Churchill sat back in his chair; in the moment he seemed vulnerable. "I know I'm a poor shadow man right now; still, my day will come again. I wasn't meant to sit on the sidelines," he ended, showing some of the old spirit he was rightly known for.

Clara felt awkward overhearing their conversation. "Please excuse me, I have work to do," she said. "It has been an honor to meet you, Mr. Churchill."

"You will meet again. Winston is no stranger to this establishment," Maze assured her. "*Travail, travail,* she is training me well. Wouldn't be at all surprised if she takes out a whip to me one of these days."

Churchill nodded. "Quite understandable, young lady. He can be a stubborn fellow, our Paul. You seem to be handling him well. The trouble is we're both artists at heart. Paul makes a living out of it. I can't. Hence, I come to him to learn to paint, and he turns to me for vocabulary. We make a good team."

Clara left them discussing world events.

CHAPTER 11

Frenchman in Khaki

CLARA FINISHED TYPING the last page of yesterday's work and was ready for the next installment.

The book had opened with an account of Paul Maze's privileged childhood in Le Havre, France. His mother was somewhat of a disciplinarian. His father, a merchant in the coffee and rubber trade, appeared quite formal, and, as a young man, Maze represented his company in London. Clara assumed it was why he spoke English well. With the early part of his life covered, the next chapters would take him into the war and the part he played in it.

Taking dictation from Maze was a challenge. Clara was so engrossed in the story she could hardly wait for the next installment. Like the Pearl White adventures on the radio, Maze left Clara in a state of anxious anticipation. What might happen next? Did the Germans capture him? How did he get away with being both French and British without either uniform?

Clara had just finished typing the incident where his motorcycle crashed on top of him in a mud-filled trench. Bullets from German guns whined above him. He could see a German platoon advancing — and that's where he'd left it. She'd wanted him to go on, but he said he had an appointment; she would have to wait 'til the next day for the rest of that story. He must have got out alive, she thought. Well, of course, he did; she wouldn't be working for him if he hadn't. I won't let him leave me with a cliff-hanger again, she decided. I've got to know what happens next!

Clara checked the typed pages, and finding no glaring errors, placed them in a folder and took them up to the studio. She knocked on the door.

"Come in," Maze called out.

Clara opened the door. The heat of the room hit her immediately. Two glowing gas fires — blazing at full blast — were placed on either side of the room. Maze stood at his easel, dressed in an open khaki shirt and shorts. A naked woman lounged on a chaise not three feet away from him.

Clara stood at the open door — more than a little surprised. "Oh, I, well, I didn't realize you were engaged. I'll just leave the chapter here on the side table — won't disturb you further. Sorry for the intrusion — I'll come back later," and she turned to make a hasty retreat.

"I'm an artist, Mrs. Simon," Maze called after her.

She paused at the door; he was most obviously speaking to her, but she kept her eyes averted and waited . . .

"Artists paint naked women. I might have set aside still life to concentrate on real life; this appointment was made some time ago. The female form is most beautiful, don't you agree?"

Clara was not prepared to answer. Her embarrassment combined with the heat was causing her to perspire profusely. It appeared to have little effect on Maze; he was in his element, dressed as if he were about to go on safari while she wore a wool skirt and jumper. It was cold outside and not too warm downstairs.

"Just about finished," Maze went on. "I'll ask Rogers to tell Mrs. Smithers to send up something delicious for lunch; we can work here. *J'ai terminé mon tableau.*"

"I find the heat too much; if you don't mind, I'd prefer to lunch in the kitchen."

"You will lunch with me — *s'il fait trop chaud dans le studio, allons dans la salle à manger.* You are not a downstairs employee."

Trying to think of some way of getting out of the situation, Clara handed Maze her finished work. "I too would have to strip if you insisted I work in this heat, and I'm not about to do that," she said, trying hard to make a joke.

Fortunately Maze was amused. "One model at a time; you, perhaps, some other time."

"That's not what I meant," Clara hurriedly put him right. "Ring for me when you're ready."

"No, stay. Let me explain. I have to keep the studio warm when I

have a model. Can't expect them to sit in a cold room now, can we?"
He dabbed at the canvas with a long brush and spoke to the model.
"That will be all for the day, Louise."

Louise draped a sheet around herself and disappeared behind the
Oriental screen.

"Same time next week?" Maze asked her.

"*Merci beaucoup, monsieur,*" Louise answered.

Clara wasn't at all surprised to find Louise was French.

"You don't have to postpone a sitting because of me," Clara quickly
asserted.

"I do, and I will tell you why after Louise leaves." Maze put down his
palette, wiped his hands on a piece of muslin and placed his brush in a tin
of vile smelling cleaning fluid. "*D'accord*, I'll turn down the heaters."

Louise emerged from the screen fully dressed

"There are maps I would like you to see," he went on. "We will go
over them after lunch. Do you have a passport?"

"Are you asking me?" Clara inquired, thinking perhaps he was
talking to the model. But then maybe not. She stepped back to give
the model room to exit through the door.

"Of course I am asking you."

"Yes, I have a passport." Clara replied, wondering what that had
to do with anything.

"Then I need not concern myself with government requirements."

What was he talking about? Clara had no alternative other than
to remain and find out.

"We will be traveling to France next week. Rogers will make all
the arrangements. I need to — *mais non* — we need to experience where
I lived the war. My memory — I have blocked too much; it will help
me and be useful for both of us. I would like to leave on Monday, if
that is all right with you."

Clara was flabbergasted. "You want me to go to France with you?"

"Of course. Rogers will accompany us, chaperone, if you like. We
will take the train from Waterloo to Portsmouth, where Rogers will
meet us with the car. From there we all take the ferry to Le Havre, and
Rogers will then drive us to my farmhouse. It will be an adventure as
well as work." Maze stood back from his easel. He beckoned her to
come closer. "*Qu'en pensez vous?*"

The only thing Clara was thinking at that moment was how she was going to break this latest development to Sidney, and not just to Sidney, the family too. She could just hear them, each one giving an opinion — Henry spluttering, Sidney quiet, Nelly pensive, thinking it over. If only she could go without telling them.

Maze, oblivious to her dilemma, stood at the easel studying the canvas he'd been working on. "I don't expect you to give a professional critique; just tell me, if you saw this painting in a gallery, would you buy it?"

"I would appreciate it. I don't think I would buy it."

"*Pourquoi pas?*"

"Wouldn't know where to hang it."

"All it needs is a wall."

"My mother would have a fit . . ."

"*A une belle femme en dishabille?*"

"*Exactement.*"

"Well, you do give an honest opinion. Does that mean you do or don't approve of my work?"

"I think men like paintings of naked women. I like your landscapes and your soldier works and the guards — my favorites, too."

He stood back from Louise. "You have to admit she's lovely."

"Yes, and I also have to admit it's far too hot up here. Can we lunch downstairs please?" she said, leaving the matter of France still hanging in the air.

Rogers had adjusted the dining room table to a reasonable size, but still it was a bit too formal.

Mrs. Smithers entered the dining room. "I have cold pheasant, lamb pie, or I can make you sandwiches. What would you like?" She addressed her selection to Clara, who sat at the end of the table far away from Maze.

Maze looked to Clara to choose.

"A sandwich would be lovely, thank you."

"And you, Mr. Maze, you will want cold pheasant, right, sir?"

"You know me too well," Maze replied.

Mrs. Smithers hurried off into the kitchen.

Now Clara prompted, "You said I should come with you to France?"

"That is correct."

"Would it not be better if you spent time there alone?"

"Absolutely not. You must come with me to record as I remember my feelings, my assignments, everything I've long tried to put behind me. You know I cannot write this book on my own. I do not wish to remember on my own." He looked away, as if thinking of the past, then shook his head as if he didn't quite believe what he had lived through.

MOST LUNCHEONS SERVED in the Maze establishment included a variety of guests. One day it would be the Archbishop of Canterbury and Paris art dealers; other times some Lord and Lady Plum-in-the-mouth sat with an actress appearing in a show in the West End; often Winston Churchill joined the guests at the table; even the Duke and Duchess of Kent turned up on occasions. On this particular day, though, it was just the two of them. Clara imagined she was going to have to carry on alone — at least that's what she thought, until there was a knock on the front door; and then there were three.

"Mrs. Eleanor Barnes is here to see you," Rogers announced.

"Elle alors! Que Dieu me délivre!"

And with that in swaggered Eleanor Barnes dressed in a black silk sheath, a silver fox fur draped over one shoulder and what closely resembled a bashed-in, man's Trilby on her head; the outfit was complete with high-heeled black patent leather shoes and a handbag to match. Her perfume, Chanel No. 5, was expensive, overwhelming and unmistakable.

"If Mohammed won't come to the mountain, oh, wait a moment," she said, "I think I'm heading for a mixed metaphor, not allowed in the presence of a writer. I should know better than that. What I'm trying to say is that we hardly see you any more, Paul." Looking directly at Clara, she added, "Now I see why."

Maze stood and let the sarcasm pass. "My assistant, Clara Simons. Have you had lunch? I can ask Maggie to bring another plate to the table."

"I have eaten, thank you." Obviously Eleanor couldn't care less about Clara. She'd already summed her up — another of Paul's conquests, no doubt. "I sent you an invitation to my party. You haven't replied. Just in case it hasn't arrived or someone hid it away, I'm delivering another in person. No excuse now; it's going to be absolutely marvelous, and you must be there. Here, open it." She handed him a white envelope.

Maze accepted the invitation and used a knife to slit the envelope; as he did so a dozen or more little shiny red swastikas fell like confetti to the floor. "And what is the point of these?" Paul inquired as he picked up one of the fallen swastikas.

"Well, dear one, that's the theme. Those Nazi people, stomping and heil Hitlering everyone, they try to look so frightening. They're not really, you know. I just thought we could have a bit of fun if we all dressed up like them, particularly Hitler, with his hair all flattened on one side and his silly little mustache. What a hoot! You can be, now let me see, which of them is the most handsome? Oh, I think its Albert Speer. Yes, he's an architect, you know, artistic like you, Paul, designed the Reich Chancellery. Quite brilliant I am told." Eleanor turned to Clara. "You take care of his appointments, I presume. Write the date down." Not a please, not a would-you-mind, she'd issued a direct order.

"I do not make appointments for Mr. Maze. Rogers takes care of that," Clara said as she returned Eleanor's demand with her own abrupt reply.

"Very well, I'll tell him then."

Maze glanced at the invitation and placed it on the table. "I'm not sure I will be in London; we depart for France on Monday, and it depends how long we stay."

"Tut, tut, Paul. I want you there. I've tried your wife, but she won't leave her beloved Scotland. Now you're running away to France. Don't tell me your tight little conclave is disintegrating."

"Not at all. I'm writing and painting, and Margaret is busy."

"You're not still on that war book! I can't imagine why you would want to live it all over again. The sooner you finish it, the better for all of us. See that he does Miss — "

"Simon, *Mrs.* Simon," Clara finished the sentence.

"Can't stay, must rush, early evening cocktails at the Bartholomew's. Will I see you there, Paul?"

"No, I have another engagement."

"Pity. You could have been my escort. Oh, well, on my lonesome again." And she swept out, leaving a trail of perfume in her wake.

Maggie began serving lunch.

"Ask Rogers to come in." Maze held his handkerchief over his nose. "Can't abide evening fragrances in the daytime. I need Rogers to open every window in the room. I'm suffocating. And tell him to fetch my box of papers from the studio."

"I can open them," Maggie offered.

Maze accepted. Turning to Clara, he said, "Eleanor's not as awful as she appears; it's mostly bravado. She is lonely. Her husband was killed on the Somme, he left her well off, doesn't know what to do with the money. She's, as you English say, off the rails a bit. Gives parties, goes to parties, looks for eligible men and hasn't found the right one. She's been after me for years. My wife can't stand her."

"There's nothing amusing about Nazis." Clara knelt to collect the remainder of the fallen swastikas. She handed them to Maggie to throw out. Clara's disgust was obvious.

"Eleanor socializes with the rich and titled, and they are not the most sensitive of people. Now let's get back to where we were before the intrusion."

Rogers brought Clara's notebook and pencil together with a box of maps and photographs. "Will there be anything else, sir?"

"That's all for now. Just make sure the car is in good order; we're taking it to France next week."

"The car, sir, is in tip top condition. I tend to it every day. Not a scratch or a dent anywhere."

"And the engine?"

"Purrs like a pussy cat, sir."

Out of the box came sketches, little pieces of paper with maps and roads marked, photographs and brochures, menus, newspaper cuttings, envelopes with receipts, a collection of memorabilia, a history of scraps, all of them important and necessary to bring authenticity to the book.

"I must have had some premonition that it might come to this." He picked up a photograph — must have been someone he knew. "I wonder if you have any understanding of what it was like over there. No, of course, you don't. How could you? No one really could unless they were actually on the battlegrounds. Anyway — you had to be quite young when it began."

"I was only nine," Clara recalled. "I heard my parents talk about it; never realized how awful it was until much later. Not much was said about it in school. We had mostly women teachers, since all the men had gone to war. I remember seeing the Zeppelins flying over us; they were huge and gray and fascinating. I don't really think I understood their significance."

"Did your family lose anyone?"

"My father's brother was killed in Mesopotamia, and my brother-in-law Mannie was badly wounded. He spent many months in hospital, and when he came out he was told the job they were supposed to keep for him was given to someone else. I understand it happened to a lot of men. Mannie was a reporter at the *Evening Star*. He's freelance now, involved in politics, gets himself into trouble for shooting off his mouth and struggles to make a living."

"When it started we all wanted to play a part," Maze explained. "The war was fought on my soil in my country; I had to help defend what was mine, what belonged to France. At first the Brits volunteered. They thought it would be over quickly. It wasn't; it just dragged on and on. Those who hadn't volunteered were forced to sign up, sent over to help us, given a gun and shoved into the trenches. I had none of that — just a pencil and pad."

Clara shared Mannie's experience with Maze. "To this day he doesn't know what they were doing there. Even the young German soldiers questioned the war. He befriended a farm boy from Yorkshire, never been away from his parents, eighteen, I think he said he was; the young lad was petrified, in total shock, couldn't respond to orders and ran away. When they caught him he was brought before a tribunal and accused of disobedience and desertion. He was found guilty and executed. If that's not barbaric, I'd like to know what is. It's hard to believe things like that happened." Clara opened the notebook and picked up a pencil.

Maze stood up and walked over to an open window to look out upon the river. After a long silence, he began, "I had been separated from my regiment; we'd been attacked, and everyone ran off in different directions. I was alone in a field of dead soldiers. When the shelling stopped I decided to try to find British Army Headquarters. All I had with me was my sketch pad and a pencil in my haversack and a few personal items. I had no identification. I was dressed in such a way to not be obvious." He turned back to Clara. "Am I going too fast?"

"No, I can keep up. Don't stop."

"A British Army car drives up and stops. Two officers get out and ask for my papers. I didn't have any. I tried to explain I was a field artist, working with both the French and the British, and my motorbike was somewhere in a field with the back tire blown out. They didn't believe me. They took me prisoner. Nothing I could say made any difference. I had not been given a proper uniform when I joined up. I wore a mixture of different regiment garments. Some British, some French. They thought I had stolen my clothes from dead soldiers. When they asked me where I was billeted I answered truthfully, 'Nowhere, really.' That made them even more suspicious. I tried to explain I worked as a liaison — I wasn't attached to any particular regiment. They pushed me into the car and took me to their headquarters. At the headquarters more interrogation; they went through my haversack. I had a razor imprinted 'Made in Germany.' They wanted to know why I had it. They put me in a cell with German prisoners. I speak German, so I spoke back to them in their language. A guard heard me talking in German to the prisoners and reported me."

Clara was taking dictation as fast as she could.

"Just hold up your hand when you need a rest, and I'll slow down," he said.

"Then, just a little slower." Clara had to admit Maze was rushing on, more than before.

"I was taken to a large tent where the Provost Marshall and the officers who had captured me accused me of being a spy. They wanted to know why I spoke German. I said I spoke French, German and English, which is why I was seconded to both the British and French armies. I could translate for both sides and sketch the areas around the battlegrounds. They asked me the name of my superior officer. I told them I didn't have one. I could not prove my connection to them or the allies. I was found guilty.

"The following morning they marched me before a firing squad. I was tied to a post and blindfolded, awaiting execution, when a small company of the Mounted Scots Greys rode in. The soldiers put down

their guns to allow the horses to pass through. One of the Scots Greys
gets off his horse and came over to take a look at me. He lifted up my
blindfold and said, 'Good God, Maze! What the hell are you doing
here?' He saved my life."

Clara saw Maze's hands shaking. Horrified by what she'd heard,
she put down her notebook and walked over to where he was standing
at the window. "An unbelievable story. It's a wonder you didn't have
a heart attack. Can I get you a drink, something?"

"No, just be with me."

"I'm here," she turned away from the window and grasped his
hand to calm him.

"I wouldn't want to go over it again; it was a very close encounter
with death, more so than any battlefield experiences I had," he admitted grimly.

"No wonder you were asked to write your story, Mr. Maze."

"Maybe so." Maze straightened, returned from reliving his ordeal
and looked at her. "I would like to drop the formalities, if you don't
mind. I will call you — Clara, and when we are away in France, *je
voudrais que vous m'appelez Paul.*"

Clara had never been on a first name basis with an employer. It
seemed strange, calling the man she worked for by his first name, but
then she'd never known anyone like Paul Maze, so why should she be
surprised?

CHAPTER 12

Confrontation

IT WAS FRIDAY evening in Aldgate and everyone was rushing to get home before dark and the beginning of the Sabbath. Clara stopped to buy flowers for Nelly. A little further on, Jack Robbins, one of the few non-Jews on the street selling fruit, called her over. "Just packing up," he said. "Here, take the last of the peaches and plums — nothing wrong with them — and give 'em to Nelly with me love."

Jack had worked his stall in the same place on the High Street for donkey's years; he knew Clara from a little girl. Every year at Christmas he gave Nelly oranges to put in their stockings, and every year Henry attempted to explain to Jack why Jews don't celebrate Christmas. Nelly, being ecumenical and wiser, won out. "Don't know what he's on about," she'd tell Jack. "Father Christmas can't tell one chimney from another."

"Thanks, Jack." Clara took the brown paper bag from him and walked on to Old Castle Street where she could see if Nelly was sitting at her window; she wasn't. It must be later than she thought. Avoiding the traffic, she crossed the road to Half Moon Passage, opened the door to Twenty-One and climbed the stairs to the parlor. The chicken soup in the big black pot simmered gently. Nelly stood at the stove rolling matzo balls. They were all there, waiting for dinner, listening to Churchill on the radio.

Henry seated next to the radio, his ear to the box, peered at the gauze over the speaker, as if he could actually see Churchill inside it. He turned 'round as Clara came in. "Friend of yours on the wireless, war monger!"

"He's not."

"Shush," Nelly said, trying to hear what Churchill had to say.

Clara had heard Churchill spouting off in person on a similar subject at the Maze residence just a few days before. It seemed strange to hear his voice coming through a speaker at her house. She'd been with him, could have reached out and touched him, and now that same man was broadcasting over the wireless coming into Nelly's parlor, as if he were there, sitting with her family as they gathered 'round the table listening:

> We are but half the strength of France, our nearest neighbour. Germany is arming fast and no one is going to stop her. That seems quite clear. There is time for us to take the necessary measures to achieve parity. No nation, playing the part we play and aspire to play in the world, has a right to be in a position where it can be blackmailed. Our weakness involves the stability of Europe . . .

Nelly popped the matzo balls into the soup and then sat down on her chair beside the stove. Friday was always a busy day; she'd been preparing dinner since early morning — and her feet hurt.

Sula, released from the hospital less than a week ago, came to sit beside her. "Your cooking is what I missed most, Mum. Hospital food was awful. I'm glad to be home."

"It's where you belong, luv. Not going to have them experimenting on you any more. Not if I can help it."

"We'll see." Sula wasn't so sure. She was able to walk with the help of a stick but still had to go back to the hospital once a week for exercises to try to strengthen her leg muscles.

"Soup's just about ready. Get yourselves to the table," Nelly announced.

The table was laid for the traditional Friday night meal. A big platter of fried fish placed in the middle of the table, two white Sabbath candles on either side of a loaf of shiny brown challah beside a decanter of sweet red wine and a Kiddush cup. The wine was mostly for show; nobody drank it except Henry when he made the blessing. The only other sign of alcohol in the Levy household was the occasional Guinness that Nelly claimed she drank for medicinal purposes.

"Don't believe a word of it," Henry said. "My Nelly loves a tipple every now and then."

All assembled at the table, Nelly got up from her chair by the stove to stand beside Henry. He took a box of matches out of his pocket and gave them to her. She lit the candles and recited from memory what every Jewish woman on a Friday night in every part of the world was taught from a very young age: "*Baruch atta adonai elohainu melech ha'olum asher kidshanu b'mitzvo tav vertzivanu lhad lich ner shel Shabas.*"

Henry raised the Kiddush cup and recited the blessing over the wine. "*Baruch atta adonai elohainu melech ha'olum borai poree hagafen.*"

Bernie blessed the bread. "*Baruch atta adonai elohainu melech ha'olum ha motzi lechem min ha'aratz..*"

And with the traditional prayers completed they tucked into what could only be described as a delicious spread.

Nelly's fried fish was, without exception, the best; no one could come near to getting their fish as well prepared as hers — seasoned just right, gently coated with egg and matzo meal — it came out of the pan golden brown on the outside and pure white inside. A fully qualified purveyor of fish, she could tell a good tasting fish when she saw one. The eyes had to be clear, the smell had to be fresh and the fishmonger down Petticoat Lane, who she'd been going to for years, treated her with the respect she deserved. It was Plaice in the winter, Haddock in summer and Halibut in between. Sometimes it was Dover Sole if the coffers allowed, though Cod did appear when Henry had a bad day at the races.

"That's enough of him," Henry decided getting up from the table to switch off the wireless. "In and out of office like a swing door he is, can't make up his mind what party he belongs to, calls himself an Independent. I'd like to know what that's supposed to mean."

"Means he's anti-Socialist," Mannie said, biting into a slice of thickly buttered challah.

"He's a good man, paid dearly for his mistakes," Sula interjected, expecting political mayhem to break out any minute.

They were all Socialists in their own way, though Henry was more of a 'sit back and see what happens' type of Socialist. If the result of an election wasn't to Henry's liking, he could always fall back on the 'I told you so' line that drove Mannie up the wall.

Mannie was as near to a Communist as one could get and wasn't ashamed of letting you know where his loyalties lay. In fact, after the last debacle, the police kept a closer eye on his activities. Sula stood with Mannie on political issues; Anna and Bernie just listened, went with the opinion of the one who shouted the loudest. Sidney, not political in any way, much preferred to boast about his Arsenal football team's accomplishments unless, of course, they'd lost; then he'd keep his disappointment to himself. Bernie, a Tottenham fan, made the two of them mortal enemies on Saturday afternoons when football games were played. The remainder of the week football was never discussed. Winston Churchill didn't interest either of them.

Clara usually joined into their discussions — not this time. She was a fan of Churchill. She didn't care about his political affiliation. He said what was on his mind. He treated her as an equal, and if Maze, who had known him for years, supported him, then she too had to respect his achievements. He was an old warrior who'd learned a few things in his time — his words, not hers. Both he and Maze had fought a war, Churchill, more than one. He'd been a reporter in the Boer War. Surely he could be trusted to recognize the signals coming out of Europe, warn the government to take notice, not to ignore them.

Anyway it didn't matter what a few Jews sitting 'round a table in the East End of London had to say; no one took much notice of them other than Oswald Mosley, and all he wanted to do was get rid of them. Right now Clara was wrestling with how she was going to tell Sidney and her family she was leaving for France on Monday.

Henry, having finished his meal, held court. "In my opinion, when the First Lord of the Admiralty, Mr. Winston Churchill, that is . . ."

"That was," Mannie corrected him.

Henry hadn't finished. " . . . sent our ships into troubled waters, which caused a massacre . . . "

Nelly at the sink chimed in, "He ain't First Lord now; he paid the penalty for what he did, and now he's back and telling us not to turn a blind eye to this Hitler fellow. We should listen to him. He knows what he's talking about."

Henry wasn't giving in. "Well, I don't think we need him. He's in love with the sound of his own voice, too full of himself. The government we have is good enough for me."

"Are you out of your mind?" Mannie stood up from the table. "This government — "

"Don't get him started; it's bad for his blood pressure." Sula gently pushed Mannie back in his seat.

Sidney chose to ignore them all and asked Clara if she'd had a good day.

"I did, and if you'd all stop fighting with each other and be quiet for a moment, I have something to tell you."

"What is it, luv?" Nelly was the first to inquire.

Clara decided not to tread meekly. She jumped right in. "I'm going to France with Mr. Maze on Monday."

That stopped them. Silence replaced their chatter. Clara knew it couldn't last. She carried on while they were still digesting what she'd just said. "Mr. Maze can't continue writing without revisiting the towns where the war, I should say, his war, was fought. He has asked me to accompany him to help with the research. I agreed. How long I'm away depends on how fast we can get the work done. This is all part of my job, and I don't want to hear anything against it or him."

Henry recovered first. "You're not going, and that's final."

"I don't think it is any of our business," Sula, always on Clara's side, declared.

"I wouldn't mind going back to France, visit the graves of my mates. Perhaps he'll take me instead," Mannie suggested.

"Well, don't just sit there, Sidney, put your foot down. Make her see some sense," Henry urged.

Clara stayed on course. "In case you haven't noticed, Dad, my job is not run of the mill. It's not nine to five employment, and 'Bob's your uncle,' you go home. Mr. Maze told me before I accepted the position my hours would be erratic, and I discussed it with Sidney before I took the position. I'm not giving it up. This is an opportunity for me to travel, for me to learn. I'm not working for some slob like Abbott ever again. Maze is, well, he's different; he mixes with important people, doesn't think the way we do."

Sidney got up from the table. "This is between me and Clara, and we'll sort it out."

This was the last thing Clara expected to hear from her husband. She jumped up and gave him a hug.

"He's an artist. Since when have they been considered important?" Henry asked.

"He's an artist, he advises politicians, and he's writing a book. I'm helping him with the book; that's my job."

"That's right, and I'm your father. I'm the one who puts bread on this table — "

Nelly interrupted, saying, "Stop it, Henry. They all help to put bread on the table. If we relied on you, we'd be living on the cat's horse meat. I've had enough of this. I'm going into the front room to sit on my chair by the window, see what's going on outside. You can join me if you want on one condition — we leave Clara and her job out of the conversation. She knows what she's doing, and she don't need our advice; if she did, she would ask for it."

Nelly had a way of putting an end to unpleasant topics. "Clear the table, remove the cloth, wash the dishes and 'do in' the parrot."

"Why does she hate Boadicea so much?" Anna asked.

"She doesn't really; it's all an act." Clara breathed a sigh of relief; the France debacle was over for the time being.

FRIDAY NIGHT WAS always a special occasion for everyone who lived in the East End. The religious Jews and their umpteen children were dressed in their finery on their way to services at the synagogue. The organ grinder stood near the Whitechapel Gallery playing music hall tunes. Nelly, at her window, listening to the music drift over and knowing all the words, sang along with him. Reminded her of when she was young; she and Henry performed in the pubs, helped them make a few bob extra from the customers who showed their appreciation. After the children came along she wouldn't leave them alone at night, didn't want to, really, and she wasn't about to let Henry find another partner, so they gave it up. Could have gone back to it when Edie came into the family, but by then Nelly had lost her enthusiasm. "Leave it to the youngsters," she said, "the new composers, lovely melodies, clever lyrics — not like our hackneyed old songs."

Clara came in to sit with Nelly, her chores completed. "What you really think about my going to France, Mum?"

Nelly didn't answer immediately. They sat at the window together. The lamp lighter came along and lit the gas lamps, bringing a warm glow to the street. A couple of drunks steadied each other in a doorway unable to agree on which pub to hit next. The stalls were closed;

in their place were men with pushcarts selling hot chestnuts and candy floss, ice cream and sarsaparilla, and children with pennies clutched tightly in their hands trying to make a choice, usually going for the candy floss. On the other side of Half Moon Passage was a music shop; it stayed open late, their amplified music drowning out that of the organ grinders. Al Jolson sang, "Climb upon my knee, Sonny Boy," bringing tears to Nelly's eyes. She loved it; could picture him in her mind, a nice Jewish boy in black face who made a name for himself. Nelly could listen to him over and over again, even had a few of his records. His song ended, replaced by something classical.

Nelly was ready to answer Clara. "I think you've got a grand job, luv. I also think you've got to be careful. We don't know these people, how they think, what they think. You're an attractive young woman, Clara; you're also married. Taking off with a man you hardly know isn't the wisest thing to do."

Clara didn't appreciate the inference.

Nelly didn't give her the opportunity to object. "I understand we can't stop you. If it's all right with Sidney, then that's really all that matters. You asked for my opinion, I gave it. Now off with you; go see what he says." Somewhat as an afterthought she added, "And knowing you as well as I do, it won't matter tuppence what your dad or Sidney says. You'll be leaving for France on Monday!"

"That's right, Mum."

CLARA FOUND SIDNEY sitting on the step outside, throwing stones into a bucket — most of the time hitting the target. She watched him for a while before he noticed she was there.

"Sit with me," he said, sharing his stones with her. "See how many you can get in."

They took turns throwing. She was hopeless. "You're much better at it than I am. . . . Everything all right between us, Sidney?"

"I'm a bit miffed about your going away, Clara. You could have asked me first."

"I only found out this afternoon. Mr. Maze made the arrangements, and I had to make a decision; it's all part of my job."

"Then I don't think much of your boss. He's inconsiderate — sounds a selfish bastard to me."

"He really isn't. Just doesn't think the way we do."

"Doesn't he know you have a husband and that I'd have something to say about it?"

"Of course he knows, but by his thinking it doesn't have anything to do with you or the family. He employed me to help him with his book. It's what I'm there for. I didn't know it would involve travel; now I find it does, and I've agreed to go. Can't get out of it, and to tell you the truth I wouldn't want to. I don't suppose I'll even have a job when the book is completed. This won't go on forever."

There wasn't much more Sidney could say; she'd accepted — and that was that. He let the matter of France drop. "Julius gave me a raise today. I felt like telling him where to put it; don't worry, I didn't. I've worked there for over ten years, and I have no idea how much the firm makes. I don't know what he takes home or even what the machinists get."

"Why don't you ask him?"

"He'd probably tell me it's none of my business; he deals with the office stuff — no need for me to get involved."

"If you're so miserable there you could leave, look for something else."

"I can't. He depends on me. I run that factory for him while he's out gallivanting, chatting up the customers."

"Would you prefer to do what he does?"

"Of course not; I'm not a salesman. Haven't got the gift of the gab like him."

"So, you do what you do best, and he does what he does best. For the time being it works. Later on perhaps you can open your own business."

Sidney stopped throwing stones. "Want an ice cream?"

"I'd love one."

They walked through Half Moon Passage onto the High Street and disappeared into the crowds. Not even Nelly could spot them from her front room window.

CHAPTER 13

Heinrich Luftmann

THE DAY BEFORE Maze and Clara departed for France, Rogers brought in the post and handed one of the letters to Clara. "Would you be kind enough to take this up to the studio? I know Mr. Maze asked not to be disturbed, but I believe this to be important."

Clara glanced at the envelope. At the bottom of the envelope she read in block letters: URGENT AND PERSONAL.

Up in the studio Maze was feverishly working on a commissioned painting, trying to put the finishing touches to it before they left. Clara, letter in hand, entered tentatively. "This just arrived in the post. Rogers asked me to give it to you. I believe you should read it now."

"Can't it wait?"

"I don't think so."

"Read it to me, please."

"Clara opened the envelope and took out the letter. She looked for the signature. "It's from Heinrich, Heinrich Luftmann."

My dear Paul,

I have a friend who is leaving for London tomorrow. He will take this letter and post it to you when he arrives. He will be staying at the Imperial Hotel in Russell Square. You can contact him there. I do not trust the post here. Please share it with Winston, perhaps he can speak about it with some of his colleagues. There is no joy here.

Today the police came to my atelier and proceeded to destroy nearly everything in it. Every painting on the wall and every unframed print. I look around and see total destruction. They put knives through my oils and threw the paper works on a fire they made outside. I am lucky they did not go upstairs where I still have some of my work. This I will have to hide. The Germany I once loved is becoming a torturous place. My girl friend Trude was with me at the time. She told them we were licensed by the Ministry in Munich. They did not care. They said they were carrying out orders from that same Ministry.

My work is now considered "degenerate." How is it that it wasn't degenerate last week? I remember the peaceful days when you and I painted together here and in England. The time we went to Blenheim Palace to be with Winston, how we set up our easels in the gardens of that grand place and spent a week just enjoying each other's company and working. Remember that painting we all did together? I think I did the trees, you did the background and Winston put in the little houses.

I wish I had better news for you, but I do not.

I will now have to do my real work in secret. I will have to pretend to carry out their wishes and just paint landscapes. I am told they are acceptable. No abstracts. No female figures.

Trude has taken a job in a new munitions factory, the previous factory was in Dachau, it is now being rebuilt as a concentration camp. That has to tell us something. Let us hope what we are going through is just an aberration and that the people will come to their senses and dismiss the people who have taken over our lives.

With fondest regards,
Heinrich

Maze put down his brushes, obviously disturbed by what he'd heard. "I'll have Rogers deliver it to Winston immediately; it is proof of what he's been telling the government for months now." He walked over to his desk and took out a file. "Winston gave me a copy of his last speech in the Commons. Here — read the highlighted portion."

We cannot look back with much pleasure on our foreign policy in the last five years. They have been disastrous years . . . We have seen the most depressing and alarming changes in the outlook of mankind which have ever taken place in so short a period. Five years ago all felt safe; five years ago we all were looking forward to peace, to a period in which mankind would rejoice in the treasure which science can spread to all classes if conditions of peace and justice prevail. Five years ago to talk of war would have been regarded not only as a folly and a crime, but almost as a sign of lunacy . . .

Clara handed Churchill's speech back to Paul and said, "My brother-in-law has been aware of this for months, actually got arrested for speaking out against it. He's held rallies in Hyde Park. He's been telling people to listen to Churchill, and he's one who helped stop Mosley and the Fascists marching in the East End; they're all part of the same problem."

"It's an outrage. I'll have Rogers take me to the Russell Hotel this evening to find the man who sent this on."

Clara thought of her Aunt Lizzie in Germany. Was she in trouble? Wasn't it time for her to come back to England? She'd thought of mentioning the letter to Nelly, then perhaps she shouldn't; no sense in worrying her. On the other hand, Lizzie had to know the situation in Germany; you would think she'd want to get out, and maybe she will. As Nelly said, "Always room for one or two more up at Twenty-One."

GERMANY WAS BECOMING, if it was not already, a police state. Europeans were aware of the inherent dangers. Britain should be taking notice. They weren't. They considered it a phase that would pass. Too proud to consider they too were a slice of Europe. No, it was better to think of themselves as an isolated island with no allegiance to Europe. They'd fought one recent war for Europe — weren't about to fight another. They weren't ever going to call themselves Europeans and cared little for their own Jews, cared less about Gypsies, despised homosexuals . . . Wasn't such a bad idea to let Germany clean up their own deviants.

Yes, it was true, Hitler had his supporters and henchman planning how this was to be accomplished, and there was little or no opposition. Making fun of the "little corporal" might be amusing, but it wasn't prudent. Hitler was a force to be taken seriously. Germans who didn't or couldn't agree with his tactics were advised to leave while they had the chance. Winston saw Germany, yet again, to be a threat to world peace. He hammered his concerns in Parliament at every opportunity; still the members would not take him seriously. He was considered to be just another speech-making politician blowing off steam.

All of these thoughts and more ran through Clara's mind as she contemplated the letter Paul had received from Germany.

CHAPTER 14

Journey to France

"WHAT CLOTHES DO you take for a working week in France?" Clara asked herself out loud just as Sula came in to help. Sula sat on the bed while Clara stood before her wardrobe looking for something suitable. Maze wasn't one for dressing up, which had become patently obvious in the short time she'd been with him. When he went out, his black cloak covered whatever was underneath, and indoors he wore corduroy trousers, cardigans and an assortment of well-worn shirts. If Rogers hadn't dressed him for formal occasions, Lord knows what he would have found to wear. On the other hand, just in case she had to meet important officials or perhaps in the evening have a dinner meeting, she must find something appropriate.

"I'll take these, and these and these," Clara decided as she folded shirts, skirts and tops. Then came her shoes, underwear and a couple of more dressy garments — the dresses she wore when she went dancing at the Palais.

"How long you going for — a year?" Sula joked, watching the suitcase beginning to bulge. "That's enough. You'll never close it."

"Just need that lovely blue jacket of yours, if you don't mind. No need to pack it; I'll wear it for the journey. I think I'm done."

"You don't look terribly excited. I'd be over the moon if it were me," Sula remarked. She sat on the case while Clara pushed down on the front catches.

"I've had to placate Sidney, not an easy bloke to reason with where I'm concerned. He's still a bit wary. And as for Dad, he just won't speak to me. I'll be better when I get away from them."

"Dad will get over it and so will Sidney. It's a new era, Clara; we don't choose to be at the mercy of our men any more. They can't keep us in the kitchen, making their beds, having umpteen kids, though I don't think Sidney thinks like that. Anyway, you're not the same person who worked for Abbott. You've found your niche. Maze is your ticket out of the East End. If I were you, I'd take it and run with it."

What Clara hadn't shared with Sula was her admiration for Paul, his ability to face up to a problem and do something about it. She wished Sidney might be more like Maze. Sidney shied away from conflict, kept it all inside, and never said a word to Julius about his dissatisfaction. He complained only to her when he came home from work. And where did that get him? Stuck where he said he didn't want to be, resenting being taken for granted, not getting paid what he was worth. His brothers had said "sod it" and left. Not Sidney. Sidney's loyalty and fear got in the way of his recognized worth to Julius, and until he saw it for himself and did something about it, there was nothing she might say that would make a difference.

Clara lifted the suitcase off the bed. It was heavy; there was no way she could drag it on and off two buses.

"You'll need a weightlifter to carry that. Take the taxi Maze offered," Sula suggested.

"It's a bit extravagant; I mean, turning up in a taxi doesn't seem right."

"Better than getting a hernia and not be able to go at all," Sula answered. "Ask cousin Nathan — he'll take you; been a taxi driver for a year now and should know how to get to Cheyne Walk."

"He's the last one I'd ask to go to Chelsea. The whole neighborhood would know what I'm up to. He can take me to Waterloo. That's where I'm to meet Mr. Maze."

"Good. We've got that sorted. Now cheer up and look forward to a huge adventure. If there was room in that case, I'd jump in and go with you."

"Nothing I'd like more, Sula."

"Come off it. Even if I had the use of both my legs, you'd turn me down. This is your life, Clara. Not mine," and under her breath Sula muttered, "unfortunately."

CLARA LOVED TRAINS. She'd never been in first class before — much nicer than third, the way she usually travelled. They had the compartment to themselves, plenty of room, she on one side, Maze on the other.

"You like seeing where you are going or watching where you have been?" Maze asked.

"Where I'm going," Clara replied. They swapped seats.

Before Clara left Chelsea the previous Friday night she'd asked Rogers to make sure to put everything she'd placed on Maze's desk in his brief case. She didn't trust Maze to remember.

"It's a bit late to ask, but I suppose Rogers has put all the papers I left in your briefcase."

"He did." Maze handed her the brief case. "*Ouvrez — le, s'il vous plaît.*"

Clara opened the briefcase to be sure all was in order. In with his other papers, she discovered two leather bound notebooks, a silver propelling pencil and a beautiful silk scarf. "And these?" she asked.

"For you," he told her. "In France you must be *'une femme française* — a scarf is absolutely necessary."

"And the silver pencil?"

"*Un souvenir.*"

"*Merci, Monsieur Maze. C'est trop généreux.* I will wear the scarf when we arrive in France."

Maze moved ahead with what was uppermost on his mind. "I read through the pages you typed. I think we have the beginning of a book." He seemed very pleased with himself. "What do you think?"

Clara took up the pages and flipped through the first few, then said, "You have a habit of putting the cart before the horse."

"I speak, you write. If I am wrong with the use of my English words, you correct them."

He ignored the comparison Clara had made — probably didn't understand the nuance. "The tables will be turned in France," she joked. "You will correct my French."

"*Bon.* Close the brief case; work begins when we get to France. I must remind you again to use my given name. This *Monsieur* Maze is too formal, seems even ridiculous."

"It will take me a little time to become accustomed to it."

"*Une fois en France, je serai Paul et vous serez Clara. D'accord?*"

"*D'accord,*" she agreed.

CLARA WAS DREADING the crossing to France. The only other time she'd visited France the boat rocked and heaved, and she was sick throughout the passage — couldn't wait to get back on dry land. This time the sea was calm and the wind slight. She walked the upper deck with Maze, letting the breeze blow through her hair, enjoying the fresh sea air.

Rogers preferred to sit inside reading the paper. He wasn't one for outdoors, especially on the open sea.

ONCE THE CAR was off the boat, and having gone through the usual landing procedures, they were cleared to drive away. It was a lovely warm day. Rogers drove through the town of Le Havre, Paul pointing out places of interest he wanted Clara to see. Le Havre was important in many different ways. For the merchants it was the coffee and cotton exchange. For historians it was the fact that it was so old with so much preserved, including its fifteenth century churches. And for the artist, he said, "There is no better natural light anywhere. The Impressionists found the light to be inspiring, see the way it plays on the sea and the buildings." He was proud of the city of his birth, and he wanted to share it with her.

Villagers along the road recognized Paul and waved. Children picked flowers from the roadside and threw them into the car. Maze was delighted with his reception. "Yvette must have told them I was coming," he confided.

Clara supposed she would find out who Yvette was before very long.

"This happens every time we come back to Le Havre. You'd think the king himself was returning," Rogers said as he stopped the car for a little girl waving to them at the side of the road. Through the open window she gave Clara a bouquet of flowers.

"*Merci beaucoup,*" Clara spoke her first words of French on French soil as she accepted the flowers.

Rogers turned into a dirt road leading to the farmhouse, then stopped before a gate. "We'll walk from here," he told Rogers. "Clara, come, dear." Maze helped Clara out of the car, and with a flourish he opened the gate, calling out to Rogers, "Tell Yvette we'll be there soon."

Paul, reaching out for Clara's hand, led her through giant poplar trees to an open space where a field of sunflowers swayed gently in the breeze. "*Magnifique*. See the little red poppies, a sprinkle of red in a field of yellow. What a wonderful sense of color our maker has. And there is more." They took a path through the sunflower field that led to a narrow running stream. "This is where I went fishing when I was a boy, just stood, rod in hand — nothing on my feet. I was in heaven."

Closer to the house were the vegetable and flower gardens. "Yvette is my second *maman*; she has been with my family since I was a young lad. My parents relied on her completely, and after they died she stayed on; it had become her home too. Her son was killed in Ypres. Her husband is long gone. She is invaluable to me in so many ways. Goes to market once a week and sells whatever we have ready to harvest."

They continued walking.

"Remember what I said about the light? Well, it is also here, not only by the sea but also in the country. I come back to paint when London becomes unbearably dreary."

Clara was entranced, the open space, the cleanliness of it all. "Why stay in England when you have all this?"

"Because, my dear, in London I meet artists, politicians, interesting creative people; here they are country farmers; they work the land, they find serenity in simple things as I do. This is my home. It feeds the soul; it doesn't feed the mind."

They walked back through the field of sunflowers, sunflowers taller than they were, with heads up to the lowering sun. "Soon they will droop. I think of them as going to sleep. Tomorrow in the morning when the sun comes up, they will rise and hold their heads up high again and follow the progress of the sun till evening."

Yvette came out to meet them, a fresh faced, round woman dressed in peasant garb: a long, full skirt, a smock-like top and a black shawl around her shoulders. She threw her arms around Maze, hugged and kissed him, speaking French, seemingly oblivious of Clara standing beside him. When Yvette finally let go, Maze introduced Clara. "*Je te présente, Madame Simon, mon assistante anglaise.*"

Yvette eyed Clara with suspicion, offered her hand and continued talking to Maze in French. She stopped to take a breath, and Maze hurriedly interpreted for Clara who then assured him she understood every word.

"I heard her say you don't come to see her as often as you used to; she has lots to discuss; and you are a naughty boy!"

"She is right." Maze laughed. "She has much to tell me. I'll take a little time with her while you rest. I will explain we are here to work. It takes Yvette a while to warm up to strangers. Come, I will escort you to your room, and we will eat together when you come down."

Clara followed willingly; she was tired and felt grubby and hungry; a quick lick and a promise would do the trick — Nelly's answer to a long and tiring day.

Clara's room was charming, decorated in shades of yellow and white. A jug with warm water, soap and a basin stood on a credenza, her case open on a luggage stand, ready to be unpacked. Paul might not be able to take this for long, but I could, she thought, comparing the room to the tight little quarters she shared with Sidney at Twenty-One. The bed, so inviting — a fluffy duvet covered in a traditional provençal pattern. The walls reflected the setting sun, and from the window she could see the outline of the sunflower field, as beautiful as any impressionist painting she'd seen at the National Gallery.

Clara breathed in the perfumed air spreading through the room from the lavender in the window box. It was, without a doubt, a perfect ending to an unforgettable day.

CLARA CAME DOWN to the kitchen refreshed, her clothes hung away, her toilet completed. Forgoing the lick and promise, she'd taken a bath. That alone had been worth the journey; the water in London was so hard and full of lime. Not here. Just a gentle touch on the soap and, *voilà*, bubbles and foam! She wore a simple dress accessorized by the scarf Paul had given her.

The scarf didn't go unnoticed. "It suits you well," Paul said as he seated himself beside her at the table.

Yvette had prepared a sumptuous meal, the table laid with pretty plates, her own freshly baked bread giving off an aroma that made you want to grab it off the table and bite into it, a cauldron of vegetables, various cold meats, quiche, fruit pies, and a jug of wine. Rogers was already tucking into the cassoulet.

"My favorite dish," said Paul. "Leave some for us, *vous êtes trop gourmand.*"

Rogers, not understanding or more likely not wanting to understand, kept on eating.

Paul explained, "The best food in the world comes from this part of Normandy — our cheese, our cream and our seafood. Rogers loves it; he spends most of his time when he's here in the kitchen with Yvette. One day I will bring Cook to learn the recipes; that is, if Yvette is willing to give away her secrets." He looked over to Rogers munching away. "If we were here more often, Rogers would be too fat to fit in the driving seat!"

Rogers' fork paused on its way to the plate. "Mr. Maze is quite right. When a treat such as this is set out in front of one, it would only insult the cook if even a morsel of it was let go to waste." Rogers had managed a sentence in between piling another helping of everything on his plate.

The food and the wine, all too much — not a spread Clara was used to. She ate pâté for the first time in her life. Even the wine, not sweet and sticky like Passover wine but delicate and distinctive. Now she knew why French wines were so sought after. Just to make sure her eternal soul would not be completely damned, if and when she reached the pearly gates, she turned down the stew — a floating pig's trotter all too visible — and just ate the vegetables.

This wasn't a free for all get-what-you-can-while-you-can meal at Twenty-One. This was dining and savoring every morsel. It wasn't rushed, and it wasn't taken away the moment you cleaned your plate. The dessert, strawberry tart in almond cream, delicate, sinfully delicious, so different to the bread pudding served up by Nelly. Not that there was anything wrong with Nelly's bread pudding, but even with the greatest stretch of the imagination you couldn't describe it as delicate.

It had been a long day. Rogers was soldiering on, while Clara couldn't find room for another bite.

Maze lifted his glass in a toast. Clara and Rogers raised their glasses. "To the best cook in all of France."

Yvette blushed.

Dinner was over. Paul pushed his chair away from the table. He thanked Yvette, who was on her way to the larder to bring out a selection of cheeses.

"*Assez, assez,* enough, enough, *merci,* Yvette." Maze and Clara thanked her. "Clara, will you walk with me?"

Clara was not averse to a little exercise. She had eaten far too much. Outside, Maze pretended to walk like a fat man, arms splayed, cheeks puffed out. "This is what would happen to me if I lived here."

Clara mimicked him, and together they waddled down the path like two overstuffed clowns. A little farther on they reached a bench beside the river, where they watched its flow.

"My family lived in the city of Le Havre, so I have a lasting love of the sea; my early paintings are of boats and sailing ships. I watched as the tides came in so close and then left so quickly, going so far out, leaving shells and strange creatures in the sand. My parents knew where to find me, always on the beach with my bucket and spade and, of course, my sketchbook. It was only after the war, after I had left Le Havre for England — I was a student in England — that I came back and wanted to enjoy the countryside too. I was fortunate to have both. My wife . . ."

This was the first time he had mentioned his wife.

"My wife Margaret loves it here, more than she likes to be in London. She is a Scot, and Scots are set in their ways. It was because of the war we met; her husband was killed in Paschendale. I was given the task of informing her of his death. She was devastated; she had five children. I spent time comforting her. We grew close. After the war we met again. A little while later we married, and we lived in her home in Scotland. Scotland is quite beautiful. I appreciated its beauty, but its landscape did not touch me. I found I could not live there, and though we bought the house in Chelsea together, Margaret could not settle in London. We are good friends and have the best of arrangements; we visit each other. I have my life, and she has hers."

"Not many people would comprehend such an arrangement," Clara said. "My father, for instance; he is of the old school, marry once and you marry for life. He does not approve of my going away with a married man."

"Tell him I'm a married man in name only."

"That would only make it worse; I think I'll leave it as it is. He has asked me why I work for a painter who wants to write — "

"Was he in the war?"

"No, too old."

"*Ah, c'est pourquoi il pose la question.* You can tell him writing is my way of trying to understand it," Maze reminisced. "Mine was an unusual assignment. I had no gun. I had a pencil, and with that pencil I traveled the battlefields on both sides, French and British, even the Germans; they were all so close. I worked with generals and with foot soldiers. I listened to both. I kept their voices, their commands in my head, even after the war ended. I had to find a way to make them go away. A doctor advised me; he said I should write — how did he put it — get it out of my mind. I cannot paint the images of war out of my mind. I tried. It does not work. I must find the words to describe those dreadful days." They sat in silence for a few moments, "No," he corrected himself, "it is *we* who must find the words." It was chilly. Thoughtfully Paul removed his jacket and placed it around Clara's shoulders.

"When Ronan first suggested I meet you," Clara ventured, her voice soft, her words carefully chosen, "I said I could not possibly be what you needed. Me? Clara Simon from the East End of London in Chelsea? Ronan insisted, gave me the confidence to apply, and here I am with you — in France!"

Paul turned to her and kissed her gently on the cheek. "I have grown very fond of you, Clara. You have made the writing of a difficult book so much easier for me. Tomorrow we will explore my little bit of France."

They walked arm in arm back to the farmhouse. It wasn't the right time to express how grateful she was — to have a job, to know him, and to share his world if only for a short time.

CHAPTER 15

In France

STANDING AT THE bedroom window Clara watched Rogers pace the pebbled pathway as he waited for her and Maze to appear. He'd dusted off the car, wiped the windows clean and took the top down. It was obvious. She'd better get a move on. It was time to go to work.

Down in the kitchen and sitting at the table, Paul and Yvette were chatting as Clara came in. Yvette insisted Clara have breakfast. It was little use saying a cup of coffee was all she fancied when a croissant with homemade strawberry jam and a slab of butter waited her arrival.

Otherwise, Yvette kept her distance, speaking in French to Paul and showing affection to Rogers, who'd given up waiting outside and come in for another cup of coffee. Clara rationalized Yvette's reticence might have something to do with the fact that Mrs. Maze was a frequent visitor and the presence of another woman, however harmless, was to Yvette's eyes a complication. Or had Yvette been standing at the kitchen window doing the dishes and seen Maze kiss Clara?

"We must be on our way," Maze announced. He got up from the table and warmly embraced Yvette.

Clara hurriedly finished off the croissant and swallowed down the last of her coffee.

"*Bon — maintenant vous pouvez sortir et bien travailler. Un bon petit déjeuner.*" Yvette, satisfied Clara had fortified herself for the morning, cleared the table.

"You have made Yvette very happy," Paul remarked as they departed. "When you finish your plate in my country, you compliment the chef."

As they drove off in the car, Maze sat beside Rogers up front, an open map on the dashboard. Clara sat in the back with a camera, her notebooks and a wicker picnic basket filled to the brim with sandwiches and drinks.

"So MUCH HAS changed since the war," Maze shouted to Clara; the wind tended to carry his voice away from her.

"Speak up or Rogers slow down," Clara shouted back as she leaned forward to catch what Maze was saying.

Maze was unstoppable, his voice emotional. "We destroyed villages, we trod on cultivated fields, we left our mark wherever we fought — thousands of white crosses scattered across the land. I have come back many times, and each time I see something new. This time is different. I look for the old — some landmark, a ruin, a sign."

They drove on in silence. Twenty minutes later Maze asked Rogers to stop the car. "I think I know where we are. Yes, I recognize the bridge."

Clara spotted a group of people in an adjacent field. She stepped from the car and began walking toward them. Maze followed. To her surprise they were speaking English. A dozen or so men were digging deep into the soil, while the women were sowing grass seed on completed graves. Caskets stood beside newly dug graves, and there were more caskets stacked on a lorry nearby.

A woman came over to her. She wore a scarf on her head and an old trench coat. She leaned on a shovel as she greeted them. "One of your loved ones 'ere?" she asked. "Don't know if we can find 'im, could give it a try. We've 'ad a few requests since we started this job."

"No, we were lucky, my cousins were too young and my father too old. We are here to do research." Clara turned to Paul, adding, "This is Mr. Paul Maze; he's writing a book about the war. He was a field artist."

"Good on 'yer, guvner; that war was a disgrace. We lost millions of our young men; my son was one of them. I'll never forgive that General Haig; he should rot in hell when it's his time to go. It certainly wasn't time for my son; he was only eighteen years old, just a lad, wounded the first week they sent 'im 'ere, and what did they do? They shoved 'im in a field hospital, patched up his leg, then ordered him back to the trenches. "He died of gangrene poisoning; 'is leg never 'ad time to heal."

"I'm so sorry." Clara walked over to one of the caskets partly covered with dried mud.

As if reading her mind the woman followed along to tell her, "Yes, we dug 'em up — wasn't difficult, covered with a bit of earth, some already open to the elements — just shoved in shallow pits, no markers, no identification and not looked after by anyone. Not even the British government; they think a white cross says it all. Well, it doesn't. Me and me husband started this group; come over once or twice a year to give these poor dead lads a decent burial. Some have identification on the caskets; others don't, so we look inside to see if we can find out who they are. They gave their lives for us; the least we can do is name them, give them some dignity. We've got an Unknown Soldier in Westminster; we don't need no more 'ere."

Clara recalled a poem she'd learned at school. Here it had real meaning. She was standing where that poem might have been written. She couldn't resist sharing it with the woman:

If I should die, think only this of me
That there's some corner of a foreign field
That is forever England.

"It's Rupert Brook, one of the dead poets, isn't it? I'm not an educated woman, but I know them poets. I know 'em all. Wilfred Owen, John McCrae . . . I 'fink I likes 'im the best . . . it's an easy one to remember: 'In Flanders field the poppies blow . . . '"

Clara recited with her:

Between the crosses, row on row,
That mark our place; and in the sky
The larks, still bravely singing, fly
Scarce heard amid the guns below . . . / We are the dead . . . /

Clara alone added the last line, saying softly, " 'We shall not sleep, though poppies grow in Flanders Fields.' "

Maze, who'd been walking the field while the woman and Clara spoke, heard the poem; he came back to where they stood, and in a choked voice made the promise, "I will make sure your work is recognized when I get back to London."

"We don't need recognition, sir — although we could do with a few more volunteers and a few bob to 'elp us carry on."

Paul reached into his pocket and took out his wallet. "Here, this is all the money I have with me; we'll be back tomorrow with more."

"Thank you, thank you, me and me mates really appreciate your generosity." She started back to the others digging up yet another casket, then stopped. "What's the name of your book, sir?"

"*A Frenchman in Khaki.*"

"I'll remember that. Thank you again, sir."

CLARA STAYED FOR a few moments, standing in the field of crosses. Each one depicted a son, a father, a husband and soldiers with families. They weren't just dead soldiers; these were young men in the prime of life. Maze was right to bring her along. She needed to be there.

"It was in one of these fields I found a German soldier;" he told her. "The chap had a terrible wound in the stomach. I tried my best to help him; it was obvious he was too far gone. He told me he had been a waiter in a London restaurant just a few weeks before war was declared. I propped him up against a tree; there was nothing I could do. He had been left behind by his battalion. He gave me his watch. I still have it. I stayed with him until he died."

Back in the car, Rogers drove on. No one spoke.

Clara, tearing up again, moved by Maze's story of the German, astonished at the devotion of the woman and the people with her, all dedicated members of a religious group who considered it their duty to carry out what those in power had either ignored or conveniently forgotten.

"I think it's down there. Stop the car," Maze said. "I'm trying to remember where I was. So much easier to view it from a motorbike, *mon dieu*, I get shudders down my spine when I think of it; I was an open target. Don't know how I survived. Just luck, I suppose."

The car came to a halt and Paul got out and walked over to an old brick shelter. He called for Clara to join him. Later she wrote a version of what he recalled:

This is where I hid and sketched, but I could not help my attention being diverted towards the sound of musketry rising and dying down, coming from the south, where at the time the Fourth Army was attacking. As soon as I had finished and got out of the shelter I became conscious of a weird change creeping into the atmosphere. Pink clouds had piled up, climbing higher in the sky. The sun became gradually obscured and an odd half-light that changed the aspect of everything crept over the landscape. Gun reports seemed to have a different resonance . . . the sky had turned a blue black. Realizing what was going to happen I quickly started back. The first big drops of rain began to riddle the dusty ground with gray holes. A streak of lightning tore across the black sky followed by torrential rain that blotted everything out in a second. I ran vainly, seeking shelter, and overtook other men who were laughing and joking, welcoming the change as though the end of the war had come. The rain falling down the shiny slopes formed streams everywhere. Steam rose from the hot ground . . . The Somme dust had turned into liquid mud . . . During the next three days the rain hardly ceased. Conditions became appalling . . . the trenches had now crumbled with the rain, and water rushing down the slopes had invaded the communication trench. The mud was a soft yellow, sticky paste that clung to one's boots and had to be kicked away at every step. Men were slipping about, tripping over duckboards sunk in the deep bogs at the bottom of trenches that were being constantly shelled: no communication route escaped.

"Twenty thousand dead, sixty thousand wounded; it was the beginning of the Battle of the Somme, and it took place in the mud, which began to form that day," Maze recalled.

A MAN ABOUT the same age as Maze stood under a nearby tree. He had a patch over one eye and only one arm. He turned and walked toward them. He raised his cap. "*Bonjour.*"

"*Bonjour,*" Maze replied and carried on a conversation. The man's dialect was difficult for Clara to understand; she asked Maze to interpret for her while she wrote.

"He said he comes here every day to say a little prayer to thank God for giving him back his life. He spent three years being shot at — when he wasn't underground in the tunnels trying to make contact on the telephones with the soldiers in the battle areas. He doesn't know what we gained; he only knows what we lost."

Clara found a log to sit on and wrote her notes; Paul and the man sat with her. Maze filled his pipe bowl, offered the man his pouch of tobacco and together they smoked their pipes. Rogers brought the picnic basket. They shared the food. They spoke of similar experiences, then suddenly with a shake of the hand the man left. They had their memories, and they had their scars. Perhaps he found it all too painful to stay longer.

"I was wounded somewhere around here, nothing terrible, just a leg wound," Maze remembered. "The stretcher bearers took me to a church that had been turned into a hospital. It was full of seriously injured soldiers. There weren't enough doctors; the nurses were exhausted. All I wanted to do was to get out of there and back to the front. *Les bonnes soeurs* told me to be quiet and wait. It was dreadful. Soldiers screaming, moaning in terrible pain, waiting to be seen by a doctor; I felt a fraud, shouldn't be taking up their time — then a young Irish girl came over to me and said if I didn't have the wound looked at, septicemia could set in and I'd be back in the hospital in a more serious state. I thanked her and kept quiet and began to sketch what I saw there. Next the matron came over; she asked me what I was doing, who I was. I told her I was a Frenchman working for the British, a field artist."

"Right," she said, "keep on sketching, and when you get back to Blighty, show your work to the politicians and the generals, that is, if you can find any; let them see what they're responsible for, and if you manage to find one with a conscience, though I doubt whether there's such a thing, maybe he could prevail upon the others to bring an end to this carnage."

THERE WAS NO shortage of graveyards and battered buildings. Close to twenty years on and the signs of war remained in the fields of graves, in the burned out shells of mines, in broken down buildings, in trenches and on stone memorials. The deeply etched lines on the faces of villagers spoke volumes of their grief. They had not forgotten. How could they? The devastation and the ghosts of those who died surrounded them.

Clara wrote as Maze spoke:

> To find a safe place to make my drawings was at times difficult. I had to use a periscope and crane my neck over sandbags quickly and peep; but the parapet was very high, and I kept slipping off. I had to avoid attracting enemy attention, for they were always on the *qui vive*, ready to snipe or to phone to their guns to fire a few rounds. The dark space one could see in places between sandbags on the opposite side were loopholes. The clump of barbed wire in front of the trench looked forbidding. So far our artillery had done little to it in the way of destruction. Our objective beyond was very undefined. A thick belt of trees bearing fresh leaves limited the view . . . bodies lying about No Man's Land broke the appearance it had of being a track. When I left a trench and said goodbye to the men who were going to attack, and with whom I had been perhaps only a few minutes, it always filled me with anxiety for them and brought home the incongruities of it all . . .

Actually being where the events took place made them even more real to Clara. Now she understood Mannie's anger and her father's grief over losing his brother. Now she also knew why Maze had to write. It was a senseless war fought by untrained soldiers. Killing for the sake of killing with nothing accomplished except humiliation on the German side and a cease-fire on theirs.

She'd heard Churchill's repeated warnings to the Baldwin government ". . . take heed of what is happening in Germany." He was saying this could and will happen again: more dead, more casualties, more widows and more orphans. Hadn't we had enough of war? Battlefields strewn with dead soldiers of all nations, young men who were forced to fight for the mistakes of governments they elected and once trusted. To go through it again would be unconscionable, utter madness.

"And this very day we have a mad man, Adolf Hitler, running amok in Germany because of the Versailles Treaty. We made them sign it, and now they have no work, little food and the shame of losing the war — while ready to start another one." Maze could not control his anger. "I fear for us all."

It was late afternoon before Rogers drove them back to the farmhouse. On her way up to her room Clara heard Maze tell Yvette, "We'll be out for dinner." Right now, all Clara wanted was a bath and a nap.

THE MAÎTRE D' recognized Maze as he entered the restaurant and welcomed him like a long lost friend. He'd reserved a special table for them, not that the place was full; it was early for French diners.

"I suppose you can say we dine while the Englishman eats," Maze acknowledged. "A rewarding day, *n'est-ce pas?*"

"A sad day," was Clara's response.

A waiter brought wine, held the bottle for Paul to read the label and then poured a little in his glass.

"*C'est très bon*," Maze approved, and with glasses filled he made a toast, "To our book, Clara."

Clara lifted her glass, "To your book, Paul."

The wooden tiles on the small dance floor reflected the soft light above them. A piano player, an accordionist and a muted saxophone played French melodies. The maître d' came over to light a wax drip candle. Behind him a waiter carried a tray with hors d'œuvres. The lights in the restaurant dimmed, their table lit only by the flickering candle.

"You seem far away — come back, tell me." Paul wanted her to share her thoughts.

"I was just thinking of a soldier I sat next to on a bus when I was quite young; he wore a blue uniform, and he couldn't stop shivering and shaking. I wanted to hold his hand, to help him stay still. My mother told me he was shell shocked." Clara paused for a moment. "Poems keep jumping into my head; I used to just say them, now I feel them. 'These are the minds the Dead have ravished / Memory fingers in their hair of murders / Multitudinous murders they once witnessed,' Wilfred Owen. He was killed right at the end of the war. Why can't we just talk and resolve our differences without having to kill each other?"

"Because we fight before we think, and we shoot before we negotiate. We send our ambassadors to speak to the aggressors, and they come back with false promises, and war starts all over again."

The sommelier refilled their glasses.

"I have been thinking," Maze took Clara's hand in his. "Perhaps we should stay on in France and finish the book here."

"I can't. I promised my husband I would not stay long. And then there's my family."

"This family of yours, tell me about them."

Where should she start? Meals at Twenty-One, she thought to herself, where dinner time was often a zoo — everyone in a hurry to eat and leave. Too many at the table; if one more happened to arrive, they all moved up one to make room, even letting Nelly take food off their plate to fill one for a late comer's plate. How could she explain so alien a concept to him?

"They are what we English call the salt of the earth, caring and loving; they haven't got much in the way of money or material things. We live an ordinary existence; don't really want for anything. My sister Sula is my best friend; she has a serious muscular condition, and the prognosis is poor — the doctors don't seem to be able to help." Clara sipped her wine.

"And your husband?"

"He's a good man."

"Do you love him?"

It was a difficult question. Did she love him? She cared about him. She wasn't sure about love, and she didn't know Maze well enough to discuss her feelings.

Instead she answered. "He's the man I married, and he loves me."

Maze, obviously charmed by her reply, said, "Do you think he would mind if I ask his wife to dance?"

"What he doesn't know won't worry him."

He led her to the floor where other couples were dancing. He held her close. A slow fox trot, a dance she knew so well, it seemed so natural to be led, to be held, to flow together, no words, just the music taking them to a place they'd never been before. The subject of Sidney evaporated, and the music played on.

THEY STAYED TWO more days in France and one in Belgium. Rogers drove them to the town of Albert to see the Notre Dame de Brebieres where a German shell fell on the base of the dome, leaving the virgin statue atop the dome, leaning dangerously. They searched records in Amiens and Peronne. They walked the fields along the Somme and spent some time in Passchendaele. In Ypres there were the monumental gates and name after name, one after the other on walls, on pedestals and in churches. Each day unlocked memories, and each town had a story to tell.

Clara had little real knowledge of the war before this visit to France; she'd heard snippets, read the papers and cried when Uncle Joe was killed. Here in the midst of the battlefields with survivors tending the graves, with amputees so prevalent, with women still dressed in mourning black, it was all too real. An opportunity to put pictures into words, add emotion to reports, none of this would she have been capable of doing if Paul had not insisted she join him. But Maze, in reliving his experiences, seemed down, and he questioned why he was asked to write yet another book on war. Who would read it? "Why bother?" he demanded.

Clara reassured him. "It will refresh memories; it's what we need right now. Perhaps those who believe war is the only answer will think maybe it isn't, maybe there's some other way to settle our differences. And if there isn't, then, as Mr. Churchill says, we must prepare for the worst."

"I hope you're right, Clara. And thank you for taking this journey with me. You have lightened my heart."

She was no longer just the secretary recording words. A recognizable shift in their relationship had taken place in France; it was deeper, unspoken and unnamed.

CHAPTER 16

Back in London

CLARA DRAGGED THE suitcase up the stairs at Twenty-One and plonked it down, acknowledging that pride had gotten in the way of common sense. She'd refused a lift from Maze, and having waved him off to Chelsea, she'd taken two buses and a train, then walked from Aldgate Station. She knew Rogers understood her reluctance; after all, horses, carts and trams traveled the High Street where she lived, not shiny black oversized limousines. Meanwhile, Clara wasn't about to tell Maze that driving her home in a posh car would start tongues wagging and bystanders gawking, and if they got caught in one of the every day traffic jams it could take forever to maneuver their way out. She could just imagine the reactions and the whistles they'd get; she'd never live it down.

When Clara came into the parlor she found Nelly dozing in her chair by the stove, a kitten on her lap, the wireless playing soft music. No one else was there. Clara tiptoed through, trying to be as quiet as she could possibly be.

"Is that you, Henry?" Nelly opened one eye.

"No, Mum, it's me, Clara."

"Oh, wasn't expecting you; come and give your mum a hug. Good to have you back, luv. I'll make us a pot of tea." Nelly eyed the suitcase. "You carry that case up the stairs all by yourself? Should have got one of the kids outside to help you."

"A cup of tea will do the trick."

"How was it?"

"Well, it was interesting and depressing at the same time."

"Wasn't a holiday then?"

"No, not that I expected it to be — an eye-opener, though. You can't believe the number of graves there, fields upon fields of them — soldiers from all over the place — ours, Canadians, South Africans, Australians. Oh, so many. It was a walking nightmare. I had no idea. Paul was right. I had to experience it first hand, to interpret correctly what he wants to say in his book."

"You call him — Paul? That's a bit bold. When did that start?"

Clara explained it was easier not to stand on ceremony with a man like Maze. He wasn't one for titles, whether they were Mr. or Mrs. or Duke or Duchess. If you became his friend, you were an equal, formalities slipped away.

"You work for him — that don't mean he's your friend," Nelly said as she poured boiling water into the teapot.

"I have become his friend; we get on well." There was an awkward silence. She should have kept calling Paul by his surname. Nelly was too astute to let the slipup pass.

"A bit of advice, luv. When the mob gets back and wants to know every detail from beginning to end, keep calling that guv of yours mister — whatever his name is. Use his first name, and you'll set the cat among the pigeons; you don't want that."

"I'll stick to his surname, but really, he's a very special man. I've got to know him better, and I like him."

"He isn't one of us, Clara, so don't get carried away."

"I'm not. If you met him, you'd understand."

"Little likelihood of that, luv. Wait, I think I hear your dad's footsteps on the stairs — he don't have to get the full account, either."

"Mum's the word, and if you don't mind, I'll take my stuff upstairs before he gets here. Plenty of time to answer Dad's questions and the others too; don't want to go over it more than once."

"Good idea. Go on, he don't have to know you're home yet. You need some time to get yourself back together again. I'll send him off on an errand, then you can come down when you're ready, and no one will know any the better."

"You're the best, Mum."

"You look exhausted. Explanations can wait."

A LETTER FROM the Lefevre Gallery was in the stack of mail waiting on Clara's desk the first day she was back to work. She went through it and selected two letters, one from the Lefevre Gallery and the other from Heinrich Luftmann. She handed the one from the gallery to Maze, the other she put aside for the moment.

"Look at this," he said. "I forgot all about the show at the Lefevre. They expect me to have twenty paintings ready in two weeks! They want new work. Read the letter." He handed it to her, then ran his hands through his hair in a great state of agitation.

"You have new paintings, the Louise nudes, the landscapes and probably a few more hiding somewhere in a cupboard. It will not be a problem." Clara tried to calm him, "They want paintings that have not been exhibited in their gallery. It has no date requirement on the work."

"Oh. Then that is not so bad. Come, you can help me choose."

"You trust my judgment?" Clara was both surprised and flattered.

"Of course. I think the seascapes; we'll have to dig them out — haven't done any for years."

Clara was ready to help. "It will be a change from war stories."

Clara followed Maze up to the studio. The paintings were stored in slots along the studio walls. There were many paintings from which to choose. They needed twenty. He pulled out twelve, and together they decided on the remaining eight. Clara called for Rogers to get them ready for delivery.

"There's a letter from Mr. Luftmann, Paul, do you want to read it now?"

Maze took the envelope from Clara and read what Heinrich had to say. "Winston needs to read this. Tell Rogers to run this to Churchill's office and see if he can meet me at the club this evening."

Churchill had spent the last few months warning and criticizing the government — blind fools, he called them. Germany was arming for war, and the British government saw no reason to do likewise. "Have they learned nothing since the war?" he had asked Maze. "Can't they see what was happening right before their eyes?"

Hitler, he claimed, was giving the Germans what they needed, and that was revenge. He made them believe Germany could once again be a proud nation; it didn't matter to the masses how he intended to implement his promises. "It's a simple philosophy," Churchill had proclaimed. "Feed the belly, close the mind."

Friends of Stanley Baldwin, the British Prime Minister, persuaded the Baldwin Cabinet to reaffirm the ten-year program, which meant that defense planning should continue on the basis that no major war was threatened within that period. And Neville Chamberlain, "that weak and ineffectual man," as Churchill called him, went along with it, saying, "Financial and economic risks are by far the most serious and urgent that the country has to face."

THE CLUB IN Upper Berkley Street was over a hundred years old and had a reputation above reproach. It was a gentleman-only retreat, frequented by the rich and titled. The right place to be seen reading *The Times*, having a drink, hiding from the wife — not entirely Maze's cup of tea. For Churchill it was where he entertained his friends and discussed private matters without the presence of women to distract him.

"I am troubled by this." Churchill held Heinrich's letter in his hand as he spoke to Paul seated comfortably just opposite him in a club lounge chair.

"He should get out before it gets worse," Maze replied.

"I doubt whether they'd let him leave, sooner lock him up. His predicament is precarious. On the other hand, it could be used to our advantage. Heinrich cannot speak directly to us. You noticed it was postmarked London again? He obviously doesn't trust the German mail." Churchill twiddled a cigar in his hand. "What is the matter with the leadership here? They don't listen; they don't comprehend. Deaf ears and no brains, that's what I have to deal with. Instead of making rearmament a central issue, Baldwin speaks only of economic depression. Well, I can tell you we'll be a darn sight more depressed when war breaks out and we haven't a gun to defend ourselves!"

Maze knew Churchill was right. Further, if Heinrich Luftmann's letter didn't show it, what did? "Stay the course, Winston, watch your health; don't want you having a heart attack. Eventually they will have to take notice. When you get home lay a few bricks or paint, take your mind off it."

"Clemmie agrees with you; she's not too fond of the bricklaying, though, says I'm in competition with the Great Wall of China. Silly woman. My wall hardly goes around Chartwell. I'm not aiming to enclose the whole bloody country!"

"I see Heinrich calls himself an Abstract Creationist now."

What's that?" Churchill asked.

"*Je ne sais pas.*"

"Each to his own. I must say I like to see a tree that looks like a tree. These abstract fellows leave me cold. Mind if I keep the letter with me? Got to think about it. Can't let it go unanswered."

"I'll see if I can locate the fellow who brought it over. There's that London postmark again." Maze and Churchill thought alike.

"Yes, that means Heinrich is concerned that his mail is censored. Don't like it, don't like it at all."

CLARA WAS NOW fully ensconced in the studio. If something came up that she didn't understand, he would be right there to explain it; and Rogers, tired of carrying the typewriter up and down the stairs, was relieved not to have to continue the chore. Clara liked the studio; it was light and airy, and her window looked out onto the river. Her one request was to be out of there when a nude model was posing.

"Ridiculous. You carry on with your work, and I will continue with mine. The human form is nothing to be ashamed of." Maze was adamant.

She lost that one. Maze, oblivious of the incongruity, kept painting. She kept her eyes glued to the typewriter and continued to transpose shorthand notes while the nude reclined on a nearby sofa.

Clara decided the best way to deal with Paul's fragmented concentration and frequent interruptions was to write as much as she could and then let him read it. If he approved, well and good; any errors, she'd correct. Having most of the material on hand, and having been where the stories took place, she felt competent to do much of the writing herself. There were a few questions she had and some points needed clarification. For instance, if he wasn't attached to any particular army unit, how could he be trusted? If he didn't have a uniform, how did the ordinary soldier know he wasn't the enemy?

"That was a problem, but I managed to talk my way through it most of the time, except, of course, when they were about to execute me."

Maze had got to know many of the generals during the war — General Gough in particular; Gough sent him out on reconnaissance. It was with Gough's blessing that had given him permission to work with the French and the British. "Remember, I wasn't considered a soldier. I was an artist mapping out positions of both the enemy and the allied contingents, and I reported back to Gough. Had I been a recognized soldier, I would not have been able to travel as freely as I did. Anyway, the Germans were far too busy digging trenches when they weren't manning guns and so didn't take much notice of a strange looking man on a motorbike. To them I probably seemed like a harmless Frenchman from a nearby village, and because I stayed within certain boundaries of the British and Allied forces, I was known to them. I moved when they moved. They needed a liaison, and I was it."

A FEW DAYS after their meeting at the club, Churchill was in the studio painting with Maze. Maze was working from a sketch he'd made in France, transferring the image to canvas. He confided in Churchill — he wanted to finish this painting to be included in his upcoming exhibition. It was a sunflower field; reclining in front of the sunflowers he'd placed a young woman. She was blond, she was wearing a white dress very much like a dress Clara wore while they were away together, with a foulard scarf draped around her shoulders.

Churchill heaved himself out of the chair to take a closer look. "I like it. Mind you, when you've got a pretty girl like that, you could put her in front of a dustbin and you'd still have a fine painting." He turned his attention to Clara. "Do I see a resemblance by any chance?"

The last thing Clara wanted was to get involved in a painting discussion. "Well, it's . . . " She stumbled, looked at the work and tried to think of something pertinent to say. "Well, it was a most beautiful field of sunflowers, and — I suppose — Mr. Maze put me in his painting for want of finding someone else."

"Well, the only other woman around was Yvette, and as much as I love her, I don't think she'd be a suitable model for a light, romantic setting, do you, Winston?"

"Your Yvette would make a great cover for a cookery book; can't see her in a sunflower field." Churchill stood back from the easel.

"It's all to do with composition; sunflowers are only a background to the figure in the foreground."

Clara decided to let them get on with it. She had a book to complete. She left them admiring the painting. She'd gotten to where General Gough sent Maze to find the Cavalry Division:

> Two German Red Cross men were stretched across the white marble steps in a large pool of blood at a Louis XIII chateau ... the door of the chateau was ajar ... Everything had been turned upside down, the place was full of German wounded ... I shook one man, but he never stirred; another gave a moaning growl. I couldn't tell which was asleep, drunk or dead ...

"Oh, I nearly forgot to tell you," said Maze. "I found the man who posted Heinrich's letter to me. I was supposed to meet him, but he was called back to Germany. Couldn't get much out of him on the phone — just that we should be concerned for Heinrich."

Churchill took his time to react. "Pity about that; but I have another idea. What I am thinking is this: you go to Germany under the guise of an art dealer — "

"*Moi?*"

"Hear me out," said Churchill. "You travel as a bona fide dealer or artist. You have the Aryan look, and your work isn't in anyway controversial — and you speak German!"

"Is that supposed to be a compliment?"

"No, your watercolors, your landscapes, they're enchanting — no hidden meanings. You can visit accepted German galleries, look at what they have and show them your work. Take some of my paper works too. I have a few innocuous ones. I'll sign them with a phony name. While you're over there, you can meet with Heinrich; far better to hear from the horse's mouth what's going on than from people who deliver letters. We know Heinrich's lady friend works in a munitions factory. She can give us information. With it, I can back up my assault on the government. If I have facts, if I can present the situation through the eyes of someone who's been there, I might get somewhere. I cannot go; I'm too recognizable. You could pass. Think about it." Churchill leaned back in his chair, puffing away on his cigar, as if it might be a done deal.

Maze, not quite sure how to react, went back to work on his sunflower painting. He had a book to complete, a show to prepare for, and he'd just returned from France. On the other hand, Clara could carry on without him for a few days, and he had twenty paintings, and one more, ready for exhibition. If Churchill was really serious about this mission, he could not refuse him. "You are a persuasive man, Winston. Don't understand why you can't be as convincing with your colleagues in the House. Give me a week or so."

"Not for one moment did I think you would turn me down, Paul. Thank you. Incidentally, that Nazi soirée you told me about, when is it?"

"This weekend."

"You going?"

"No."

"I'd like you to. Tell me who's there. Listen to what they have to say. Take that pretty assistant of yours."

"A Jew at a Nazi theme party?"

Churchill chuckled. "She's a Jew? Well, I never — even better."

"I'll suggest it, not sure she'll agree." Maze had his doubts, even though he rather fancied the ides of taking Clara to an aristocratic gathering. "She'll be a rose amongst many thorns, Winston."

"I think she may relish the idea. You mark my words. You can be your charming self. Mrs. Simon can take mental notes. You'll be a good combination. Bet you the Astors, Mitfords, Duke of Windsor and that American woman of his, they could be there too. All of them, sympathizers — one way or another, turncoats — if you ask me."

"Mrs. Simpson?"

"Right. What he sees in her is beyond me. And Joe Kennedy — don't trust him farther than I could throw him. More money than sense, hobnobs with the Nazis."

"Is Eleanor Barnes that well connected?"

"Well, you'll find out when you get there. If not the ones I mentioned, there'll be others; why else would they attend such an event? If they're not Nazis themselves, they have to be sympathizers."

"Clara has a husband." Maze reminded him.

"What difference does that make?" Churchill wasn't one for beating about the bush. "You're taking her, not him!"

Chapter 17

Mannie

Every Saturday night Johnnie Mansfield sat at the old pub piano playing and singing a medley of vaudeville songs, old reliable favorites, songs they heard their parents sing, songs they'd heard from the moment they could distinguish one melody from another.

Too proud to beg, too honest to steal, I know what it means to be wanting a meal: My tatters and rags I try to conceal, I'm one of the shabby genteel.

When he came to that last line, "I'm one of the shabby genteel," they'd roar with approval and stand up and twirl around, the women lifting up their skirts, the men pulling at their trouser legs.

"Give us a few verses of 'Can't Do My Belly Bottom Button Up,'" a chap somewhat in his cups shouted out, "'cos I can't get mine to reach the 'ole!"

Johnnie Mansfield obliged. There wasn't anything Johnnie couldn't play or sing. If they wanted Scottish ballads, he'd give them Harry Lauder's "Just a Wee Doch and Dorrie." Anyone who'd drifted in from up north, say Lancashire, for them he'd perform Gracie Field's "Biggest Aspidistra." And as for the cockney requests, there was always, "Knocked 'em in the old Kent Road."

In an alcove at the back of the pub Mannie waited for Sula. He sat as far away as he could from the patrons, cupping his ears to block out their off-key voices, smoking his cigarette and trying to concentrate on the *Evening Standard* newspaper. Mannie wasn't one for sing-alongs — let them make idiots of themselves, no need for him to join in. With a tankard of lager and a shandy for Sula he was content to read his paper and sip his beer until she showed up.

He'd arranged to meet her 'round about now. He looked up to see her, pushing her way through the mob, using her stick more as a weapon than a crutch. Finally she reached a clearing, spotted Mannie, and limping noticeably, made her way to where he sat.

"How was your day?" Sula asked, shouting above the noise.

"Well," he hesitated, "it was interesting. I got an offer of a job."

"Great, tell me more." She sank down in the chair opposite him. "I was called before the Aldgate Committee; Harry Isaacs heard I needed work. They asked a lot of questions, liked the fact I'd been arrested — that really tickled them. Then after some humming and hawing, they offered to send me to Spain to report on the civil unrest there; they want an honest written account."

Sula could not believe what she was hearing. "Are you out of your mind?"

"I haven't accepted . . . just said I'd think about it."

"Then you are out of your mind."

"Calm down. I want to discuss it with you."

"There is no discussion. There's a civil war brewing in Spain. Look at you. Do you honestly think you're physically able to dodge bullets, to face Franco's army, if it comes to that? You paid your dues in the last one — don't need another suicide mission. I won't let you go."

"You're beginning to sound like your father. At least give me a chance to think about it."

"It's out of the question." Sula was adamant.

"I'd be there to write, not fight." Mannie felt demoralized — his livelihood slipping away from him.

"It is not our job to keep the League of Nations going. If you want to write about trouble, there's enough here to keep you occupied. You don't need to go abroad looking for more."

"It would get me back into the swing of things, Sula."

"You can tell the committee you'll write for them here. Spain has nothing to do with us."

"It has everything to do with us, you wait and see," Mannie replied.

Mannie, of course, realized he wasn't up to the task when they'd offered the assignment. It felt good just to be considered. At the time he knew they chose him because they couldn't find anyone else. Still, it didn't hurt to stall a bit. He'd asked for the evening to speak to his wife. "What she got to do with it?" the secretary had asked. Mannie ignored the question. He wasn't altogether pleased with the way they conducted business; theirs wasn't the most kosher of organizations. If he'd been honest, he'd have said, "No," on the spot. He wasn't about to give them the satisfaction of an early reply, and he certainly wasn't going to own up to the fact that the last thing he wanted was to be in the middle of another war zone.

SITTING THERE, LOOKING at Sula, his mind strayed to their first meeting. They both attended evening classes at Toynbee Hall. He took writing classes, had a gift for words, wanted to write and be a reporter. She encouraged him. He applied for jobs at a number of newspapers, couldn't find anything permanent, got the occasional assignment, and after joining the Socialists wrote pamphlets for them. He submitted articles to magazines, some were taken, others rejected. It was Sula who suggested they live together and share expenses, an unheard of arrangement. He agreed. They rented a bed-sitter in Wentworth Street and to save money had all their meals up at Twenty-One with the family. A few months later they got married in a Registry Office and told the family about it after the deed was done.

When Henry heard they'd tied the knot he had a fit. "Haven't the decency to invite us. My daughter married in a Registry Office? That's a disgrace!"

Nelly wasn't pleased — said she'd like to have been there; still if that was the way they wanted it, then so be it. "What's done's done," she told Henry. "Think of it this way. We didn't have to pay for the wedding!"

Mulling it over for a few days, Henry performed what he considered his paternal duties and had a talk with Mannie. "You'll look after our Sula, you hear me, and if I ever hear you as much as touch a hair on her head, I'll march you down to that 'ere Registry Office and have your marriage annulled on the spot."

"Point well taken, Mr. Levy." And with that Mannie was off the hook, and Henry regained his rightful place, telling Nelly, "I gave him a what for, Nelly. Must say he took it in the right spirit."

"Good on yer, Henry. A father must do what a father must do, and you done it."

Sula took a job as a bookkeeper for a cabinetmaker, earned enough to pay the rent, and they managed all right until she was taken ill. The only alternative then was to move back to Twenty-One.

Mannie hadn't had steady work for years. He'd spent nearly a year in hospital, recovering from his wounds, then another eighteen months in rehabilitation. Before being called up he was apprenticed to a large printing company in Tottenham. It was a family tradition, his father and his uncles worked there, and during the war, when the men left to fight, his mother and his aunts took their places. At seventeen he volunteered and was put in a division of the Fourth Army. At eighteen he was badly wounded at the Battle of the Somme. He spent weeks in a field hospital before being sent home, his left leg amputated at the knee. Out of the ten young men conscripted from his place of work, he alone survived.

When he was released from rehab the foreman from the printer's shop came to his parent's home to tell him his job was safe; he could start work again. They were very decent that way. Magnanimous, his mother called it. Mannie turned the job down, saying he wanted to do more than stand at a machine all day. They offered a desk job; he refused. His father thought him selfish, breaking a family tradition. Mannie, not one to stay silent, said he wanted to write the copy, not print it. The boy who'd gone off to fight returned a man. He was determined to do better than his family stuck in low paying jobs because, like their mums and dads before them, it was safe and they were assured of a weekly wage.

At the pub the drinkers were more than getting in their stride. Johnnie played "Knees Up, Mother Brown," and everyone joined in . . . "under the table you must go" . . . and under the table two of them went, knocking over the drinks, offering to replace them and knocking them over again. A fight started. Harold, the bouncer, employed for just such a situation, took hold of a couple of drunks by the scruff of the neck and literally threw them out of the pub. He returned to spot a few more inebriates and dealt with them too. And there were more to follow, all of them landing up on the pavement outside the pub bemoaning their fate.

Alfred, the pub licensee, realizing the rowdiness was getting a bit much, asked Johnnie to play less raucous pieces; he requested a lullaby. "Something gentle," he said.

"Naw — they won't go for that. How about 'Shine on Harvest Moon'?"

"Try it," Alfred said as he counted the minutes to closing time.

"Do us a favor, Johnnie, no funeral marches; we 'ain't dead yet. Liven it up a bit, for Gawd's sake!" a drunk at the bar demanded.

"Sorry, old man — orders from the boss. Drink up and sing along with me. 'Shine on, shine on harvest moon, up in the sky, I ain't had no lovin' since January, February, June or July . . . '"

"Neither have I," said Mannie, helping Sula up from her chair.

"Nonsense," replied Sula with a wide grin. "I'm ready for a bit of lovin'. Let's go."

Mannie finished his beer, leaned over to Sula and gave her a kiss. "Just wanted you to know they thought me worthy of the offer; made me feel good at the time."

"I know, luv. Fight your wars on your own turf. They don't need you in Spain. Anyway, if Nelly got wind of it, she'd have you committed."

CHAPTER 18

Clara and Sula

I T WAS SATURDAY afternoon at Twenty-One, and all was unusually quiet. Henry and Bernie had rushed out the door the moment Nelly left with Anna; Henry was eager to take as many bets as he could before the afternoon horse races began. Bernie, his eager assistant, had gone with him to learn the ropes.

"Keep an eye out for the copper on his beat," Henry instructed as they walked swiftly down one of the side streets. "If you sees him, pretend you saw a thief or some other excuse — keep him occupied. I'll do a runner and stay out of sight 'til 'es gone."

Nelly, off to Boris the Photographer, was perfectly aware of Henry's on-the-side business but managed to let her disapproval remain unspoken; she was up to her neck in arrangements for Anna's upcoming nuptials and hadn't the time or the inclination to do much about Henry's unsavory diversion. And, if truth be known, she wasn't exactly averse to having a few extra quid in the coffers. Jewish wedding albums were always "Best By Boris." He hadn't changed his group arrangement for thirty years. There stood the bride, her long bridal train draped gently down three steps, next to the groom in morning dress, top hat in hand, both placed in a sideways pose. The bridesmaids lined on incremental steps either side, heads turned looking directly at the camera. You couldn't tell one wedding portrait from another.

Mannie was locked in an upstairs room writing and had asked not to be disturbed, and Sidney had left early to avoid the crowd soon to be gathering at the Arsenal football ground. Today's match would be mayhem, Arsenal playing Chelsea — two London teams with a long history of rivalry. Sidney wouldn't be back for hours.

When Maze asked Clara to accompany him to the Eleanor Barnes soiree, she thought he was joking. "Why me?" she asked. Surely there were others better suited to attend a posh "do" in Belgravia. But when he quite seriously told her that Winston Churchill had suggested he take her, well, then, what could she say? She could turn down Maze, but she couldn't possibly refuse Churchill.

With everyone out and about, Sula and Clara had the parlor to themselves — even Boadicea was taking a nap. Sula, the only one in the family Clara had confided in, was helping her prepare for the upcoming dreaded evening. To say Clara was anxious was putting it mildly. She was petrified. She washed her hair, and while Sula set it, Clara did her nails. Her dress and shoes were waiting for her in Chelsea. Apart from the newly polished nails, no one would suspect Cinderella was going to the ball in just a few hours.

"It wasn't a casual invitation, Sula," Clara explained. "Not just from Mr. Maze. Churchill suggested I go."

"Why not Mrs. Maze? What's wrong with her?"

"His wife is in Scotland. Rogers told me she wouldn't come down to attend any party Eleanor Barnes arranged. He said Mrs. Maze disliked Eleanor Barnes intensely; in fact, he'd overheard her say that Mrs. Barnes was obnoxious and rude, and had a strange collection of friends."

"Still, out of all those people who trot in and out of that house you were the only one he wanted to take? Doesn't make sense to me."

"It's a job; he's supposed to mingle, while I — snoop."

"Snoop?"

"Yes. I have to listen to conversations, make mental notes. Don't think I didn't balk at the idea; I even suggested he take someone else. He reminded me it was an important function attended by Nazi sympathizers, and Churchill wants to know who they are. We had no choice; we had to attend. He's appalled at the theme, but there are times, he said, when personal feelings must be set aside, and this is one of them."

"He's asking too much of you, Clara. Doesn't he know you're Jewish?"

"Of course he does. That's not the point."

"Then — what is the point?"

"I told you — to listen and to report back to Churchill. He wants to know who our enemies are; some of the guests, he said, are actually friends of Hitler."

"Glad it's you and not me, that's all I can say. So, what are you going to wear? There's nothing suitable in your wardrobe."

"Maze took me to an exclusive boutique in Knightsbridge. I tried on half a dozen dresses. I suppose you'd call them gowns. Two French women hovered over me for an hour. Finally I chose, with his approval, a full-length ivory satin gown with a beaded neckline. I wish you could see it, Sula. It's exquisite. Unfortunately it will have to stay in Chelsea; I can't bring it back here for obvious reasons."

"What if the newspapers are there? You could be on the front page of the *News of the World!*"

"Not likely to be *News of the World,* more likely *The Times.* No one reads *The Times* in Whitechapel. Anyway, I'll have Mum's fan, the one Uncle Naffy brought back from China. I'll hide behind it."

"You really like this Maze bloke, don't you?"

"I, well, I find him interesting." Clara hesitated for a moment. "He's different than anyone I've known before."

"Mannie thinks he's taking advantage of you."

"It's really none of his business. What do you think?"

"I think," Sula smiled and gave Clara a hug, "I think you're probably one of the luckiest girls around, and I'm totally envious."

"If Mannie met Paul, he'd like him. They actually have a lot in common."

"And Sidney?"

"Chalk and cheese. Sidney would be intimidated."

CLARA HAD ALERTED Sidney at the beginning of the week; she might be needed in Chelsea on Saturday night. He showed little interest when she'd tried discussing the work she was doing with Maze. All Sidney wanted was for her to look for another job, something closer and less time consuming. She had to find some way of placating him while keeping her job at the same time. She decided the best strategy for the upcoming Saturday engagement was to inform him in stages. He knew her working hours with Maze were often erratic. He'd accepted that. This time, because it was a Saturday night, she'd intimated she might be needed, starting with, "There might be a possibility . . ." then changing the approach a few days later to "could be a probability . . . " He hadn't reacted. In actual fact he didn't know she'd be going back to work that evening, and she certainly wasn't going to let on Maze was taking her to a party in Belgravia.

"You'll have to tell him when he comes in; you can't just disappear," Sula advised.

"Of course I'll tell him. I don't need to be there for another hour or so. Anyway, I did try — he wasn't interested, said it was my business, not his. I've reminded him countless times that when I first interviewed in Chelsea, Maze told me the job entailed more than typing and I might be needed at odd times. It wasn't a nine-to-five job. Sidney knew it and actually said the overtime pay would help us save up for our own home. The book is only part of what I do; there are art shows to attend to, meetings with important people and other duties — like this party. Maze wears a number of different hats. He's called upon by people in government. He paints and has gallery shows and some of the work he involves me in, well, it's secret."

"You're not being honest with Sidney."

"That's unfair, Sula. I've tried; he's not interested. I keep from Sidney what he cannot accept. He complains about being stuck in a job he dislikes and does nothing about it. I move on. I can't live his life, and I can't allow him to dictate mine."

Sula nodded and kept her silence.

"I admit traveling and social gatherings weren't mentioned when I was first interviewed for the position, and I did question France, why he needed me there; but having gone, I understand why."

"But a Nazi celebration? Don't you think that's a bit much?"

"They won't know I'm a Jew, and I'm certainly not going to announce it."

Sula, realizing nothing she could say would have any effect on Clara, dropped the subject. She tested to see if Clara's hair was dry before taking out the curlers. "How do you want it, up or down?"

"I don't know. How do Nazi women wear their hair?"

"How the hell would I know? You'll wear it down; it's easier."

"No, put it up; it's more sophisticated."

"It's not long enough."

"Stretch it and remove those wave irons; they're tearing at my scalp."

"You want to look beautiful? Then suffer, preferably in silence." Sula, at least in this instance, took charge.

Sula was putting the finishing touches to Clara's hair when Sidney came in. You could tell by his face Arsenal had won. Nothing made him happier than an Arsenal win. "Three to one!" He announced the score with tremendous pride. "Chelsea didn't have a look in. Eddie Hapgood! What a kicker, what a mover! Did you know they made him England's captain?"

Neither Clara nor Sula had a clue about football and could care less. It didn't stop Sidney's enthusiasm. He carried on, unperturbed. "Look out, Scotland. Watch it, Ireland. Our boys were all over the place. It will be a black day when Hapgood retires; never be able to replace him.

"That's for sure," Clara agreed, giving Sula a look that said, "What the hell is he going on about?"

"Where is everyone?" Sidney didn't wait for an answer. "How about a cup of tea? We'll go out for a good celebration meal tonight, you and me, Clara."

Sula excused herself; she wasn't about to get involved in what would probably turn out to be a drawn out confrontation. She left Clara and Sidney together in the parlor.

"We'll have a cup of tea — and then I have to leave," Clara informed Sidney.

"Leave? Where you going?"

"I told you at the beginning of the week I might have to work tonight, that I wasn't sure. Well, I do have to work, and I can't get out of it."

"Saturday is our night, Clara. Put him off."

She paused in thought — to soften the blow. "I'll try not to let it happen again."

"Have you told him you're a married woman? Or doesn't that matter to him?" snapped Sidney.

"Of course he knows."

Clara had never seen Sidney so angry. He'd planned the evening, and she'd ruined it. The job was causing a rift in their marriage, and he'd had enough of Paul Maze and Clara's involvement with him. He'd gone along with it up to now, but when it interfered with his Saturday night out with his wife — and Maze taking precedence — it was unacceptable.

"You're pushing it a bit, Clara. I'm not the only one who disapproves. The family doesn't like it, either, and it doesn't affect them as it does me. I'm the one left without a partner on the weekend. I'm the one who looks duped. They take me as a damn fool, not being able to stand up to my wife. Well, I'm sick of it. First France, now this. What next?"

Clara retaliated. Her life was not going to be taken over by a committee or a husband who resented her working for a man who asked more of her than she first realized. "Things change, Sidney. I work for a man who isn't run of the mill. He has his finger in lots of pies. He's important in many different ways, and I'm lucky to work for him."

"Really? Lucky? I'd say you're a darn fool to put up with his demands. What about me? What am I suppose to do on a Saturday evening, sit at home and twiddle my thumbs?"

"Listen, Sidney, I don't interfere with your going to football matches every Saturday afternoon or when they play on week nights. Do you ever give a thought to us doing something together on Saturday afternoon? No, never. Arsenal comes before me every time. And what about Fanny Francis' daughter's wedding? I had to go by myself because you were stuck at the Arsenal and wouldn't leave. Why is your rotten football game more important than my job?"

"That could not be helped. The game was a draw. They were playing overtime. No one walks out of a game in overtime. I caught up with you later, didn't I?"

"Yes, but only after I attended the synagogue alone and sat down with an empty chair beside me at the reception," Clara reminded him. "One Saturday evening without me isn't the end of the world, Sidney. Take Sula to the pictures. Mannie's locked himself in the room upstairs. Sula's at a loose end; give her a night out."

"I don't want her. I want you. Just go, Clara. Don't tell me who to take or where to go. I'm quite capable of going to the pictures alone. I don't need an escort."

It wasn't a disagreement over a stupid Saturday afternoon football game — she just threw that in to get even; she really didn't care about his football games. Every husband she knew attended football matches on a Saturday. It was relaxation, harmless entertainment. It had more to do with who Sidney was, a man who refused to take a risk, who chose to play second fiddle to his brother. She'd encouraged him to go out on his own, he hadn't the guts to give it a try. What else was she supposed to do? One of them had to make a move, and she took the opportunity when it presented itself.

For her, working and wanting to be with Maze was far more complicated than she'd ever let on to Sidney. Looking at it honestly, it had everything to do with who Sidney was in comparison to Paul — Sidney, a predictable, simple man, Paul, an exciting unpredictable charmer. And the truth was: Paul had won her over.

Before Paul entered her life, choices were limited; now, in what seemed a very short time, they were limitless. She had successfully entered a new world, a chance in a lifetime, and she achieved it by standing up against Abbott, an anti-Semitic bully. Sidney could have taken her move as an example. He didn't. So, he was stuck, and she was moving on.

How ironic it now was that she would soon be entering a room of upper class anti-Semites with the intention of helping a politician persuade his government to take notice of Germany's rebirth and its headlong path to inevitable war.

Clara was in the right place at the right time, and if it meant going against her family's wishes, then so be it.

Nelly's motto, nothing for the dumb, came to mind, and tonight Clara was proving, once again, Nelly to be right.

CHAPTER 19

Belgravia

CLARA GAZED DOWN on the satin gown laid out on the bed in a guest room in Maze's Cheyne Walk residence, hardly believing it was for her.

"Can I help you, Miss Clara?" Maggie tapped on the door as she entered the room. She carried a ruby red wrap over an arm and a white beaded pocketbook in her hand. "If you'll step into the gown, I'll zip it up for you."

Clara sighed. The time had come, and she slipped on the gown and waited for Maggie to help her.

"You're a *picturre* to behold," Maggie remarked in her soft Scottish accent. Mr. Maze'll be *verry* proud to have you on his arm this evening."

"I'm afraid to move," Clara said and examined her image in the Cheval mirror.

"I spotted the wrap in Mrs. Maze's cupboard," Maggie explained. "Thought you might like to *borro'* it to keep you warm. And look at this wee beaded bag. Just what you need for your lipstick and handkerchief. I'll put them back where I found them tomorrow; she'll never *knoo*. And you *nee'* not worry; Mr. Maze suggested it."

Maggie and Clara had become good friends, both finding themselves in unfamiliar surroundings and having to adapt. London was a lonely place for a girl from the Highlands, where sheep were more plentiful than people.

Maggie nudged her, saying, "He's a waitin' for you downstairs."

Clara slipped the wrap around her shoulders, picked up Nelly's precious fan and the beaded white bag and made her way from the bedroom, a little wobbly on new shoes. She held on to the banister as she gingerly took each step down to the foyer where Maze, handsome in evening dress and a new black cloak, proudly watched her every move.

ROGERS' LONG AND arduous task of polishing the car did not go unnoticed. It gave a blinding reflection off the light beaming down from street lamps.

"If you don't mind me saying, Mrs. Simon, you look smashing this evening."

Clara blushed at Rogers' compliment. Amazing what fine clothes could do. "Thank you, Rogers — you've made the car look as if it had just now come from a showroom."

"It's an excellent machine, served us well, deserves a bit of spit and polish every now and then." Rogers stroked the door panel as he would have stroked a loyal old dog.

"He won't let me purchase another. Won't hear of it," Maze said petulantly.

"There is nothing wrong with this one, and she will not be put out to pasture while I'm around to look after her." Rogers was adamant in his defense of the vehicle he loved.

It was a chilly, clear evening with a near full moon. Clara was thankful for the wrap around her shoulders; and with Nelly's fan, her talisman, she felt protected.

They sat at the back of the car, a blanket over their laps. "We will ignore the theme," Maze said, "drink the champagne, eat their food, listen to the gossip, then dance the evening away." He had the evening planned.

"And when they ask you who I am, what will you tell them?" Clara asked cautiously.

"Oh, I'll think of something; anyway, you can be sure Eleanor will inform all present that I have brought along my assistant!"

"Oh, God, I'm really not looking forward to this." Clara practiced opening and closing the fan and remembered a poem she had been taught when she took a deportment class in school. She spoke the verses silently to herself hoping it would take her mind off what she was dreading.

"You're very quiet, Clara."

"Actually, I was reciting something to myself to calm my nerves."

"Want to share it with me?"

"You know me; just another poem running around my head — bit silly really."

"No — I want to hear it."

Clara began:

If you want to learn the lesson of the fan,
I'm quite prepared to teach you all I can,
So, ladies, everyone, pray observe how it is done,
this simple, little lesson with a fan.
If by chance you are invited to a ball,
and you see someone you don't expect at all,
If you want him close beside you, but a dozen friends divide you
Of course you know it's most unladylike to call.
So you look at him a moment, nothing more,
Then you cast your eyes demurely on the floor.
With your fan you go, just so, towards you, don't you know?
It's a delicate suggestion, nothing more.
When you see him coming over, simple you,
just be very, very careful what you do.
With your fan you'll idly play, and you look 'round,
as if to say, it's a matter of indiff-er-ence to you.
You flutter and you fidget with it so,
and you hide your little nose behind it, so
Till when he begins to speak, just lay it on your cheek,
in the fascinating manner that you know.
Then when he tells the old tale o'er and o'er,
and vows he will love you ever more
Gather up your little fan; secure him while you can,
It's a delicate suggestion, nothing more.

"Charming. What a memory you have for poetry. Who wrote it?"

"Mr. Anonymous!"

Clara's recitation eased any concerns Maze might have harbored. She was, without doubt, a beguiling young woman. Paul took Clara's hand in his. "It's a lovely night for a drive. Rogers, drive us through the park, please."

"It's a long way 'round, sir," was Rogers' mindful response.

"That's all right; we're not in any rush. I love London," he said, looking out the window. "It is my second most favorite city — Paris then London. One day I will take you to Paris, Clara, to the galleries, to the Louvre, to the restaurants. The food in France, well, I don't have to tell you. Yvette proved my preference for French cuisine."

Clara wasn't having his Paris outdo her London. "We have the Tower, Buckingham Palace, Westminster Abbey, The National Gallery . . . "

" . . . and lots of fish-and-chip shops!" Rogers added.

They were coming into Belgravia; Clara braced herself for their arrival. "I will use the fan to signal you."

Maze gave Clara's hand an affectionate squeeze. "Have no fear; I won't be far from you at any time."

A row of chauffeured cars stood alongside Eleanor's residence, each one ready to discharge their passengers onto a red carpet where an attendant, dressed in Nazi uniform, waited to usher them through the open double doors.

Rogers joined the queue. As the car in front moved forward, he moved, too, until he reached the dropping off point where he jumped out and ran to open their door. No Nazi was going to take his job from him.

"This is more than I can take," Clara whispered to Maze.

At the entrance another uniformed Nazi took Clara's wrap and Paul's cloak.

"Will we ever see them again?" Clara asked as they walked away.

"Eleanor may have to sell them to pay for the party," Maze joked.

ELEANOR'S GREAT ROOM had been turned into a ballroom. Round tables with white tablecloths surrounded the dance floor. Nazi banners flowed down the side of the walls. Men in evening dress had tufted black mustaches pasted under their nose and hair plastered down with the one little bit falling over their forehead. The women, if they weren't dressed in Tyrol costume, were scantily dressed in flapper silk. They looked as if they'd been thrown out of some degenerate nightclub in Berlin. Others were more discreet in designer gowns.

Meanwhile, to top it all off, the band was dressed in lederhosen.

Their dead-white knobby knees sticking out from dark woolen socks, and little green hats with feathers stuck in them, made them appear as if they might be fugitive elves from a Hansel and Gretel tale. They interspersed Strauss waltzes with German folk songs, which one of them sang in a nasal falsetto while playing an accordion.

Where did Eleanor find them? Did she bring them over from Germany? Eleanor spotted Paul and Clara standing at the threshold of the ballroom. "Paul, how nice of you to grace us with your presence." She paused, giving him the once over. "You're welcome, even though you haven't carried out the theme as I requested. And you brought Miss — uh, your assistant with you. I take it your wife is indisposed." Her sarcasm was obviously aimed at Clara.

"You know as well as I do, Eleanor, my wife is in Scotland."

"Oh, well, her loss. Your table, I believe, is number eight. Now I must do what all good hostesses do, swan around and make sure my guests are well looked after."

Paul settled Clara at their table where two seats were reserved for them, the others already occupied. "What would you like to drink, my dear?"

"A delicious French wine, of course. What else would one drink at a German soiree?" Clara laughed.

Paul nodded and went off to collect their drinks.

An older woman at the table introduced herself. "I'm Harriet Latimer. This is my husband, Sir Cedric. I might be speaking out of turn, but I have to sound off to someone. I cannot understand why anyone in their right mind could think this is an appropriate theme. In fact, if you ask me, it is an utter disgrace. We should all walk out."

Sir Cedric hesitated. "Too late for that — should have known when we got the invitation with those bloody awful swastikas."

"We were invited because Annabelle, our daughter-in-law, is related to Eleanor," Mrs. Latimer explained. "Annabelle refused to attend, but our son, Sebastian, wondered what Eleanor was up to, so we offered to give them a run down when we return. Anyway, Cedric never refuses an invitation where the champagne flows and the food's abundant."

"Absolutely right, old girl; last week we attended a *do* for some obscure titled fellow at the House of Lords. Wouldn't do that again — catering not up to snuff. I intend to have a word with the chef there, probably some foreigner who can't cook a good English meal!"

Clara watched Paul at the bar talking to someone she thought she recognized but couldn't put a name to. She asked Mrs. Latimer who he was.

"Oh, that's Lord Halifax, changed his name from Lord Irwin recently, just inherited the title from his father; nice enough fellow and quite handsome, friend of Ribbentrop, I understand."

A man sitting next to Clara who wore the Great War decorations on his army dress uniform overheard their conversation. "Halifax! He'll have them goose-stepping down Whitehall, if we don't hurry up and stop them. Better start listening to Churchill before it's too late. I'm making my statement by wearing our uniform; British and proud of it! Not that dirty little Austrian corporal's outfit some of these idiots think amusing. They won't think it so funny when another war's declared, and it will be, you mark my words."

"Bit of a blow hard, Churchill," another at the table joined in. "Endless speeches — loves the sound of his own voice; I know we're in for a numb bum session when he gets the eye of the Speaker."

Paul returned to the table with the drinks. "Goebbels is visiting from Germany, staying with Halifax. Halifax is regarded as one of the architects of appeasement."

"Halifax? That man makes more trips to Germany than he does to Westminster," a man at the next table countered.

Clara, lifting her fan to her lips, asked, "Who's that man?"

Paul whispered, "George Lansbury — been accused of hawking his conscience around. I don't trust him."

"I thought it was Ribbentrop staying with Halifax," a fellow in army dress next to Cedric spoke up. "Mind you, it's difficult to tell one from the other these days."

Cedric lit a cigarette. "Wouldn't trust any of them; don't believe a word they say. They plan to take over Europe, and we're not doing anything to stop them!"

"Oh, I don't know, those Hitler types shout themselves hoarse, and, poof, they're gone." The guests at the table were waking up.

Ernest Bevin came to join them. "He has a point about those Jews; far too many of them. Weeding them out is a bloody good thing, if you ask me."

"It's not the Jews who cause the problems in this world; its ignorant people looking for a scapegoat, and it's always the Jews they pick on," Clara spoke up courageously.

"One might think you were one of them!" Bevin said, looking directly at Clara. "Some are all right, I suppose; wouldn't want them as my friends, though." He left to take a place at the bar.

"Once working class, always working class," Cedric muttered. "Bevin is a grand example with his thick West Country accent; much of the time I can't understand a word he says."

Further discussion was halted by the Master of Ceremony's announcement: "Dinner is served. Please make your way to the dining room."

Maze gave Clara a word of advice as the others left the table. "Listen. Don't react. You're going to hear a lot of pro-Nazi remarks here."

Clara was in no hurry to adjourn to the dining room. "Wait," she said. "I want the place cards. Need to know all their names. You take that side; I'll do this. Where was Halifax sitting? Who else was at that table?"

A waiter offered to help, Clara recognized him. "Aren't you Sam Lotoff's son, Jake? Your dad's the caterer, isn't he?"

"Yes, I'm the head waiter."

"Well, if that isn't ironic. Eleanor Barnes employing a Jewish firm to cater a Nazi party! Jake, please don't tell anyone you saw me here."

"Of course not, Mrs. Simon. I'm not exactly proud of it, either."

With Maze's pockets bulging and the beaded bag full of place cards they stood in line waiting for the Master of Ceremonies to announce their names.

"Mr. Paul Maze and Miss *Simone*." Clara's last name was pronounced with a French accent.

Just then, a tall, Aryan looking gentleman approached. "Aubrey Hoffman," he introduced himself. "And you are the famous painter, Paul Maze — friend of Mr. Churchill."

Paul nodded.

"Then we are here for the same reason," he half-whispered shaking Paul's hand — "and this lovely young lady?"

"Clara," Paul understood. "Clara Simon."

"How do you do." Aubrey took Clara's hand. Then his name was announced. "So lovely to have met you," he said, departing toward his table.

They were seated near Eleanor's table, where her partner for the evening, a Sir Rupert something or other, was becoming more intoxicated by the minute. Eleanor wasn't lagging far behind. The younger set, all dressed as Hitler Youth, were seated farther back, tanked up and singing, "*Deutschland, Deutschland über alles, über alles in der Welt,*" until a steward silenced them.

Also at their table was Eleanor's late husband's commanding officer. Before dessert and while Paul was table-hopping, he moved over to sit beside Clara. "You're the young lady working with Paul on his book." He held out his hand in greeting. "Bart Harmon."

"I know the name. I have you in my notes."

"I'm just one of many; did what we had to do. Certainly don't like this sort of thing." He surveyed Eleanor's table. "We can make fun of the Germans all we like, but there's really nothing funny about them. They're a gang of criminals." He paused for a few moments. "We can wine them and dine them and even pretend to like them, but it won't stop them."

Clara noticed Paul stopping to speak to the handsome German fellow, Aubrey Hoffman, before he came back to the table to make sure Clara was coping. "Glad you two met. Bart's a good man!"

Eleanor came over to waft Maze away. "There are people you just have to meet, Paul." Maze left grudgingly. Clara, uninvited, stayed put.

"Take no notice of Eleanor; she's three sheets to the wind," Bart said. "Can't help feeling sorry for her, lost soul really." Harmon appeared to be looking for an excuse for Eleanor's behavior. "And those young people over there are going to have to fight it all over again; they may rue the day they put on those hideous uniforms."

DINNER PASSED WITHOUT further incident. The party moved to the ballroom, where a flashing ball of light turned, giving an eerie effect as it reflected the hanging swaths of red cloth decorated with swastikas that threw ominous shadows against the walls.

As they danced, Paul told Clara, "Bart's quite famous. He commanded the Third Cavalry, friend of Churchill's — glad you got to meet him. Probably here for the same reason we are. I think it's pretty obvious who the sympathizers are. What worries me is there are more of them than there are of us."

"It's like we're in a Marx Brothers movie." The more intoxicated the crowd became, the louder the band played, Gershwin and Cole Porter music of the day replaced by German polkas. "This isn't a joke, Paul," Clara added. "The majority of these people are obviously pro-German."

"I've had enough," Maze raised his voice above the increasing noise. "Not sure we've accomplished much, but at least we made the effort. Churchill will know more about his opponents with the list we make from the place cards."

In time, they slipped away before Eleanor noticed their absence.

Driving home, Clara exploded, unable to help herself. "How can you stand those people? Don't ever make me do anything like that again!"

"I avoid them as much as I can. The only good thing I can say about them is that some of them buy my work."

BACK AT THE house in Chelsea, Clara went immediately upstairs to change into the clothes she'd arrived in from Whitechapel. She looked longingly at the gown, laid it on the bed where Maggie first placed it. Once in a lifetime gorgeous, she thought to herself. Then she dressed in the clothes she had worn there, closed the door behind her and came down to Maze waiting in the foyer.

"I don't want you to leave; stay with me." Paul slipped his arms around her and kissed her on the lips — and she had melted into his embrace as if it might have been the most natural thing in this world to do. It was late, no servants around — Rogers down in his little room in the lower quarters and Maggie safely tucked away in bed. "I cannot let you go. Stay with me tonight, Clara." They kissed again. "I don't want the evening to end like this."

Suddenly Clara found herself pulling away. "No, Paul, I . . ." Words failed her.

Maze took her in his arms again, kissing her passionately, his lips soft against hers, so practiced and assured, so unlike dear, sweet Sidney — and she found herself holding on to him, her desire so strong it took all her willpower to resist. "I have to go, Paul. You have to let me go," she whispered.

Reluctantly, Maze stood back.

Clara looked up at him, tears falling down her cheeks. "It will spoil all we have together, Paul. You're free, I'm not. I'm afraid to love you, I can't live deceit. Tonight was wonderful and awful at the same time. You made me feel like a princess."

"And I — the ugly frog?"

"No — you were, you are, the handsome, seductive prince."

"You played your part. You made me very proud."

"I hope so," She looked away, as if to end the conversation.

Maze called down to Rogers, then helped Clara slip into her coat. "I let you go only because I know you will come back to me when the time is right."

Rogers was with them now. "Take Mrs. Simon home, please."

"I'll bring the car around." And Rogers hurried off.

"I go to Munich in a weeks time — just for a few days. I have an errand to carry out for Winston."

"Errand?"

"A bit of spying needs to be done on his behalf."

The mention of Munich reminded her of her aunt Lizzie; impulsively she spoke out, "Take me with you."

"Not this time, Clara."

"My mother's sister is in Munich" Clara explained. "We don't know what's happened to her. Our letters are returned address unknown. I survived the Nazis this evening, Paul. I know I can do it again."

"That was pretense, Clara; this will be real. Give me your aunt's information. I will find out for you."

"If I am good enough to take to France, I can accompany you to Germany." Clara insisted.

"It is too dangerous."

"The Nazis cannot touch me. I have a British passport."

Paul stood back from her, as if to study her.

Clara wasn't the reserved young thing who'd come to work for him a few months ago. She'd gained self-confidence and mixed well with his friends, no matter their social standing. She was a tremendous asset, attractive, held her own against the Nazis pretenders stomping their way through Eleanor's party. She had matured into a poised young woman; he could take her anywhere. Perhaps having her with him in Munich would cause less suspicion than if he went alone. Still, he had reservations, and he said, "I would like nothing better, Clara, but — "

"No buts, Paul. This time it is my decision. I never thought I'd be thanking you for taking me to Eleanor's; you've opened my eyes to the arrogance and self-righteousness of those horrible so-called upper classes."

"It's why we French had a revolution, my dear. Won't happen here; they are too — how do you say it — full of themselves and have far too much power."

"You stood by me at that frightful party. The beautiful gown you chose helped me pretend I was one of them. I snooped for Mr. Churchill, and I can do the same for my family."

"You made me proud, Clara." He kissed her again and held her in his arms — until she reluctantly pulled away.

"I have to leave; it is very late," she told him.

Unwillingly, Paul accompanied her to the car and opened the rear door.

"No, I'd like to sit in front with Rogers. Thanks for a strange and rewarding evening. I'll see you on Monday, and we will go together to Munich." She opened the front door herself, got in and closed it.

Maze closed the back door, and Rogers, nodding acknowledgment of the situation, drove off, leaving Maze on the pavement watching until they were out of sight. He'd chosen to accept Clara's decision; he had found it hard not to go along with it.

"Did you get a chance to speak with the other chauffeurs?" Clara asked as Rogers motored through the deserted streets.

"Yes. They were angry when they saw the Nazi get up. Couldn't fathom it out; no love lost between them and the Germans. Most are old army blokes, count themselves lucky to be alive. Can't say they like the toffs they work for, only do it for the wages, easy money. I'm lucky in that regard. Mr. Maze treats me right; you won't hear any complaints from me."

OVER WESTMINSTER BRIDGE they drove, turning on to Parliament Square, past the Houses of Parliament and Westminster Abbey with Big Ben standing at attention beside them. At night the majesty of the architecture against a moonlit sky gave added strength to the

indefatigable importance of the structures. Much had happened inside those walls over the years — history written and history forgotten.

"Not sure the way from here," Rogers said.

"Just follow the river as far as you can go, then we turn left somewhere; I'll recognize it when I see it."

"I live on the other side of the river near Wandsworth, not far
from the prison actually. Not too bad. If I had kids it'd be different.
It's just me and my wife."

"How did you come to work for Mr. Maze?"

"Met him over in France during the war. I was a driver and a bit
of a mechanic. Someone told him to bring his motorbike to me; he'd
crashed it, and it was in a right mess. I did the best I could with it; at
least I got it to go. Saw him a couple of times after that, then just at
the end of the war we met again, and he said if I ever needed a job in
London I should get hold of him. When I was demobbed, the people
I worked for before the war had gone out of business, and there wasn't
much available; I was just about on my uppers."

"Happened to a lot of returning soldiers; my uncle's employers
wouldn't take him back."

"That's the thanks you get for putting your life on the line. Anyway, I kept looking, wasn't going to take on cheap labor day jobs —
plenty of that — wanted something more permanent. I was reading
the paper one night, and I read Mr. Maze was having an art show in
Bond Street. So the next day my wife and I dressed up and took
the bus to Bond Street. It wasn't exactly our scene. Mr. Maze recognized me the moment I walked in, and, well, as they say, the rest
is history."

They were approaching The Minories when they were forced to
stop. The police had barricaded the road. A constable came up to the
car. "Can't let you through here. Where you headed? "

Clara told him. "Aldgate, High Street, number Twenty-One."

"You'll have to take Mansell Street, turn right at the end, and
you'll be close to your destination."

"What's happening then?" Rogers asked.

"The usual Saturday night brawls, only this one ain't just the
Irish. We've got the Socialists and the Fascists thrown in. They've
been throwing anything they can find at each other, dustbin lids,

rocks, rotten fruit, you name it. Mosley's lot, out of control, think they rule the bloody world."

"They should be locked up, the lot of them." Rogers wasn't happy with the detour.

"I'm not getting into the whys and wherefores. Lock your doors and drive on."

Rogers turned the car around and took the road the constable suggested. There were a few stragglers on the streets, some holding handkerchiefs to their heads, others with arms around pub friend's shoulders, steadying each other, their night out over, staggering home to their wives and kids. Paycheck Friday, night out in the pub Saturday, broke by Monday. She couldn't understand why their wives put up with it.

"I've just realized something, Rogers, about that party in Belgravia. Those people are no different than the hooligans on the streets down here, slinging whatever they can lay their hands on. It's only money that separates them."

"Always the same, the rich get richer, and the poor do the dirty work for them. Can't see it changing in my lifetime."

They'd reached Half Moon Passage. "Thanks for getting me home safely, Rogers. Sorry to keep you out so late."

"It's all part of my job, Mrs. Simon." He made sure she was safely through the door of Twenty-One before driving off home to Wandsworth.

Upstairs, Sidney was sitting in the parlor waiting for Clara. "What time do you call this?" he demanded.

"I know it's late. I'm home now, and I'm tired. Let's go to bed."

"I won't put up with it, Clara. It has to stop. You'll give notice Monday morning, do you hear me?"

"We'll discuss it in the morning."

"Your dad says I give in to your every whim; I'm weak. Well, from now on you'll see who's the boss. I won't play second fiddle to anyone."

Clara couldn't cope with Sidney's recriminations right now. "Come to bed, we'll talk tomorrow."

"I'm not ready for bed. You and I have to talk."

If Sidney wanted to stay up all night and argue, that was his choice. Clara headed for the bedroom too tired to think about anything other than sleep.

CHAPTER 20

Sunday at Twenty-One

ORTHODOX JEWS REST from sundown on Friday to sundown on Saturday. But Nelly, never a stickler for convention, took time off on a Sunday.

"I don't need to parade in all my finery down the High Street on a Saturday. I'll leave that to the *frummes*," she said, using a derogatory term for the ultra religious.

Still, what the Levy family lacked in their religious practices they made up for by their observance of the *kashrut*, the Jewish food laws. On Sundays when friends and family gathered for lunch she made sure any food brought in passed her inspection.

Solly Tenser turned up at Twenty-One in the same way Boadicea arrived; someone dropped him off. No one remembered who brought him nor did they know what he did for a living and where he disappeared to every now and then.

"Where you been, Solly?" Nelly would ask, knowing full well he'd avoid answering the question.

More than likely he'd been serving at His Majesty's pleasure in Wormwood Scrubs Prison. Not that he did anything really bad, just got caught every now and then in what some would term a shady deal. Still he was a good friend, never let them down, and if you could find him and you needed something, he was there to oblige. You knew not to ask Solly to pick something up for you — that would be tantamount to giving him permission to pinch whatever it was and wherever he happened to see it. But with Nelly's request for smoked salmon, Solly couldn't go wrong. It was kosher, it was easy to find and it was a luxury the Levy family couldn't afford.

Markey Marks, Henry's barber, brought the chopped liver. Anna's routine task on a Sunday morning took her to Petticoat Lane to buy bagels from the ever-present Yetta on the corner of Wentworth Street; and Sidney had a standing order at Morries, a delicatessen in Stoke Newington where the best *gehuckta* herring awaited him. Sula, the only health conscious one among them, took charge of healthy food with plenty of fresh vegetables. Meanwhile, Nelly made the cream cheese by pouring soured Guernsey milk through linen gauze at the beginning of the week, allowed it to drip over the sink for a few days, and it was ready to be served by Sunday. And so, with all present and a few stragglers turning up at various intervals everyone tucked-in.

This particular Sunday morning they went ahead without Clara, Sidney having told them she'd got in very late the night before and was still sleeping.

"Who's this bloke she's working for? Why'd she leave Abbott?" Solly asked, licking his fingers to remove the last morsels of strudel.

Sula answered before Henry got going. "Abbott was an anti-Semitic bastard. The man she's working for now is writing a book, and she's typing it for him."

That was all Solly needed to know. "I'll make a point of remembering that. You say Abbott's his name? Won't be 'avin' any of my customers knocking on his door. What about this book bloke? You know 'im?"

Nelly was quick to reply, "Oh, it's a temporary job; she'll be finished with it soon. No one you know, Solly."

"Well, as long as she's happy, that's all that matters. And now I gotta be on me way. Lovely spread, Nelly, thanks. Got a bloke in the market selling some of me stuff — somebody's nephew, don't know him from Adam. So, before he puts all the proceeds in his pocket and buggers off, I better get going."

CLARA, UP IN her room, heard the commotion going on downstairs and was not about to come down until she got the all clear from Nelly. Solly was the last person she wanted to see; it would've been easier to face the Spanish Inquisition.

She'd been awake for some time, going over the night before. What a strange experience it had been. Downstairs they'd never understand that. Likewise, they were not going to take the news of her going to Germany any better than they greeted her French trip. At least this trip had a family reason — she suspected Aunt Lizzie's silence had much to do with the plight of the Jews in Germany. From what Clara gathered from conversations she'd overheard at Eleanor's party, Lizzie might be homeless, forced to move or, even worse, held by the Gestapo. Nelly's three letters to her sister had all come back unread and marked: *Nicht bekannt unter dieser Adresse.* It wasn't difficult to translate what that meant. All contact had been lost, and Nelly was beside herself with worry. Paul had unwittingly presented a unique opportunity for Clara to locate her aunt, and she was determined to go with him to Munich.

Clara knew Sula would stand by her; the others would say it was just another excuse for being with "that man." Well, in a way it was. There was still a perfectly good reason to go, though. Meanwhile, Nelly would eventually come 'round. Henry would rant a bit. Sidney was a different problem. He'd been mad as hell last night . . .

How to explain it to Sidney was going to be a major event. She had mixed feelings — after Paul's kiss last night, after what Paul had said to her, after her reaction and the pleasure she felt, her guilt was palpable.

THE SUNDAY AFTERNOON ritual was in full swing. They'd cleared the table and retired to the front room. Markey Marks played the piano, Henry stood beside him, turning the pages of sheet music — not that Markie needed music; he probably couldn't read it, and anyway he had a good ear. If it were a song Henry liked, he'd sing along, reading the words instead of making them up. Nelly, too, she loved a good old sing-song.

Meantime, Sidney had helped Sula do the washing up. Now she could feel the tension rising.

Sula turned to see Clara coming into the parlor. "I saved a bagel for you, wasn't easy with that load of vultures. Want a cup of tea to go with it?"

"Love one. Thanks, Sula."

"You two on the outs?"

"I came in late last night, kept him up. My fault," said Clara. She took a bite of the bagel.

Sula poured the tea. "Then give him a kiss and say you're sorry."

"A kiss won't do it," Sidney asserted as he wiped another plate and stacked it. "She's got to make up her mind. It's either him or me. That's all there is to it."

"I'm not making a choice, Sidney. I'm tired of having to explain everything. If you can't accept it, then I'm afraid it's just too bad."

"See why I can't get anywhere with her? I don't matter to her — it's obvious." Sidney threw down the dish towel and faced Clara.

She sighed and said, "Well, you might as well know. I'll be working longer hours, and there will be more travel. Mr. Maze is going to Munich next week, and I'm going with him. Now before you start yelling, I was the one to suggest it, and he tried to talk me out of it. I wouldn't let him. Aunt Lizzie lives in Munich. Mum can't get hold of her. I intend to find her and see if I can bring her back."

Sidney came over, picked up Clara's half eaten bagel and slammed it down on the table. "You know what I think? I think you've gone off your rocker. This job has gone to your head, and none of us here are good enough for you. What's got into you? You really believe you can go to Germany and find your aunt Lizzie? You've got delusions of grandeur. You're not thinking straight. He's putting ridiculous ideas into your head. You'll not go anywhere with him again and certainly not to Germany. That's it, Clara. And the sooner you give up that job the better. You've pushed me far enough."

Sula picked up the dishcloth and wiped the bagel remains off the table into her hands.

Sidney walked away and into the front room, shouting above the singing, "You know where Clara thinks she's going next week? Germany. That's where she thinks she's off to. She has it in her mind to find Lizzie. And I'll give you three guesses who's taking her; come to think of it, you won't need three — one will do!"

The music stopped. Henry, for once in his life, was speechless.

Now it was dead quiet.

Nelly gave the news time to settle in before she spoke. "There must be other ways of finding Lizzie. I'll go to the Board of Deputies. We can put a notice in the *Jewish Chronicle*."

Clara, having followed Sidney, defended her reasoning. "And what do you think that will do, Mum? They've not done much up to now.

The only way to find out what's happened to Lizzie is to go there. They're rounding up Jews, relocating them, sending them God knows where. Munich is no exception. The Nazis are confiscating property, taking their jobs, stopping them going to universities. The last letter you got from Lizzie said they'd closed down Uncle Franz's business. Lizzie probably doesn't have the money for the fare home. We can't just sit here and do nothing. I have the chance to do something, and I'm going to do it."

"The girl's gone mad." Henry was no longer speechless. "Germany? You think you can walk into Germany — just like that?"

Clara stopped for a moment, wondering whether she should tell all. What the hell, she'd gone this far. "There's good reason why I was out late last night. I had to go to a party with Mr. Maze in Belgravia — very posh and totally nauseating. I was asked, as was Mr. Maze, to listen to conversations and report what I'd heard to Mr. Churchill. I know you think I'm fantasizing, and you may not believe a word I'm saying, but I assure you I'm telling the truth. The party, like all these overblown, upper crust shindigs we read about in the papers, had a theme. They dressed up as Nazis with all the trappings! A disgusting display of the rich making a mockery of Jews at the hands of the Nazis, having fun at their expense. It was frightening. These people are Nazi sympathizers; they support Hitler and his regime. They excuse themselves by mocking the Führer. Its one big joke to them, but deep down they accept him."

"You lied to me, Clara!" Sidney exploded.

"No, Sidney, I just didn't tell you exactly why I had to work on a Saturday evening. I went because I was asked, not my choice; in fact, it made me sick to my stomach."

Mannie interrupted, "So, you propose going over to Germany and asking some Nazi if he could help you find your aunt. I can just hear it: 'Excuse me, Mr. Nazi, I'd like you to help me find my Jewish aunt.' 'Vot you sey? Jewish aunt? Vell yunk lady, I sink dat ees not possible; zee Jewish aunt is vith ze Jewish dogs — and vee don't know, and we don't care ver zay are, eider!'"

"Leave her be, Mannie." Sula tried to restrain him.

"No, I'm with Sidney on this one. She's out of control — gone too far this time."

"How come these trips all have something to do with that French-man of yours?" Sidney ranted. "It's all too convenient for him. He's got you tied around his little finger. If he said, 'Come and hunt elephants in Africa,' you'd find some excuse to go there as well."

"Don't be ridiculous. I'll tell you how come: it's because that Frenchman, and he has a name and I wish you'd use it, has contacts, and those contacts, in this instance, might be able to help us."

"Help *you*, more like it."

"That's uncalled for, Sidney. If you can't accept my explanation, well, that's just too bad. I've made up my mind. I'm going to Munich and that's that."

Markey stood up from the piano, took Henry by the arm and suggested they go down to Lyon's Café for a cup of tea.

Sidney left in disgust, probably to kick a ball in Shadwell Park.

The rest remained in the parlor — talking over Clara's latest announcement.

NOT TOO MANY trams ran on a Sunday, so Nelly could see across the street, something she couldn't do during the week. The kosher shops were open; Bernard Bernstein, the tailor, was closed. People were lining up outside the Rivoli picture house buying tickets for the afternoon performance, and the Jewish Free Reading Home had a sign outside welcoming readers. The only restrictions on Nelly's life were those she put on herself. She could go where she liked any time she liked. If she wanted to venture farther, she and Henry could take a ride on a bus up to Oxford Street or Regents Street to look at the shops. Her thoughts were of Lizzie. Of course, there was anti-Semitism in England; the likes of Mosley made sure it was kept alive. But by all accounts Lizzie had it much worse.

Unlike her sister, Nelly was free in the city they were both born in. This was her London; it was also Lizzie's, and it was where she should be now. She didn't belong in Munich, that's for sure — a place where Jews were called subhuman, ridiculed, their homes and possessions taken from them. Clara wasn't a stupid girl; she was a mature young woman with a fine head on her shoulders. If she thought she could find out what happened to Lizzie, then who were they to stop her. As for Maze, it was pretty obvious Clara was infatuated with him.

So what? She'd get over it in time, and Sidney would take her back, no doubt about that.

Sidney had fought hard enough to win her in the first place; he'd fight even harder to keep her. He'd come 'round eventually. Nelly recognized he lived in his self-made safety bubble, had his football, had his wife — stayed loyal to both. Clara, well, she always was a bit of a risk taker. He must have known that before he married her. If you don't take a few risks in life, you're not going to get far. She wasn't too worried about Sidney — he wasn't going anywhere; his anger had more to do with pride than anything else. And Henry, her lovely old Henry, too old fashioned to accept Clara's impulsive ways. She couldn't expect him to understand what motivated Clara. Nelly knew Clara's intentions weren't all selfless — ulterior motives might well be at play — but at times like these, if the opportunity arose, then wouldn't it be wrong to tell her not to go?

Clara pulled up a chair beside Nelly, sat with her, looking out the window.

"You're taking a chance, luv."

"I know, Mum, but when Mr. Maze told me he was going to Munich, Aunt Lizzie came to mind immediately. Honestly, the suggestion didn't come from him; in fact, he said he would try to find Lizzie. Well, I couldn't expect him to concentrate on an important mission and at the same time look for one of our lost relatives. I said I had to go with him, and finally he gave in. We're heading for another war, Mum; Aunt Lizzie's life is in danger. If you could have heard what they were saying last night, your blood would have run cold; it made me determined to do something, anything — I can't just sit back and do nothing."

Nelly put her hand on Clara's lap. "I'm worried, luv, can't say that I'm not, but on thinking it over I know you're doing the right thing; you have to do what you can. Maybe the others are envious; perhaps they wish they were in your shoes. To my mind they should be praising you instead of judging and throwing out insults. As for Sidney, well, you'll have to sort him out. If I was fifty years younger, I'd be doing just what you're doing."

Henry appeared at the door. "And you don't care that your daughter is putting herself in harm's way?"

"How long you been there eavesdropping?" Nelly asked.

"Long enough to hear you giving permission to Clara to take off without a by-your-leave from me."

"Sometimes, Henry, you have to stop thinking about yourself and look what you can do for others."

"You're beginning to sound like the preacher outside the Salvation Army shelter. If you wait a minute, I'll get you a tin plate and you can join him."

"It's nothing to joke about, Henry." Nelly had on her serious face.

"I'll say it's not — it's crazy. Where's Sidney? What's he doing about it?"

"I don't know, and right now I have to say I really don't care. Our Clara is doing what she feels she has to, and neither you, nor I, nor Sidney are going to stop her; we may as well accept it and let it rest."

Clara continued to sit with Nelly, watching the comings and goings on the High Street. "It's like being at a picture show, Mum, sitting up here and looking down on it all."

"And the best thing about it is you don't have to pay to go in," Nelly replied, now taking little notice of Henry still standing at the door. "Your dad will come 'round, he always does."

Henry had the last word. "Not this time, Nelly. Not this time."

CHAPTER 21

Recollections

MAZE MADE THE final touches to a commissioned oil painting of a quaint French village that he'd been working on all week. He stood back to examine it from a distance — to satisfy himself it was finished . . .

No, he decided, nothing else was needed.

He placed the painting on a table near the window to dry, looked at it for a few moments, then returned to his work table to clean his brushes.

Clara, who had been waiting patiently, asked, "Are you ready to resume work on the book, now? Tell me if you like the way this reads:

> I loved being on solitary roads, left to my own reflections while the early morning mist gradually vanished and the first burst of sunshine flooded the country. A battle going on in the distance would strengthen my feeling of being in a pocket of peace outside the circle of the rising cyclone.

"I said that?" Maze seemed genuinely impressed. "Not bad for a French painter!"

"Not bad at all," Clara agreed. "More or less your words — certainly they're your thoughts. I just try to make the sentences flow a little smoother."

"Excellent — "

"No, no," she added. "That's not what I mean. It has to be your voice. Perhaps I've been a little presumptuous. From now on I will put down every word you say and not embroider."

"No. I leave it to you. I'm the painter; you're my writer."

"So, let's move on to the next chapter," Clara said, determined to get him back in a writing mode.

Maze wasn't ready to dictate. "All in good time. I want to tell you about the meeting I had with Winston at the club. I gave him the place cards and the list you prepared. He was impressed with the comments you made on the back of some of the cards."

"I'm glad he found them helpful; something good had to come out of that dreadful experience."

"It has. He said you established an innovative way of getting information to him, which is more than his paid assistants seem to manage."

"Then it was worth the effort." Despite the hard time she'd had with Sidney, Clara felt a little better hearing Churchill's comments.

"I told Winston you were coming with me to Munich. That really got his attention. You might become his number one spy! He wants you to give a report on the search for your aunt, what the everyday German has to say and, if we get the chance, see if anyone speaks out about the camp in Dachau. I'm told it's only ten minutes by train from Munich. He's certain our friend Heinrich knows more than he dare put down in a letter."

Whatever guilt might have remained in Clara's mind about attending Eleanor's Nazi charade disappeared. She had used her time well, and she intended to use it well again when they arrived in Germany. As for the embrace she'd shared with Paul when they returned to Cheyne Walk from the party, the pleasure of that moment stayed with her.

Maze had turned to examine his painting.

"Back to the book, Paul; and come away from the window. The painting will dry without your hovering over it."

"The book? I have to take off my painter's beret and put on my author hat; give me a moment."

While she waited for Paul's attention, her mind focused on the trip to Munich. She'd not convinced everyone in the family; she certainly hadn't convinced Sidney. They'd stopped harassing her, but she knew she hadn't gotten their approval. Like Sidney, Sula questioned her sanity. Her father hadn't softened one bit. Only Nelly supported her; it wasn't that she wanted Clara to go — it was just that she understood why she felt the need to go. She'd said, were she younger and given the opportunity, she'd have done the same thing. And as for Anna, well, Anna found it difficult to find her way to Petticoat Lane, let alone Germany.

MEANWHILE, CHURCHILL WAS taking up more and more of Maze's time. They painted together, they discussed politics, and often they'd just sit in the studio critiquing one another's work. All of this encroached on Clara's schedule and took away from the time Maze was supposed to allocate to the book. Maze couldn't be cajoled into anything unless he was in the mood. Her flare for writing made it relatively simple to elaborate on the facts she'd accumulated and make them readable. At times she had the impression Maze wouldn't have minded if she wrote the entire book for him; after all, he'd much prefer to paint than write.

"Excuse me, sir." It was Rogers. "The receptionist from the gallery phoned to say they are sending a van around in an hour to collect the pictures for your opening on Wednesday. Do we have them ready, sir?"

Clara answered, "I've stacked them over there in the corner. Mr. Maze has chosen the pieces he wants to show." Clara flipped the pages of the notebook to where she'd compiled a list of the paintings. "I see you've crossed out the sunflower piece — "

"I am keeping it for my private collection," was the quiet response.

Clara put down her notebook. She could see they weren't going to get back to the book until the art work was out of the way. She continued itemizing the paintings; better not to comment in front of Rogers, though she couldn't help but be flattered by Paul's decision to keep the sunflowers. She realized the show was important to him; it was how he made his living. Still, it did conflict with the writing of the book, and there was a deadline to meet. The publisher had asked for the first hundred pages of the manuscript, and they were only on page sixty.

While he was busy with the art show, she'd kept busy with the memorabilia — old family portraits, scenes from his childhood, letters and the usual collection of stuff one keeps just in case one day it might be of use. Maze, as she well knew, had no perception of time, so it was up to her to get him back to the book. Now that the art work had been chosen, it might be easier.

Clara helped Rogers maneuver some of the larger paintings downstairs and came back to find Maze fiddling around with his newest toy, an HMV gramophone blaring out a medley of Strauss waltzes. "Doesn't it make you want to dance? One, two, three. One, two, three." He waltzed 'round the studio, arms outstretched, waiting for Clara to join him.

"We have a book to work on," she said sternly. "What do I tell the publisher when he rings?"

"*Dites-lui que vous avez une leçon de danse.*"

"I will not tell him I'm having a dance lesson. Come on . . ." It was no use. He folded her into his arms and twirled her across the room, avoiding his easel and the model's chaise while bumping into tables, knocking off jars of water and making an effort to step over the puddles collecting on the studio floor.

"I have to sit down; the room is going 'round," Clara protested, feeling giddy.

Maze steadied Clara and guided her to the chaise. He danced on, alone.

Rogers returned, unperturbed by the loud music or Paul dancing by himself in the middle of the room. "Is there anything more to go to the gallery?" he asked.

Maze waltzed over to the window to take another look at the watercolor he'd placed there to dry. "I like it, and I know it will sell. So, do I keep it or give it away?"

"I cannot make that decision, sir."

"Clara?"

"Sell it."

"The lady says sell, then I shall sell. Needs a frame, Rogers. Arrange, please."

"Very well, sir." Rogers picked up the painting, holding it carefully by its edges, as if it might be an unwashed pair of knickers.

Maze, a little out of breath, walked over to the gramophone to put on another record. The needle came down on Beethoven's "Third Symphony". The sound filled the room. Maze stood at the window looking out over the River Thames, listening intently to the music.

After a while he turned off the gramophone and spoke to Clara, who was still seated and slowly recovering from the waltz he'd inflicted on her. "What I find so amazing about the Germans is how they can compose and appreciate such beautiful music, and the next minute become barbarians threatening to murder everyone in sight. There has to be something very peculiar in their make-up." He brought a chair to sit beside Clara. "You recovered? I'm ready to go on with the next chapter now."

Clara, her notebook and pencil in hand, listened carefully. His mood had changed; he had become more somber and introspective. He was once again a man with a story to tell.

"Let me tell you about the German fellow who was handed over to the regiment. He was in civilian clothes; he had deserted during the night. He didn't understand the seriousness of the situation he was in. There were orders from the Cavalry Corps that had captured him: he must be shot. He said he wasn't a spy, just a deserter. It made me think; I had been in a similar position. I felt sorry for him. I asked him if he wanted to write a letter to his relatives — I would see that it was sent to them. I left him with the escort for a while and rushed to General Gough and implored him to spare the fellow. I did not get his permission to do so.

"I was on my way back to get his letter when I met the firing party coming up the road, making for the spot chosen for the execution. When I got back to him, the escort was ready to take him. The poor man had two letters in his hand, one to his mother and the other to his girl friend. I asked the escort to give me a little more time. Again I rushed back to the general and implored him not to shoot the man. 'One German more or less is not going to affect the ultimate result of the war,' is what I said to Gough.

"Gough was in his car and ready to leave. He shouted out, 'Do what you like with him.' I ran back as though I had wings and saved the young German from being executed. The cavalry guard gave him back his watch and chain and shook him by the hand. I often wonder whether he made it through the war. He might have been caught and shot by his own countrymen for all we know. That's the hypocrisy of war."

Each time Maze related these personal accounts Clara tried hard to keep her emotions at bay; she had to be able to concentrate on just what he was saying. It was when she read back her shorthand notes and typed them that she got the full impact of what it must have been like to be there, to bear witness to the carnage, to be part of a slaughtering army, to actually be on the battlefields in France and Belgium. He was reporting, sketching and informing.

Massacre after massacre, soldiers given orders by their superiors to kill, generals commanding boys of seventeen and eighteen and sending them out to battle, knowing full well they were sending lads in the prime of life to their death. Waves of them shot down by enemy bullets and then, like a field of chaff, their bodies cleared, and the next contingent sent in to take their place.

Why was it allowed? How could it continue? What were the generals thinking? Was life so cheap, so dispensable? Did no one give a thought to their families, their wives and their children, those who would never see their loved ones again? There had to be relief; no reader could go on with a book that spoke only of atrocities.

"We need more stories like that one, Paul, and maybe the occasional amusing anecdote to relieve the tension."

Shoulders sagging, Maze said, "Our book is about war, Clara. There were brief moments of quiet — no escape unless you deserted. I'm afraid I can think of nothing amusing."

CLARA HAD ACCEPTED the position with Maze not knowing what to expect, willing to take on the challenge. At the law office she had worked on difficult cases, some unpleasant civil suits and wife battering, even a murder, but nothing compared with what she was hearing and writing about now. She was an innocent when she began; her knowledge of the war and what it was like came from Mannie and some of his friends. Mostly they refused to talk about it, thankful to be back and safe. Maze told it to her factually and honestly, as an artist and a liaison, from all sides, French, British and German. He was telling their story as well as his, if for no other reason than to get it out of his system and let it be known what they went through and validate the position that no other soldier should be put in the same position.

Paul's accounts prompted Clara to read the poetry of the war poets again. She took the books out of the library — the works of

Rupert Brooke, Wilfred Owen and Siegfried Sassoon. Only Sassoon
was spared, and he continued to write, as Maze was doing now, pro-
testing and presenting prose to all those willing to read and learn.
"We must not forget," he wrote. It was for those who could not speak
for themselves.

When Clara first read the poems, they spoke of sadness and sense-
lessness, but now they read as laments of waste and treachery. And so,
like those poets, Paul spoke of ghosts, watching for the dead. He spoke
of the beginning and end of life. He spoke to those who'd lost a loved
one and couldn't express their sorrow. He did it for them.

What of the millions who lay buried under the fields of white
crosses in Flanders Fields? What might they have brought into the
world had they been given the chance to express themselves, become
husbands and fathers, to give life to future generations? Mannie spoke
for them when he could; his was a voice in a wilderness of disinterest.
England — the precious few who came back.

Every November Eleventh — Armistice Day — the fallen were hon-
ored by those who'd made it back. They paraded down Whitehall,
some in wheelchairs, others on crutches, their numbers dwindling as
physical conditions deteriorated.

"Abide With Me," the military band played. Did we? Did we abide
with them?

Those proud, damaged men remembered on that one day with
poppies in the lapels of the solemn crowds who stood on the pavements of Whitehall, silently watching as the veterans made their way
to the Cenotaph. Christian and Jew alike, standing side by side as
prayers were spoken by clerics, speeches given by politicians, the King
and the Prime Minister laying wreaths. Their motto: *Lest We Forget.*

The entire Levy family attended the service at the Cenotaph every
year. Clara could view it now with greater understanding as an absurd, deplorable phase in the long history of European conflicts. If
Churchill was right, and they were heading for yet another war,
there would be many more wreaths of red poppies to add to the base
of the Cenotaph.

It was becoming more and more obvious that the fragile peace
agreement Britain and Germany had signed in Versailles in 1918, on
the eleventh day of the eleventh month at the eleventh hour, was

falling apart. Germany was preparing for another war, a war already begun against Jews and perhaps even others as innocent as Aunt Lizzie.

Churchill, against tremendous opposition, continued to speak out against the government's complacency. *The Times* quoted him as recently as a couple of days ago:

> You go on, in strange paradox, decided only to be undecided, resolved to be irresolute, solid for fluidity, all powerful to be impotent.

Eloquent Old Churchill, they called him, and they weren't being complimentary. Well, let them call him what they liked; Clara was determined to find Aunt Lizzie and, at the same time, be the spy Churchill told Maze he wanted her to be.

CHAPTER 22

Heinrich and Trude

DACHAU, A MEDIEVAL town fifteen miles from Munich, once housed a munitions factory, which closed when the need for the type of weapon manufactured there became obsolete. In 1933 Heinrich Himmler, Police President of Munich, reestablished it as a "Concentration Camp for Political Prisoners". These were mainly artists, intellectuals and Jehovah's Witnesses. In time gypsies and homosexuals were rounded up as well.

Some of the artists interred in Dachau were friends of Heinrich Luftmann. They became part of the labor force to transform the factory to Heinrich Himmler's specifications. Like the others they'd been taken from their homes and sent to Dachau without explanation. There they were interrogated, humiliated and tortured. If they survived, they were put to work. If they complained, they were starved and beaten. Some were released after a few months when their health failed; others bribed the guards with money, often raised by Luftmann and his antiestablishment colleagues.

Luftmann and his girlfriend, Trude Graff, as young teenagers were members of the German Youth Movement, a liberal, sports-minded association where many felt superior to what they considered the increasingly popular, somewhat primitive Nazi alternative, The Hitler Youth. The Nazi regime did not allow any youth groups to be separate from The Hitler Youth. Those who refused to join were pursued and made to comply with the Nazi edict.

Heinrich Luftmann, who'd recently written to Paul Maze, wrote again, and this time used Aubrey Hoffman as his courier. Hoffman, a regular visitor to London, agreed to deliver the letter to Churchill in

London via Maze. Maze had met Hoffman at Eleanor's party and had struck up a friendship when they realized they were both there for the same reason, and it wasn't to enjoy the company! Hoffman, domiciled in Munich, was of German origin and a close friend of the Mitford family, known Nazi sympathizers. He had easy access to them and their Nazi friends. His parents were divorced: mother lived in England, father in Germany. If questioned by authorities in either country, he could always say he was visiting family. Only Churchill knew he was an MI5 agent.

The British Security Agency, later known as MI5, had been formalized prior to 1914 and became increasingly active in the years before the beginning of The Great War. They recruited young men to serve as spies and double agents. It was a small, elite operation that grew as the need for information became more pressing. Hoffman was able to travel between Britain and Germany with considerable ease, and, knowing this, Luftmann trusted him to deliver his letter.

"Remember the German who introduced himself to us at the party — Aubrey Hoffman?" Maze asked Clara. He held up the envelope meant for Churchill. "He sent it 'round by courier last night."

"Yes, he was that tall, good looking German. How could I forget?"

"I rather like the fellow. Had the feeling he was summing me up at the time. Now I know why. Winston asked me to read it before sending it to him. It has to do with the concentration camp in Dachau."

Winston was concerned that Luftmann's artist connections might hamper Hoffman's cover; he considered it unwise for Hoffman to risk being seen as Luftmann's friend. It was Hoffman who'd suggested to Winston that Maze go to Munich to collect information gathered by Luftmann's girlfriend, Trude.

Trude had moved to Berlin to continue her art studies. When the university was forced to close its doors to Jews, Trude returned to Munich and applied for a job in the design department of a recently opened munitions factory. "It's a way to infiltrate, to learn the Nazi agenda and get paid at the same time," she'd said.

Luftmann, concerned they'd find out she was a Jew, tried to dissuade her, "You're walking into the lion's den," he warned.

"I have to find out what they're up to," she'd insisted. "I've had the interview; they've accepted me, and I'll be fine."

"Did they ask about your parents, their background, any of that?"

"No, they needed my design skills. All they asked was if my allegiance was with the Führer. I lied, of course. I said, 'Would I be here if I wasn't?'"

Luftmann realized nothing he could say would deter her. "Concentrate on the work they give you and don't socialize."

"I have no intention of becoming a best friend to anyone," Trude replied. "I'll do my job and go home."

TRUDE WAS ONE of only two women in the art department and had little contact with the workers on the factory floor. The second woman, Elsa, was a member of the Nazi party and Trude had to appear on good terms with her. Occasionally they would have a sandwich together at lunch. Trude kept conversation to the projects they were working on and showed an interest in Elsa's family — her three children, all proudly enrolled in the Hitler Youth movement, and her husband, who worked in Dachau as an interrogator. Elsa spoke nonchalantly about Dachau and what was going on there. "Dachau will teach those Communists to behave. Adolf Hitler rules with a firm hand, and I believe he has every right to save us from those who wish to destroy us."

Of course Elsa supported Hitler. He was her idol, the right man at the right time. He was just what Germany needed, a strong, compelling leader. Trude never let on that she had friends in Dachau. Neither did she speak much about her home and family. Elsa was a factory friend, and Trude got from her what she needed, learning every day the way Germans felt about their Führer, their distinct hatred of the Jews, and how clever Hitler was to recognize it was because of the Jews that Germany had suffered all these years.

LUFTMANN KNEW IF he were seen with Trude, she'd be marked immediately; he had to be very careful. He decided to ride his bicycle near to the factory and follow her when the closing siren sounded. They'd be safe then; they'd get lost in the crowd of workers leaving the factory.

He waited for Trude near the main gate. Standing behind a large oak tree, he could see the factory workers leaving, picking up their bicycles or walking to transport waiting to take them back to where they lived. Trude never took the bus; she found it simpler and less conspicuous to cycle to work.

He heard the siren. Trude would be along shortly. He watched from his lookout point. The workers began to filter out — in time hundreds of them; it wasn't until the crowd began to thin that he finally saw her. She walked over to the bicycle rack and threw her rucksack over her shoulder. She was about to get on the bike when a guard approached, blew a whistle and shouted for her to stay where she was. The wind was in the right direction; it carried the guard's voice. Heinrich could just about make out what he was saying.

"Remove your rucksack," the guard ordered.

Trude did as she was told.

He opened it and looked through it. Finding nothing of interest, he handed it back.

"May I go now?"

The guard jammed his foot on the front wheel and put his arm around her waist. Trude moved away.

"Such a pretty girl. I would like to take you out tonight."

Trude tried to stay calm. "I'm sorry, I have plans for the evening, perhaps another time. "

"I will watch for you and ask you again." He was obviously disappointed.

Trude smiled and waved goodbye as she cycled off, giving him hope that she might accept his invitation sometime soon.

Luftmann, still hiding behind the tree, breathed a sigh of relief. He gave her what he considered a reasonable lead and then followed. When she turned onto a dirt road, he caught up with her. "He let you off easy."

"You heard him?"

"Not quite — but I felt like punching him in the nose. What did he want?"

"To go with him for a drink."

"You going?"

"What you take me for? I told you to stay away from here. There are guards all over the place."

"We're just two people on bikes riding together; they'll think I'm one of the workers."

"Our bikes have license numbers; they can tell who works at the factory. You must not come here again."

"Get me a license."

"Impossible — just stay away, please," she pleaded.

"I had to speak to you. My friend Paul Maze will be here in a couple of days. He's traveling under the guise of an art dealer with a lady friend. He'll have paintings suitable for German buyers."

"That's all we need in Germany right now, more art! Look what they did to your work at the atelier."

"No, just listen. There's a method to this madness. You know what's going on in the munitions factory, what they're planning, building, developing. Where it is stored, designs, numbers, allocations, steal it if you have to — plans, diagrams, anything of importance."

"You tried to talk me out of taking the job, now you need me to spy on them?"

"I was worried at the time."

"You're over that now?"

"No, but you can get what we need. If that guard asks you out again, much as I hate the idea, go. It will look like you're one of them."

"That's asking too much. I don't know him, and I don't intend to get to know him." Trude pedaled faster to get ahead of Luftmann.

"You don't have to marry him, Trude," he called out as he caught up with her. "Just have a drink with him."

"He might not be on duty next time. The guards change every day."

"I know his type; he'll find a way of seeing you. You're not that easy to forget."

"Enough with the compliments. If I do manage to get the information — and I can't promise I will — what do you plan to do with it?"

"I'll give it to Paul, and he'll pass it on to his team in London. He'll have with him a portfolio of works for sale. In return I will hand him my work to sell in London; we've agreed they will all be collage."

"Why collage?"

"It will be easy to hide information under the torn paper cut outs — no one will ever know. I've already done some. Flowers and farm scenes; you'd call them chocolate box paintings. The kind of art you hate."

"And how do you expect me to hide information when the guards go through my rucksack every time I leave?"

"I told you. Go out with the one who asked you; maybe flirt a bit with the other guards. Tuck the information away in your underwear; they'll search your rucksack again, but they won't touch your clothing, not if you're nice to them."

"You tell me who we're doing this for? It better be someone worthwhile."

"Winston Churchill."

"You've got to be joking."

"I'm not. It is Churchill. Churchill and I and Paul, Paul Maze — he's a well known French artist — painted together in Brittany."

"You never told me you knew Winston Churchill."

"I'm telling you now."

They kept on cycling at a steady pace.

"I will do what I can, but you must not come near the factory again; if they recognize you, they'll start watching me, and then I'll be of no use to any of you. And you must know — the last thing I want to do is go out with that guard!"

"Just have a drink with him."

They came to a junction in the road, and not stopping, Luftmann called out to Trude as he turned down the road away from her, "I'll see you at the weekend. I love you."

"I love you, too," she responded and cycled on, unsure about the assignment she had just been given. It wouldn't be easy; there was always someone looking over your shoulder. Her job was highly secret; she'd been surprised they took her on when she applied. Being blond and Aryan looking probably helped.

While other girls worked in the actual factories on assembly lines, very few were given jobs in the offices. She'd have to work out a way of hiding the information; that is, if she could even find what they wanted. She didn't fancy stuffing papers in her underwear. Better to open the lining of a coat or a jacket perhaps.

Luftmann had taken the long way back to his atelier in Munich.

Trude cycled her usual path home.

Neither of them had noticed a man in a khaki raincoat focus a camera on Trude just before she turned on to the dirt road. He'd watched through binoculars. He'd seen her talk to the guard. He saw her get on her bicycle and be followed by a young man also on a bicycle. He photographed the guard, the girl and the young man. He slipped the camera in the pocket of his raincoat and took out a note-book and pen and began to write.

CHAPTER 23

Passover

THE DATE MAZE booked to leave for Germany coincided with the beginning of Passover. That Clara would even consider not being present at the family Seder, the one traditional holiday never to be missed, was the final straw. Having insisted on going with Maze she found herself in an untenable position. Should she put off the trip or ask him to change the date? The way things were in Germany time was against them — still he might accept going a day or so later.

"All right," she reluctantly agreed, "I'll ask him to postpone it if he can, but just for a couple of days, and then I'm going. I don't want to hear another peep out of any of you."

At work the next day Clara summoned up enough courage to ask Maze if he might delay their trip. "I have a problem. The Jewish Festival of Passover happens to start on the day we're booked to leave. I'm determined to go with you, but it is a problem."

Maze hesitated. He had not fully accepted Clara's decision to accompany him, even though she was determined, and now she'd given him a way out if he wanted to take it. Did he want to go alone? No. Would it be wise to have her along, probably not, but he wanted her with him. And there was Winston — he had to take what he said into consideration.

"It's two days," Clara went on. "Instead of leaving on Saturday, as we planned, could we leave on Monday? It's just that our Passover is one of those festivals where families and friends get together, and if I'm not with them, they'll feel cheated. As it is, they nag me constantly about Munich, and it's getting to be unbearable. Please — all I'm asking is to postpone our journey for a couple of days."

"Heinrich's expecting me."

"Is Mr. Hoffman still in London?" Clara asked.

"He leaves later today."

"I could call the hotel. He'll let Mr. Luftmann know."

"Tell him we will leave first thing Monday morning. I can't delay it any longer, Clara."

"Monday — it is." Clara telephoned the hotel, Hoffman had not checked out. She left a message for him, and with that she was off the hook with the family; she'd overcome the Passover hurdle. At least they couldn't throw that one at her again.

THE EIGHT DAY celebration of Passover began with two consecutive nights of reading from the Haggadah the book describing the Israelites release from Egyptian bondage. For the Levy family one night was enough, and that night, as per tradition, was always followed by a meal of extraordinary proportions.

Nelly loved preparing for Passover — dozens of eggs were hard boiled, she chopped up three different types of fish for the gefilte fish, bought a rooster for the soup, made matzo balls, braised the brisket, and sent Henry to Grodzinskis to buy a Plaver cake.

Sidney, raised by Orthodox grandparents, had watched them bury dishes in the garden for fear they might be contaminated by unleavened bread crumbs. The truly religious took the eight days of Passover very seriously. Sidney's grandfather stumbled through the house with a lit candle and a feather to ensure there wasn't an iota of leaven food hiding in some hitherto unseen crevice. His grandmother rescued their once-a-year Passover cutlery and crockery from the attic, washed it, and kept it in a separate sink to make sure it went uncontaminated. Nelly, on the other hand, put leftover bread in a bag and gave it to Anna to feed to the pigeons — that was the extent of her religious adherence.

Clara, Anna and Sula helped Nelly with the preparations. They arranged the Passover plate with bitter herbs, *charoses*, a lamb shank, a burned egg and parsley dipped in salt water and placed it in the centre of the table, all symbols of rough times in Egypt centuries ago. They made sure Henry got the Passover service right and didn't turn two pages in order to get to the end quicker. They knew when to leave the door open for the Angel Elijah to enter, and they also knew at the precise moment when their aunt Peggy would walk in with a tea cloth on her head, taking the place of Elijah who she said had too many homes to visit and she was helping him out. They sang *"Had Gad Yah"* to the melody of "one a penny, two a penny, hot cross buns," which was absurd, considering it was an Easter song commemorating the crucifixion of Jesus, and they drank the syrupy red wine marked Kosher for Pesach. It was the one and only time of the year Clara saw Henry get a little tipsy.

The Levys and their guests managed to get through the first half of Passover and occasionally dragged it on to the second portion where there was always heated discussion. They'd talk at cross purposes, they'd argue politics, they'd eat too much and linger too long. On this particular night they got stuck in the Exodus story!

"Never understood why we had to wait for Moses to come along to lead us out of Egypt. Why did we put up with them for so long?" Clara asked.

"And another forty years after that," Mannie reminded them.

"'Cos he lived with them 'gyptians and knew what was going on. No one knew 'nuffin before that." Henry took another swig of wine.

Solly Tenser, who'd been dozing 'til then, woke up and hypothesized, "I'd say it was an inside job. Moses had the ear of the Pharaoh."

"I'd have done something about it sooner than that," Nelly piped up.

"And what would that be?" Mannie inquired. "Have us all jump on a camel?"

"Oh, I dunno — crept out in the middle of the night maybe," Nelly supposed.

"There were thousands of us. Don't you think the Egyptians would have noticed?" Clara asked.

"Bet they had a pyramid night shift going; them pyramids look to me like they took years to build — they'd never be allowed to escape," Solly put in.

"And why is it their daughters aren't mentioned? Everything's male oriented in our religion," Clara observed.

"That's because we were the ones 'schlepping,' building their palaces, all that kind of stuff; t'aint women's work." Henry felt exhausted just thinking about it.

"No, it's because we were shoved in tents, cooking and flattening out the matzo," Sula reminded him.

"And some of us are still stuck in the kitchen," Anna muttered.

"Or taking flights of fancy to godforsaken lands." Mannie ducked as Clara picked up her Haggadah; she was ready to hit him on the head.

"'Nuff," Nelly announced. "Your dad's beginning to slur and the chicken soup's ready, so let's eat."

Everyone enjoyed Passover except Bernie, who couldn't stay away from matzo; the unleavened bread, known as the bread of affliction, was rightly titled for Bernie. It caused him terrible constipation. And as for the hard-boiled eggs, well, those made Bernie's condition worse, and by the end of the final days of Passover Bernie's acute stomach ache became a cause for alarm.

"If matzo, sent from heaven, was good enough for the Israelites wandering in the desert," Henry began . . .

Nelly interrupted, saying, "Manna was sent from heaven, Henry, not matzo!"

"Whatever, matzo, manna, they didn't have sandwiches. Bernie should get special dispensation if matzo blocks 'im up."

Unfortunately Bernie, Anna's fiancé being the most devout Jew in the entire Levy ménage, felt it would be sacrilegious to go against what the Haggadah mandated, and so he ate and endured the pain. Bernie continued to suffer, though not in silence. Everything prepared for Passover gave Bernie indigestion — the brisket, the matzo balls, the bitter herbs, the almond macaroons, the coconut pyramids, and, of course, the dreaded matzo. He didn't mind the *charoses*, the sweet grated apple and walnuts soaked in honey, which the family passed around the table. No one was sure what it signified, but by the time it got to Bernie most of it was gone anyway so even that delicacy didn't momentarily ease his discomfort.

"You still going to Munich, Clara?" Sidney brought the subject back to Clara's trip. "You think they have Passover there?"

"Do you really think any German Jew would be allowed to have a Seder service this year? The Nazis have forbidden everything that has the slightest connection to Jews. They've closed their shops, their factories, they've burned their books, it's over for us in Germany."

"And she's still going there," Sidney blurted out.

"Look, we've discussed this 'til I'm blue in the face, and the subject is closed."

"If I thought there was any chance of you finding Aunt Lizzie, I'd back you; but from what I read in the papers, you are taking a risk, and we're all worried." Mannie took a different approach, hoping kindness would win over anger.

"Mannie's right. Aunt Lizzie would have written to us if she could."

"That's just the point, Anna, she hasn't," Clara replied.

"What if she's moved? That's the most likely scenario. And as for those bloody Germans, they're not likely to forward the post now, are they?" Mannie proposed.

"I've got it worked out. I'll go to the address Mum has, and if Aunt Lizzie's not there, I'll ask around. If another family's in her place, I'll ask them if they know anything. Mr. Maze won't let anything happen to me, and, anyway, he has connections, and I know they'll help."

Aunt Peggy took the tea cloth off her head and got serious. "We all know you're doing this with the best intentions, luv, but when you say you're searching for your aunt — and, believe me, they'll know why you're there — you think they won't put two and two together?"

"They can't touch me. I'm a British citizen. We've been through this a hundred times. I know Mannie has a valid argument, I'll give him that, but he won't change my mind — so I suggest all of you drop the subject. I stayed for Passover. It's enough." Clara, weary of their constant battering, pushed back her chair and prepared to leave the table.

Sidney stopped her. "We've got to do the ten plagues! Not a Seder without them."

Henry took his glass, dipped his finger in the wine and recited each plague with each drop. "Blood. Frogs. Vermin. Beasts. Cattle Disease. Boils. Hail. Locusts. Darkness. Slaying of the first born." When he'd finished he licked his finger and put down the glass.

"And they've every one of them and a few more in Germany right now. That's why I'm going. That's why Aunt Lizzie has to be found." Clara was almost shouting. "If we had a Moses today, he'd lead the Jews out of Germany; but we haven't, and as I have a chance to lead just one Jew, then I've done something other than sit on my behind and agonize when I read the paper. If this Seder service is to mean anything to any of you, then just give me your blessing. Let me go and be done with it!"

Henry had been unusually quiet during the discussion. He'd gotten nowhere with his daughter in previous conversations, and he didn't see the point of carrying on the subject any longer. It was Passover, and he'd just read the portion of how Moses led the Jews out of Egypt. Who knows, maybe Clara might be able to lead Lizzie out of Germany! He raised his glass. "Next year in Jerusalem," the eternal Jewish prayer, and in unison they all simmered down and raised a glass to repeat, "Next year in Jerusalem."

Nelly added, her glass still raised, "Let's hope it's not next year in Dachau or in some other concentration camp."

Clara reacted somberly now, saying, "I have to tell you it was that party I had to attend in Belgravia that made me determined to go with Mr. Maze. It made a lasting impression on me, and it's not a good one, but I know now why I had to attend. I believe in fate, I believe I was supposed to be there to meet the man who asked me if I'd heard the latest German slogan. Obviously he was not one of the sympathizers. He recited it to me: 'Dear God, make me dumb that I may not to Dachau come.' Don't you think that says it all?"

CHAPTER 24

Munich

MAZE AND CLARA arrived in Paris in time to board the night train to Munich. The following morning they were having breakfast in the dining car when the train suddenly came to a screeching halt.

Clara, confident and sure of herself at the outset of the journey, panicked. She leaned across the table to Maze and said in a hushed voice, "Why are we stopping?"

"We're at the German border."

"What are they doing? What's all that clinking?"

"They're detaching the French carriages and replacing them with German ones."

"I thought we were on a French train."

"We were. They change trains and crew at the border."

"What about our suitcases?"

"They'll be switched over."

Clara could see German guards with guns in holsters and swastika armbands boarding the train. Maze instructed Clara to remain silent as two of them entered the dining car and stopped at their table.

"Passports. *Ist diese Information richtig?*"

"*Ja,* but can you speak English? My German is not so good," Maze lied. He handed over their passports for inspection.

"You are the French one? Her?" He pointed at Clara. "English?"

"Yes, m . . ." Maze hesitated, "my assistant."

"Destination?"

"Munich."

"What is in Munich for you?"

"Business. I am an art dealer."

The guard took their passports and handed them to the other guard, who turned every page of each document. He handed them back to the first guard, who put them in a leather brief case he held under his arm.

The first guard handed a printed form to Maze and spoke to him in German; Maze responded, this time in German. Finally the guard clicked his heels and raised his right arm. "*Heil Hitler.*"

Maze barely nodded, then turned to Clara who was now as white as a sheet.

"It's all right. He asked me the reason for visiting Germany and why I needed an English assistant who couldn't speak the language. I told him you had a good eye for art, and I could interpret for you when necessary."

"We haven't set foot in their country, and I'm shaking like a leaf." Clara was getting a taste of what she might face later on.

"Oh, and he said we should have a good time in the New Germany!"

"What about our passports?"

"We'll get them back when we reach Munich."

FINALLY ARRIVING IN Munich, they registered at the Hotel Bayerischer Hof. Here they were again asked by the desk clerk to produce passports. He opened them to where they'd been rubber-stamped.

"*Ich sehe keine Aufenthaltserlaubnis. Diese wird an der Grenze ausgestellt. Das Hotel braucht sie!*"

"What was that?' Clara didn't like the clerk's tone of voice.

"Something about a permit — please send someone over who speaks either French or English, I am having difficulty understanding you." Paul tapped his fingers impatiently. "We've had a long journey and need to rest."

The clerk called to his manager and showed him the rubber stamp in Clara's passport.

"There is a problem," the manager reported. "You do not have permission to stay."

Maze remembered the printed form he'd filled in at Customs. He quickly pulled it from his coat pocket and handed it over.

"This allows you to stay five days, then you must leave."

"We have no intention of staying that long," Maze assured him.

"What is in your luggage — the leather portfolio?"

Maze opened it. He'd thrown in a few of his students' works.

"And you expect to sell these here?" The manager was either being sarcastic or expected better work.

"Sell or exchange," Maze replied.

"We will keep them here until you request them."

"They are mine. I do not see why they have to be held by you."

"Policy."

"And our passports and suitcases?"

"The suitcases you will have, the passports stay with the art work."

The manager summoned a blond youth dressed in khaki shirt and short pants. "He will show you to your room; your luggage will follow shortly."

Clara lagged behind, whispering to Paul, "They'll find nothing in mine."

"Nor mine." Maze laughed softly. "Wasn't worth making a scene over the portfolio or the passports — the case might be useful, but I think we'll get it all back." He laughed again. "They weren't impressed with the contents, were they?"

CLARA SAT IN a comfortable armchair, trying to relax and taking in the room, actually a suite of rooms. A sitting room separated two bedrooms. Next to her chair on a carved wooden credenza was a large bowl of fruit, a full, open box of chocolates and an exquisite flower arrangement in a crystal vase with a note attached. "What does this say?"

"*Wir heissen Sie im Hotel Bayerischer Hof willkommen. Wir wünschen Ihnen einen sehr angenehmen Aufenthalt, Heil Hitler.*" Paul had read the words with a flourish. "They're happy to have us here."

"Could have fooled me," Clara answered. "I suppose I better get used to it."

"I'm afraid so. I need a drink." Paul walked over to the bar and poured himself a brandy. "What would you like, my dear?"

"To go home!"

"I warned you it would be unpleasant. Obviously it's not going to be easy — take a deep breath and have a drink."

"I'd like a cup of tea."

"I'll call room service."

Paul sat down beside her. "Aubrey Hoffman called me in London just before he left; we arranged to meet this evening."

"Can I come with you?"

"No, this I have to do alone. Please do not attempt to leave; I will have a meal sent up."

"Well, all right." Tired from the journey, she gave in easily.

"I picked this up for you at the desk." He handed her a map. "I suggest you study it. Find where your aunt lives and mark it. You must look as if you know what you are doing and where you are going. Sorry to be so, well, so German, but we are both here for a purpose, and every second counts."

"I understand. But don't be gone too long."

"I'll try not to." Maze went into his bathroom, washed, changed his shirt and was ready to leave. "Stay here, do not leave the room. Promise?"

"I promise."

AUBREY HOFFMAN WAITED for Maze at a table in the lobby of the Bayerischer Hof Hotel. He saw Maze exit the lift and walk to the reception desk to hand in his key. Hoffman put down his newspaper, drank the last drop from his coffee cup, stood up and slowly made his way to the exit.

Maze, keeping his distance, followed. At a café, not far from the hotel, Hoffman stooped as if to remove something from the bottom of his shoe and then walked on, a signal to Maze that this was where he would be meeting Luftmann.

Maze entered the café.

Heinrich Luftmann turned and beckoned to him from a table where he waited. They greeted each other formally, and Maze sat down with him. Luftmann took out one of his paintings and showed it to Maze. "Look as if you're interested in my work," he said.

A waiter came over. Maze ordered two glasses of schnapps. Luftmann looked around to make sure no one was close enough to hear them. "It's so good to see you," he said softly.

"Good to see you, too. Wish it were under different circumstances," Maze replied.

"It is what it is. We are sinking into the abyss. They even attempt to limit our imagination!"

Maze examined the painting as he spoke. "Your letters were most informative; how are you managing?"

"As best I can. I meet my girlfriend, Trude, in secret. She is under constant scrutiny at the factory. An artist friend of ours was hauled off in the middle of the night and held for ransom because they knew his family had money. When they paid up he was released; now he lives in fear of being abducted again." Luftmann paused as the waiter brought them their drinks, then moved on. "I don't know how long Trude will be able to stay at the munitions factory without them finding out she's a Jew. It's very bad for the Jews. I don't have to repeat what you already know. Just a few days ago there was another edict — their bank accounts have been appropriated and their possessions confiscated, and no one will employ them."

"Is there no stopping this?"

"What can we do? Go against the Nazis, and you're sent to a concentration camp."

"In London our newspapers print very little of this; the English, it appears, are more interested in Edward, the soon-to-be-crowned King and his love affair with Mrs. Simpson. Edward's friendship with Hitler hasn't affected his popularity one bit, and the government pays no attention to Winston's warnings."

"I have to get to the reason for your visit," Heinrich said. "I never know who's watching; it is why I do not like to stay in sight too long. Tomorrow morning you will take your portfolio to Gerhard Buchman. He will show you his collection of collages. You will choose the pieces you want, and he will buy the work you brought. He will write out a bill of sale and obtain the necessary export certificate. The information Winston requires will be inserted beneath the collage." He slipped a diagram across the table to Paul. "I have marked the location; it is close to your hotel. I will try to be there around eleven."

"How do you know you can trust him?"

"He's a good man; been in the gallery business for years. He's forbidden to show or sell work by Jews, though he still has some art by lesser-known Jews. To stay solvent he represents artists who paint what Nazis like — landscape and portraits, nothing abstract. He has a few pieces of mine hidden at the back of his gallery. He gives us money when he can."

"Leave Munich, Heinrich. Come back to London with me," Maze urged his old friend.

"Paul, this is my country, I cannot desert it now. We, all of us gentiles, must find ways to get our friends out of Germany. I have a meeting — if you like, you can come with me; well, not exactly with me, behind me. You will learn more there than I have time to tell you now. Turn right when you leave the café; I will wait a few yards down the street at a crossing."

Maze paid the bill, took the painting, and keeping Luftmann in his sight, followed.

THE MEETING WAS held in the basement of a bookshop. It had a back entrance, which Maze would never have found had he not kept Luftmann in sight. He was stopped at the front door. "Who is this?" a young man asked Luftmann.

"An old friend from Paris — lives in London now. He's Paul Maze, a fellow artist. We worked together as students. I have known him a long time. He will help us. This is Raoul Levie, Paul, he runs this group."

"I've seen your work." Raoul recognized the Maze name. "You had an exhibition here some years ago."

"I did. Not much chance of having another, I see."

"Not in this Germany!"

Inside, Luftmann sat with Maze at the table. "We are preparing leaflets, anti-Nazi propaganda," Luftmann said. "We distribute them in the early hours of the morning. Hitler makes law by decree, and he has the right to override the constitution. In his acceptance speech as Chancellor he made it quite clear any protest against the regime is considered treason — 'treason shall be stamped out with ruthless barbarity.' We continue, knowing full well what that means."

While the group worked, Maze asked questions. He learned Dachau was not an ordinary prison; it was a slave labor camp on the outskirts of Munich. Everyone knew what went on there, yet few raised a voice in protest. These brave young men and women felt compelled to take a stand against a regime that constantly humiliated and tortured anyone they considered unworthy to be a German.

By the time Maze got back to the hotel it was midnight. He looked in on Clara; she was sleeping soundly. He hesitated, wanting to lay beside her, hold her close, needing the comfort of her warm body. Reluctantly he turned away and went to his own room.

CLARA WOKE EARLY. The sun was rising just above the chimney stacks on the other side of the road. Seven in the morning and the city was bustling. Pedestrians, cyclists, buses, trams and a lorry parked with the engine running just a few feet away from the hotel. Workers in striped uniforms carried dustbins on their backs as they dumped the contents into the back of the lorry. Strange, she thought, dustmen in London wore ordinary working clothes; these men all dressed alike. Were they prisoners? Here she was in a suite in a luxury hotel where nothing seemed untoward, while outside uniformed men with swastika armbands seemed to be everywhere. And soon she would be among them.

She put on her dressing gown and came into the sitting room. Paul's jacket, thrown on an armchair, proved he was there. The night before he'd arranged for coffee to be sent up in the morning. It hadn't arrived. She rang the operator who spoke no English, although she seemed to understand the word coffee.

A knock came at the door; it must be the coffee. Clara opened it to find an older man holding a silver tray. He entered and settled the tray on a table. To her surprise he spoke English. "Breakfast is served between seven-thirty and ten. Will you have it up here or in the restaurant downstairs?"

"Here, please."

"The kitchen needs a definite time."

"Eight o'clock then."

"It will be arranged."

He was definitely British, she decided. Must be one of those Nazi sympathizers; he certainly had an attitude. Why else would a Brit be in Germany now? He poured her a cup of coffee. "You will find it stronger than what you are used to," he said. "Is there anything else?"

"No." She wanted to ask him what on earth he was doing in Munich but decided not to. He was right about the coffee, a stronger blend than anything served in London.

She carried the cup to her room, had a bath, dressed and came back to the sitting room to find Maze up and dressed.

He came to her immediately and kissed her on the cheek.

"How was your evening?" she asked.

"Disturbing. You were fast asleep when I came in."

"Sorry, I was tired."

Maze sat beside her, taking her hand in his. "The people I met last night strongly advised me not to go into the Jewish area with you."

"I didn't expect you to."

"We'll have breakfast downstairs then; I'll demand our passports back."

"Then cancel room service."

"I'll do that at the desk." Paul handed her a wad of notes from his wallet. "You cannot be without money."

Clara looked at the paper in her hand. "I have no idea what this money represents. Is it a lot? Who would I bribe?"

"I will pay the taxi driver. If someone looks like they want to give you information and is holding back, just take out your purse, and they will get the message. Use whatever you need. Did you mark on the map where your aunt lives?"

"Yes. I found it quite easily."

"Do not enter into conversation with anyone. Just speak about your aunt. I mean it, Clara. You have to be very careful."

Maze lifted the newspaper off the coffee tray and translated a paragraph from a front page article.

In Munich yesterday, thousands of school children watched as books described as Marxist were burned. As the books went up in flames, they were told let this also burn into your hearts the love of the Fatherland . . .

He put down the paper. "We must not discuss or give an opinion or criticize. Observe and stay silent. Go directly to the address you have. Ask the taxi to wait. If your aunt is not there, leave."

Maze handed her a piece of paper with the name and address of the gallery. "This is where I will be."

The clock in the square outside their window struck nine. Clara stood up, picked up her coat and handbag, ready to leave.

"I'll come down with you." Maze finished his coffee, and they left the suite together.

As the doors of the lift closed, Paul drew her to him and held her close. "Remember — no matter how friendly they may seem, they are not your friends."

The lift all too quickly reached the ground floor. They drew apart as the door opened. A different concierge was on duty when they stepped into the lobby. But he was talking to, or more likely being questioned by, two uniformed soldiers. It was a frenzied conversation Maze wasn't about to interrupt. He pulled Clara aside, as if in deep conversation, and held her attention until the soldiers departed. Only then did he hand in their keys to their room, then turn to Clara and direct her from the lobby into the breakfast room.

"What were they saying?" Clara whispered.

"They were asking for information he did not have or wasn't about to give. You saw the card he produced; it proved his membership in the Nazi party which is probably why they accepted whatever he was trying to explain."

"I'm not hungry," Clara admitted. "I just want to get this over with; help me get my passport back."

"Just have a piece of toast, you'll need sustenance." Paul insisted.

Clara obliged. Once seated at a table she ate toast, sipped coffee and waited for Paul to finish his eggs and sausages. Finally back at the desk, Maze demanded their passports from the clerk who, unlike the clerk on duty the night before, was polite and forthcoming. Maze escorted Clara to the revolving hotel door. Outside the doorman called for a taxi. One came up moments later. Maze tipped the doorman, then helped Clara into the taxi.

He spoke to the driver in German and handed him the address. "*Wieviel kostet die Hin- und Rückfahrt? Ich möchte, dass Sie auf meine Freundin warten und sie hinterher zum Hotel bringen.*"

The driver raised an eyebrow but made no comment.

"I paid the fare both ways and tipped him extra for waiting. He will bring you back to the hotel." He paused; she could see the concern on his face. "Well," he said quietly, "remember what we spoke about." He kissed her on the lips, then added, "*Bon chance.*"

"I'll be all right. I came here with a purpose, and now I have to carry it out."

A sobering look clouded his face as he closed the door on the taxi and waved the driver away. It took all of his reserve not to jump in and go with her. But he had his work to do, and she had hers, and the sooner they'd accomplished their separate missions, the sooner they'd be able to leave . . . she seemed so vulnerable, sitting there, his heart went out to her. He admired her determination, he loved her spirit, he said a silent prayer.

Clara settled into the back seat of the taxi, she touched her lips with her fingertips, his kiss lingered. He would be there for her whatever the outcome — he was in her life now in a way she could no longer ignore.

Maze watched the taxi pull away. With a sigh of resignation and resolve he straightened and reentered the hotel, collected his portfolio from the front desk and examined the contents; everything seemed in order. A sticker with a swastika on the front of it indicated the case had passed inspection. The desk clerk, now a pretty blond girl, asked if everything was satisfactory.

"Yes, thank you."

"We like our guests to be comfortable." She was flirting with him.

"And you have," he said. "As much as I would like to spend time with you, I must, unfortunately, be on my way. *Guten Tag.*" He picked up his portfolio.

"I'm off at three." She hadn't given up.

"I won't be back by then," Maze replied and dashed her hopes.

THE GALLERY, AS Luftmann had said, was in easy walking distance of the hotel. Not wanting to hang around, Maze strolled at a leisurely pace and still arrived at the gallery earlier than expected. *JUDEN KUNST,* Jew Gallery, in newly applied black paint, was slashed on the window. He crossed the street, picked a vantage point and waited until he saw Luftmann approach.

Luftmann paused, read the sign and tried the door. He looked around, spotted Maze, and disappeared into an alleyway beside the building. Maze, crossed back over the road, entered the alleyway and followed him to what seemed to be an empty red brick building. Luftmann entered, left the door slightly ajar and waited for Maze inside.

Luftmann fumed as he greeted Maze, "Ach, they've closed him down! No one will dare come to this gallery now. I'll have to find another outlet for my work, damn it!"

Very little light came into the warehouse; the windows were filthy, and it smelled musty. Luftmann lit a match. Piles of rubbish were strewn across the floor. They found Buchman sitting at a desk he'd concocted out of planks of wood placed over crates. He was going through his inventory. Luftmann introduced him to Maze.

"I am sorry for the inconvenience," Buchman said. "That writing was on my window when I came to open up this morning. I'm not a Jew, but I have shown the work of Jews. I will have to speak to the authorities."

"Buchman's gallery is one of the most prestigious in Munich. If they can do this to him, then none of us will be able to sell our work." Luftmann, on the verge of panic, wrung his hands in despair.

"I think perhaps we may have to use the past tense," Buchman stated sadly.

"Yet another loss to this city; we will end up with Nazi posters all over the place and illegally acquired art in government offices." Heinrich controlled his anger sufficiently to outline his plan. "I have received the information from Trude. It is mostly numbers and charts. They don't make much sense to me, but she tells me your people will be able to decipher them."

"I have already started work on Heinrich's collages," Buchman stated. "He's prostituted himself, done country scenes, a barn and different perspectives in the same genre; but then it's all for a good cause, and he will get paid. The barns will be the major cut out, large enough to accommodate the information. Leave me three pieces of the work you have with you, Herr Maze, and they will be replaced by these collages."

"Call me — Paul, please." He turned to Luftmann. "Not exactly your style, Heinrich."

"They destroyed my style; I have no style, so why should I not make a complete mockery of my work and be useful at the same time?"

They spoke by candlelight. The flickering flames cast an eerie glow to an already sinister setting; their conversation matched the mood. They spoke of the crisis artists and their benefactors faced and what Buchman could do, if anything, to avoid prosecution. If he stopped showing Jewish artists, would he still be allowed to keep his gallery open? Would it be seen as giving recognition to the regime? It was both a moral and a financial dilemma. And, of course, there was the dreaded fear of being denounced as a Communist; if he disobeyed their commands, it would land him in Dachau. It seemed prudent to lay low for a while, to make sure his hiding place was safe and to hope what was occurring in Munich was just an aberration of short duration.

Luftmann was the first to leave. Maze followed a few minutes later, having arranged to meet at a beer garden on the Maximilianstrasse. Buchman declined. It was all too much for him; he had difficult decisions to make.

CLARA WONDERED IF the driver was purposely taking her the long way 'round to her aunt's place. It had to be on the other side of town, for they drove through the city and out into the suburbs, passing some quite lovely homes before coming to an open market and turning off on to Sonnenstrasse into a working class area. They were now on Himmler-Strasse where block buildings lined both sides of the road; the buildings were similar to some of the poorer construction in London.

"*Das war einmal die Karlstrasse, jetzt ist es die Himmler-Strasse,*" said the taxi driver.

Clara understood; the name of the street had changed. Lizzie had not given them that information. It could be why Nelly's letters were returned.

The taxi driver slowed down. The blocks were numbered; he was looking for number seven, and it was not on his side of the street. He motioned her to get out and pointed to the other side.

Clara stepped out of the taxi and stood for a few moments on the pavement to get her bearings, surprised that Lizzie had chosen so remote an area. It was nothing like the bustling environment she had been born into. Well, maybe it was her husband Fritz's choice, block after block of concrete buildings with small windows. She turned 'round and realized her driver had driven off and was disappearing down a side street. So much for paying a return fare; she wouldn't be seeing him again.

She noticed a nearby play area with children on swings and a riding roundabout. An old lady carrying shopping bags walked past her. A little farther on she saw youths kicking a ball. She moved on to where the boys were playing. They stopped their game and waited for her to pass. She'd brought with her one of Nelly's returned letters in which Lizzie mentioned a park where she walked her dog. This had to be it. She crossed the road. Since the street name was not the one on the envelope, she wondered if the numbers had been changed, too. Then she looked up to see a young man approaching her.

"Can you speak English?" Clara asked, her fingers crossed.

"I study English at the university," he said and smiled.

She showed him the envelope. "I'm not sure where this is."

"Come. I can show you." He escorted her to the right apartment. "We have problem here. We have new street names. It is difficult for us also; we have to make sure where we are. I too get lost sometimes. I am Rudi, and you are?"

"Clara."

A middle-aged woman answered the door.

It wasn't Lizzie. Clara introduced herself and went on to try to explain in broken German who she was looking for. "My *Tante* lived here. Lizzie Schmidt." Clara handed the woman a photo of her aunt.

The woman looked at it, returned it and slammed the door shut.

Rudi knocked again; the woman opened the door. He repeated Clara's question in German. She shook her head and spoke rapidly.

To Clara it was evident Lizzie wasn't at this address anymore. Before the woman closed the door again, Clara asked Rudi, "Can you find out how long she's lived here?"

"She tells me her family moved in four months ago. They waited a long time for the apartment, and she doesn't know anything about a Lizzie Schmidt, and you should leave her alone."

Neighbors came out on to a balcony to see what all the fuss was about. The young man suggested they leave. "To find your aunt it is better you go the police station," Rudi explained. "There have been many changes here. The Jews were ordered out. These people, all of them, are with the Nazi party. It is why they are in these homes. They call it the allocation of the deserving."

"Can't I try again? Perhaps the neighbors know," Clara pleaded.

Rudi passed the photo around. A few took a look, shrugged and passed it on; others scuffled back into their homes and closed the door. An elderly man took the photo and examined it more closely, saying, "*Ja, ich glaube, dass sie hier mit ihrem Ehemann gelebt hat.*"

"He said she lived here with her husband, she doesn't now."

"None of them want to help us?" Clara could see the hopelessness of their situation.

"I will go with you to the police station; it is not far," Rudi offered. "You will not get information from these people."

Maze had told her specifically not to talk to anyone and to come straight back to the hotel. But how? There was no taxi, no sign of any transport — she may as well continue her search. The least she could do was to try to find out where the authorities had relocated Jews. Rudi seemed a nice enough fellow and was willing to help. She decided to take the chance.

On the way to the station Rudi spoke about the summer he spent in England hiking in the Lake District. "It was so beautiful. I walked where Wordsworth wrote his poems and where Constable painted. I was sad to leave. I could have stayed forever, but I was in school in Heidelberg and had to finish my studies. I am not happy with what is happening in my country right now. We cannot question. We can only obey. I had Jewish friends at the university; they had to leave, whole families have been taken away. Some of my friends have left Germany; I think I, too, must go."

At the police station Rudi translated for her. The desk officer told her he wasn't in the housing business, people moved every day, and they didn't tell him where they were going, and, what's more, he wasn't interested. They were wasting his time and theirs, and a German, referring to Rudi, should not be assisting a foreigner.

Clara said she realized he was a very busy man, but she had come all the way from England to look for her aunt. "Surely, Officer, people cannot just disappear."

The Officer banged his fist on the desk, angry that she dared to question him. "*Gehen Sie! WIR haben keine Juden hier und es wird auch hier nie wieder Juden geben. Gehen Sie zurück. Wir haben hier Wichtigeres zu tun!*" It didn't need translating. It was quite obvious what he was saying. No Jews — never again Jews . . .

Rudi ushered her out. "I think it better you leave. I must go, too."

Clara opened her handbag, took out the wad of notes Paul had given her, picked out three of the largest denominations and gave them to him.

"It is not necessary, Frau Clara."

"It is, Rudi; you have been very helpful, and I must say the most polite German I have met since my arrival here. Thank you."

Rudi gave her a hug. "You are very kind. I will put this with my savings. I will always remember you as the one who helped me gain my freedom." He hurried away, leaving Clara standing alone outside the police station. She tried to remember in which direction the main street was. She shouted out to Rudi. "Which way do I turn for Sonnenstrasse?" but he had already disappeared around a corner.

Here she was in a hostile environment, not speaking the language and not knowing where she was going. If she could find her way to Sonnenstrasse, she could perhaps see a bus or preferably a taxi to take her back to the hotel. She kept walking. A black Mercedes pulled up beside her. Two men got out, one in Nazi uniform, the other in plain clothes wearing a blue suit.

The man in the blue suit came up to her and said, "*Sie sehen aus, als ob Sie sich verlaufen haben. Wohin möchten Sie? Haben Sie Papiere?*"

"I am English. I do not speak German."

"*Haben Sie Papiere?*" he repeated.

She fumbled in her bag and found her passport. He took it, looked at it and spoke to her in English. "Where do you stay?"

"The Hotel Bayerischer Hof."

"You have good taste."

Clara explained to him that the taxi driver who brought her was paid to wait and take her back to the hotel. "He drove off. I don't know where he went. I have no transport. Perhaps I can find a train, maybe a bus?"

"That was most dishonest of him. We will take you."

The uniformed man opened the back door of the black Mercedes and invited Clara to get in.

"So you came here for what reason? Surely not for a holiday," Blue Suit said as they drove off.

"No, I came to find a relative, my aunt."

"And you have been successful?"

"No."

"Perhaps she has moved. What is her name?"

"Elizabeth Schmidt."

"You have some documentation?"

"I have a photo."

"Give it to me, please."

The two men up front spoke in German. Clara heard the word —
Juden.

"We will keep this photo; perhaps we can find where she is," Blue
Suit finally told her.

Clara didn't believe him. She asked for the photo. He refused. No
other conversation with Clara followed until they reached the hotel.

Here Blue Suit advised her not to walk the streets of Munich
alone. "You are here for a very short time; you do not want to be here
for a very long time. Understand?"

Clara understood.

MAZE WAITED FOR Luftmann at the beer garden. He'd been there
for over an hour, and there was still no sign of him. After three cups
of coffee and being constantly asked if he was expecting someone, he
was advised it was getting close to the lunch hour, and they would
need the table. He was just one person having only a beverage, unless
he wanted a meal.

"I do not wish to dine alone," Maze told the waiter and paid his
bill. He decided instead to go to Luftmann's apartment. He'd been
there on a previous trip; he knew more or less where it was. After a few
wrong turns, he found it. The door was open. Paul checked inside.
Heinrich was nowhere to be seen; he decided not to wait.

He left a cryptic note where he knew it would be found, pinned
to Heinrich's smock. The smock itself resembled a work of art, hardly
any of the original white linen showing. It had seen better days; knowing Heinrich as he did, it would never be replaced, might even be
framed one day. He wrote:

Roll paintings. Place them in tube. Paris train tomorrow 10
a.m. Paul.

Heinrich would understand. Germany was no place for a Frenchman and a British Jew.

Out on the street Maze hailed a taxi and requested the driver to
take him to the train station; there he would exchange their tickets for
an earlier departure.

At the station he joined a long line leading to the reservation window. The line moved slowly. His impatience and concern for Clara growing, he did not want to leave her too long by herself, thinking for sure she'd be back in the hotel by now. Eventually it was his turn. *"Meine Pläne haben sich geändert, ich muss mit dem Zehn-Uhr-Zug nach Frankreich."*

He was told the train was full. He opened his wallet and placed a large denomination note on the counter.

The clerk took the money, held it up to the light, saw it wasn't a forgery, put it in his breast shirt pocket, said nothing, and exchanged the tickets.

Mission accomplished — it was worth the wait. Outside the station he searched for a taxi, luckily finding one quickly. He was confident Heinrich would find the note and bring the art work to the train.

Back at the hotel, presuming Clara had long ago returned, he went directly to their suite. The door was locked. A maid opened it for him. Clara was not there. He did not wait for the lift; he ran down the stairway to the reception desk to find both keys still in their box. Clara had been gone for over four hours.

Paul did not recognize the concierge — he was not the same person on duty as that morning. He thought it unwise for him to try to find the aunt's apartment, though he was tempted. Still and all, Clara had the address with her, and he'd only glanced at it on the map. She was probably on her way back; at least he hoped she was. It would be better just to wait. There was a lounge area in the lobby. He sat near the window where he could see the taxis come and go through the circular driveway.

Half an hour went by — still no Clara. He had a drink at the bar. He paced outside the main entrance. It was over an hour before a large black Mercedes pulled up. A soldier in Nazi uniform, stationed outside the hotel, left his post to open the front door of the Mercedes with a Heil Hitler salute. It had to be an official vehicle. The back door of the car opened, Clara stepped out. Up front, Blue Suit nodded to the uniformed soldier and stepped out of the car. Paul moved cautiously to where he could overhear the conversation.

"Thank you for bringing me back. I appreciate it," Maze heard Clara say.

Maze stayed where he was; after the gallery humiliation, he, too, might be marked.

"May I have the photo of my aunt? It belongs to my mother."

Clara held out her hand.

"*Auf Wiedersehen, Frau Simon.* I hope you enjoy the rest of your visit to Munich." Blue Suit clicked his heels and returned to the Mercedes. No response had come from him about the photograph.

The hotel's uniformed soldier closed the car door, gave the Hitler salute and returned to his post. The Mercedes sped away and disappeared in traffic.

Clara entered the hotel where Paul swept her into his arms and held on to her. She was shaking and near to tears.

"What happened? No, don't tell me — not until we get to our room. I was so worried. I was wrong to let you go alone."

It was only when they arrived in their suite and closed the door that she finally spoke to him. "I had to go alone. It is not your fault."

"Why the police? Where was the taxi driver I paid to stay with you?"

"He disappeared the moment I got to Aunt Lizzie's flat. It was awful, well, except for Rudi."

"Who's Rudi?"

"A student, he helped me, but no one would tell us anything. My aunt has vanished along with the other Jews who lived in the same apartment block. Rudi said he'd heard the Nazis moved all the Jews, and he'd seen women and children thrown into the back of a lorry. So, I went to the police."

"You went to the police?"

"Rudi suggested it. He stayed with me, he didn't have to. I don't know what I'd have done without him. The police dismissed us, told Rudi to mind his own business and not speak to foreigners and go on his way. I gave Rudi some money; he didn't ask for it. He wants to leave Germany before they grab him." Clara babbled on. "There was no sign of Aunt Lizzie. One man said she had lived there and then shut up like a clam. I hate this place. It's evil."

"Who were the men in the Mercedes?"

"Special Police, I think; they picked me up when Rudi left. I hope I haven't caused him trouble. I was trying to find some strasse or other, can't remember the name. I had no idea how I was going to get back. One of them asked a lot of questions. I showed them the photo of my aunt, and they refused to give it back."

"You need a drink. I need a drink!" Paul offered her a brandy.

She refused, saying, "No, I have just one more place to contact. Need to keep my wits about me."

"Enough, Clara, you've done all you can."

"One last try. Please call the switchboard for me and ask them to connect me to the British Consulate."

"It's useless, Clara."

"Please, Paul. Just one more try."

"All right, and that has to be the end of it. I've changed our reservations. We are leaving in the morning." He went to the phone, carried out her request and handed the receiver to her.

Maze listened as she explained her predicament; he could see her becoming more and more frustrated. Finally she banged down the phone.

"Tell me, what did they say?" Paul demanded.

"I don't know who I spoke to, some mucky muck in the Consulate."

"Mucky muck?"

"Someone of importance who said there was nothing they could do as my aunt is married to a German and technically that made her a German, too, and since Hitler has become Chancellor they are guided by his proclamations. In other words, bugger the Jews."

"No suggestions? No advice?"

"Nothing, and that's not all. He had the audacity to refer to my aunt as 'those people.' Imagine, 'THOSE PEOPLE'! The disdain in his voice — he said they are probably Communists. He agrees with the German government. None of them have any sympathy for Communists. He's as guilty as the Germans."

"They are bound by German law."

"Don't make excuses for them, Paul. They should close the embassy down — that would be the right thing to do. I wonder if he's the same pompous ass we met at Eleanor's party? The one who said he was with the British Foreign Office here in Germany. I think he said he was in Berlin; anyway, there are hundreds of them over here. This is why Mr. Churchill keeps on at the government. He knows the mentality of these Nazis. He doesn't believe a word they say, all lip service and idle promises, and he is right, it will lead to another war." She took a deep breath and demanded of Paul, "What more could I do to find Aunt Lizzie?"

Maze took Clara in his arms. "You have done all you can. There is nothing more you can do."

IT WAS THEIR last night in Munich, and Munich was known for its fine restaurants. "Would you like to go out for a good Deutschland dinner?" Paul asked, half hoping she would turn him down.

"Thank you, but, no, thank you; let's dine here."

"Exactly what I hoped you would say. I'll order room service."

"Just you and me together this evening, Paul."

Clara had tried and failed to find Lizzie, and she realized, even if she had unlimited time, she still wouldn't be able to find her. The authorities weren't talking. The flat occupants were all Nazis on to a good thing; why should they want to help? The police showed absolutely no interest. There was an overall sinister feeling in the city. She was still reeling from the morning's encounter, and Paul was concerned for Luftmann. He'd not heard from him.

After a quiet dinner in their sitting room together, Clara bathed and got ready for bed.

Paul went to his room to undress, put on a robe, then came back to the sitting room and poured himself a night cap. Clara had left her door ajar. He could hear her sobbing.

"May I come in?" he called out.

"Please."

He entered her bedroom to stand by the bed. "When you insisted on coming with me, Clara, I had no idea how bad things were here. Had I known, I would have been more adamant, I'm so sorry."

"I'd have come anyway. You should know that about me now. I don't give up easily. Stay with me. I don't want to be alone tonight. I'm frightened."

Paul removed his robe and lay down beside her. "I've wanted to be with you like this for a very long time." His words were gentle as he held her and caressed her. "Far too long."

Clara turned to him. "You, Paul, are . . ."

"No need for words. Just love me as I love you."

For the remainder of that night in Munich, in Germany, the horrors they had learned about, the inhumanity they had witnessed, were put aside; there was nothing more for them to do other than to make love in a land that, at this time in history, knew only how to hate.

CHAPTER 25

Munich Railway Station

PAUL AND CLARA arrived early at the Munich railway station, where a porter unloaded their luggage onto a cart and escorted them through the hoards of frantic people determined not to miss their train as the seconds of its departure slipped away unmercifully. Clara felt physically sick — children were crying, mothers carried babies and held toddlers by the hand, men balanced cases on their heads, even dogs pulled at their owners' leashes.

It was pandemonium.

"I don't know how you're going to find Heinrich in all this," Clara shouted, trying to be heard above the noise of the crowd. "All these people wanting to leave at the same time? It's crazy."

"There are three trains scheduled for Paris today, as well as two for Amsterdam and two for Zurich," the porter told them in English as he literally thrust his way through the masses. "If they don't get on the first one, they'll be in line for the next. It's like this every day."

"They'll have to put on more carriages," Clara stated.

"They make nothing easy for refugees, that's what they are, rejected by their own country," the porter explained. "It's a disgusting state of affairs, if you ask me."

"Your English is very good," Paul noted as he and Clara followed the porter with increasing difficulty.

"My mother is from Dover. We speak English at home," the porter yelled back. "Won't be surprised if she doesn't get her marching orders soon. He stopped abruptly to look at the departure board. "Your train leaves from platform seven. Took a couple there an hour ago; looked pretty full then. Hope you reserved seats." Finally they reached their gate. "I have to leave you here." The porter lifted the cases off the cart and gave them to Maze. "They won't let me go to the train."

"Thank you. We'd never had made it without you," Paul said as he handed over a generous tip.

"Thanks, sir. I hope you have a good journey back to civilization. Wish my mum would listen; says she won't leave my dad — he's German."

There wasn't an inch to spare on the platform. Paul pushed forward, carrying his and Clara's cases. "Hang on to my jacket — do not let go," he told her.

Clara had no intention of letting go; she'd never seen so many people in one place at one time, not even in Petticoat Lane on a Sunday morning.

Walking the platform, they could see the corridors of the train were solidly packed with people and luggage. The porter was right — not an empty seat in any of the carriages. There were men and women hanging out of windows saying goodbye; others stood vacantly staring into space with children on their shoulders and mothers weeping beside them.

Finally Paul, with Clara still attached to his jacket, reached the first class compartments. There were name cards on the windows, designating reserved seats. Still, every compartment they passed was full. Eventually, in the next to last carriage, Paul located their names. "You go ahead and get on the train, Clara, and find someone to help as I pass the cases through the window."

Clara held on fast, wouldn't let go of his jacket.

"Please, get on the train. There's no way we can get these cases through the corridor."

Clara reluctantly let go and boarded the train. Theirs were the last two seats left free in their compartment. She stood looking helpless at the open window — no one offered to lend a hand with the cases — Paul lifted the first case and pushed it through the window. Clara took hold of it and dropped it beside her. Then came the other. "I'll wait 'til you get on, then you can put them on the rack. These people don't appear to be a very helpful lot." She addressed her remark to the passengers in the compartment who were oblivious or just didn't care to help her.

"Just push the cases into the compartment. Right now I have to find Heinrich." Paul was already on his way back to the end of the platform.

Clara glanced at her watch. "The train leaves in thirty-five minutes," she shouted after him — he hadn't heard her. With that, Clara gave up and collapsed in a seat beside a very large German man and a rather small French lady. She looked around at the other people in the compartment, four, including her on her side; Paul's seat was empty and opposite. Perhaps one of them would offer to change seats when the train got going. She would wait for Paul to come back and let him do the negotiations.

A guard came into the compartment accompanied by a Nazi officer; he requested their tickets. Paul had left with the tickets in his pocket. She had to remain calm, explain when he got to her. She was next.

"My companion has my ticket. He just left to say goodbye to a friend. He'll be back very soon."

The guard asked again. She repeated what she had said. He shook his head, not understanding a word. Clara showed him her passport. He opened it and proceeded to slip it into his pocket.

The large German man in the compartment spoke to the guard. "*Ihr Freund hat ihre Fahrkarte. Er kommt bald zurück.*"

"*Sie hat eine Karte, mein Herr. Sie hat sie nur nicht bei sich.*"

"*Sie kann mir keine Karte zeigen, daher muss sie mitkommen!*"

"He says you must go with him; he says you have no ticket, and you must go with him to the guard's van."

"If he will wait just a few minutes, my friend will be back with my ticket," Clara tried again.

"*Im Wachabteil hinten im Zug. Wenn wir ihre Karte nicht haben, bevor der Zug abfaehrt, muss sie raus!*"

"It is better not to argue with him," the German cautioned her. "I will tell your friend when he comes back."

Clara, terrified, hesitated. The guard was indifferent to her plight and stood his ground. He ushered her out of the compartment and she found herself sandwiched between two uniformed Germans, a policeman in front of her and the guard a step behind; there was little room to move. Passengers were wedged in the corridors with suitcases at their feet. The policeman barged his way through, shoving cases aside, pushing passengers against doors, determined and with a sense of urgency to get to where he was taking Clara.

MAZE SEARCHED FOR Luftmann. He stood on a bench to see over the heads of the crowd. He jumped on the back of a luggage wagon without the driver knowing he was there. Finally he spotted Luftmann way back at the other end of the train. Fifteen minutes had gone by. The wagon turned toward the station exit. Maze got off and navigated his way through to Luftmann. "I should have waited for you yesterday."

"I'm sorry. I was called before the leaders of our protest group. They told me I had to concentrate on what was happening here in Germany, not run around with a French art dealer who lives in England."

"Well, tell them the art dealer has gone back to where he came from — "

Luftmann interrupted, "Not to worry about them. When I told them the real reason for your visit, they wanted to know what they could do. I couldn't get away, and I had no way of contacting you."

"I should have made the explanation myself."

"I was more concerned about the art work," He handed Maze his portfolio. "I was worried that the collage might get unstuck if it was rolled. I laid them flat in the portfolio. The other pieces are of no consequence; they'll certainly pass inspection. And my barns — you will expect to see cows coming out of them, they are so realistic."

"Thank you for all you have done for us, Heinrich, and if it gets too uncomfortable for you to stay, come to London; there will always be room for you and Trude in my home."

"Thank you." A guard blew his whistle; the train began to move. "Go, I will try to stay in touch." Luftmann dissolved into the crowd.

Maze, holding the portfolio tightly, jumped on the train; immediately he felt a heavy hand on his shoulder, a customs inspector, pointed to the portfolio.

Maze made a quick decision; he spoke in English. "I am an art dealer. The portfolio contains art work to sell in London."

"*Haben Sie eine Ausfuhrlizenz — *"

Maze gave him the necessary papers and opened the portfolio.

"*So, Sie interessieren sich auch für deutsche Kunst?*"

"Yes, I have an interest in German art."

"*Diese sind nicht, was ich unsere besten Werke nennen würde. Sind Sie Franzose?*"

"I agree, not the best of German works, but they sell and that is why I come here to buy them."

"*Man hat mir gesagt, dass die Engländer einen schlechten Geschmack in Kunst haben.*"

Maze decided it was best to agree. "You are quite right; it is not fine art, not good enough for Paris, which is why I intend to rid myself of it as soon as I get to London."

His answer had the desired effect; it amused the inspector. They shook hands, and the inspector allowed him to move on through the train. Maze held the portfolio above his head as he pushed his way through the packed corridor. When he reached their compartment Clara was not there.

"Where is the lady who sat in that seat; I left her there. Did she leave? Where is she?" Maze demanded an explanation from any or all of the seated passengers.

The fat German explained, "She is in the guard's van at the back of the train. She had no ticket. You must go quickly; the train is due to leave in four minutes."

Maze wedged the portfolio onto the luggage rack. The train was at least two dozen carriages long, their first class compartment at one end, the guard's van right at the other — ironically, where he'd just come from. The train on the other side of the platform had departed; the crowds were beginning to thin out. He decided it might be better to get off the train — that way he'd probably get to the guard's van quicker than the corridor route. He arrived at the guard's van with two minutes to spare — to find Clara seated on a wooden box with a Nazi guard beside her. Out of breath, both relieved and angry, he insisted on an explanation, saying, "Why is she here? What has she done? Let her go immediately."

The guard ignored his demands and asked to see Maze's passport. He gave it back and told them both to get off the train.

"No. Please. Let me explain," Clara pleaded. "You had the tickets, Paul. I couldn't get him to understand you'd be back any minute. All he wanted to see were the tickets."

Maze immediately produced both tickets. *"Hier haben Sie jetzt die Karten."*

"He has my passport," Clara told Maze.

The policeman understood the word passport. *"Wir werden ihren Reisepass zurückgeben, wenn wir die französische Grenze erreichen."*

"You give her back her passports immediately."

"Nein, damit sie uns nicht aus dem Zug springt."

"He says he is keeping your passport until we reach the French border because you might want to jump the train and stay beyond your permit limit."

Clara was about to say she'd sooner go straight to hell than stay in Germany when Paul put his hand on her arm. "Don't," he whispered, then turned to the guard and politely told him in German, *"Ich verstehe, dass Sie nur ihre Pflicht tun, und hoffe, dass jetzt alle Missverständnisse geklärt sind."*

The guard let Clara go as the train pulled out of the station and indicated they should return to their seats. Clara couldn't stop shaking. "What did you say to him?"

"I told him I understood he was only doing his job, and we were pleased the situation had been cleared up. It is always best to humor petty officials; makes them feel good and doesn't hurt us one bit."

"What about Heinrich?"

"I have the art work; he seems determined to stay."

Back in the compartment the fat German offered his seat to Maze, which he accepted gracefully. Now Clara cuddled up to Paul, needing his protection, wanting him close. "It will be all right. When we arrive at the border I will speak to one of the French guards; they get on before the German bastards get off. The Germans have to exchange papers with them. Remember we are not wanted in Germany; they won't hold on to your passport."

"If you'd left me with the tickets, none of this would have happened." Clara was pouting.

"I'm sorry; I was concentrating on finding Heinrich. You're safe, and you're with me, and that's all that matters for now."

If this wasn't an I-told-you-so situation, then nothing was. Clara had failed in her effort to find Aunt Lizzie, and she had broken her marriage vow. So many thoughts were running through her head. It wasn't a planned affair; it just happened. She and Paul had made love, but then he had a reputation; he loved many women. Was she different? Did he really love her or was it just the circumstances? How could she face Sidney, the family? Nelly, with her wily intuition, would know immediately.

No one was speaking in their carriage; the passengers appeared to be deep in their own thoughts, aware of what they had left and perhaps wondering what awaited them in another land. It was no longer Maze and Mrs. Simon — it was Paul and Clara. Their time in Munich had broken down barriers, the safety net removed. Her relationship with Maze had gone from employer, to friend, to lover. Before she embarked on the journey she thought she was invincible, could accomplish anything she set out to do. She was wrong. Germany destroyed her naiveté; it had changed her. She was no longer an innocent.

Paul had the information he was sent to get. Clara came to Germany with all good intentions and left an angry yet helpless onlooker. Unless a miracle occurred, and the likelihood of that was nonexistent, Lizzie's destiny was already determined. Too much was happening at the same time. Even if she wanted to stay on to keep searching, she couldn't. And in any case, what good would it do? She had done her best. Her head was throbbing, her mind raced around in all directions, and she felt guilty for being able to leave this awful, dreadful deplorable country — too many others were not so fortunate.

Evil ran rampant in the Fatherland; she'd seen it and experienced it. "I never, ever want to come back here," Clara told Paul as the train took them away from Munich and all its destructive forces.

"Just as well," Paul replied. "Don't for one moment think I would let you."

CHAPTER 26

Anna's Wedding

CLARA RETURNED HOME from Munich in time for Anna's marriage to Bernie the following Sunday. It was to be held at the Great Garden Street Synagogue, the same house of worship where she and Sidney made their wedding vows.

"Our Anna would have married much sooner had millions of eligible blokes not been killed in the war," Nelly told her friends, in defense of Anna's prolonged spinsterhood.

When Bernie turned up they grabbed him, even if his war experience only amounted to filling sandbags, which were rarely, if ever, used.

"We don't need no more 'eroes," Nelly announced at the time of Anna's engagement. "Someone had to do the scut work," she'd add, reprimanding anyone who dared question Bernie's allegiance.

Nelly commandeered Henry's horse race winnings, Bernie put his portion of Henry's ill-gotten gains under his bed, and Anna paid five shillings every month into her post office savings account. The day they long awaited had finally arrived.

Two taxis tied with white ribbons stood outside the Half Moon Pub. Cheering patrons, together with the family, waited for Anna who came down from Twenty-One accompanied by Henry and Nelly. Henry ushered Nelly into the first taxi, raising his topper to the crowd before getting into the taxi beside his wife.

Keeping a respectful distance, Clara and Sidney entered the second taxi with Sula and Mannie, and off they went through the crowded streets of Aldgate.

At the synagogue Clara helped Sula climb the stairs to the upper level where women sat. It was difficult enough for Sula to walk, let alone climb steps. They took it slowly. Sula held on to the banister, and Clara held on to Sula.

"Once again tradition favors the man; why we put up with it I don't know," Clara remarked as they reached the top of the staircase. "Can you tell me where in the Torah or the bible it says men get to stay downstairs while women have to crawl up?"

"Maybe they think we deserve to be closer to heaven," Sula stated, thankful for finding an aisle seat. "And, if I have to do this again in my state of health, it might just get me there sooner than you think."

The sanctuary was packed with aunts and uncles, cousins and cousins of cousins, and what seemed like all the shopkeepers and stall owners who traded in Petticoat Lane. Looking down on the men below, Clara could see Mannie and Sidney, both looking handsome in their hired Moss Brothers suits. As for the rest of the men, with prayer shawls draped and heads covered, she couldn't tell one from the other.

Henry led his daughter up the aisle to where Bernie stood in morning suit and top hat as tradition demanded. Henry gave Anna to her soon-to-be husband. Bernie's parents stood on the left side of the canopy, and Henry joined Nelly on the right. The Rabbi read the service in Hebrew.

"You think Anna understands a word of what the Rabbi's saying?" Clara whispered to Sula.

"Doubt it. The Rabbi arrived from Russia last week; he hardly speaks a word of English!" Sula giggled.

Anna hesitated for just a few moments and then very slowly repeated the words the Rabbi had taught her. She'd spent the entire week memorizing, "*Ani l'dodi v'dodi li.* I'm yours and you're mine!"

The Rabbi placed a glass under Bernie's right foot. With a very heavy stomp Bernie smashed it to smithereens, and the congregation shouted out, "*Mazletov!*"

Anna and Bernie were husband and wife.

JEWISH EAST END weddings were interminable, and Anna's was no exception. After the service came the signing of the Ketubah, a document written in Aramaic that no one understood but had to be signed by the wedded couple. Next came the serving of sweet wine and light refreshments in the synagogue. The required Boris portraits followed,

then a two hour respite for the guests to go home to change from day
wear to evening wear, and finally the party at night where a ten course
supper was served. After all that, if you could still move, the band
played the wedding waltz, and the real celebration began.

Table arrangements were always a diplomatic nightmare, and Henry
had worked on them for weeks. You couldn't put your doctor with
one of his patients. You were in big trouble if you placed rival merchants next to their competitors. Cousins always wanted to sit together. The tables seated eight, and there must have been at least twenty-
five cousins — Henry couldn't please every one of them. Older relatives had preference over younger ones, and they complained if they
were seated at the back; still they requested not to be seated too close
to the dance floor — it was too noisy, and they couldn't hear themselves speak.

"I'm prepared for disagreements," Henry warned Nelly as he
handed her his plan. "The only people satisfied at a Jewish wedding
are them seated at the 'ead table with the Rabbi and his wife, and the
immediate family. So, I've got the newlyweds, Bernie's parents and
the best man with us, while the kids' table is just off to the side. Gawd
knows, I've tried to seat the rest of the guests in order of importance."

"You've done your best, love, that's all you can do." Nelly was
relieved he hadn't passed the job on to her.

Solly Tenser and his latest love sat with Clara at the closest relative table with another couple who none of them knew, a man, about
the same age as Henry, and his much younger wife. He introduced
himself. "I'm Alf Mendes, a cousin on your father's side, and this is
my wife Consuelo. I've been living in Portugal for some years now.
Just happened to bump into your dad the other day in the market,
and he invited us to the wedding."

Henry's family were Sephardic. Clara didn't know any of them
well, and she wasn't in the mood to get to know them better now. She
could not get into the swing of the party. She sat through the solemn
ceremony and attended the wedding breakfast, but now as the music
got louder and the guests became rowdier, it was more than she could
stomach. She danced with Sidney a couple of times, a limp doll in
his arms. The band played Yiddish music, not for the Levy family,
they played for the guests who expected it, and they were having a

wonderful time. Men danced the Kazastska, women twirling until they were almost too dizzy to stand up, and old widowed ladies danced together to their own beat. Clara wanted to be anywhere but here.

Back at the table, Sula saw Clara's detachment and suggested they go to the ladies' room. "It's your sister's wedding; you could pretend you're having a good time."

"I can't, Sula. If you'd been with me in Munich, you'd find it difficult too," Clara said as she sat looking at herself in the mirror. "We're free, allowed to be who we are while right at this moment German Jews, no different than us, are prohibited from walking on the same pavement as gentiles, torn from their homes, sent to God knows where." Clara had tears in her eyes as she ranted on. "And back in that hall relatives and descendants of those same Jews dance and sing as if all is well and nothing can touch them. Well, it can, and it will, and I cannot bear to watch them. It just makes me want to go up on that stage and shout, 'STOP, take the blindfolds off!'"

"Being miserable here isn't going to help the Jews in Munich."

"They need to know. I want them to know."

"It's not your day, Clara, it's Anna's. Let it be. And anyway, what do you think they can do about it?" Sula asked.

"Support the few who speak up, make the government take notice."

"This is a celebration, Clara. You can't expect people to sit and mope about what's going on hundreds of miles away."

"That's the point. It isn't that far away."

"Well, it's not on our doorstep."

"Not yet, but it will be, Sula. Mark my words."

"Look, they may not know as much as you, Clara; still, I'm pretty sure they read the papers. And let's face it, if you couldn't find out anything about Aunt Lizzie, and you were actually there, what do you think we can do from here?"

"I don't know, Sula. It just doesn't seem right me being here." Clara wiped the tears from her eyes. "It is all too much."

"How much of this has to do with Maze?"

"Maze? It's not him, it's them. I can't join them, not now, not today. For me it's a bit like going to the circus and seeing a lion tamer walk into the lion's cage knowing one day those lions are going to attack him."

"What about Sidney?"

"Tell him I needed a breath of fresh air," Clara replied as she left.

"You can't just walk out and leave him," Sula called after Clara.

The cloakroom girl handed Clara her coat and the shoes she'd worn when she arrived. "Good thing you got these. Them high heels are a bugger to walk in. Leave 'em here. I'll look after them for you."

Clara nodded and put on the lower heel pumps. "Thanks, put the heels with my husband's coat; it's hanging next to the one you just gave me. He'll take them home for me." Clara placed a shilling in the tip plate. She looked up to see Sidney approaching.

"Where do you think you're going?" Sidney demanded.

"I have to get out of here."

The cloakroom girl perked up. This was going to be interesting — could brighten her evening. Her job had to be the most boring in the whole world. She only did it for the tips, and most of the time they weren't worth much. Mind you, the Jews tipped well. The Irish weren't too bad, if they weren't drunk and out of their minds. The rest of them, the Church of England lot, she'd be lucky if she got a threepenny bit from them.

"You can't leave now." Sidney tried to remove Clara's coat. "Come back to the table. It's Anna's day. Show some respect for your family."

"I've been with the family since early morning, and I'm tired. I don't feel like dancing, Sidney, and if I sit at the table like a wallflower, they'll pull me over to join them. This way they won't even notice I've gone."

"We've one more hour to go. Take your coat off and wait it out."

"No, my head feels as if it's about to explode. I can't take the noise, just not in the mood for any of it."

"If this is because you couldn't find Aunt Lizzie, it's not your fault. There's nothing else you can do."

"I know, but she's my mother's sister, and she should be here with the rest of us."

"It was her decision to marry a German."

"What difference does that make?"

"I'm not stupid, Clara. You used it as an excuse — that's the difference. And it's even more obvious now, right here where there's an ongoing family celebration — and you can't stand to be part of it!"

"One has nothing to do with the other."

"You've not been the same since you got back, and I'm not the only one who's noticed."

"This isn't the time or the place to discuss it, Sidney." Clara walked toward the exit door.

Sidney shouted after her, "There never is a right time with you!"

"Go after her," the cloakroom girl said, giving Sidney a verbal shove and his coat. "I'll keep the shoes, I'll give 'em to one of the family if you don't get back in time. Get a move on; don't let her leave like that."

"You're right. Thanks." Sidney took his coat and moved quickly to catch up with Clara. He had more to say, and if he didn't say it now, it might never get said.

Clara walked in the direction of Aldgate; it looked to Sidney as if she might be going home. He stayed well behind her. She kept walking, and just before she reached the High Street, she stopped at the St. Botolph's bus stop. A bus came along, she got on and went upstairs. The bus took off, Sidney ran after it, jumped on and sat downstairs.

"Shouldn't do that, mate, very dangerous; always another one bringing up the rear," the conductor scolded him.

It was the same bus Clara took every day to Chelsea, except on Sundays it altered its route and went directly to the Kings Road. Pity it didn't do it during the week, had something to do with the traffic or the passengers who worked in the West End. Still, it would take her close enough to the Maze residence. She knew Paul had a gathering at his home that evening and had wanted her there. She'd turned him down, wouldn't have gone even if it weren't Anna's wedding day. She was alone at the top of a bus taking her to a place she could only visit and where she knew she couldn't stay. That one night with Paul had changed everything; now she was living a double life, feeling uncomfortable and guilty.

Sula had hit a nerve when she asked whether Maze was the problem. Had he made her dissatisfied with a life she once seemed to enjoy? She thought about the people at the wedding — not the relatives, you couldn't choose them — the others. Good sorts, all in sequins and satins, guzzling food as if it were their last supper, anticipating the next course, having a rare night out at another's expense.

Clara hated herself for thinking this way. Were they really any different from Eleanor's hangers on? Of course they were, but in a far more positive way. No princely inheritance for them, no pretense, no cover up; they were hard working Jews, mostly immigrants or children of immigrants who hadn't yet made the money, didn't have the refinement of the upper classes. Some would make it, move away and start afresh with a bit of money behind them. Others would stay, either out of choice, like Henry and Nelly, or because it was familiar, what they had always known.

Most of the wedding guests were Henry's friends. Just a few were Nelly's; she chose more carefully than he did. His were the ones whose inhibitions vanished after a few glasses of wine, as they lifted their skirts, and sang and danced, leaving their problems outside just for this one night of celebration. "Knees Up, Mother Brown," they loved it. "The Conga," they'd form in a long line, holding on to each other's waist, snaking 'round the room, knocking chairs and tables as they went, having a wonderful time.

Nelly was classier in many ways. Years ago she and Henry had sung in the music halls, could have been professionals, but she chose not to. Her life revolved in and around Twenty-One. People came to her; she attracted them. She was good company, 'one on her own,' Henry called her, and Clara took after her.

"Oakley Road," the conductor called out her stop.

Clara carefully maneuvered her way down the stairs.

"A pretty girl like you shouldn't be alone at this time of night. Where's your bloke?"

"Oh, got fed up with him," Clara joked as she got off the bus.

Sidney waited until she was safely on the pavement. The conductor rang the bell for the driver to move on. Sidney got off at the next stop. He ran back and caught sight of Clara walking up Oakley Road, then turning onto Cheyne Walk. She waited for a couple of cars to pass before crossing over to the embankment side of the road.

Sidney had never set foot in Chelsea, had no reason to. The only thing he knew about it was the Chelsea Football Club; the team wore blue, rivals of the Arsenal Football Club who wore red. He'd seen them play against each other; both had good players. Just about on a par, though he wouldn't own up to it if he happened to be with a Chelsea supporter.

Just a little way down Clara stopped in the shadow of a large elm tree. It was quiet on the embankment; the sound of the flow of the Thames was soothing. She stood opposite the Maze residence. His guests were leaving. What a difference from the party she'd left in Aldgate. Bet they didn't have to hire their evening suits, she thought. The men escorting the women dressed in haute couture gowns, their furs slung casually around their shoulders, their diamond necklaces gleaming, catching the light from the street lamps, as they waited for their chauffeur driven cars, lined up to take them back to their homes in Knightsbridge, Mayfair, Sloane Square. Not one of them was going back to Aldgate!

Sidney watched too. He'd probably made some of those fur coats the women were wearing! Even the men had fur collars on their over-coats. He wondered if they ever gave a thought to the poor sods who sat in factories making the clothes they wore. It was like watching a film in the picture house. What was Clara thinking? Did she really want to become part of the scene playing out in the house across the road? Him, standing there like the Artful Dodger, skulking and hid-ing, feeling as a stranger must in a foreign land. He had to confront her, put his cards on the table. "Clara?" he called out softly.

She froze, startled at hearing his voice. She turned. "Sidney? What are you doing here?"

"I could ask you the same question, Clara."

She walked over and sat on a bench beside the river.

He paced and pointed across the road. "Is this what you want? Are they who you want to be with?"

"It's not them; it's not the trappings."

One or two yachts, their cabin lights dimmed, were anchored a little way out on the river. A couple of tugboats made their way slowly down stream, she supposed to the docks at the East End, her end of the Thames. She could see the lights of Battersea and Vauxhall on the other side, Chelsea and Lambeth Bridges, opening and closing, and up the river, farther on, Kew and Richmond.

"Then what is it? Why can't you let me give you what you want?" Sidney leaned against the embankment wall, facing the street. "Look at them in their expensive outfits, their Rolls Royces and Bentleys. It's like opening night at the opera. Is it the glamour, Clara? Is that what you hunger after?"

"No, I despise them; they're a bunch of anti-Semites." She did not know that but imagined it was so.

"Then it has to be him. It has to be Maze."

Clara's silence gave Sidney his answer.

"What happens when the book is finished?" he ventured.

"I don't know. Anyway it isn't finished, and I still have a job to do."

"You're breaking my heart, Clara. Don't do this to me. I love you."

Clara rose from the bench and walked away, unable to say what Sidney wanted to hear. He'd always loved her; he was her anchor, her road back. Nelly had warned her she was straddling two worlds, and sooner or later she would have to choose one or the other. It wasn't the glamour that interested her. They could keep it. It was Paul.

She'd overcome the feeling of inadequacy she'd felt in the early days. She could hold her own with Maze's friends and the interesting people who came in and out of his establishment. How could she compare any of them with the Millie Garfinkles of Aldgate whose only interest seemed to be gossip and whether the herrings on the slab at the fishmongers were fresh enough to buy? There was no comparison. Her mother and father had long ago settled and made peace with where they were and what little they had. In contrast, her life was taking a different path, and she had to move on. Aldgate could not be the beginning and end of it all. There had to be something between where she came from and this, Chelsea, with its strange mixture of artists and pretentious aristocrats. Maze had found his niche, sorted the chaff from the wheat. She was still searching.

Sidney hailed a cab. "We're not taking a bus back. I can at least offer you a little luxury every now and then."

His remark brought tears to her eyes. Sidney was a decent, good man; she'd hurt him deeply.

There were no answers for Sidney or Clara that night. They had journeyed from the ridiculous to the sublime in a matter of hours with no conclusion in sight.

CHAPTER 27

Gestapo

HEINRICH LUFTMANN HAD changed out of his more Bohemian garb and dressed in the modern, more severe, acceptable German manner to deliver the portfolio to Maze. He'd borrowed a gray suit and a tan raincoat from Gerhard Buchman, and after donning a Trilby that his grandfather had given him a long time ago, he felt sufficiently indistinguishable from any other man of similar age at the Munich station.

He'd no trouble delivering the portfolio containing the information required by Churchill; it was only after Maze was safely back on the Paris train that he became aware of a man, also in a tan raincoat, watching him over the top of a newspaper. Heinrich turned to leave platform number seven, and, as he did so, he saw the man fold his newspaper and slip it into his trench coat pocket. Taking a quick glance back a few moments later, Heinrich realized the man was just a few yards behind him — he was obviously keeping him in sight.

Heinrich walked ahead slowly — he needed time to think. The mysterious man slowed his pace, too. Should he confront him? No. Not a good idea. At that precise moment Heinrich recognized a train that served the local community coming in on platform number eight. As it screeched to a halt, Heinrich crossed over to the number eight platform. The alighting passengers headed toward the exit gate. Heinrich moved ahead against the throng, hoping he'd lose his follower in the crowd. A minute or so passed, the guard blew his whistle and the train began to chug slowly out of the station. Heinrich made a dash for it and jumped on. He wasn't sure whether the man had seen him. He stayed on board for two stops, then jumped off the train — nowhere near where he lived.

Later, safely back in his atelier, Luftmann settled down to work for a few hours, painting pretty pictures. He hated having to lower his standards, but since Buchman had been given permission to reopen his gallery on condition he show only what was now defined as acceptable art, Heinrich agreed to the assignments. He did so for the sake of his parents who were too old to work and needed his financial assistance.

The Nazis definition of fine art, other than what they'd stolen, had to be of pleasant landscapes, innocent blond children and flowers in a vase. No nudes. No abstracts with hidden meanings. No political statements. It was art for the indiscriminate buyer, art for chocolate boxes and art for tourist attracted to pretty scenes.

Buchman's clientele had changed overnight. No Jews. No serious collectors. No protest art. Now he was forced to show innocuous works, something pleasing to hang over a couch, fill a space on the wall or take home as a souvenir.

The Buchman Gallery had been taken over by the Nazis, and it made Heinrich and his friend Buchman feel like collaborators. The authorities threatened to put Buchman out of business — until he offered a substantial bribe — and it was only then they reluctantly allowed him to open again with their conditions attached. He had little choice. His was a family concern, run by his father and his father's father before him. Gerhard Buchman had money, but not knowing how long or even if his gallery would survive, he could take no chances. Compromise was the name of the game, and the only way he could allay his guilt was by working secretly against the regime.

The cuckoo clock on the wall struck seven. Where did the time go? Trude was due to arrive at Heinrich's atelier any moment, and here he was, still in his German, borrowed business suit. She'd think he'd gone mad, not a good beginning for a romantic rendezvous. He was looking forward to the evening and being with Trude; they hadn't been together in a long while. He had a quick bath and came down stairs to set up a small table close to the fireplace with glasses, plates, cutlery and candles. Nothing fancy — he had nothing fancy. He'd bought the wine, his one extravagance, and removed the cork, allowing it to breathe. The chicken was roasting nicely in the oven. He poured himself a drink — and waited and waited.

Two hours later Trude arrived.

"What happened? Why are you so upset? Did they find out? Do they know about the information you gave us?" Heinrich asked, both worried and guilty at the same time. "Oh, God, it's all my fault."

"No. Well, yes, in a way, but they'd have found out sooner or later anyway. It happened outside the factory. I was leaving when two men, who said they were Nazi officials, came up to me and shoved me in their car. They took me to their headquarters and interrogated me. They showed me a photo of some woman I had never seen in my life, said something about some art dealer who had just left the country — must have been Maze. Asked me whether I knew him, what he was doing here. It just went on and on. I told them I had no idea what they were talking about. Finally they let me go." She sank down on a chair at the table.

"They've linked you with me; we'll have to get out of Munich." Heinrich paced the floor. "I'll make inquiries in the morning. We can't stay here — it's too dangerous."

"No, don't panic, it's over; they won't bother me again. I'll have a bath, and I'll feel better. I will not give in to them."

Heinrich wished he could be as determined as Trude; she was amazing. "Want me to wash your back?"

"No, you see to dinner. I'll just have a soak and be down to join you very soon."

"Don't rush. My dinner can't get any worse than it is already. Just put on one of my robes, and we'll have a glass of wine before we dine on my overcooked chicken and mushy vegetables."

"Thanks, Heinrich."

"Those bastards," Heinrich groaned to himself. Not only do they destroy my art, they ruin my cooking! He tried to hide his fear with a light touch. But he knew Nazi officials were to be taken seriously, and this wasn't the time to tell Trude he'd been followed at the station.

THE FIRE WAS warm and the wine superb. Glad to be together, Trude wouldn't discuss the interrogation. "Let's put it aside," she said. "We don't have to bring them home with us."

She was right. He'd been through a few of these experiences himself. They both knew that one must never give out any information.

One must act normally and appear, if not stupid, then certainly unaware of any wrongdoing.

"I don't suggest you give up art to become a chef, but, on the
other hand, the chicken was delicious and the wine divine. We spend
so little time together; it's a treat just to be here with you."

They went up to bed when the fire died down and made love. It
had been a romantic evening. They lay snuggling, falling asleep,
wrapped around each other, only to be awakened an hour later by
banging on the front door.

"I'm not opening it," Luftmann muttered in his sleep. He held
Trude closer.

It didn't stop. Whoever it was kept banging, then the sound of an
object hitting the door and the latch breaking, boots on the stairs.
Two thugs in Nazi uniforms stood at the open door, ordering them
out of bed. "*Nackte Schweine, zieht Euch an.*"

Downstairs Luftmann could hear what he gathered to be henchman hacking their way through his studio. The one Brown Shirt standing at the foot of the bed gave Trude no time to find her shoes. He
pushed her from the room and down the stairs. The other waited
impatiently for Luftmann to dress. "*Beeilen Sie sich, wir haben nicht die
ganze Nacht. Wo Sie hingehen, müssen sie nicht gut aussehen.*"

"Where you taking her? Leave her alone!" Heinrich shouted.

The Brown Shirt ignored him, telling him once again he hadn't
all night to wait.

Outside they were thrown into the back of a covered lorry. The
Nazis jumped in after them. The driver took off. As his eyes became
accustomed to the dark, Luftmann could see familiar faces among the
women and children; some were members of his group. Trude, on the
other side of the lorry, was scantily clothed and shivering. He asked if
he could sit next to her.

"*Bleiben Sie, wo Sie sind.*"

Not allowed. He stayed where he was.

They drove for about ten minutes. When the lorry stopped they
were herded out and marched into a church cemetery. There they
were lined up against the cemetery wall. Trude ran to be next to Heinrich. As she came to him the order was given to shoot — she fell.

The execution squad continued to fire; they fired until every one had fallen. The commander ordered a marksman to make sure they were all dead.

He marched to the wall, kicked each body to see if it might still be alive, got no response and reported back, *"Alle tot, Kommandant."*

They jumped back into the lorry, pleased with their accomplishment, and left.

Luftmann was wounded; when kicked he'd played dead. It had all happened so quickly. One moment they were in the afterglow of sated passion, the next they were in front of a death squad. Trude, the woman he adored, lay three bodies down. He inched toward her, lifted her and held her in his arms, trying to revive her. It was useless; she was dead. He examined the other bodies. They were all dead. He pinched himself to make sure he was still alive, not having a nightmare. The pain alone should have assured him, but it was all so quick, so terrible . . .

He removed a shirt from one of the bodies and tore it into strips. He tied one of the strips around the bullet wounds in his left leg to create a tourniquet. Another bullet had grazed his ear; yet another had gone through his arm. He took another strip and bound his arm. He couldn't leave Trude there. With an almighty effort he summoned sufficient strength to drag her away. He held her, caressed her and stayed with her, sobbing, sheltering her under a tree until sleep overcame him.

With the first light of morning a bird singing in the branches above woke him. Trude lay dead at his side. His leg throbbed, and the bandage on his arm was sticky with blood. He thought he heard a voice. He lifted his head. Was that a priest kneeling beside him? What was this? A vision, a dream?

The vision spoke. "How long have you been here?" the priest asked. "Who did this?"

"I don't know, a few hours, a few days?" Heinrich was incoherent.

"Come, let me help you. Can you walk?" the priest asked.

"I don't know," Heinrich answered.

The priest helped him up. "Put your arm around my shoulder, the church is just over there."

Heinrich wasn't a religious man, couldn't remember the last time he'd been inside a church. But someone, something, was looking after him. Maybe it was God. Then why, his mind demanded, didn't God save Trude?

"I can't leave her, my Trude. A doctor, she needs a doctor, please . . ."

"She's gone. You cannot bring her back." The priest gently removed Trude from his embrace.

"They, those pig Nazis, there are bodies on the other side of the wall. I don't know who they are . . . Yes, I do, they are Jews, Jews in a lorry, women, children — "

"We will pray for them; it doesn't matter to us that they are Jews. We are all God's children."

The priest placed his cloak over Trude. "We will bury her and the others. And when this nightmare is over I will arrange to have the bodies moved to one of their cemeteries. As long as I survive that is my promise to you."

Heinrich thanked God for early morning mass. Had the priest not come to perform mass he would not have survived. He removed the ring he'd given Trude and placed it on his own finger. He lifted Trude one more time, kissed her on the forehead. "They will pay for this, my darling."

"Come . . . " The priest helped Heinrich to stand, and, with his support, Heinrich hobbled toward the open door of the church.

CHAPTER 28

Nelly

NELLY SAT IN her favorite chair beside the stove listening to the radio. Occasionally she'd nod off or, as she preferred to call it, lose herself. Henry, who rarely slept in the daytime, chided her for falling asleep in the late afternoon, especially when he was bursting to tell her his latest accomplishment. He held off until she was fully awake.

"Put the kettle on, Nelly. We've got important business to discuss."

"I was just resting my eyes, imagining you and me dancing to Harry Hudson's Band all those years ago."

"Get away with yer," Henry joshed, knowing that dancing to Harry Hudson's band was no more on Nelly's mind than flying in the air. "Pull yerself together."

"No peace for the wicked," Nelly said as she begrudgingly got up to fill the kettle. Henry had just come back from a meeting with Solly Tenser. Generally, on principal, Nelly was dead against anything involving Solly Tenser; but when Henry presented Solly's proposition, it did, on the surface, appear legal, and it didn't actually involve Solly. It came about through a mate of his who'd opened a small chemist shop in Leather Lane.

"Solly said he wouldn't be seen dead working a stall, that's why he offered it to me."

"What's the catch, Henry?"

"There ain't one. It's just not up his alley; he don't like to be confined to one occupation."

"We all know that. The more he stays out of sight, the less likely he is to be caught." Nelly was onto Solly and his shady deals.

"Be that as it may, it's not for him. I wouldn't have to lay out a

233

penny. I'd get me stock from the shop inventory, and the owner would get a percentage of me sales."

"I dunno, Henry. Solly's a good friend, but I wouldn't touch him with a barge pole when it comes to business."

"Solly swore to me, on the Pope's life, it was all kosher, and he wouldn't accept a penny as the intermediary," Henry assured her.

"The Pope? He swore by the Pope?"

"What's wrong with that?" Henry asked.

"I'd have believed him more if he'd used the Chief Rabbi!"

"You're nit pickin', Nelly."

"Someone's got to see a bit of sense 'round here. You given this any thought? You'll be standing outside in all weathers. Is that what you want again?"

"It's not like I'm wiv the penguins in the Artic. If it gets too cold, I'll pop into the shop and 'ave a cup of tea!" Henry answered. "Bloomin' sight better than Titchfield Street. No caffs there; you could freeze your bloomin' balls off in Titchfield Street in the winter."

HENRY HAD A series of jobs since marrying Nelly. In the first few months of their marriage he was a conductor on the buses until the transport unionists called a strike. After that he never went back. Then he tried working in the Spitafields Meat Market — dead animals and blood all over the place, coming home each evening looking as if he'd committed murder. It made him sick to his stomach. Nelly had to steep his overalls in a big iron tub on the stove and boil them till the stains came out. The steam from the daily wash engulfed the parlor so much so the wallpaper started to peel off the walls and played havoc with their girls' hair. Henry left the meat business.

He did his bit in the war effort — working for a company that made buttons for army uniforms but was laid off when the man he replaced returned, unharmed, and took his old job back. For a short time Henry worked for his uncle Moses, toffee-maker supreme, and brought home bags of sticky cut off bits. The kids couldn't get enough of it, but it was so hard it either broke their teeth or caused deep cavities, and Nelly had to take them, often screaming in agony, to the dentist. When adding up the pros and cons the toffee interlude made no financial sense, especially when the dentist's bills outweighed the pittance Moses paid him. For a while Henry was a bookie's runner — illegal as all get out — until Bernie came into the family and took the job over. Then he opened the stall in Titchfield Street, too far from Aldgate and never a successful enterprise.

"What yer think?" he asked, hoping Nelly would jump at the idea.

"I think I haven't had time to think," Nelly answered. "Give me time, can't suddenly drop something like this and expect an immediate answer."

Nelly did give serious consideration to the offer of a stall in Leather Lane. Number one, she thought, if it takes him away from betting on the horses — at least during the week — that alone would be worth it. Number two, he'd be out from under her feet, and number three, purely for financial reasons, it might be a good idea. Anna's wedding had cost them a packet, and Nelly still had the caterer to pay.

Nelly's lot in life was to look after her family. Mannie was making a bit of money now, but it wasn't a regular job. In her estimation, writing was what you did in your spare time. If you didn't get a pay packet at the end of every week, you weren't — to her mind — gainfully employed. Sula, in her condition, could hardly go looking for work, and what little they had, Nelly couldn't take from them. Sidney and Clara both had good jobs and insisted on paying their way, but she expected they'd be moving out soon and that money would stop. She put her cup back in the saucer, poured a second cup and slowly gave her verdict. "We're not on the bread line, yet, Henry, but we're not far from it. Take the stall, do your best, and keep Solly Tenser as far away as possible from it."

CLARA WAS IN a nervous state after she came back from Munich, Nelly observed. Hadn't been the same since the day she left, couldn't even make it through Anna's wedding celebration. And Sidney, well, he wasn't the same either — walked around as if he'd lost a shilling and found a penny.

Clara had done her best, but Lizzie was still missing, and Nelly knew she had to keep up the search. She'd made a visit to the Jewish Board of Deputies, met with a Mr. Bloom who expressed his sympathy but could do very little. They were inundated with inquiries, he told her; there were hundreds of cases like hers. A few Jews were getting out, but it was a losing battle.

"We're doing all we can. I'll put your sister's name on file," Bloom promised. "If I hear anything more, I'll contact you, but don't get your hopes up; communication with the authorities in Germany have broken down, and we're — well, to tell you the truth — stymied."

"What about the foreign office?" Nelly asked.

"Oh, you can forget them, they're useless, and I'm beginning to think they might be in cahoots with the Germans."

IT WAS SHORTLY after the war in 1918 that Lizzie Solomon announced she was going to Europe. All hell broke loose in the Solomon family, not unlike what occurred when Clara declared her intention to leave Abbott, except this upheaval was decidedly worse. Lizzie's parents, Abe and Sarah Solomon, had already chosen a husband for her: Arnie Rappaport. Lizzie declined Arnie's advances. "He's a *schlemiel*," she stated flatly.

"Yes, but he's a rich *schlemiel*," Lizzie's father proclaimed.

"Well, that's not a good enough reason to marry him," Lizzie declared, and Nelly agreed with her.

The matchmaker found another prospect: not as wealthy, reasonably presentable and nice enough. He too was rejected. Eventually, after the numerous offerings, along came Jonas Liebowitz from a very religious family. It was after Jonas that Lizzie informed her parents she had no intention of marrying a man she herself hadn't chosen, especially a religious one who would saddle her with umpteen children and keep her slaving in the kitchen.

"I'll find someone for myself," she declared. "The lot you've come up with are," she found it difficult to put it into polite words, "well, they're all right, but they're not right for me, especially Jonas."

Jonas' father took himself off to the synagogue and stayed there praying for Lizzie's redemption, while Jonas' mother hid her head in shame. Jonas Liebowitz, done in by it all, packed up and moved to Palestine.

Nelly took it all in her stride, did the shopping for her family and for the Liebowitzs, who feared they might be ostracized for Lizzie having turned down their son. Nelly, the eldest of the eleven Solomon children, supported Lizzie's decision, which sent her own father, together with Jonas's father, back to the synagogue for another three days of prayer. Up until then, Lizzie's father hadn't set foot in a synagogue since the day he was married. He must have thought a curse was upon them and only God could do something about it! The fathers together asked for guidance since never again did they want to go through what they had just suffered with Lizzie. To add insult to injury, Lizzie took a job as a lady's maid to a wealthy gentile family who owned a villa in the south of France.

It was in France that Lizzie met Fritz Schmidt, a Lutheran and a German. Lizzie wrote to her parents, telling them she had met the man of her dreams, and she was going to marry Fritz. First they forbid her, then when Lizzie ignored them and married Fritz in Munich, Mr. and Mrs. Solomon sat *shiva* for the full seven days and stayed in mourning for a year, which is what orthodox Jews do when one of their own married out.

Nelly stayed in touch with her sister without her parents knowing, and it wasn't until both parents died that Lizzie was welcomed back into the family. Lizzie and Fritz came to London on holiday and stayed with Henry and Nelly. Fritz, with his few words of English, amused them by trying to learn the language and mixing in German and Yiddish, neither of which Nelly or Henry understood — but it didn't matter. Fritz and Lizzie made a fine couple, and they were happy.

With their parents gone, Nelly and Lizzie could talk freely about their upbringing and why they both abandoned the orthodox way of life. It was stifling. It made chattels out of the women and tyrants out of the men. Although it hadn't made either of them reject their heritage; it did make them look at it in a different way.

Nelly married Henry, her choice not theirs. She was lucky; she happened to meet him before the matchmaker was called in. Her parent's only objection to Henry was that he came from a Sephardic background, and they were Ashkenazi. The Rabbi said it was perfectly permissible for them to marry. Henry passed the test. They brought up their children as Jews, neither Sephardic nor Ashkenazi, just Jews. Lizzie, having no children and married to a non-Jew, assimilated. She never denied her background. Having accepted Germany as her home and Fritz as her husband, how ironic it was for them both to be punished for what she had forsaken so many years before.

Nelly recognized a similar situation arising with Clara; in many ways she was very like her Aunt Lizzie, headstrong and intelligent and wanting to get out of the day-to-day existence of Aldgate. It was obvious Sidney would never be Clara's intellectual equal. When Clara met Sidney she was studying French, taking night classes at Toynbee Hall with other young women and men wanting to better themselves. Sidney was a worker, not an educated man; still, he worshipped her and proved it in many ways. He gave up his most precious possession, his motorbike, he stayed committed to her while she dated other men, and he stayed away before finding an excuse to meet with her again. He still loved her when she looked like a purple spotted Dalmatian, and he only went to football matches on Saturday afternoons when Arsenal played at home. Clara had done everything in her power to dissuade him, but his tenacity won out, and they seemed happy until Paul Maze came into the picture.

Nelly understood Clara's attraction to Maze. Even if she hadn't met him, she figured he was everything Sidney wasn't. He'd introduced Clara to interesting people, he'd given her the chance to travel and he'd treated her as an equal. And now they'd gone away together, to France, to Germany, and Nelly knew the attraction had to have gone further. Even if it wasn't physical, and she wasn't so sure of that, there was a lot more to stimulate Clara in Chelsea than there would ever be in Aldgate. Clara saw in Maze what she would have liked Sidney to be, someone she couldn't tie 'round her little finger.

NELLY HEARD THE door downstairs slam and Henry's huffing as he climbed the stairs; she had to get him to a doctor before his lungs collapsed. Twenty Woodbines a day, a cheap cigarette said to be made of the sweepings off the floor in the tobacco factory, was what he smoked. "That's what's causing it," she'd told him so many times.

"My gawd!" She looked at the time on the old clock on the mantelpiece. "I had no idea how late it is — got to get on with the dinner."

"And what is the specialty of the house tonight?" Henry inquired.

"Wait and see." Nelly gave him her usual answer.

"We had that last night!"

"And you're getting it again! How'd it go?"

"We're in business, Nelly. Monday, next week, I'm moving my stall from Titchfield Street to Leather Lane. Going to make it look smashing, redesign it, clean it up. Got it all planned." Henry was backing toward the door to the bedrooms, one hand behind his back.

"What you got there?"

"Oh, it's just a little something. I was going to give to you on your birthday." Henry put the package on the table.

"I can't wait six months. Who knows what could happen by then? Might be dead for all we know."

Henry slowly unwrapped the package. First the newspaper. Then the brown paper. Then the tissue paper. The last layer he left for Nelly to remove, and when she did there appeared the most beautiful Dresden china figurine of the Yardley Lavender Lady and her three children. Her face flushed with pleasure. "Where'd you get it, Henry?"

"Well, Mrs. Levy, you're married to a fully authorized purveyor of Yardley soaps and creams; from now on this house will smell of all things lavender. What do you think of that?"

Nelly jumped up and gave him the biggest hug she could imagine. "Henry Levy, you really are a miracle man!"

"Well, you have to agree it's a bit better than coming home smelling of rotten meat from Spitafields Market!"

CHAPTER 29

Maze Residence — Chelsea

ROGERS HANDED CLARA a letter as she was about to leave for the day. "You might want to read it before you go." He stood by while she opened the envelope.

The letter came from the publishing company. "Oh, dear," she said as she read, "they require the first ten chapters of the book by the end of the week. We're still two short."

"May I suggest you insist he concentrate on his writing. His art show is organized, he's done his research in France and your Germany trip is over."

"I've tried, Rogers. It's not easy; it's the constant stream of visitors — they take up so much of his time." Clara groaned.

"I'll endeavor to keep the visitors at bay; you keep him focused on the book," Rogers replied. He understood her predicament.

"I'll keep trying." Clara marched back up the stairs and pushed open the studio door. "Here, Paul, read this; it's from your publisher."

"What does it say?" Paul continued working on a painting.

"The editor wants to know if you have any intention of finishing your book." She was close to shouting as she attempted to be heard over the third movement of Beethoven's "Fifth Symphony". She knew she was stretching the truth a bit, but something had to get his attention. "First thing tomorrow morning we need to concentrate on the next two chapters."

Paul put down his brushes and stood back from his easel. "Why wait for tomorrow? I know exactly where we left off. We can start now. You ready?"

"It's late, Paul. Tomorrow is soon enough. I said I'd be home for supper."

"You tell me I have to write, and then you say you have to leave. I have no plans for the evening, and I'm in the mood to write."

"You're impossible!"

Paul came to her and placed a kiss on her cheek. "Let's begin before I forget what I have to say. Rogers purchased a dozen new notebooks for you. They're in a carton under the table."

Clara crawled under the table to retrieve one.

"At one of my billets . . . "

"Wait a minute. Turn down the music; I can't make out what you're saying."

Maze obliged and lifted the needle from the record. "You ready now?"

"Yes."

"At one of my billets there was an old woodcutter who couldn't read or write. He had three sons, all in the army. His wife had a little education, and she would read their letters aloud to him. 'It's always the same,' he said. 'They always tell us we are winning, yet we never win.'"

"Paul, that does not follow your previous dictation. It's come out of nowhere." Clara thought for a moment, "It needs an introduction."

"What I'm trying to say is this woodcutter knew his sons were fighting a losing battle, and he could do nothing to save them."

"Then that's what you should write."

"Which reminds me," Maze picked up a clipping he'd taken from *The Times*. "I marked a paragraph for you to read; it's from a speech Churchill gave at the Oxford Union Society last week. Here, read it."

I think of Germany, with it's splendid clear-eyed youth marching forward on the road of the Reich singing their ancient songs, demanding to be conscripted into an army; eagerly seeking the most terrible weapons of war, burning to suffer and die for their fatherland.

Clara returned the clipping to Maze.

"If the Prime Minister thinks he can work out an agreement with Hitler, he's dreaming. They're worlds ahead of us in preparations."

Maze hesitated. "You realize the terrible weapons reference comes from Heinrich's friend Trude."

"I'm glad our trip to Munich was of some use."

"I know how hard it was for you in Germany; you were very brave."

Clara put down her pencil. "It was the situation, and we had only each other."

"Your family must be deeply concerned for your aunt's safety."

"They are." Clara wanted to move on.

Maze turned his attention back to his dictation. Words tumbled out. He was eager to tell his story, to describe the effect war had on those who served.

Clara took it all down in shorthand; he spoke so quickly she'd filled page after page, and it was getting late. "I need to transpose this while it is still fresh in my mind, Paul." She looked at the clock on the wall; it was past eight. "I have to go. I can work on this at home."

"Stay the night."

"Don't be ridiculous. I'm in enough trouble as it is. I'll be back in the morning, early."

"We should be together. We should finish our work together."

"No, Paul. I have a home to go to — and a husband."

"I forget. I try to forget."

"I can't." Clara turned away and went to tidy her desk. That done, she started downstairs. It was then she saw Rogers, taking two steps at a time, in a great hurry on his way up. "What is it, Rogers?"

"Mr. Maze, you must come down now, sir," Rogers demanded as he stood on the landing outside the studio. "There is a Mr. Luftmann in the foyer — "

"Heinrich?" Paul, who'd gone back to his painting, dropped his brush, came hurrying out to push Rogers out of the way and rush downstairs to the foyer. Clara and Rogers went tumbling after him to find Heinrich resting wearily on a walking stick, his clothes far too big for him, his left arm bent in a makeshift sling and blood stains on his right trouser leg.

Rogers and Maze helped him into the living room and seated him in an armchair. Rogers rang for Maggie to bring a basin of hot water and towels.

Heinrich was exhausted and close to tears; he wanted to explain. "I, I . . . "

Paul stopped him, putting his arm around his friend's shoulder. "Time enough for that — you must be starving. What can I get you?"

"A drink, water . . . "

"Brandy, you need a shot of brandy."

Clara found the tray holding decanters and glasses, and brought it over to Paul

"Phone Dr. Cunningham, tell him we have a man here who needs immediate attention," Maze yelled out to Rogers, who was already on his way out the door to the telephone.

Paul poured a brandy for Heinrich and one for himself. Mrs. Smithers, Maggie, Rogers, all came into the room, none of them knowing quite what to do.

"Soup, that's what he needs," Mrs. Smithers decided and ran back to the kitchen. Maggie now stood beside Heinrich, gently wiping his brow with a damp cloth.

Doctor Cunningham, who lived close by, arrived a few minutes after Rogers' call. He knew Maze was not one to panic. If he called, it had to be something urgent. After examining Heinrich, he suggested he should be in the hospital. "He's dehydrated, and, untreated, the leg wound could become gangrenous — not sure you can look after him as well here."

"If at all possible, it might be best to keep him out of hospital." Paul took Cunningham aside and spoke quietly. "It's a political thing; don't want the newspapers picking it up."

"I'll look after him, I know I can," Maggie told Cunningham. "Up in the Highlands we have no doctor; we look after each other. Just tell me what to do."

"He'll need a nurse, Maggie, but you can assist her," Cunningham said kindly. "He'll need constant attention. I know a nurse I can call upon at a moment's notice — you can trust her. In the meantime, Maggie, run a warm bath. Maze, you stay with him in the bathroom, and I'll be back with medical supplies. The bullet looks like it came out on the other side. I'll check on it more closely later. As for his arm, it's muscle injury — he must've injured it somehow in his escape. Needs a more supportive sling on it. Still, it's a miracle he's still alive."

"Then you think you can keep him out of hospital?" Paul asked again, needing the reassurance.

Cunningham nodded. "Oh, I think that can be arranged. Considering what the man has obviously endured and the distance he traveled, he's in relatively good condition. Mentally? Well, that may be another problem. First we'll take care of his physical side."

"Thank you. I knew I could depend on you." Maze felt a load lifting from his shoulders.

"That's what the Hippocratic Oath is all about, Maze." Dr. Cunningham replied in the matter-of-fact way most doctors have of making little out of what appears to others as insurmountable.

Clara, looking on, was feeling completely helpless. "What can I do?"

"Hold his hand. That's probably the best advice I can give you. He needs the warmth of a woman, and he'll have you and Maggie, not just a bunch of old fogies hanging over him," Cunningham replied.

Heinrich smiled. "Two pretty girls. I must have arrived in heaven!"

THE MOMENT SHE arrived on the premises, Nurse Collins took charge. She dismissed Maze and Rogers, saying she and Maggie would see to the bath. Later, after the doctor had examined Heinrich more carefully, she dressed the wound on Heinrich's leg, fashioned a new sling to support his arm and shoulder that provided relief, and settled him back into the bed in a spare bedroom on the ground floor with a bathroom adjacent — the perfect location in Maze's large house, comfortable and convenient, while not revealing his presence.

"Cook will feed you, Maggie will spoil you, and Clara and I will be here for you," Maze assured Heinrich. "I've sent Rogers over to Winston's flat here in town. I want him to hear your story first hand."

"Hope I don't fall asleep before he gets here," Heinrich said, wearily settling back against goose feathered pillows and drawing a blanket up to his neck with his uninjured hand. "I'll try to stay awake . . ."

Rogers announced Churchill's arrival.

Winston came in his slippers, wearing a dressing gown over striped pajamas.

"You didn't have to dress up for the occasion," Paul noted wryly.

"You want me, you take me as I am — don't need a top hat at this time of night!" It was only then that he first laid eyes on Heinrich. "My God, man, what have they done to you?"

"You should have seen him when he arrived. I thought he was about to drop dead on the spot. I'm truly sorry to have disturbed your rest, Winston. I was only trying not to have Heinrich repeat his ordeal more than once," Maze apologized.

Rogers, Maggie and Clara stood back, allowing Maze and Churchill time with Heinrich.

Churchill waved away Paul's concerns. "When a fellow is pulled out of bed in the middle of the night there is no time for sartorial elegance. I do apologize, Mrs. Simon."

"Nine o'clock is not the middle of the night, Winston," Paul informed him.

"It is for me, my friend. I have to catch sleep when I can; far too often it eludes me."

Rogers waited while their repartee continued, and seeing that it might not, cleared his throat and interrupted, saying, "Will there be anything else, sir?"

"I'd like you to drive Mrs. Simon home a little later, Rogers."

"Of course."

"Maggie, could you make a cup of hot cocoa for Mrs. Simon?"

"And you, sir, would you like one too?" Maggie addressed Churchill.

"That would be very nice, young lassie. Very nice, indeed."

HEINRICH, FEELING MORE comfortable than when he arrived, related his experience from the moment the Secret Police barged into his home. Clara sat with him and held his hand.

"We were at home, Trude and me. The storm troopers broke down my door, held us at gun point and threw us into a truck with many other frightened people. We were driven to a cemetery. They lined us all up against a wall and fired, execution style. Trude died instantly. The Germans made sure we were all dead, except they made a mistake with me. I pretended to be dead. I stayed where I was all night, then I dragged myself to the church close to the cemetery where a priest took me in. I stayed there about a week; it might have been longer — they tended my wounds as best they could. I lost all recollection of time.

"Two of the priests there were being relocated to Belgium. They provided me clothes from a bag of old clothing they kept for the poor. Then they gave me a cassock to wear over those clothes, and some money, and I went with them. Finally I got on a train going to Le Havre. There I caught the ferry to Dover and eventually the boat train to London. I had Paul's address hidden in my shoe. I walked from Victoria Station."

"You walked — in your state of health?" Winston was flabbergasted.

Maze couldn't hide his guilt. "I feel terrible, my — our being there must have alerted them."

"No, Paul, I was being followed before you came, and Trude's days were numbered; she knew they'd find her somehow. A Jew in a munitions factory had little hope of surviving. Once you're signed up for government work, you can't leave. She was stuck." Heinrich broke down in tears. He'd not slept for days — and his eyes kept closing in search of sleep.

"Trude's sacrifice will be recognized. The information she gave us is invaluable. I'm using it to change the minds of stubborn members of Parliament. Get some rest, Heinrich, I'll be back tomorrow — we'll talk more then."

Nurse Collins tucked Heinrich in for the night. Clara said good night to one and all and waited outside the front door of the house for Rogers to bring the car around, thankful she didn't have to take the bus. Meanwhile, Winston and Paul settled in to finish the carafe of brandy.

"If this doesn't prove what I've been going on about for the last few months, I don't know what does," Churchill said. "What will it take for our former prime minister, that India rubber man Ramsay Macdonald, to wake up? Mind you, I'm told he speaks to his dead wife every night, wonder at times whether he's all there. Wish she'd talk some sense into him." He added, "The present one, Stanley Baldwin, ain't much better."

Maze chuckled.

"It doesn't amuse me in the least." Winston's anger had surfaced. "They try everything they can to discredit me and isolate me. I won't let them. Refuse to let them. We cannot. We must not stand by and allow a villainous, errant, rarely muzzled, uneducated Austrian corporal to take over Europe. And we've got to get rid of the blinders on our damned half-witted government. They must put me back on the front benches of Parliament where I belong. We have to prepare for war. It's as obvious as the nose on my face and that ridiculous little mustache on that very dangerous ugly man's visage!"

CHAPTER 30

Half Moon Pub

ALF, THE PROPRIETOR of the Half Moon Pub and an old friend of the Levy family, was one of a host of marriageable men Lizzie's parents had long ago suggested — and Lizzie rejected. Her refusal had much to do with Alf's chosen profession. She couldn't see herself in the role of a publican's wife. Nevertheless, his feelings for her had not diminished, and when the news of her disappearance became common knowledge he looked at the larger picture, at all the missing Lizzies, and felt he couldn't ignore the situation any longer.

After the excitement of Anna's wedding had abated, Alf climbed the stairs at Twenty-One to have a cup of tea and a heart-to-heart with Nelly. He found her in the parlor, staring into space, lost in thought.

"Hello, luv, got a few minutes for an old friend?" he said as he came through the ever-open door.

Nelly turned to see Alf in the half-light of the parlor. "For you, Alf, always," she replied. "I'll put the kettle on."

"Can't have a decent conversation in the pub; don't let me alone for a minute down there. Wanted to see how you're doin'."

"Worried about Lizzie, of course. Clara did what she could. Can't ask for more than that, can we?"

"Terrible what's going on there. Perhaps when things settle down we'll have a clearer picture."

"It ain't going to settle down, Alf. It gets worse every day."

"So I hear, Nelly. I've been goin' over the Germany problem in me mind, mainly because of a bloke 'oo came into the pub the other evening, not a regular, mind you, but we got talkin' — said he was a captain of a small ship. After a few drinks he told me 'e'd just brought in a couple of 'undred refugees, dropped them off in Yarmouth and says there's an organization that takes 'em in. Couldn't do it legally — government's dead against it — but did it anyway. I wasn't about to ask no questions, said 'ees prepared to do it again, but the people 'ee brings in need 'elp. The lucky ones, the ones 'ee gets out, arrive with nuffin' — just the clothes on their back, not a penny to their name. Who knows, Lizzie could be one of them one day."

"From your mouth to God's ears," Nelly said as she poured the boiling water from the kettle into the teapot.

"I think the Jewish Board of Deputies might be in on it," Alf assumed.

"I went to them; they weren't optimistic."

"Their hands are tied, Nelly; they have to appear to abide by the law. Still, what they do behind our backs, we really don't know."

"I hope you're right, Alf."

"But we can do our bit, too. We can support that captain and 'elp the refugees when they get 'ere."

"I dunno, Alf. The wedding cost a mint. We're still paying that off."

Alf took a deep breath. "It's not your money I want, Nelly."

"Got plenty of old clothes; they can have them."

"That too, but I need something else. Remember my Friday Music 'all Evenings? I'm starting them up again. I'll charge an entrance fee, not much, maybe a shilling or two, and have a jar on the bar for spare change; the proceeds will go to a fund for resettlement of the refugees. I've signed up a few acts. All of them doin' it for gratis, and you and Henry are on my list of preferred performers."

Nelly looked at him as if he'd completely lost his marbles.

"And before you turn me down I want you to think of Lizzie and all the others like 'er. You can't refuse me, Nelly, not when you know who we're doin' it for — "

"That's what I call emotional blackmail, Alf."

"Call it what you like, Nelly. You and Henry have to take part. I've got some of the Aldgate lads putting up notices in the shops, the shul and the markets, even got one at St. Botolph's. And, by the way, your 'enry knows all about it, and 'e's ready and willing."

"Didn't say anything to me."

"He asked me to tell you when he wasn't about."

"Couldn't do it himself, eh? I'll be having a few words with him if he ever dares to show his face up here again."

Alf could see Nelly was warming to the ideas as he continued to persuade her. There couldn't be a better cause; she had to agree on that.

"All right, Alf," Nelly said, tapping her fingers on the table. "You've worked on me conscience, and it's done the trick."

"Done the trick, done the trick," Boadicea repeated.

"That perishing bird!" Nelly got up from the table to throw a cloth over Boadicea's cage.

"The sailor never came back then?" Alf noted, half smiling.

"If you ask me, he never had any intention," Nelly replied. "Still, I have to admit the bird adds a bit of color to the room. But don't you ever tell anyone I said that. Of course, we'll have to do a bit of warbling up here before we perform again downstairs. Don't even know if I've got a voice these days; might need a handful of Boadicea's birdseed to get going. Mind you, Henry's not bad to listen to when he sings in the bathtub on Friday nights!"

"You'll be like two nightingales singing in the woods." Alf chuckled.

"More like two owls hooting in the dark!" Nelly came back at him, never lost for a quick retort.

"It's them poor souls who land on our shores, that's who we're doing it for."

"I know, and I respect you for it, but don't expect miracles from us. It's been a long time since we sang in public."

Alf had completed his mission successfully. "Thanks for the tea, Nell. Got to go — deliveries in ten minutes — have to be down in the cellar to count the barrels."

The talk at the dinner table that night was Henry and Nelly's upcoming performance. No question as to whether they should participate; it was more about what would be appropriate for them to sing. Lizzie was never far from any of their minds, and with the exception of Sidney, they agreed Clara had made the right decision to go to Munich.

They had all their old sheet music stored away up at Twenty-One — some in the piano bench in the front room and a box of it in the attic. Clara and Anna gathered it all up and placed it in neat piles on the parlor table.

"Well, I'll tell you what I think," Henry announced, "I always had a soft spot for 'Silver Threads Amongst The Gold' and, for light relief, 'I Do Like to Be Beside The Seaside.' Maybe I'll don me bathing trunks for that one."

"You'll do nothing of the sort. The seaside's out!" Nelly put her foot down.

"What's wrong with it then?" Henry complained.

"We're not by the seaside, we're not likely to be beside the seaside, and I don't particularly like the seaside. If you think I'd let you go on stage with those skinny white legs of yours sticking out of a pair of trunks that are now three sizes too big, you have another think coming!"

"Since when don't you like the seaside?"

"Since we went to Brighton in the freezing cold and you forgot the chairs, the birds ate our sandwiches and the stones hurt my bum!"

Clara jumped in — they'd go on at each other forever if someone didn't stop them, "How many songs do you need?"

Henry gave the question consideration. "Well, we usually had two or three to start, then we did an encore, and if they liked us, we added one more."

"And if they didn't, we rushed off the stage before the tomatoes hit us and the hook got us!" Nelly added.

Finally, after much disagreement and differences of opinion, they settled on five songs.

Henry got his wish with 'Silver Threads Amongst the Gold' — "Have to keep me handkerchief ready to wipe me tears when we sing that one, Nelly."

"My Heart Is With You Tonight" was a romantic piece approved by all.

" 'In the Shade of the Old Apple Tree,' we all know that one," Anna remarked as she began to hum a few bars and was immediately told to shut it.

"Danny Boy" came next. "How many Irishmen do you know?" Sula asked.

And, finally, to liven things up a bit, "When Father Papered The Parlor," which Nelly thought appropriate. Most of the Jews she knew were incapable of changing a light bulb let alone hanging wallpaper. "When your dad knocks a nail in the wall, the man next door gets a coat hanger!" Nelly couldn't help herself; she had to get that one in.

Rehearsals began immediately. Nelly and Henry moved into the front room to practice, Sula accompanied them on the piano while Clara directed. Anna turned the pages of the song sheets, and the door to the parlor had to be shut tight to stop Boadicea singing along with them. Music had returned to Twenty-One.

ON OPENING NIGHT a long queue formed outside the Half Moon Pub. It seemed as if the entire population of Aldgate had turned up. The first fifty or so crowded into the pub while the rest stood outside straining to hear Alf announce the evening's entertainment.

"Good evenin', ladies and gentleman. Tonight is a special night. We're 'ere to raise money for the refugees, those that managed to get out of Germany. They come with nothing other than the clothes they wear. Everything has been taken from them, and they need our 'elp, and we're goin' to give it to them."

The crowd roared their approval.

"We offer you music and songs. With the money we collect we could bring a little bit of hope and dignity back into their lives."

There was loud applause inside and outside the pub.

Friday night at the Half Moon Pub soon rivaled the Rivoli picture house down the street. Alf's promotions did the trick, and money for the refugees was coming in — his one regret being his pub couldn't accommodate the numbers turning up. He'd hired a waiter to take drink orders from the people waiting outside, each hoping to be the next to squeeze in. They could hear the music, didn't have to pay an entrance fee, so they put money in the hat when it came 'round. Still, they would have preferred to see the performers in person, and Alf faced a financial dilemma. How could he double donations, please his customers and still make a profit?

Nelly had the solution. "We'll do the show twice a month. All profits to go to the refugees on the first night and just half of what you take in the second night."

"I'll go broke." Alf groaned.

"No you won't," Nelly assured him. "You'll make the same as you would on an ordinary night. More customers, more money and half of more is the same as half of less."

"Since when did you become a mathematical genius?" Alf inquired.

UP AT TWENTY-ONE Sula was not doing well. Her eyesight was affected, and she tired easily. The treatment she was receiving was painful and, so far, not helping. She'd just spent another week in hospital receiving gold injections. Although Nelly and Henry were aware of Sula's condition, only Clara and Mannie really knew how tough it was for her. Sula begged them not to tell Mum and Dad; let them think she was on the mend — it was better that way.

Clara was also feeling a bit under the weather. Without telling Sidney, she'd gone to the doctor only to find, unlike Sula, her case was curable. What she had would take nine months to heal; she was six weeks pregnant.

She and Sidney had always taken precautions. She knew they weren't fool proof, but suddenly the thought struck her: perhaps it was the result of the one night with Paul in Munich. How could she know? She put the thought aside. She was now trying to fight her way to Twenty-One; crowds outside the Half Moon blocked her way.

"You got influence, Clara, get us a ticket. Pay you for it; keep the change or bung it in the bucket," a bloke she knew from the market said.

"Not me, Harry, sorry. Try again next week. Put your money in the glass on the bar and listen to the show outside. "

"I likes the real thing, Clara. I'll wait."

"Sorry, keep trying," she told him and finally managed to climb the stairs at Twenty-One, where Clara found Sula sitting there alone. "It's a madhouse out there. You'd think Alf was giving away free booze."

Sula looked up. "The only thing you can say for it is they're raising a few bob for a good cause. I made a pot of tea. Have a cup. You look knackered." She poured Clara a cup of hot tea.

"I am."

"Maze working you too hard?"

"No. I've just come back from the doctor. I'm pregnant."

Sula's face lit up. "That's wonderful. Mum will be a grandma; she'll love it."

"You could have knocked me over with a feather. I asked the doctor if he was sure. He said he'd been an obstetrician for thirty years and hadn't been proved wrong yet. I told him we use birth control. He looked over the top of his glasses and said, 'Accidents happen. You're having a baby, Mrs. Simon, and you better get used to it.'"

"He's right. You should be over the moon, thrilled."

"It's a bit of a shock, Sula. I mean, I didn't expect this."

"It's a blessing; it's a new life. As for Sidney, all he wants is for you to stop working with Maze. He's been on about it for ages. Now you have a reason to leave."

"I'll leave when the book is finished. Maybe a couple of months; Paul's well into it now."

"Then you have the perfect reason to hurry him up; can't go waddling to Chelsea when you're seven or eight months pregnant. Anyway, Sidney wouldn't want you to, he doesn't now, so you can imagine what he'll say when he finds out."

Clara agreed. Her tea was growing cold. Mum always said cold tea made you beautiful. Where did that come from? Probably because she rarely had time to sit down and have a hot cup. Nelly rationalized things like that. Clara wished she had the same ability. She didn't feel very beautiful right now; cold tea wouldn't hurt! Thank God for Sula, so levelheaded — always managed to put things in perspective.

They were still sitting in the parlor sipping tea when Henry and Nelly came in from their rehearsal. They'd added a few songs by popular demand. "I dunno," Henry said as he removed his tight-fitting boots. "I think we're getting a bit long in the tooth for this."

Nelly put on her apron, ready to get the evening meal started. "Well," she said, "I'm giving serious consideration to our final encore. I'm beginning to think we should change it from 'Danny Boy' to 'Ain't It Grand To Be Bloomin' Well Dead'!"

Henry and Nelly's patter lightened their mood. Sula came up with the suggestion that perhaps "Good Night, Sweetheart" might be better.

Clara agreed and said no more. This wasn't the time to announce her news. She had Sula swear not to tell anyone for now. She had to tell Sidney first.

Still, the gnawing feeling would not go away, for neither she nor he would ever know who fathered the embryo now growing in her belly.

CHAPTER 31

Crossroads

WINSTON CHURCHILL FOUND painting with Paul Maze to be the one relaxation he could enjoy in London.

After a frustrating day in the House of Commons, he'd instruct his driver to take him to the Maze residence. Up in the studio at his own easel — palette in one hand and brush in the other — he'd let off steam without being called a blow hard or some other pejorative term unfit to be uttered in front of a lady.

Clara, working on the book at her desk, assured him that, coming from the East End, she'd heard far worse. Heinrich, recuperating in a lounge chair nearby, was immune; the memory of what he had experienced weighed heavily on his mind. But from time to time, as the days passed and his health improved, he listened to the conversation that passed between others more closely.

These were Churchill's black dog days, his depression made worse by his inability to convince his colleagues of Germany's intransigents. He'd accused Ramsay Macdonald of being personally responsible for the deterioration in policy for the previous four years "which had brought us near to war and made us weaker, poorer and more defenseless," and it hadn't endeared him to the members in the House; in fact, he was described by Stafford Cripps as being "thoroughly mischievous."

"I'd say that was a compliment coming from him," Maze remarked.

"I told them that given the choice between war and dishonor, and you chose dishonor, you will have war," Churchill proclaimed. "Bloody dishonor — who do they think they're dishonoring?"

"No one but themselves, Winston, certainly not you," Maze reminded him. "Perhaps they'd listen to Heinrich."

"Me? I'm the enemy; they'll have nothing to do with me."

"Perhaps," Churchill acknowledged. "Still, you never know. I think I recognize a few who might be on my side. The others, well, they stubbornly refuse to recognize what is staring them in the face; they're more concerned about losing their seat in the next election than doing the right thing."

"Invite them here," Maze said. "You don't need the press hounding you outside your own residence."

"Worth considering," Churchill replied, bucked by Maze's suggestion. "Heinrich's tragic encounter might influence the nay sayers."

"I can try," Heinrich said with a trace of renewed spirit. "For Trude and all the others . . ."

"Yes, yes. For Trude and all of those poor lost souls murdered alongside her," Churchill said with a sad sigh. He was accustomed to criticism, but what he couldn't abide was the stubborn disregard of facts he forced his colleagues to face. "I have to say Stanley Baldwin wasn't much better, and as for Neville Chamberlain being considered for the highest post in government — Prime Minister — well, I find it hard to hide my disgust. You have to know, Paul, our regard for each other is notoriously unfriendly."

Nevertheless, Churchill kept on hounding the government, providing examples of Germany's readiness for war and Britain's failure to face facts. He would not let up.

"You're like a bouncing ball, Winston. They keep hitting you against the wall, and you rebound, landing up in their court, waiting to be hit again," Maze observed.

Churchill rubbed his nearly bald head as if searching for bruises. "Considering the world and its occupants, I wonder what God thinks of the havoc we have created. Really, it surprises me the way He's watched us destroy everything in our wake; but then I suppose He has many challenges to attend to — can't just concentrate on us. I wouldn't have His job for anything. Mine is hard enough, but His is much more difficult. And," Churchill humphed, "He can't resign!"

"Maybe not resign, but I do think, at this moment, He might be taking a short vacation," Maze replied and looked up to find Rogers standing at the door. "What is it, Rogers?"

"Sir Michael Reynolds has arrived to collect the painting he commissioned. He's waiting for you in the sitting room."

"Ah, there is a God after all. You'll excuse me? Michael's a valued patron."

While Paul was out of the room Churchill said to Clara, "I'd like to write an introduction to Paul's book. What do you think, Clara?"

"He would consider it an honor, sir."

"Won't tell him, though; we'll keep it a secret — I love secrets," Churchill stated gleefully, "and very good I am at them, too. One has to be in my line of work!"

"It's safe with me," Clara assured him.

A FEW DAYS later Paul spoke to Clara about his future plans. "When the book is published, I'll need you to hold my hand at interviews and bookshops, and write letters to those who love the book — and maybe to those who hate it. Then I'll go back to painting full time — and you can arrange my art shows, and . . . " Maze continued on, spilling out one idea after another.

Finally Clara stopped him. "Don't let's discuss what we're going to do after the book is finished. Let's concentrate on getting it done."

"*Tu es si pratique, charmante et pratique, quelle combinaison.*"

"You can remain charming; I have to be practical." Clara pointed out.

"So, where was I?"

"Somewhere in France, or was it Belgium?"

"I believe it was Belgium," Paul replied remembering Ypres. And he was off and planning their future.

Clara gave up and let him plan. It was no use, not now. However, the time would come, and then there'd be no backing off.

Heinrich had started to paint again. He was frustrated; what had once been second nature was now an effort. He confided in Clara, "I have lost all that is dear to me, my country, my Trude, and now my art."

Clara's heart went out to him. Heinrich didn't ask for pity, he simply needed to regain confidence in his art. "Look at Paul," Clara urged. "He lived his nightmares for years before someone came along and suggested he write about his experiences. You could do the same."

"I have no talent for writing."

"But you can talk, Heinrich. You must make yourself known in

London. Paul knows everyone worth knowing. You are Winston's eyes, his witness. It's no coincidence you survived; you must speak up — as you once suggested to Churchill, tell them what's going on in Germany, speak about Trude and all those who disappear or are taken away."

Heinrich set aside his paint brush and sought his easy chair where he sank down with a sigh. "When I think back to the early part of this decade, Germans were desperately looking for a leader," he reminisced. "For artists and writers, the philosophy of Communism seemed to be the answer; we were, however, sadly in the minority. We had little food and no work. There were three million unemployed in Germany. Then Hitler came along and promised bread and work for everyone. Goebbels had stated early on: 'He who can conquer the street can also conquer the masses and thereby conquer the state.' Hitler took those words literally. And so the Weimar Republic disintegrated, became a lawless society, and the people saw the solution to it in Adolf Hitler. They made a terrible mistake, and once he was in power, it was too late to rectify it. I should have insisted we get out; instead, I — along with many others — thought we could change things. How stupid we were!" Heinrich stopped for a moment. "What's the use of ifs; our whole life can be made up of ifs. How do we know at the time what we think we can do and believe we can accomplish will turn out to be nothing more than wishful thinking? We lost. I still see Trude lying dead in my arms. What's just as bad, I know what is happening to my friends — to the Jews."

CLARA WAS LIVING the First World War with Paul and the threat of another from listening to Heinrich and Churchill. She had a new life taking form in her womb. Was this the right time to bring a child into the world? A Jewish child? Should she be thinking about abortion?

A girl Clara had worked with at Abbott's had the address of an abortionist. She could never consider an abortion. What worried her more was the paternity. She would allow no doubt to enter Sidney's mind, but then again this child could be his. It was for her to live with the uncertainty, not Sidney. Paul need never know; besides, there was no way of knowing for certain it was his. She herself wasn't sure. If she carried to term — Sidney, who wanted a son, would be a loving father, boy or girl. He'd often spoken of wanting children, and that was all that mattered.

She was thankful that, so far, she hadn't suffered morning sickness. That was all she'd heard from pregnant friends: how every morning they threw up; how nothing stopped the nausea until the third month. She was now in her second month. Soon she'd begin to show; she wouldn't be able to keep her secret much longer.

It was important to stay focused on the book. Once that was done she could leave, give Paul a plausible excuse. He was eager to finish the book; he had put aside his painting and was concentrating on the final chapters. They were just a week over the deadline, not bad, considering the interruptions and time taken off.

Clara pleaded with the editor for just a few more day's grace; she hadn't received the preface from Churchill. She waited, then finally took it into her own hands and phoned his secretary. It arrived two days later.

Churchill had written just over two pages and, as only he could do, captured the essence of the content of the book and the character of the man he was proud to call his friend — one artist to another, expressing in words a painting on an untouched canvas. Both Paul and Clara were moved by the final paragraph:

> For the rest we have the battle-scenes of Armageddon recorded by one who not only loved the fighting troops and shared their perils, but perceived the beauties of light and shade, of form and color, of which even the horrors of war cannot rob the progress of the sun. This volume should be acceptable alike to the artists and the soldiers of the two great nations whose cause of freedom its author so ardently and enduringly espoused.

Clara sent the last chapters with the preface off to the publishers, and now it was time for them to celebrate with Churchill and Heinrich.

Paul opened a bottle of champagne and made a toast. "To a job well done." Churchill lifted his glass, adding, "And to Clara who kept Paul's nose to the grindstone!"

"Without my dear Clara, there would be no book," Paul acknowledged.

"Perhaps now you will allow me to ask for the hand of this lovely lady," Churchill said, anticipating a positive reply.

"*Mon dieu!* And what do you think Clemmie would say?"

"Her helping hand, you idiot; my secretary upped and left last week. Think she's gone over to the other side."

"Sorry, there is much I would be willing to share with you, but not Clara; we still have plenty to do," Paul said somewhat loftily.

Heinrich found their cordial spat over Clara amusing and actually laughed out loud. "I thought slavery was abolished. Is she to be put on a block and sold to the highest bidder?"

They could banter all they liked; Clara knew her working days were limited. Motherhood loomed. Perhaps it was the few sips of champagne she had enjoyed going to her head, but now the arrival of the new baby consumed her, and with the toast she silently vowed she would take the question of the child's paternal identity to her grave.

ON CLARA'S WAY home that evening, she had an overwhelming desire to see Sidney. She took a small detour and dropped by the factory. His brother Julius greeted her warmly; he never hid his affection for her. Clara played up to him for Sidney's sake, but she had never really liked him. He was a big man, over six feet tall, much taller than Sidney, and ten years older. Julius was a presence in any room. He towered over his workers, used his size to intimidate. His wife, Rose, a sweet woman, gave into his every whim, and his sons kept their distance. If it hadn't been for Sidney's craftsmanship, Julius would have been in trouble. Still, he never gave a thought to making Sidney a partner. Sidney, in theory, could inherit the business, as Julius had from their grandfather, but the likelihood of this happening was remote.

"Got back yesterday from America," Julius announced in a boastful tone in greeting Clara.

"What was it like?" Clara dutifully enquired.

"New York is, well, it's hard to describe — skyscrapers everywhere, the Empire State Building. You get a stiff neck just looking up at it — the lights of Broadway, the Statue of Liberty. I've never seen anything like it. It's not all what it's made out to be, though; out-of-work men line up for limited jobs, homeless roaming the streets, soup kitchens, beggars come up to you. The Depression's taken its toll. I thought their economy was recovering, not much sign of it; furs remain a luxury, and there's little money around. Made a couple of sales, nothing of any consequence, got enough to keep Sidney going, no worry on that score."

"I'd like to go to America one day."

"Well, just say the word, Clara, always room for one more."

"Then that someone shouldn't be me, should it, Julius?" He wasn't getting away with that remark. "Anyway I've come to see my husband." She stressed husband.

"Something wrong?"

"Just wanted a word with him."

"He's on the floor. Want me to get him for you?"

"No, I'll surprise him, if you don't mind." Clara walked into the factory. The combination of sewing machines and hammering on wooden boards as the sewn furs were stretched and nailed made a dreadful racket. She picked her way through the bits of fur on the floor. It was sickening to think that these were free roaming wild animals, snared for the rich to parade in coats made from their skins.

Sidney looked up and saw her. "What you doing here?"

This wasn't the welcome she'd expected.

Sidney continued with stretching the skin he was nailing; it seemed when he saw her he brought his hammer down even harder. "Sorry, can't stop, if the ermine skin dries, it will tear."

Ermine was expensive, and Sidney only worked on special orders; two other furriers did the bread and butter work. They were paid less. None of them were paid what they were worth.

"Just came to say we've finished the book. I wanted you to be the first to know."

"Glad to hear it. You finished with him?"

"Not completely, but I will be."

"When he's out of our lives, we'll talk."

"I thought you'd be pleased."

"I've got to get this coat done by the end of the day, Clara. Julius is giving it to some important customer. Bribery, if you ask me. Go home. I'll see you there."

Clara left, gloated over by Julius, snubbed by Sidney. Why had she bothered? All it accomplished was to emphasize the glaring distinction between the charm and worldliness of Paul and the limited possibilities with Sidney. She understood Sidney's disenchantment, but if they were ever to make a go of it, he had to put the past behind him. Sidney was good at holding on. He held on to a job he detested with a brother he loathed, and he held on to her with deep resentment. He never took a stand. She'd have had more respect for him if he had given her an ultimatum.

Of course she had to admit her connection to Paul angered Sidney, but he wasn't the only one; it had repercussions on her family, her religion and now the baby. She would never give up her family. And how could she continue to be part of Paul's life and still go back to Twenty-One every night? They were totally incompatible, and one would have to go. Perhaps she'd talk it over with Sula again, but how far would that get her? She knew what she had to do; procrastination wasn't the answer. As for Sidney, non-confrontational Sidney, she would never put doubt in his mind. She'd given him a hard enough time as it was. Clara knew this decision would put her on a road that led out of Chelsea and directly back to number Twenty-One.

Her time with Paul had been an unexpected and wonderful adventure, but it was only an interlude, and the reality hit her hard. Perhaps the best way was to simply tell Paul she was pregnant. Or should she just tell him she had to leave because it was causing trouble with her husband?

Would he accept that? Probably not; after all, he had problems with his wife, and they seemed to have come to an amicable agreement.

Where did she belong? she asked herself for what might have been the hundredth time. With Paul? Yes, he wanted her with him. In Chelsea? No, she'd yearn for her family. Still, it had to be one or the other.

Paul was who he was, a man who adapted to any situation. She was a visitor to his lifestyle, a Jew in a gentile world. She recalled the night when she ran away from Anna's wedding celebration and stood outside Paul's home on the embankment — on the outside looking in — and Sidney coming up to her, standing at her side, watching the guests leave in their finery and posh cars. She would never be the same naïve girl who stood up to Abbott and his anti-Semitic outburst, that's for sure. But her mother was right. It didn't matter whether you mixed with the dregs of society or the so-called aristocrats; they viewed Jews as pariahs, money-grabbing disposable outcasts. She'd dined with cabbages and kings, she'd learned and grown while becoming a different person; but deep down, very deep down, she knew she must take what she'd learned, stay with Sidney, move to the suburbs out of Aldgate and make a life with him for the child soon to be born.

PAUL WAS CALLED back to France when Yvette died, and as much as he cared for his childhood home, he could not live there permanently. Yvette was irreplaceable; it was she who kept the farmhouse going, but it was old and needed repair. Should he sell it, keep it? Hard decisions. His estranged wife loved France, but she lived in Scotland; her occasional visit didn't warrant the upkeep. England was where he made his home. France? There was still the little flat in Le Havre; he'd keep that.

"Come with me, Clara, help me make a decision."

"I wish I could. I can't, not this time."

"*Ah oui . . . ton mari . . . je comprends. Je n'aurais pas dû tu demander.*"

"Of course you should ask. We have been so close, but I have no choice. I promised my husband I would give up work, Paul," she blurted out, "I'm pregnant!"

"*Oh, ma chère Clara, un bébé?* When?"

"In May."

"After the baby is born, you will come back?"

"No. I won't work, not for the first few years."

Maze was stunned. She was so much part of his everyday life. He couldn't imagine being without her. He'd lost Yvette and now Clara was walking out of his life. It was all too much. He felt abandoned and told her so.

"We had our time together in France, Paul. In those few days we came to know each other. You spoke from your heart, and I no longer had to imagine war. I saw it through your eyes. I learned so much. I will always cherish those memories. And Germany, dreadful, terrible Munich, without you by my side I would not have had the opportunity or the courage to make that journey."

"It isn't only France, Clara. I'll miss your smile, your humor, even your whip, and I learned from you, too. *Tu m'as donné une nouvelle perspective*, I see it all so differently now."

"Take Maggie with you to France this time; she's a lovely girl, and she will do everything for you. And Rogers, he'll never leave you; he'll always be at your side."

"At my side, not in my arms," he replied as he came and embraced her.

Clara could not hide her tears. It was so hard to explain and not sound a hypocrite. She treasured her job; she had never met anyone like Paul, and to give him up was a sacrifice she didn't want to make but had to — it was time for her to leave. Two people from diverse backgrounds, neither of them free, had fallen in love. It wasn't supposed to happen, but it did. In France and even Germany, it was just the two of them — no wife for him and no husband for her. With Paul, Clara realized what had been missing in her life: romantic love, intellectual stimulation. It was an escape for both of them. Maybe it started as infatuation, but when they made love it all changed. She was won over with genuine compliments, with the way he spoke to her, challenged her intellect and treated her as an equal. He was everything she could ever have wished for in a partner, and she loved him dearly.

She had escaped from a humdrum existence in a working class environment to an exciting and sometimes overwhelming love affair with a charming Frenchman who would never be hers. She no longer had illusions about remaining permanently in Paul's life. It was fine being his secretary, but being his lover and staying married at the same time was unthinkable. There had never been a divorce in Clara's family, and there wasn't going to be one now. A promise given was a promise kept, and she would not break the chain.

CHAPTER 32

Clara and Sidney

CLARA RETURNED FROM her third month prenatal appointment to find a brown paper package conspicuously placed on the parlor table at Twenty-One. She picked it up and read the label:

HC Publishing Company
Mrs. Clara Simon, 21 High Street, Aldgate, London EC1

There was no mistaking what the package contained.

Clara sank down on a chair and tried to stop her hands from shaking, chiding herself for procrastinating and eventually summoning up the courage to open it. Careful not to awaken Nelly dozing beside the stove, she quietly removed the wrapping. And there it was, a beautiful, linen-covered, golden brown volume with a band of the French tricolor running across the top and bottom of the cover. The title and the author's name were embossed in a brilliant blue:

A FRENCHMAN IN KHAKI by PAUL MAZE.

She looked for a note; there wasn't one. She turned the first two pages, and there on the left-hand side of the third page in Paul's handwriting she read:

To Mrs. Simon,

Whose help and devotion was a factor in writing this book which the author will never forget. In memory of the days when she entered my room with that refreshing smile of hers that led to her present happiness.

Paul Maze

No wonder there wasn't a note — he'd written what he wanted to say right in the book. She studied that line about "her present happiness" and wondered to what he referred. Could he mean the baby? Turning the pages slowly, she recalled each sentence, each paragraph, what Paul had said, when he said it and how she interpreted it. She hoped he was pleased with the finished product.

She read Churchill's opening; it made her proud to be connected in a small way to him. A chapter heading recaptured the time she and Paul spent in France, their first kiss and the day when he asked her to pose for him in the sunflowers. It was a lovely painting, one he said he would not sell. She thought of Yvette, her kitchen, her food — and Yvette's love for Paul, replacing the son she lost.

Out of a serendipitous meeting with Ronan had come a small miracle in the shape of a book. It had impacted the way she thought, the way she lived and the way she would see life in the future. It removed the mundane and replaced it with the knowledge that the opportunity to better oneself was there for everyone. All one had to do was pursue it, recognize it and run with it.

When Clara first met Paul he told her he wanted to write a book to warn against and to describe the horrors of war. At first she'd felt inadequate, not educated enough to accomplish what he asked her to do. He'd assured her she was capable, and his belief in her gave her the confidence to be what he wanted her to be. He taught her, she learned from him — more than she would ever have learned in school. He was her professor and, in time, he became her lover. He'd opened up new frontiers and proved that determination and a bit of luck could move mountains.

Just as Clara put the book back in the box, Nelly woke. "You got the package?" she asked.

"Yes, Mum, just a few papers from the publishers, nothing much," Clara lied. It was her book, and she wanted to read it by herself before sharing it.

It was precious.

On the following Sunday Clara suggested she and Sidney take the bus to Regent's Park. "We can have tea, maybe a piece of cream cake and then listen to the band playing in the Pavilion."

Sidney, who should have been a gardener, not a furrier, never needed a second invitation to enjoy the flowers and unusual plants that grew there.

"I'd like that," he said, obviously happy to have Clara to himself again. He'd persevered through a difficult time, his pride injured and his devotion tested, but it was worth it; he'd won the battle, and she was there, safe in the bosom of her family.

They walked arm in arm along the pathways to the rose garden. The roses were in full bloom, every color you could imagine — even black.

Clara, feeling a little tired, stopped to sit on a park bench next to an old man. "Mind if I join you?" she asked.

"Not at all, nice to have a bit of company for a change." He offered to share his bag of stale bread.

Clara accepted a handful of crust.

Sidney nodded his approval and walked over toward the rose gardens.

"I come here every day to feed the pigeons," the man told Clara. "Shouldn't really; they can be a bit of a pest. I save some for the swans, beautiful creatures that they are; a bit nasty if you get on the wrong side of them, protecting their territory." He shrugged. "Well, I suppose they have to protect their territory as they all belong to the King."

"How about the sparrows?" Clara asked; she was concerned for the smaller birds. "Can't they have a few bites?"

"The little London sparrows? Of course, they belong to all of us. They get their share. Pigeons don't give them much of a chance. I do my best to shoo them away when it's the sparrows' turn." He seemed a lonely old man, eager to talk. "My wife died last year," he went on. "We used to come here every Sunday. So now it's me by myself, and I pretend she's right beside me. We were married for forty-five years — that's a long time. No complaints; she was the light of my life."

"My condolences," Clara said softly. She felt his loneliness. A sparrow perched on the arm of the bench. She crumbled a crust. The sparrow ate from her hand.

"I know I'll see my Betty again," he continued. "When the Good Lord decides he's ready for me to join her she'll be there waiting for me. May want to know why I took so long. Don't have an answer for that." He emptied out the last few crumbs, stood up and tipped his hat. "Got to get on my way, nice talking to you, and, by the way, that little sparrow that ate from your hand, well," he laughed softly, "that was Betty."

SIDNEY HAD PICKED up a rosebud that had fallen to the ground. He carried it from the garden and handed it to Clara. "Park attendants watching. I couldn't pick the rose I wanted for you," he said, as if in consolation.

"Here, sit with me," Clara said, her voice just as soft as it had been with the old man. "I have something to tell you."

"I'm all ears." Sidney sat down and diligently waited.

"I'm pregnant. We're going to have a baby."

"We're what?" Sidney, not a man who showed enthusiasm over anything other than the Arsenal football team, jumped up and took a leap in the air; he nearly collided with a man and his wife taking an afternoon stroll. "Awfully sorry, just a bit excited; you see, my wife just told me — we're going to have a baby."

"Congratulations, young man." They wished him well and walked on.

"What about me?' Clara asked, alone there on the bench.

"Oh, yes!" He kissed the top of her head. If he'd won the Irish Sweepstakes, he couldn't have been happier.

FOR AS LONG as he could remember it had been Sidney's dream to have his own home away from the East End. He might have been born in the city, but he wasn't a city boy at heart. Every night he'd turn to the advertising section of the *Evening Standard* looking for a house they could afford. Then in the *Sunday Express* an advertisement caught his eye. "Here, look at this," he said to Clara. His words carried an air of excitement.

Clara bent over his shoulder and read with him.

In a northern area of London a new estate, Garden Suburb, is well into its third phase of construction. Affordable homes are being constructed to accommodate families with children. Schools and shops in easy walking distance, good size gardens with each property.

"That's what I want, Clara — I want a garden," Sidney said. They read on.

The underground has recently been extended. A car, though convenient, is not necessary.

"Get your coat on, we're going there," he told Clara.

"Now?"

"Yes, now."

She'd never seen Sidney so motivated. He literally pushed her out of the door and onto a bus, then to a train at Tottenham Court Road Tube Station. They arrived at the Woodside Park Station an hour later.

"Where do we go from here?" Clara asked, bewildered.

"We walk 'til we find it." And find it they did — over a mile from the station. Up and down hills, no buses, very few cars and open spaces. They breathed in the fresh air, saw horses grazing and cows munching in green fields. They walked on newly laid pavements and newly tarred roads. They looked at a semidetached three-bedroom model with all modern conveniences, and they found out they could choose from a variety of plans. Bay windows if they wished. A garage, if they wanted, and even a low interest mortgage. There was no question about it, they loved one particular design. As tired as she was, Clara went along with Sidney and a salesperson to visit available sites — shoes covered in mud — they eventually found a plot that they both agreed was right for them.

"You will be in a circle of houses, north and south, separated by a main road; you're looking at the south circle. Five minutes from the school, ten minutes from the shops. How much better situated could you be? Have to use your mind's eye for this. Remember what you liked in the brochure and then try to imagine it built here." The salesman escorted them back to the office hut. "Make your choice, and it will be yours. Take your time; it's a big decision. But I must caution you, they are going fast."

"The plot we saw on the south circle," Sidney said. "That's the one for us."

Clara was so exhausted; she'd have opted for the hut — if it had been for sale! Their house would be completed six months from the date of signing. They had chosen their first home, far away from the tumult of the East End, far away from the grime of smoking chimneys and belching buses.

Standing on a barren piece of land, Sidney would only have to wait a few more months. He'd have a house, a baby, and, more precious than anything else, he'd have his wife!

THE JOY WENT right out of Twenty-One when Sidney shared the good news with the family.

Henry felt he was being deserted. "I want my family close by," and by that Henry meant living at Twenty-One.

"You've still got Sula and Mannie, and Anna and Bernie are just around the corner. We'll visit. You haven't seen the back of us," Sidney assured him.

Nelly, as usual, took it in her stride and placated Henry. "The rest of the world turns up at Twenty-One, and you couldn't possibly miss a couple of kids who aren't kids anymore, and, what's more, having a kid of their own!"

"I know, luv," Henry responded as he studied the real estate brochure he'd been forced to read. "It's nice looking and all that. Can't say I've ever heard of it; must be on the other side of nowhere."

"It isn't, Dad, it's at the end of the Northern Line," Anna put him right. "Where did you think they're moving? To Scotland?"

As far as Henry was concerned, anything north of London and at the end of a railway line had to be in Scotland. His world was East, and East it was going to stay.

TO SET HENRY'S mind at rest Clara arranged a family outing to Woodside Park. Henry had been to Brighton, to Southend and once to Hastings. He had not before this taken a tube farther than Piccadilly Circus, and now he'd been shoved on a train traveling at breakneck speed far away from his natural habitat.

"Why do they call it the underground when we come out into the open at East Finchley?" Henry asked, the sunlight hitting him as the train came from the tunnel.

"Because it starts underground, Henry," Nelly explained. That shut him up for a while but not for long.

The walk from the station caused more trouble. Henry and Nelly were accustomed to having every convenience on their doorstep.

"Should have put on me hiking boots," Henry groused.

Nelly wished she'd put on more comfortable shoes but wasn't about to let Henry know she agreed with him.

When they finally got to where they were going, Henry stopped dead in his tracks. "It's in a field. You're going to live in a field!" Henry was beside himself and demanded to see the foreman.

The foreman, accustomed to questions from buyers, had walked out with them. "Now what's the problem, Mister? I don't understand."

"I don't want my daughter living in a field! We're not farmers; we're city people."

Armed with the plans, the foreman unrolled them and pointed out to Henry exactly where his daughter's house would be placed.

Henry dug into his pocket for his reading glasses, put them on and studied the plans, although he didn't have a clue what he was looking at.

The foreman hurried on to explain, "Let me assure you, by the time this development is completed your daughter will have a very nice house on a street with pavement, with electricity, with gas and running water and with shops about five minutes down this road." He pointed to the area, and as he was rolling back the plans, he noticed Clara's tummy. "Oh, and I almost forgot — with a school. Now, if I'm to complete all we've promised, I better get on with it. They'll be on a tea break soon; you know what British workers are like, three hours on, one hour off. How we built an empire, I'll never understand." And he was off, leaving Henry to complain to Sidney, to Clara, to Nelly . . .

"I dunno, Nelly," Henry said as he walked around the pipes and wires sticking out of the ground. "Looks a real tip to me."

Clara took over. "Look, Dad, over there. See? People are living in those houses. That's what ours will look like when it's finished."

Henry wasn't convinced. He muttered all the way back to the station — couldn't understand why his daughter and son-in-law would choose to live in a field miles from anywhere.

"What's wrong with Stamford Hill or Finsbury Park?" Henry kept at it. "That's where most of the young Jewish couples are going — just a bus ride from Aldgate. Why do they have to move out to the boondocks? Not a *shul* in sight. And another thing, how do we know they allow Jews there?"

They'd passed a newly built church. "See, it's for gentiles, not for us."

"Hush up, Henry," Nelly ordered. "They've found what they want. It wouldn't do for me, and it wouldn't do for you. We're not buying it, they are. And just out of curiosity — when did you last go to *shul?*"

Henry ignored the question and muttered, "I'd go crazy with the silence. I could hear my watch ticking, for gawd's sake."

"We won't need a watch at weekends, Dad." Clara caught on to Henry's arm. "The birds will wake us in the morning, and when it gets dark we'll go to sleep. Sidney will have his garden, and I'll walk our baby in the pram without worrying about crossing busy roads or shopping in crummy markets."

"Crummy markets? I'll have you know the best food you can find anywhere is in what you call crummy markets, and don't you forget it, my girl." Nelly proudly defended her territory.

Finally they made the train and were at long last heading back to Twenty-One. Almost immediately Henry fell asleep and snored most of the way home.

"It's the fresh air," Nelly decided. "Your dad never could keep awake after a day in the fresh air!"

Henry opened one eye. "I heard that. I'll tell you one thing, if I had to do this journey every day, I'd never leave home."

"Let's face it, Henry, you couldn't manage the buses, let alone a train!" Nelly had had the last word.

Since Clara was no longer working, she spent her time looking for furniture and fittings for the house. Anna and Sula helped. Nelly threw in the odd suggestion, but she wasn't up to date with modern devices. Twenty-One was a relic from the Victorian era, and she liked it that way. So much more was available now. Gas stoves in place of wood burning ones, electric fires built into the walls. Lots of cupboard space. Separate bathroom and lavatory — that alone was worth the price of the house. No one would have to wait, hopping on one leg while the occupant of the bathroom spent his or her one night a week soaking in the tub.

Paul Maze's name was never mentioned.

Clara saved a special place in her heart for him and kept his book, covered in brown paper in the drawer of her bedside table. *A Frenchman in Khaki* was hers to read in quiet moments, to recall and help keep close those special days she'd spent with Maze.

CHAPTER 33

Victoria

IT WAS A beautiful day in May.

Clara sat in Clissold Park watching Sidney's team play cricket when she felt warm water dripping down her leg — followed by a sharp pain. This had to be the beginning of labor. Not one to cause a fuss, she quietly told the captain's wife, who being very British and somewhat reserved, listened, nodded, then walked onto the field to inform her own husband about what was happening. He immediately called a temporary halt to the game.

It was Sidney's turn to bat, and he was ready to wallop the opposing bowler's ball to kingdom come. He waited impatiently to find out the reason for the delay. The captain approached the wicket. "Your wife is having a baby, Sidney."

"I know that. Can't I finish my innings?"

"No, Sidney. She's having the baby right now, right here. I think perhaps you should go to her."

Sidney, dressed in white from top to toe, his red face contorted in sheer panic, now stood there bewildered and frozen to the spot. "So what do we do?"

"Well, for starters, I'd say we get her to the hospital," another cricketer suggested. "Don't think she should give birth on the grass, old boy. Anyone here got a car?"

Sidney came to his senses. "I'll get a taxi." He rushed off the field and into the club house to phone for a taxi.

"We'll break open a bottle of champagne when we know," the captain shouted as the taxi took off like a bat from hell with Sidney beside Clara in the back seat.

274

Luckily it was a Sunday afternoon, very little traffic on the roads, and this wasn't the first time the taxi driver had had an expectant mother in the back of his cab. "Got three little ones me'self, not to worry, done it before. I'll get you there."

They arrived at the Royal Free Hospital twenty minutes later, Clara having contractions all the way. Sidney jumped out before the vehicle came to a complete stop and commandeered a wheel chair. A nurse chastised him for absconding with hospital property then took charge. "Come back in two hours," she said, helping Clara into the chair. "We'll let you know how far she's got."

"But — "

"Fathers aren't allowed in until the mothers have delivered. Visiting hours posted on the board over there. Only two at a time." And with that she disappeared with his Clara down a very long, shiny corridor.

Up at Twenty-One none of them had an inkling of Clara's imminent delivery. Nelly, in the front room with Henry, sat at her window seat, looking out on the youngsters, tottied up, all walking in the direction of Gardner's Corner, hoping this would be the day they met the boy or girl of their dreams. Henry, on the other hand, could've cared less about the comings and goings on the High Street; he was engrossed in the Sunday paper. Mannie and Sula came in from the parlor to join them.

"Have you seen what Churchill had to say in Parliament the other day?" Henry passed the paper on to Mannie. "Here, read this out to us."

However calmly surveyed, the danger of an attack from the air must appear formidable. No one can doubt that in a week or ten days of intensive bombing upon London would be a very serious matter indeed. One could hardly expect that less than 30,000 or 40,000 people would be killed or maimed. The most dangerous form of air attack is . . . by incendiary bombs . . . The flying peril is not a peril from which we can flee. It is necessary to face it where we stand. We cannot possibly retreat. We cannot move London. We cannot move the vast population, which is dependent on the estuary of the Thames . . .

"I've said it before, and I'll say it again, he's a war monger," Henry said.

"You're wrong, Dad, he's warning us, trying to get the government to wake up," Sula commented.

"Hitler wants Europe, not us just yet," Mannie joined in, and then they got into a shouting match. "And when he gets it, where do you think he'll go next?"

"You young fellows, always looking on the dark side."

"Because there is a dark side, Dad. We won the war, remember? They haven't got over it and never will. Hitler spends every waking hour reminding them. He wants revenge, and he'll stop at nothing to achieve it."

Nelly tried changing the subject. "We should be talking about happy things, like expecting the new baby."

Mannie would not be put off. "In case you haven't noticed we're part of the Thames Estuary; it's where Churchill thinks Germany will hit first. And he's quite right; they'll go for the docks first and then the Jews. The Germans know where the greatest concentration of Jews live. Churchill's reminding our half-witted government that if there is a war, it will spill over in our shores. It won't be like the last one where France took the brunt of it; it will be us with bombs dropping out of the sky. Germany is rearming. We're just sitting here, waiting to be annihilated."

"We had a few bombs, too — those zeppelins came here," Henry reminded them.

"Why would Germany rearm if they didn't have the intention of going to war? Why is Hitler singling out the Jews? He's found his scapegoat. The Jews were successful. They had money; they were the bankers, doctors, lawyers and big store owners when the ordinary, everyday Germans couldn't even find a job. He's blaming them for all the ills of Germany — and the people are buying it. They're a one party dictatorship. He's dismissed the League of Nations. There's no opposition party, and he can do exactly as he pleases."

"There won't be a war. The last war was the war to end all wars, or so they said," Nelly reminded them.

Mannie was right, though, and he knew it. The speech frightened the life out of everyone except the British government, though the recently reelected Prime Minister Mr. Stanley Baldwin did commit to allowing the power of the Royal Air Force to be on a par with that of the Luftwaffe. That was a partial victory for Churchill, but nowhere close to what he asked for. Hitler had made himself head of state after President Von Hindenberg died. Thus the Nazification of Germany was sealed.

SIDNEY DISMISSED THE taxi and took a bus to Aldgate. At Old Castle Street he got off and ran for all he was worth across the High Street into Half Moon Passage and up the stairs of Twenty-One. "Clara's having the baby," he announced. "She's in hospital. Nurse told me we have to wait for visiting hours — two at a time, no more."

Sula laughed, delighted. "Sidney, catch your breath, and, Dad, make a pot of tea. Clara's having a baby — not a heart attack."

VICTORIA ARRIVED EARLIER than her expected birth date, weighing in at seven pounds three ounces, fingers and toes intact. Clara stayed in hospital for ten days. When Nelly found out she was allowed to visit for only ten minutes in the evening, she climbed the fire escape to enter the hospital and locate Clara's room, bringing a jar of chicken soup. Sidney brought her flowers, and Henry had tears in his eyes every time he looked through the glass window at his first grandchild.

Clara, Sidney and Victoria stayed with the family while their house in Woodside Park was being built. Sula and Nelly babysat and were only too pleased to have Victoria to themselves. Anna wanted one of her own, but Bernie hadn't quite settled down to being a husband — wasn't sure he was ready to be a father. The birth of Victoria brought Clara and Sidney closer, and even Henry was getting used to the idea of their moving to what he continued to refer to as "the other side of nowhere."

One Saturday when Sidney was at the Arsenal, Clara persuaded her dad to come with her to the suburbs; she wanted him to see the progress on their new house — to convince him they wouldn't be living in the middle of a field. To her amazement he agreed.

Great changes had taken place since his last visit. Roads and pavements were in place. Street signs up. People were actually living there — walking around. Kirby's opened a green grocers, Hayes, the grocer, was next door to Garners, the news agent and sweet shop. Mr. K.

Ashton Painter, the chemist, had opened for business as well. All of this was praised, and it was only the butcher — pork bellies hanging in the window — who caused Henry concern. "Need to find yourself another butcher, luv."

What the butcher sold was the least of Clara's concerns; anyway, she was sure he had beef and chicken too.

"Then tell him to keep the pork away from them!"

The new home looked ready from the outside. Inside, carpenters and plasterers were still working. While Clara was discussing paint colors with the foreman, Henry decided to have a further look around. He found a field with no building going on; in fact, it was an open field with a big sign that read: Rest Home for Tired Horses.

Henry stood looking at the horses, all in good condition, roaming freely, not in any hurry to get back to the stables he could see at the far end of the field. It was quiet and peaceful, and he liked what he saw. When he finally got back to Clara, who was frantically looking for him, he'd made up his mind. "One of these fine days, Clara, I might well be your neighbor. I've found my retirement home, just around the corner from you — Rest Home for Tired Horses. Might even know a few of 'em; always wondered where they went when they couldn't race no more."

"What are you talking about, Dad?" asked a puzzled Clara.

"Come. I'll show you." And together they took a walk to Henry's newly discovered abode.

"We can find you something better than this, Dad." Clara smiled, though it was a lovely sight to look out at rolling fields with horses munching away and no one to bother them. "Can't see Mum here." Clara went along with his joke. "She'd more likely be in the barn making theirs beds."

Clara loved her dad; he was witty and easygoing most of the time; and this was a rare opportunity to spend time with him alone. So many people up at Twenty-One, and Nelly with her definite opinions and strong personality often overshadowed him. Now they talked about his job; he liked his stall in Leather Lane, much better than Titchfield Street. Nicely situated, had a better clientele — it was close to Hatton Garden, London's diamond center and " . . . those blokes don't seem to mind what they pay for a bottle of perfume as long as it's for a girl friend and not a wife." He got on well with Max Friedman, a good customer who had a shop there, and he felt secure for the first time in his married life. It was a good move, and he was glad he'd made it.

"I know I was a bit hard on you with that job of yours in Chelsea," he admitted. "I was worried you'd be out of your depth. We oldies aren't as adaptable as you young'uns."

"I got used to it soon enough, Dad, enjoyed it while it lasted."

Henry gave her a hug. "Well, it's good to have you back again with us; it's where you belong."

Henry would never know the real reason for her leaving Maze, although Clara suspected Nelly did. Nelly hadn't said anything — not yet anyway. All attention was on the new baby and their new home.

SIDNEY HAD BEGUN work in his garden long before they moved into the new house. He'd planned it for years. In back of the house he planted a Worcester pear tree and Cox's apple. He dug an area for a vegetable patch and hid it with privet bushes. He laid sod and planted perennials in flower beds, along the fence he set raspberry and logan-berry climbers, and pushing the boat out a bit, he purchased a shed to house his lawn mower and garden tools. Little did he know that in less than three years he would have to replace the shed with an Anderson Shelter in an effort to keep them safe from the bombs.

Satisfied with the back garden, he turned his attention to the front of the house while it was still under construction within. There he put down more sod and planted lilac for the spring and holly for the winter — roses too, lots of roses, all different varieties, many of which he'd grown from cuttings he'd snipped when no one was look-ing in Regent's Park.

Sidney was a furrier by day and a gardener in the evenings. By the time they moved into the house, grass was growing, his flowers were bloom-ing and the first shoots of his vegetables were peeking through the freshly dug soil. And when the horse that pulled the milk cart came by and deposited the milk on the front step and droppings on the street, Sidney was the first out the door with his bucket. "Horse dung," he whispered to his infant daughter Victoria, "is the very best fertilizer for gardens."

By the time Victoria was three years old she had her own shovel and her own little bucket. She followed Sidney, who followed the horse, and together they brought back bounties to feed the plants.

As for Clara, she settled in too. It wasn't Chelsea, and it wasn't Aldgate. It was something somewhere in between. Clara reckoned she'd manage to find the best of both worlds there, given time.

CHAPTER 34

In-Between

IN THE SUBURBS Jews lived beside gentiles in peaceful surroundings. Children played and attended school together in a clean and modern setting of safe playgrounds and bright classrooms, and the children came home for lunch and got back to school in time for the afternoon session. By just living outside the city limits — thirty minutes by train from Piccadilly Circus, a bit longer from Aldgate — they could still call themselves Londoners.

On weekends after the garden had been attended to, Sidney, with four-year-old Victoria balanced on his shoulders, took long walks across the fields, finding openings in hedges, climbing over stiles and coming out onto footpaths, which he hoped would eventually lead them back to where they began. Having been cooped up for so many years in his grandmother's dark house and the crowded flat at Twenty-One, he was now in his element. He could plant what he liked, dig where he liked and harvest what he liked. He was free to share with Victoria his love of nature, the earth beneath his feet and the open spaces. They discovered country lanes and cow pastures. They picked wildflowers for Clara. They fed carrots to the tired horses and giggled as the horses nosed their way into the empty bags hoping to find just one more.

"See that one over there? It's an oak tree — must be over a hundred years old. We have to touch it," said Sidney to his daughter.

"Why, why can't we just look at it?"

"Because Mummy says when trees are that old they are wiser than we are, and we have to show them respect and look up to them and put our arms around them to show we love them."

"What will that do?'

"I don't know — make the tree happy? And that one over there is an elm, and there's a chestnut tree." He picked up a nut that had fallen to the ground. "Look. It's prickly outside and has a shiny conker inside," he said as he peeled it apart. "Horses like to eat conkers."

"If the horses eat the conkers, they'll be too full to eat carrots." Victoria began to cry.

Later at home, after she was assured carrots would still be on the menu, Sidney taught Victoria how to play a game called conkers. "First you take something with a point to make a hole in the conker." Sidney paused in thought for a moment. "No, on second thought, I'll do that; it's a bit too dangerous for you. Then you thread the piece of string through the hole like this and make a knot at the end of the string." They worked together on the project, and soon Victoria had a shiny brown conker on the end of a string — and she was ready to attack!

"Now, if your friend has her conker on a piece of string, and you hit her conker with yours and it breaks, then yours becomes a one, and she'll have to find another one to see if she can break your one-er."

"And if I break Pamela's conker, does mine become a two-er?"

"Absolutely. And if we find a really big, strong conker, you could be the season champion — maybe even get as high as a five-er."

Victoria ran off to find a champion conker with Sidney not far behind, and Clara, not understanding a word of their conker discussion, watched them leave on their conker quest. She stared out of the window at the wash hanging on the line. Dolly, the cleaning lady, had been in a day before, and there was nothing to dust or clean. Her thoughts often turned to days spent in Chelsea — a job attached to a forbidden romance with no future. She was twenty-nine, married with a child, living the role of a suburban housewife. Her life so far divided in chapters: Aldgate, where she grew up and played in the shadow of history, then Chelsea, where she didn't belong — and now this.

She appreciated her new home. The surroundings were lovely, and she had few complaints, except it was all just a bit too perfect, too new. No alleyways to explore, no side streets where Samuel Pepys and later Charles Dickens roamed. No old buildings with built-in mysteries. No river just a few yards away. When the sun went down in the suburbs, the streets were deserted, the breeze rustled leaves in the trees, and only the occasional ping of a spade hitting a stone as it was pushed into the ground disturbed the silence.

SHE LED A sedate, quiet life in suburbia, occasionally missing the bustle of Aldgate; but it was still there, if she wanted it, had been for centuries, and nothing had changed London's East End. Here the roads were clear except for a few cars and bicycles. They weren't dangerous to cross, not like Aldgate where you took your life in your hands every time you had to make it to the other side. When Clara first heard the names bestowed upon this new estate, she thought they sounded like something out of *Gulliver's Travels*: Offham Slope, Cissbury Ring, Chanctonbury, Singleton Scarp, and Lullington Garth. Where did they come from?

On Mondays the coalman, carrying a sack of anthracite on his back, unloaded it into the bin at the side of the house. Every day the milkman's horse waited patiently as his master filled a wire basket with bottles to leave at the door. In early spring the man from Bretagne rode in on his bicycle, onions swinging from his handlebars; and the gypsy knife sharpener from Basque-country came by on his borrowed donkey wagon. Once a month the rag and bone man came looking for junk, not too successfully; he'd have to wait a while for his rewards. Suburbia's scrap hadn't yet accumulated.

A constant presence was Alfred the road sweeper, friend to all children, a storyteller and everyman philosopher, an old soldier in old clothes, a finder of lost dogs and stray cats, a man with a long past and an unspecified future. His wasn't a strenuous job, just a few leaves and some cigarette butts. Still, he kept on sweeping invisible dirt because, as he said, "What you don't see could be verrrrrry interesting," and then he put on his serious face, and shaking his head added, "and it might be risky, too."

Nothing much was known about Alfred; he never spoke about himself. He had his territory: the two rings, north and south, a couple of side streets, the main road. Alfred pushed his yellow cart up the hills and down the slopes, shovel standing at attention in the back and his special sacking bag hanging from a hook at the side to hold what he called his special "'fings." Alfred was their man for all seasons, and Victoria loved him. He was her friend. When Alfred swept her street, she ran out to be with him. He always had a story for her.

"Yer see that very straight standin' up man over there with his head bent down? Once a Grenadier Guard, and I calls 'im Mr. Lost-a-Penny cos he never looks up. Now, Victoria, if I'd called 'im Mr. Lost-a-Shilling, then I'd know he was a man wiv a lot of money — lives in a little cottage near the tired 'orses so 'ee can't be rich. And 'ee can't look up, cos 'is 'ead got 'it by a shell from a German gun in the war. Poor old 'fing."

"Poor old 'fing," mimicked Victoria. "If we give him a penny, do you think he'd look up?"

"No, darlin', he won't be lookin' up no more, certainly not for a penny, not even for a five pound note! That's what war does to a Tommy."

EVENINGS SIDNEY CAME back from his work in the city, tired, resentful of his brother, hating the fur trade, and still unwilling or perhaps unable to risk finding alternative employment. Meanwhile, during the day, Clara often took Victoria up to Twenty-One. Each time she marveled at how she'd lived in such cramped surroundings for so long.

Guess I didn't know any better, she concluded to herself. But she missed them; fact was, all too often she begged Sula to come live near her. Mannie said he'd go crazy in the suburbs, and Henry and Nelly would never move. Aldgate was where they were born, and Aldgate was where they would die. As for Anna and Bernie, they were living in Stamford Hill, only a couple of miles away, and they wouldn't think of moving.

Sidney's standard joke to Bernie was, "Wouldn't be a bad place to hide out, Bernie, when a copper's after you."

"Not for me," Bernie would reply. "I'd rather give up the bookie business than move out there." Bernie had come to a never-to-be-challenged assumption that the suburbs were where gentiles lived — not Jews.

Nelly so enjoyed Clara's and Victoria's visits; she preferred having them up at Twenty-One where she felt comfortable and at one with the surroundings — not for her the cows mooing in the meadows or horses with riders clip-clopping their way outside her house. And even Henry, who'd once said he'd like to live in the rest home with the horses, decided he wasn't ready to be put out to pasture.

Cats were Nelly's preference; always two or three up at Twenty-One, and, more often than not, a basket of kittens in a corner of the parlor. Victoria longed for a puppy; she was four years old, a bit of a tomboy, and wasn't interested in dolls.

"Cats are all right for your house, Grandpa, but me and Daddy take long walks with my friends, and they have dogs, and the dogs come with them."

Victoria sounded as if she was the most underprivileged child in the world, and Henry fell for it. He signaled to Victoria. She came over and sat on his lap. He whispered in her ear, "Next Sunday you and me are going to Club Row. We'll say we're going for a walk."

"What's a Club Row?"

"It's a street where people come to sell pets, puppies, birds, kittens and, well, I've even seen snakes and turtles there."

"Not snakes, Grandpa."

"No, of course not. I'm going to find a puppy for you. Now it ain't going to be easy 'cos you'll fall in love with all of them, but I know there will be one puppy that looks at you and sort of says with its eyes, 'Take me 'ome,' and that's the one you'll choose."

"And then what do we do, Grandpa?"

"We'll go back to Twenty-One, and by the time we get there the market will be shut down. If they gets' mad and says take it back, we'll just say, okay — next Sunday when the market opens again."

Victoria's lower lip quivered. "But I don't want to take it back, Grandpa."

"Believe me, it won't happen; your mum and dad will love the puppy as much as we do, and it will be yours forever. Not a word to anyone, promise?"

Victoria was fit to burst with excitement and threw her arms around Henry. "Remember, it's a big secret, just between you and me," said Henry with a hug.

The following Sunday Victoria and Henry set out together for Club Row. Victoria went from one puppy seller to the other; hers was a very difficult decision. Finally she chose a fluffy black Scottie that licked her face and snuggled warmly in her little arms.

"I love him, Grandpa . . . Oh, look, he loves me, too."

"Then 'ee is yours. Now we 'ave to buy 'im a collar and a lead."

There wasn't much of a to-do when they got back to Twenty-One. Clara had a suspicion Henry was up to something; he never did manage to cover anything up.

Victoria was ecstatic, and the puppy was really sweet. "What are you going to call him?' Clara asked of Victoria.

"I don't know."

"How about — Bonnie? He's a Scottie, and that's a sort of Scottish name," Clara suggested.

"I like it. Come, Bonnie, me and Grandpa are going to take you for a walk."

"We'll take a ride to Shadwell Park and walk him there," Henry said, putting on his hat and jacket. "Don't want to frighten the life out of the little thing — taking 'im for his first outing on the streets of Aldgate."

PAUL MAZE RETURNED to France with Rogers, Maggie and the cook. He'd left Chelsea with the intention of selling the farmhouse, but as he drove up the driveway of his beloved childhood home, memories came flooding back and his intentions flew off on the wings of a bumble bee. Here was his past and his recent present, the time spent there with Clara, the beginning of their love affair, a brief moment in time. He'd give his all to have it over again, but it, like so many other things in his life, was gone, and all he had to help him remember was this rundown and overgrown property standing forlorn in the afternoon's fading light. Yvette had been a proud and stubborn woman. She'd refused to accept help, but as he knew only too well, there comes a time in everyone's life when another has to take the reins.

Sunflower remains, brown and wilted on the ground, brought back images of happier days, the vibrant picture of Clara he'd painted as she sat shaded by the tall stalks of the majestic sunflowers in full bloom. Weeds grew in the cracks between the cobblestones, and birds nested in the eaves of a sagging roof. No flowers, no vegetables, just a dry, sad shadow of a once welcome home. He'd been back for Yvette's funeral; it had been an emotional time — too emotional to make decisions. He'd been there with Clara to research his book. It seemed eons ago. He wanted to remember it as it was; he felt compelled to bring it back to life, to live and paint in it again.

Rogers drove him into the old town of Le Havre, and he'd set up his easel on the waterfront. Paul kept away from domestic chores and let the others get on with it. He painted the boats and the fisherman bringing in their catch; he sketched street scenes, then carried the sketches back to the cottage to transfer onto paper or canvas. He remembered telling Clara how remarkable the light was in northern France; it enhanced the color, brought life and warmth, and it made the old streets and buildings of Le Havre come alive. If only she were there with him now. He missed her, everything about her — that smile that lit up the room, her gentle companionship and their love, gone as fast as it began, and though it ended abruptly, she would always remain a presence in his life.

Clara had fulfilled his need to put into words what he'd carried in his mind for close to ten years. He couldn't have done it without her, and he would forever be grateful. Yet he was troubled with the onerous threat of the new Germany, Hitler and his Nazi Party, making promises and breaking them, making threats and carrying them out, causing the years between his war and what he feared would soon be the next to appear only as a lull between that which he fought and another soon to be declared.

Winston Churchill came to visit Paul in France. They painted, and they talked. Winston was convinced war was imminent. Hitler had broken every agreement, every promise and every condition. He could not be trusted; yet the British government was still trying to appease. Hitler offered himself as a rallying point for all disillusioned Germans, and his country was full of them. He convinced the people that democracy was superfluous.

Heinrich still had contacts in Munich and somehow managed to smuggle out information, which he passed on to Churchill. Standing at their easels Churchill confided in Maze, "It's unbelievable what's going on — Hitler is mesmerizing the nation. They look at him as a God."

Maze mimicked him: "Accept me as your Führer. I belong to no class or group. Only to you."

"We cannot afford to underestimate his power. He's initiated the

SS — the Schutzstaffel — try and get your tongue 'round that one. He's enrolled so-called superior physical specimens who swear to him." Churchill rummaged in his pockets to find the quote Heinrich had sent.

> . . . to thee, Adolf Hitler, As Führer and Chancellor of the German Reich, Loyalty and Bravery. I vow to thee and to the superiors, Whom thou shall appoint, Obedience unto death, so help me, God.

"Had the audacity to bring God into it." Churchill returned the quote to his pocket. "If I had my way, I'd put him in chains in a dungeon — even that's too good for him."

"Winston, take a deep breath. You'll have a heart attack, calm down."

"I can't. I have little or no support in Parliament. They're against me for my demand for rearmament, they're worried about spending for up-to-date airplanes, and, God help us all, if they nominate Neville Chamberlain — who's more interested in appeasing than arming — we are done for."

"Put it out of your mind for now, Winston."

"All right — but I have to show you what one Dr. Tom Jones said about me, impudent devil." Out came another rumpled clipping that he handed to Maze, who read aloud:

> When Winston was born lots of fairies swooped down on his cradle handing out gifts, imagination, eloquence, industry and then one fairy said, 'No person should have so many gifts.' So they picked him up, gave him a shake and judgment and wisdom fell out! And that is why we delight to listen to him in the House, and we do not take his advice.

Maze shook his head in dismay and admonished, "You have a pocket full of insults, Winston. Get rid of them!"

"No. I keep them to remind me. I have to continue the fight!"

1939

CHAPTER 35

Declaration of War

B RITISH PRIME MINISTER Neville Chamberlain received the information he was dreading from Britain's Ambassador to Germany, Sir
Neville Henderson. On behalf of the British government, Chamberlain had delivered the following ultimatum to the Third Reich in
Berlin: "Either Hitler withdraws his troops from Poland or war between the two countries will exist."

On the morning of September the third, every wireless in Great
Britain was tuned to the BBC. From Land's End to John O'Groats,
people listened together with neighbors, family and friends to hear
what they had expected for some time. Germany had not responded
to Britain's request. Still and all, at 11:15 that morning the Prime
Minister was prepared to make a statement.

In the East End a barrow boy, helping his dad in Wentworth
Street market, hung his mum's wireless on the side of his barrow, its
long wire running down the road and over the pavement into an
electrical outlet on the wall of a nearby dress shop. "Nearly electro-
cuted myself doin' it, but it works," he explained.

Shoppers and stall owners crowded around as they heard crackles
from the boy's wireless come over the air. "He's made the connection,
and it's working," his dad announced proudly. "Come and listen wiv us."
The crowds gathered as they strained to hear Neville Chamberlain speak.

In a quiet and defeated voice Chamberlain came on the air and
made the announcement everyone was dreading:

I am speaking to you from the Cabinet Room at Ten Down-
ing Street. This morning the British Ambassador in Berlin

handed the German Government a final Note stating that, unless we heard from them by 11 o'clock that they were prepared at once to withdraw their troops from Poland, a state of war would exist between us. I have to tell you now that no such undertaking has been received, and that consequently this country is at war with Germany.

Everyone in the market stood frozen in place, all in a state of shock. It wasn't as if they weren't expecting it, but hearing it from the mouth of the Prime Minister, well, as one of the crowd said later, "That put the kibosh on it." It must have been a full minute or more before the silence was broken. A silent minute in the middle of the day in a busy market could seem like an eternity.

Once again Britain was at war with Germany.

The barrow boy's dad pulled on the wire attached to the wireless to release it from its socket. He'd heard enough. "Remember when Chamberlain came back from Germany wiv a stupid piece of paper in his hand and told us, 'Go home and get a nice quiet sleep.' Wonder if he 'finks we're going to have a nice quiet sleep now?"

"'Oo did 'ee think he was kiddin'?" his mate replied. "Sure sign he'd never bin down 'ere. There's never nuffin' quiet down 'ere, war or no war."

"The Territorials been up the road recruitin' for months; they must 'ave known a thing or two. Mind you, if you ain't got a job, few quid from the army ain't bad, even if you do have to sign on the dotted line."

The corned beef slicer at Bloom's Salt Beef Shop wasn't about to be left out — had to add his three-penny's worth. "We're in it up to our necks. Nineteen Fourteen all over again. Won't be a choice now; the army will get us whether we want to join or not."

The owner of the dress shop came out of his door and followed the snaking wire. "Who's been stealing my electricity?" he demanded.

"Take your pick," the barrow boy replied. "We all 'ave."

Up at Twenty-One, Nelly and Henry were in the parlor, glumly sipping on cups of tea. Having heard the Chamberlain speech, they had no appetite for lunch.

Clara arrived around two in the afternoon with Victoria. Victoria ran to jump on Henry's lap. Clara gave Henry a kiss on his bald head, Victoria hopped down, took off her coat and sat beside Nelly.

"Cup of tea, luv?" Nelly got up to get a cup for Clara and a biscuit for Victoria.

"I had no one to talk to at home. Just had to come and be with the family. You all right, Mum?"

"As right as I can be, considering what we just heard. Mind you, I never thought I'd live to see another war, not in my lifetime."

"We needed someone stronger than Chamberlain, bloke who comes from a working class family; wouldn't you think he'd recognize a con when he sees one? Did he expect Hitler to stand down?" Henry, the king of hindsight, put in.

Mannie had come into the parlor and stood his ground. "Chamberlain had to know what was going on unless, of course, he's deaf, dumb and blind, which I'm beginning to think he might be."

"It was very obvious to me in Germany, and I'm no politician," Clara commented. "I told you to listen to Mr. Churchill. He's been telling us this for months."

"There's none so blind as those who will not see!" Nelly had heard it all before. "Anyway, what could we do about it? Took us forever to stop the Fascists marching in our own streets. How were we supposed to stop the Nazis in Germany?"

Manny paced the room. "And what did the League of Nations do? Not a 'dickey bird'. In their eyes it was a German problem to be sorted out by Germans."

"My poor Lizzie . . . " Nelly realized there was little chance of hearing from her now.

Clara could find no words to comfort Nelly. She'd spared her parents much of what she knew when she came back from her trip with Maze; they had enough on their minds, and she didn't need to add to it. Now the continued lack of communication could only mean Lizzie had been moved to one of the work camps Luftmann spoke of when he'd arrived in London; if Paul knew Dachau was only ten miles out of Munich, he hadn't let on. Could Dachau be where they sent Lizzie? Clara reached out for her mother's hand in consolation.

Henry poured another cup of tea and sat at the table, stirring his cup endlessly.

"Put down the spoon, Henry, before you shove it through the bottom of the cup." Nelly's voice raised a pitch or two; she had to let out her emotions on someone.

Henry kept on stirring, his mind on what his war effort might be. "I wish I was a bit younger, I'd join up."

"It's early days," Clara reassured her dad. "Sooner or later everyone will be involved one way or another. The country will need all the help it can get."

Henry, bucked by Clara's assurance, carried on, saying, "I was in the West End last week, went to visit Ernie and Lenny in Titchfield Street. It was right at lunch by the time I got there, so they pulled down the tarpaulin on their barrows and closed up; never were hard workers, those blokes. We took a walk around and, gawd, what a sight it was. You should have seen it — sandbags and police all over the place. Windows strapped up. They knew this was coming. Barriers everywhere, they even had signs pointing to shelters. Didn't know we had them."

"We don't, not down here," Mannie reminded him.

Clara had come to Aldgate to find comfort for herself, and now she felt she needed to comfort them. "You will stay with us 'til we know a bit more. We've been offered an Anderson Shelter; it's a corrugated iron thing. It goes over a sort of pit; you dig four feet down, and this thing goes over it."

"And me and Grandpa can play in it, can't we, Grandpa?"

"We'll have to see about that, luv."

"Sidney says it looks like a green carbuncle, doesn't want anything to spoil his garden. If it's a matter of safety, he'll have to give in." Clara was already planning where she would put them all.

"I'm not moving." Nelly was adamant.

"You may have to, Mum."

"They'll have to drag me out of Aldgate."

"No sense arguing over it now, but the time may come . . ."

Nelly had heard enough; she got up from the table and left them. "I'm off to the front room to sit at me window. I can think there without any of you telling me where I should go or what I should do. The war only started today; it's a bit soon to plan the rest of our lives. It could all be over in a week or so."

"Not this one, Mum. Not after what I saw in Germany," Clara told her, "They've had much longer to prepare than us; we're at least two years behind them. I don't think Churchill will get much pleasure out of saying, 'I told you so,' but they'll have to listen to him now."

CLARA KNEW HER mum only too well; no one was going to move Nelly away from her East End. They could offer her Buckingham Palace, and she would turn them down. This was her domain, her Twenty-One, where the world — scoundrels and riff raff, peasants and paupers — passed below her window. It was better than going to the pictures. It was an endless changing scene; whether it be in peace or in war there was always something going on outside on the High Street.

Unlike Clara and Sidney, who'd escaped to the suburbs and lived what she consider a dull life in a sweet smelling vacuum where nothing happened — every day the same. Sure they had nice houses and privet hedges; but it still lacked Nelly's window on the world.

Everyone beneath her window had a story, nothing easy, nothing given to them or inherited. Each one of them strived to better themselves, educate their children, offer a better life than they'd had. The funny thing was the ones who left still came back to the markets to do their shopping, visit their friends, a way to stay in touch with their past, and even if they didn't own up to it, to get the freshest food at the best prices — out in the open where it could be seen and touched and bargained for. No pretense where she lived; the merchants wouldn't get away with it if they tried.

Nelly's contemporaries worked seven days a week to make a living, maybe save a bit for a rainy day, never thought of retiring — didn't run away to a posh place and look down on where they started. It was their offspring who left the East End, wanting something better — and maybe what they found was — but not for her. It wouldn't be right for her. Anna and Bernie in Stamford Hill. Sula and Mannie soon to move to Finsbury Park — she didn't mind that so much, it wasn't that far away. Mannie had found a ground floor flat with easy access. She'd still be able to keep an eye on Sula.

Sitting alone at her window she recalled their trip to Brighton, a week's holiday with Henry; it was years ago. They'd stayed in a bed and breakfast in Brighton. At bedtime they put out the light and stayed awake all night. "The silence was deafening," that's how she put it. Like the world had disappeared. She'd tried to sleep — not a tram, not a person, not a sound.

"Can't have this, Henry," she said. "Can't have a silent holiday."

The next day they moved to a place nearer the beach; at least there she could hear the waves lapping against the shore and the hurdy-gurdy man on the promenade.

Nelly's parents and their parents before them had lived all their lives within a mile of Twenty-One. If it was good enough for them, it was good enough for her. War was no stranger; she'd watched her uncle march up the gangplank of the ship taking troops to fight the Boer War in South Africa. She'd seen her brother join up in the War-to-end-all-wars. She'd known young men who volunteered to fight in Spain. Even before Chamberlain spoke she'd seen parents queuing at railway stations with their children, sending them away, frightened by threats of gas attacks and bombs. Hasty retreats were not for her, far better to wait and see. She didn't approve of youngsters being separated from their families. Families stayed together, and hers would too. Already there were barrage balloons in the sky and civil defense men trying their best to frighten the life out of her. What to do in case of an air raid; how to put on a gas mask; where to go when you heard a siren. They didn't need none of that in the last war, load of rubbish, probably wouldn't need it in this one either. Gave the older fellers something to do, made 'em feel important.

Clara left Aldgate that afternoon concerned for her family, realizing their proximity to the docks, and understanding the East End would probably be one of the first targets in London. Germany had planes. Germany had bombs. She watched Victoria skip along High Street on the way to Aldgate Station, happy as the day was long, unaware of what all the fuss was about. No need to frighten the child. But if they were bombed or worse still, invaded, what then?

THE WEEK AFTER Chamberlain's announcement, an ARP bloke came up and showed Nelly how to make a bed under the table, as if she didn't have the sense to do it herself. "If an air raid occurs, Mrs. Levy, and a bomb falls on your abode, you'll be safe under that table."

"If an air raid occurs and a bomb falls on Twenty-One, none of us will be in any state to get under the table, so I suggest you go somewhere else and tell them."

The ARP bloke was about to leave when the siren went off, "Just practicing," he said.

Nelly told him if they had to practice could they please arrange to do it somewhere else and not on a Sunday afternoon.

"This is very serious," he told her. "We chose the weekend on purpose; more people around saves us time. Don't have to repeat ourselves quite as often. Here." He offered her a pamphlet.

"What's this for?"

"It instructs you on how to put out a fire."

"You're teaching your grandma to suck eggs, young man. I know what to do. We've had a couple of them, fat spitting out on the stove, bucket of water and out it goes."

"I'm talking about fire bombs, lady."

"A fire is a fire, don't matter what causes it. If anything drops through this roof, it will have gone three floors by the time it reaches the parlor, and by then I'll have run like hell to the fire station down the road."

"Read it and keep it where you can refer to it." He wasn't taking any more of Nelly's lip.

The Women's Voluntary Service also had a go at her with their representatives stationed at the corner of Aldgate High Street and the Minories. They'd set up their own barrier, couldn't get past them if you tried. They handed out lists of instructions: what to do in case of an emergency; what to store in case shops had to close; what to do in an air raid.

Nelly got a new list every time she walked past them. "Thank you very much," Nelly said when she read the food suggestions. "We don't eat bacon, we don't touch lard, and we certainly don't approve of potted pork." What she didn't tell them was her liking for jellied eels, equally un-kosher as some of the other items on the list, she wouldn't have objected to them in the least. Bit of a hypocrite at times was Nelly.

In the last war she and Henry watched from the rooftop as the zeppelins flew over, quite a sight they were.

"Never quite sure what they were supposed to do," she told Clara. "We heard they might have something to do with surveillance.

Nothing happened to them, and nothing happened to us."

Against her better judgment Nelly had to admit this war might be different from the last one. Hitler was marching his troops through Europe; he'd taken Czechoslovakia, annexed Austria, threatened to invade and had carried out his threat in Poland, and now had his eye on France. If he got to France, England could be next — and that worried her. The war had at last gotten Nelly's attention.

1940

CHAPTER 36

England

A SKED BY THE King to be Prime Minister and to form a coalition government, Winston Churchill recognized he'd have little time for painting. With his wife Clemmie's blessing, he snatched a weekend break in Normandy with Paul Maze.

"Whatever happens, you must not give up painting," Maze warned. "It has served you well in the past, lightened your dog days and produced good work."

"Time, my friend, it will all be a matter of available time," Churchill replied.

"The people are on your side, Winston."

"I sometimes wonder if we could have averted war if I'd been more demanding, if I could have found a way to make those fools in government see what I saw so clearly."

"Even if you had, Winston, Hitler is not a man who listens to reason. Do not blame yourself," Maze cautioned.

Still, Churchill could not hide his disgust of Neville Chamberlain. "I cannot believe the man was so naïve and so plainly submissive. I have to tell you I am ashamed of my government's unabashed friendship with the German Foreign Minister, Joachim Von Ribbentrop. I warned them again and again to stand up to Hitler, and for that I've been ridiculed, humiliated or, what is worse, ignored. Makes a man's dog days look like a walk in the park!" He dabbed angrily at his painting.

"No need to let it out on the canvas," Maze admonished, as he worked away on his own canvas.

Churchill put down his brush, pulled a cigar from his breast coat pocket and struck a match. A few deep puffs and his mood changed.

"By the way, whatever happened to that young pretty secretary of yours?"

"Clara?"

"Yes, Clara."

"She became pregnant and chose not to work any more." Maze poured a glass of wine from a flask. "Must say I miss her — she was . . . well, you probably realize she was more than just a secretary to me."

"Had a soft spot for her myself." Winston smiled, obviously remembering Clara's beauty. "I wouldn't have let her go quite so easily."

"Circumstances were against us. I was married, she was married, and with a baby on the way . . . she had to leave."

"So, you are not in contact?"

Maze put brush to canvas. Memories came flooding back; Clara had been with him in Normandy, standing exactly where he and Winston were now. Those were lighthearted days, the dawning of their affair, all gone, all vanished.

Churchill let the subject of Clara rest; he could see it pained Paul to talk about her. "I must complete my painting." Back at his easel and dabbing at the canvas, he commented to his friend, "I believe this is the last picture we shall paint in peaceful surroundings for a very long time."

WITH THE GERMAN Army intent on occupying France, the reports from every front were becoming more ominous with every passing day. All eligible men, eighteen to forty-one, were notified to appear before the army medical board. Sidney, at the age of thirty-five, fell in that category. "Says here, Thursday of next week." He had read his notification aloud to Clara.

"Then you'll have to go. Don't worry; they probably won't take you."

"Why'd you think that?" He wasn't sure whether he should be pleased or upset by her remark.

"You've got a back problem. They'll have plenty of healthy youngsters." Clara didn't seem at all concerned.

With Clara's words ringing in his ears Sidney reported to the enlistment office the following week, only to be disqualified ten minutes after he'd said good morning to the doctor. Clara was right about his back condition, but she had no knowledge of a heart murmur, and neither did he! Anyway, the doctor said there was nothing they could do about his back — wasn't serious — and sent him on his way.

Julius had sleepless nights wondering how his factory could carry on if Sidney was called up. He slept well, however, after Sidney told him he'd been rejected, but he had another surprise in store. There were strings attached to Sidney's release.

A government inspector came to the factory a week later, and without a by-your-leave announced, "You're out of the fashion business. Your factory is to be turned over to war work."

Julius could see his profits flying out the window.

"You will be making fur coats for Russian soldiers and allied troops serving in cold climates. We'll supply the skins and patterns. You'll be paid on delivery of the finished garments. The more you turn out, the better the reward."

Julius's world collapsed before his eyes. The fashion fur coat mogul of London's East End had met his match. No more selling, no more flirting with the models, no more stacking wads of money in his private safe; he'd been taken over by the government's recently passed National Service Act, and there was no escape. Neither would Julius be appearing in fashion salons or displaying Sidney's creations on the runways. From being a man about town with an entrée to the top fashion houses, Julius was now a driver collecting cheap skins from government warehouses, while Sidney's fashion talent was relegated to routine, everyday, boring, repetitive work.

Sidney's on and off decision to leave Julius and the fur trade was no longer an option. The war put an end to his agonizing. He was stuck in it for the duration. Not much glamour for him or his brother, but, at last, they were equal.

FOR THE FIRST year of the war, the ARP advised everyone to be cautious and gave suggestions. Clara opted to sleep in the cupboard under the staircase in the event Germany might suddenly decide to attack London.

Victoria stamped her foot and said, "I won't go in that cupboard; it's scary. Witches on brooms live there, and daddy longlegs, and Cuddles won't like it." Cuddles was an oversized doll Julius had brought back for her from one of his earlier trips to America.

"I'll be with you, and we'll keep the door open," Clara assured her.

Two months of sleeping under the stairs was enough for Clara. They'd been offered an Anderson Shelter that had to be sunk in a six-by-six-foot hole. It broke Sidney's heart to dig up his garden to accommodate such an abomination, and to add insult to injury, the first time it rained the shelter filled with ankle deep water.

"Get rid of it, Sidney," Clara announced after a few nights of sleeping in it, "We'll catch pneumonia or worse, rheumatic fever, if we stay in it a moment longer."

Sidney, who'd slaved for weeks over the confounded thing, took no notice.

But it did not end there.

After the Anderson came the Morrison Shelter — a contraption that looked like a cage with a flat steel top; it substituted for a dining room table. Sidney refused to get in it; Clara called it a rat-trap; and Victoria wouldn't venture anywhere near it unless accompanied by her puppy Bonnie, her doll Cuddles and her mother.

Panic was beginning to set in. The cold war had come to an end. Bombs were falling on London. More than half of London's children were evacuated to the countryside, and Clara was advised Victoria be one of them. Reluctantly she and Sidney let Victoria go to a farm recommended by the Women's Voluntary Service. Mrs. Gould, a farmer's wife, had agreed to take in a few deserving children from London.

Victoria, clutching Cuddles, joined a group of children on a bus heading for Derbyshire. Clara tried unsuccessfully to hold back tears and Sidney's lower lip trembled as the bus pulled away. They waved goodbye together with other mums and dads, all as distraught as Clara and Sidney were at the removal of their children. It would be three weeks before they'd see their children again.

At the end of the third week, Clara travelled alone by train to Derbyshire. Sidney had a quota to fill and couldn't go. It was a warm, sunny day. The countryside surrounding the farm was beautiful, the accommodation dreadful; the farmhouse was dilapidated, old as the hills, a rambling shack. Cows, goats and chickens seemed to be everywhere. Mrs. Gould's children, Clara counted five and another four evacuees dressed in dirty dungarees, clothes too big or too small, and with little or no supervision, were everywhere, up trees, jumping in muddy water, even plucking dead chickens.

Victoria's hair, once long and golden, was a dull grey color and impossible to brush. Clara checked her daughter from tip of her head to the bottom of her toes. She discovered Victoria's black eye was actually coal dust, her neck ingrained with the same, her clothes not the ones she was sent with, and when she wiped away the dirt on Victoria's knee she discovered a large scab. "What's this from?" she asked, never having seen her daughter in such a state.

"I fell down a coal mine," Victoria owned up nonchalantly.

"You did what? There's a coal mine close by?" No one told Clara her daughter was in a mining area. "What were you doing in a coal mine?"

"Not really in it, Mummy, just 'round about it. I chased a rabbit."

That was enough for Clara. She went directly to Mrs. Gould and lodged a complaint.

Mrs. Gould assured her the children were well fed and the reason for their somewhat disheveled look was due to a water problem. A pipe had burst, her husband was in the army, and her oldest son didn't know how to fix it. They had sent a messenger to the plumber in the village, and he hadn't yet arrived. She'd heard since that he might've been called up.

"My children might look a bit scruffy," she said, "but a bit of dirt never hurt anyone. You sent them here to keep them safe, and safe they are. That's all that matters as far as I'm concerned."

"Safe? My child fell down a coal mine. You call that safe?" Clara exclaimed. "I'm taking her home!"

"Do what you like," Mrs. Gould replied; she had so many kids, one more or less wouldn't make any difference.

Victoria started to cry. "I love it here, Mummy," Victoria pleaded. "I've got lots of friends; we play together on the slag heap near the coal mine. We only have to bathe once a week, and we don't have to go to school. I love the chickens and the goats and the cows . . ." Victoria went on and on. "And I told Uncle Fred I can't go near the pigs 'coos I'm Jewish, so he let me feed the chickens."

"Who's Uncle Fred?" Clara implored.

Mrs. Gould answered. "He's my brother, won't take him in the forces; he's a bit slow but loves my kids, all of them, Mrs. Simon," and she repeated, "all of them."

Who knew what Uncle Fred might be up to? Clara's imagination ran wild. She took Victoria aside. "Mrs. Gould has been very kind to you, my darling, but soon you'll have things crawling in your head, and your knee will become septic."

"Well, you're wrong, Mummy. I want to stay here, and Mrs. Gould said we should call her Mother."

If nothing else convinced Clara to remove her daughter from Mrs. Gould's clutches, that did it.

"If we are destined to be wiped out, Mrs. Gould, at least we'll be wiped out together, and we'll arrive at the pearly gates clean!" Clara made her move.

"Got five more kids coming next week," Mrs. Gould shouted out as Clara left, pulling an unwilling Victoria by the hand. "Pity your Victoria won't be here to greet them."

"I'm reporting you," Clara shouted back.

"Won't do no good; they can't find enough places for city kids. Got to take what they can get."

VICTORIA CRIED ALL the way home. And she cried when she reached home. And she cried for a week after reaching home.

"Is this because we took you away from Mrs. Gould?" Clara asked.

"Yes, Mrs. Gould looked after my ear, and you haven't."

"Ear?" Mrs. Gould had not mentioned anything about her ear.

"Mrs. Gould put oil in my ear and made it better. Now it's bad again."

"I knew it. She's picked up something at that dreadful place. Phone the doctor, Sidney." He didn't have to be asked twice.

Dr. Stewart came later that day and made his diagnosis. "Serious infection, she'll have to be admitted to Great Ormond Street Hospital. It's a bit of a way, but I'll drive you there; mustn't waste any time with this sort of thing."

"It's all my fault," Clara cried, beside herself with guilt as she packed night clothes for Victoria.

Sidney lifted Victoria and wrapped her in a blanket. "It's all right, sweetheart, the doctor will make you all better."

Once again they were met with a draconian matron. "The surgeon will see her in the morning. You must leave now."

"Surgeon? Leave? I'll do nothing of the sort." Clara stood her ground.

"Doctor's diagnosis," she read the admission paper, "mastoid."

"What's that?"

"Mastoid. She'll need surgery to remove disease from the bone behind the ear."

"Oh, my God."

"God cannot perform the surgery, Mrs. Simon, neither can Dr. Stewart; he's a family doctor, not a surgeon. We'll give her something to sleep, and by this time tomorrow she'll be a lot more comfortable."

Victoria yelled and screamed.

Clara wept while she filled in the forms.

Sidney paced and an air raid warning wailed outside. "There's a shelter in the basement — if you wish to use it," Matron advised.

Sidney glanced at Clara, looking for an answer. "No, we'll take our chances." They left with Victoria in the hospital crying hysterically, while waking up an entire ward of sick children and being told to keep quiet by a staff nurse who'd been summoned to "shut the child up!"

Aldgate was closer than the suburbs. "I need my mum, let's stay in Aldgate tonight." Clara held on to Sidney's arm. "I shouldn't have left Victoria with that awful Gould woman."

A building burned brightly in the distance, searchlights swept the sky.

"I don't know, Clara. I hate to have her away from us. What if the hospital gets bombed?"

Clara didn't need any reminders about the awful situation they were all in.

SIDNEY PACED UP and down Nelly's parlor; no sooner had he reached one end he turned to go back to the other. It was a small room. Finally he gave up and sat at the table, drumming his fingers.Clara had no patience for Sidney's nervous habits; they unnerved her even more. "Stop that, Sidney. Have a cigarette, take a walk."

"You're crazy, Clara. There's been no 'all clear' sounded."

Henry came down in his dressing gown. "What's all this?"

Nelly answered, knowing he'd be in a right state when he got the news. "Sit down, luv, its Victoria; she's at Great Ormond Street with a bit of an earache."

"You just left her there?" Henry was appalled.

"They asked us to leave, Dad, when the raid began. Said they had enough trouble looking after the kids; they didn't need us there, too."

Henry and Nelly, Clara and Sidney sat looking at each other, cringing every time an explosion rocked the building; it was a nightly occurrence. They never knew whether they'd be around to tell the tale the next morning.

"Want to go under the table?" Henry asked, trying to be helpful. Their silence answered his question. Two hours later the "all clear" sounded.

"Clara, take the couch in the front room," Nelly directed. "Sidney, there's an air mattress, a lilo, in the cupboard for you. And, Henry, you want to sleep under the table, be my guest, I'm going to bed." And Nelly left the room.

MONDAY MORNING SIDNEY left for work, and Clara took a bus to the hospital. It was not an easy journey, with the debris from the bombing and the smoke from smoldering buildings.

Arriving early for visiting hours, Clara was prepared to wait, desperately wanting to know how Victoria was doing. She approached the main desk where the Women's Volunteer Service was set up. "Can you tell me how my daughter is?" Clara gave the woman Victoria's name.

"Let me see, my dear. Awful, isn't it, having to send the poor dears away like this? Mind you, better than having them here; a bomb hit down the street last night, shattered our windows and caused a bit of a ruckus." She continued nattering, while she searched for Victoria's name."

It hadn't registered with Clara what the woman had said. "Could you just tell me how she is?"

"Right, dear, our little Victoria is — such small print — can't make it out . . . "

Clara snatched the list from her.

"You can't do that!"

"Here, I've found her. Why didn't someone tell me she's been moved?" Clara read on. "Hemel Hempstead? Where the hell's that?"

"Go to the man over there, he'll tell you." The woman was furious with Clara. "Next, please."

Hemel Hempstead turned out to be a cottage hospital, miles from anywhere. "Oh, it's a lovely little place is Hemel Hempstead," the man "over there" reported. "Mentioned in the Doomsday Book, dates back even further, Eighth Century, I believe."

Clara hadn't asked for a history lesson, she just wanted to find her daughter. "How do I get there?"

"Oh, well, that's another story. Train's your best bet. Not sure from where, though."

What should she do? Go to Sidney at the factory? No, too far out of the way. Tell Nelly and Henry? Not a good idea. She decided to go it alone; she'd find a way to get to Hemel Hempstead.

Clara had left Aldgate before nine that morning. She eventually arrived at the hospital in Hemel Hempstead at four the same afternoon, only to be met by another stern faced matron.

"Sorry, what did you say your name is?" Matron inquired.

"Clara Simon. You have my daughter here. Victoria Simon."

"Right. She was operated on yesterday evening in London and sent down here by ambulance." Matron shuffled through a series of files to find Victoria's name. "Here it is."

Clara waited impatiently

"It says Victoria Simon is resting, and I see notes for the medical staff here." Matron placed the file back in the pile.

"That's it?"

"She's not the only patient in the hospital, madam!"

"I have to see her."

"I'm afraid that will not be possible. Visiting hours for children are over for the day. You can take a peek through the ward window if you like."

"Peek? I've just taken a bus, a tram and three trains and walked a mile to get here, and you have the gall to say I can't go in to see my daughter?"

"I don't make the rules, Mrs. Simon. If we allowed all parents in after visiting hours, it would be impossible to control the children. We're overcrowded as it is, and I can't allow one set of rules for them and another for you."

"I live miles from here."

"That is not my problem. I suggest you do what I say — don't let her see you — and then leave. Come back tomorrow. She'll be better and so will you."

VICTORIA REMAINED IN hospital for two weeks. Sidney and Clara visited over the weekend, and Clara went during the week, although the bus and train schedules were impossible to rely upon. When Victoria was finally released, Clara prevailed upon her taxi driving cousin to bring her home, which he did with the help of Solly Tenser, who just happened to have some black market petrol coupons hidden in his back pocket.

Thereafter, Mrs. Gould was cursed daily, but not by Victoria, who was ready to go back — if only Clara would let her.

"Over my dead body," Clara muttered.

"Why can't I go back to Mother Gould?" Victoria asked Sidney, her left ear still covered in bandages, her hearing had not altogether returned.

Sidney had to come up with some explanation quickly. "She said Mrs. Gould isn't taking children from London any more because . . . "

Clara jumped in, saying, "Because she's got lots of animals and lots of children, and she can't take on more."

"She was going to teach me to milk a cow. Now I'll never know, it's not fair." If Victoria had thoughts of becoming a farmer in her later years, all hope was lost.

CHAPTER 37

London's East End

Up at Twenty-One, Henry's predictions came true. The East End was under attack. "Told you so," Henry announced, "told you we'd be the first to be clobbered."

"The one time when you should have got it wrong, you get it right." Nelly groaned as she cleaned up glass from the shattered window in the front room.

"Well, I knew it in me bones, and we ought to do something about it."

"Like what?" Nelly stopped sweeping — waiting for his answer.

Henry wasn't sure what he should say, so he said nothing.

Mannie stood on the steps of St. Botolph's before a hostile crowd demanding the East End be allocated more shelters. "Who's getting bombed every night? Not you, Lord Dunamucks!" Mannie referred to imaginary members of the House of Lords, the cockney moniker for the titled few. "You and your lot move to your country houses. We would too, if we had one! This is where we live, near the docks, in a flat, in a room where every night incendiary bombs drop all around us, and we go up in flames. You've evacuated our kids, you've looked after yourselves, and while we get the brunt of it, you're sipping gin and tonics on your manicured lawns. It's not right, and it's not fair, and we're not going to put up with it."

Always the spokesman for the working man, the years had not dimmed Mannie's passion. He'd fought for the rights of soldiers from the last war, and he was doing the same for them and for their families now. He might not have a rifle, but he had a voice, and he was

311

using it for those who were unable to speak for themselves.

In a way, Clara thought, listening to Mannie, it's what Paul accomplished in his book. He portrayed the suffering of the ordinary man, the soldier sent out to do the bidding of the generals. Mannie despised the upper classes — them and their unearned privileges. In his eyes, Paul Maze was one of them. But Mannie was wrong. Paul wasn't like that. He was as much a man of the people as Mannie was. Hadn't he also fought in the Great War, volunteered, in fact, in the trenches with the foot soldiers?

And her Sidney, duty bound, never one to shirk his responsibilities, got himself the title of Fire Watcher, First Stirrup Pump, and though he was the most un-mechanical man on the planet, he became the keeper of the fire hydrant a few yards away from where they lived. "God help us all if he's called to use it," she remembered telling her neighbor Shirley. "He hasn't a clue how to connect the pump to the hydrant." They had a good laugh that day at Sidney's expense.

The laughter ceased when a fire bomb fell down their shared chimney. Gordon, Shirley's husband, ran out, completely forgetting he had a wife, and closed the door behind him. Shirley, hanging her ample bosoms over the window ledge, yelled to be rescued. Gordon, in his pajamas, had not only left his wife, he'd forgotten to take the key to get back in. Clara woke to find the house cloaked in smoke, and Sidney rushed to find his stirrup pump.

A passing warden shouted, "Put the bloody light out," and Clara answered him, "I'll put the bloody light out once you put the bloody fire out!"

Eventually Shirley clambered down the warden's ladder, her bloomers floating in the breeze. By the time Sidney managed to connect the pump to the hydrant, the wardens had the fire under control.

Clara became aware of Mannie's voice again. She'd been lost in thought, day dreaming, or maybe reliving a near nightmare, she supposed. She had to get her mind back to the present.

"Join me," Mannie was saying. "Tomorrow we march on Westminster — we'll let them know we mean business, and by that I mean equality. What's good for them has to be good for us!"

The crowd cheered.

THAT NIGHT ANOTHER air raid siren woke Henry and Nelly. A warden yelled up to them, "Get out of there immediately. Baskets of incendiary bombs are falling from German planes, and your building is on fire."

Henry jumped out of bed to put on the light, only to find there was no electricity. He grabbed a candle, found a match and was about to run up to rescue his stock in the storage room . . .

Nelly grabbed his nightshirt and held him back. "Put the candle out, there's enough fire up there to light the length and breadth of the High Street. You don't have to add to it, and you're not risking your life for a few bars of soap!"

"It's our livelihood," Henry lamented.

"It's our lives," Nelly replied. She threw him his dressing gown and put on hers. Fortunately the staircase was still intact, and they rushed down to the parlor.

"Get Boadicea," Nelly ordered.

"I thought you hated that bird."

"I do. If anyone's going to roast it, it'll be me."

"Everything we own is in here."

"Just grab the box with our papers — "

"But Nelly — "

"Don't Nelly me, we've got to get out of here. I can hear the fire engines; perhaps they'll be able to save some of our stuff."

Nelly's cats mewed, waiting desperately to be let out. Henry fiddled with the doorknob; it was hot to the touch. Nelly threw him a cloth, and with a bit of coaxing the door opened. Together they made their way through Half Moon Passage and on to the High Street where crowds were gathering.

A warden shouted through a megaphone, "Keep moving, make your way to St. Botolph's. Stop gawking, it's too dangerous, won't do no good."

Henry and Nelly were pushed along with the crowd, all heading for St. Botolph's, where they were herded into the church basement.

"Never thought I'd be happy to be in a church," Henry said, sitting on a cold bench and holding the parrot cage on his lap.

"It's made of stone; stone don't catch fire," an unknown voice advised.

"Could get a direct hit," some pessimistic bloke reminded them.

"Then we wouldn't know nuffin' about it, would we?"

"So put a sock in it," said another lost soul.

A chaplain came around handing out blankets. "Anyone want to pray?" he asked. He got a few customers; the rest stayed where they were, mulling over thoughts and memories.

Nelly, pensive, asked, "How long we been up at Twenty-One, Henry?"

"Must be forty years if it's a day."

"It's been good to us."

"It has, luv, I got no complaints. Have to see what's left of it when they let us out of here."

"Won't be much," said an old bloke sitting next to Henry. "My place blew up five minutes after I got out. Bloody lucky, I'd say. Mind you, there were a few rats running around — not altogether sorry it's gone."

"None where we live," Nelly assured him. "Our cats saw to that. You should've had cats."

"No matter now, does it?" an old codger answered. "I'll go and live wiv me daughter — if them Germans 'aven't blown her place to smithereens."

"Looks like we'll all land up with our daughters," Henry said dejectedly.

"We'll see about that." Nelly opened the blanket and shared it with Henry. "Put that perishing parrot down. Come closer to me; we'll use the other blanket for our knees. It's damp as all get out down here. Two Jews in a perishing cold church; now if that's not a turn up for the books, I'd like to know what is!"

A priest walking by stopped when he heard Nelly complain. "This church has stood for over a hundred years," he said in a preacher tone. "One has to expect a certain amount of condensation to build up in that time."

Nelly, duly admonished, wrapped the blanket 'round their knees and moved closer to Henry, feeling the warmth of his body next to hers. She closed her eyes; all the years they lived up at Twenty-One playing out before her — memories of better days flooded in. The day she met Henry on the beach front in Brighton she'd gone down for a day's outing with Lizzie, and it was just after Queen Victoria's funeral.

Henry was very handsome then, he in his white spats, trilby and gray suit. She wore her new lace dress down to her ankles and spruced it up with a Lily Langtry hat. Henry sang and she joined in, "and he walked along the promenade with an independent air, you could hear the girls declare, 'He must be a millionaire'" — music and words, that's what they had in common.

They courted for a couple of years, and when they'd saved up enough they got married, started a family almost immediately. All born at Twenty-One — couldn't buy the place, never had enough to do that, just rented it. They'd collected a few things over time, nothing of great value, still all their worldly possessions were up there, pictures and photo albums, the piano and the sheet music, the gramophone, records — didn't bear thinking about. Lucky the girls had moved out and taken their stuff with them. Would there be anything left?

Nelly forced herself to stay positive, to think of what they'd had, not of what they might have lost. She glanced over at Henry. He'd aged; two years of war had taken its toll. Never one for wearing his heart on his sleeve, still, it showed on his face. Good thing he had his stall in Leather Lane — something to go back to in the morning — if it was gone, it could be replaced, not like a home, bricks, mortar and wood . . . "

"Don't like it down here, Nelly. Don't seem right!" Henry muttered in a dreamy sleep, his head on Nelly's shoulder. Henry was remembering his girls, just kids, sitting on the floor of the stock room counting out hairpins. He'd given them a job — fifteen to a bundle. When they'd finished with the hairpins he'd get them to wrap soap. Solly Tenser specials, probably rejects, they made them look nice.

Imperial Leather Soap came already wrapped, bestseller that one. And the Yardley Lavender Ladies — Nelly's favorite, be a shame if they got smashed. Nelly held on to Henry, not realizing until now how much she loved him, warts and all; never been another man in her life. Henry had his own ways, bit of a dreamer really. Dreamed he would win at the races. Dreamed the stall would bring in good money; it did all right but no great fortunes to be made there. They'd never be rich, but they had enough — and they had each other.

Nelly's thoughts turned to Sula, had hopes of swimming the channel; a bit far fetched, she thought at the time, but that was a long ago fantasy. She was back in the hospital. And Clara, the arrival of Victoria probably saved her, way out of her league with that Maze man. Was it only a fling? She hoped so, gave her a look at the outside world, didn't take her long to see she'd never belong there. Sidney saw that; he was wise to take her off to the suburbs. Aldgate might not be the place for Clara, but it was right for Nelly. And if she couldn't return to Twenty-One, where would she go? Not away from London; she couldn't bear the thought of it. The suburbs? Oh, dear God, please, not the suburbs.

"All clear!" a priest shouted from a makeshift pulpit. "Make your way slowly and follow me."

Henry was snoring; Nelly gave him a gentle nudge. "Got to go, luv, time to get out of here."

Henry came to, not quite knowing where he was. "Where we goin', Nelly?"

"Home, if we still have one."

"Don't think I can take it, luv,"

"You got to, Henry, unless, of course, you'd like me to go by myself and come back to give you a report!"

"Don't be ridiculous."

"Then move yerself; we've got cleaning up to do."

Henry and Nelly, with Boadicea in her cage, walked slowly up the old stone steps of St. Botolph's, their eyes gradually adjusting to the light of early dawn. Smoke filled the air. Fire trucks, ambulances and police vans blocked their way, dead and injured being carried out of bombed buildings, people in shock standing in disbelief outside their broken homes. Bricks, rubble, stray cats and dogs, a confusion of agonizing destruction left after the worst raid ever on London's densely populated East End.

"Can't go through there, lady," said a policeman. "Where you live?"

"Twenty-One, on the High Street."

"I suggest you cut through to Middlesex Street, when you get to Wentworth Street . . . " He was about to give them better directions when Nelly stopped him.

"It's all right, officer; we've lived here all our lives, we know the way."

It was a tedious, heartbreaking walk, an obstacle course over fallen bricks, smoldering wood and shattered glass; pieces of furniture blown out into the street, people digging among the rubble, sitting on torn chairs, throwing buckets of water over smoldering sofas — destruction everywhere. They reached Old Castle Street, crossed over to Half Moon Passage and looked up at Twenty-One.

"Well, the outside's still standing, that's a miracle." Nelly gripped Henry's arm.

"Got no windows," Henry noted.

"Don't matter; we already lost some in the last raid."

Henry and Nelly stood among hundreds, maybe thousands of desperate people, not sure where they were going, all landmarks destroyed, turning left, turning right, couples holding on to bedding and old ladies clutching their treasures in pillow cases. A man cradled a basket of kittens in his arm; a boy carried a bicycle on his head because there certainly wasn't a place to ride it. Tea ladies setting up tables, firemen aiming hoses at burning buildings, ARP with the Civil Defense searching for signs of life — and added to all the commotion, Boadicea woke up, squawking away like a mad thing.

"Shove your jacket over her, for gawd's sake, Henry."

"No one's going to take any notice of a perishing bird, Nelly."

Shopkeepers had begun to board up gaping holes where windows had once been. Barrow boys and stall owners searched in vain for clear spots; there weren't any. Fire fighters were running out of water.

"We'll have to get it from the river," one of the firemen shouted.

"My son-in-law's got a stirrup pump, could give 'im a ring for yer," Henry offered Sidney's help.

"Won't do no good here, the hydrants 'ave dried up, and if yer 'fink the telephone's workin', 'fink again. They ain't. 'Fanks anyway, mate."

Henry spotted Alf, standing outside his pub. "You all right, Alf?"

"Looks like an Irish wedding in there; don't know where to start."

Up at Twenty-One it wasn't much better. The front room was a disaster, glass shards and splinters stuck in the three piece suite, curtains ripped and scorched, carpet smoldering but, to Nelly's delight, The Lavender Ladies had survived.

Henry lifted the lid of the piano and hit a couple of notes, "Still got a song left in it's 'eart, Nelly." He swiveled on the bench to estimate the damage. "Mind you, the rest of the place don't look too good."

Nelly more concerned about her home, and knowing Henry wasn't one for chores, made a suggestion. "Why don't you go downstairs and talk to Alf. He needs a friend."

"What about all this?"

"Leave it to me, Henry, and stop walking around with that parrot. Put the cage back on the stand."

Henry left reluctantly. She'd be better off without him; he wouldn't know where to start. She could scrub and clean till the cows came home; it wouldn't do much good. The place would be condemned, it had to be. No one could live in it. The upstairs might collapse any minute, and anyway it wouldn't be up to Nelly whether she stayed or not. They'd be ordered to leave, she was sure of that. Still, cleaning up would give her something to do, even if it was a waste of time — better than sobbing her heart out. She'd eventually have to see reason. This wasn't the first raid to hit them, and it certainly wasn't going to be the last. Perhaps they'd let him get his stock from the attic. What was he thinking? The attic was on fire before they fled, and there was nothing left.

Henry, too emotional for the moment to go down to Alf, sat on the landing of Twenty-One, a lifetime of living gone in a matter of moments. He remembered the day he met Nelly, couldn't call her pretty, handsome, yes, and, in his eyes she still was. The pretty ones he once knew lost their looks as the years passed by, but not his Nelly.

He recalled when he told Nelly he loved her; she'd got that funny look of hers and said, "I hope that means you want to marry me, no funny business, Henry."

They'd had a good life together, three lovely girls, and three good sons-in-law. Only wanted the best for them. Pity he couldn't give them the education they deserved, they'd done all right in spite of it, especially Clara, his favorite. He wondered if she still hankered after that Frenchman; none of his business, really. And so it went.

What would it take to convince Nelly to leave Twenty-One? She wouldn't listen to him; the authorities would have to take over, carry her out bodily, if necessary. He just hoped she would come to her senses before she was forced. Enough holding on to the banister rail; it's like me, he thought, hanging on by a thread.

The back door to the pub lay on the ground, blown off by the blast of a bomb. Henry cautiously picked his way through the rubble to find Alf sitting at what was left of his bar, nursing a whisky.

"Want a drink, Henry?"

"Not one for booze meself, but, under the circumstances, yes, I'll join yer."

They made a toast among the remains in the Half Moon Pub: "To Hitler — strung up by his balls." Alfred swigged down what was left in his glass and poured another.

"He's only got one." Henry reminded him.

"One will do!" Alfred figured.

"Think we're done for this time, Alf, probably bring in the bulldozers and level it. Gone in one fell swoop, our history, our pub, our street, our singsongs."

"Gone," said Alf.

"Funny the way you miss what you've got when you can't have it anymore." The drink was going to Henry's head.

"Too bloody right, Henry," Alf was also getting in his cups, "Can't keep crying over spilt booze, that's what I say; just have to turn out the light and call it a day."

"Can't turn out the light, Alf, electricity's off."

Alf searched for the right words. "It's me fate, got to accept it. What's done is done." Alf held on to his glass as if it were the last item of worth he still owned. "Where's Nelly?"

"Cleaning!"

"Ain't that a waste of time?"

"No stopping her; yer know what's she's like, takes her mind off the inevitable. I'll tell you what, Alf," Henry said, putting his arm around the shoulder of his old friend, "come on upstairs with me. Nelly will make us a nice cup of tea, that is, if she can find the teapot. If not, we'll use the chamber pot!"

Henry surveyed the damage in the pub. The front entrance blocked, no one could get in, and the outer walls were intact. The ceiling was caved in toward the back. Didn't look too good from where he was sitting. It was a wreck, a goner. Alf's pub was no more, and Twenty-One was a goner, too. "Come along, Alf. We'll join Nelly."

As Alf reached the top of the stairs at Twenty-One, he whispered to Henry, "I'm sticking to whisky, not drinking no tea out of no chamber pot!"

KING GEORGE AND Queen Elizabeth came to the East End. They walked along the bomb damaged streets and mingled with the people, and they had something in common now with their subjects: Buckingham Palace had also been bombed.

A short time later Winston Churchill made a visit, surveyed the damage and let the people know he wasn't going to let them down. Cigar in mouth and getting back into his vehicle, he tipped his hat and gave the V for Victory sign. If it did nothing else, it gave the East Enders the satisfaction of knowing they weren't altogether alone or forgotten.

And in the suburbs, a few days later, Clara walked Victoria to nursery school. She wondered why it was so quiet. She soon found out. There was a sign pinned on a notice board hung on the gate, and it read:

School closed indefinitely due to bomb damage incurred in last night's raids. **We urge you to find alternative educational facilities . . .**

Here was a reminder to Londoners living in the suburbs that there was really nowhere to hide.

CHAPTER 38

Blitz

PROFESSIONAL FOOTBALL, MORE or less suspended for the duration of the war, meant Sidney could no longer attend the Arsenal football games on Saturday afternoon. Their grounds at Highbury had been taken over by the Air Raid Precaution Centre. Victoria and Clara were the beneficiaries of his disappointment. In place of football came family jaunts to the West End.

London had shifted into an austere period; anything worth looking at had been put away or barricaded. Climbing the stairs from the underground station up to Piccadilly Circus, they looked over to the center island where gray hoarding now hid the Statue of Eros.

"They've boxed in Eros," Sidney observed.

"What's an Eros, Mummy?"

"He's a little angel with a bow and arrow, and he sends love arrows to everyone he loves."

"Why'd they put him in a box, then?" And as quickly as she asked the question, she answered it herself. "I know. To save him from the bombs."

"That's right," Sidney, said. "Not to worry, he'll come out when the war's over." They continued walking from Piccadilly Circus down the Haymarket to the picture house where the Disney film *Fantasia* was playing.

"Can we see it?" Victoria asked.

"Wait, I'll see what time it starts." Clara came back to announce the sad news; they were twenty minutes into the film already.

"Not to worry," Sidney said as tears welled up in Victoria's eyes. "We wouldn't want to miss the beginning of such a special picture. We'll come back next week after we've done our gardening."

"Goody!" Victoria clapped her hands and skipped ahead to feed the pigeons in Trafalgar Square.

THE FOLLOWING SATURDAY, before the promised outing, Victoria worked with Sidney planting carrots and potatoes. Bonnie, Victoria's little dog, was beside her. "We're digging for victory, Mummy," Victoria shouted to Clara. "Lord Woolton said carrots help us see in the dark."

"Do you know who Lord Woolton is, Victoria?"

"He's the Food Minister."

How she knew that, Clara had no idea. Somebody must have told her, probably Nelly who used him as a warning when Victoria refused to finish food on her plate.

"And when we're done, Daddy's taking me to see *Fantasia*. You can come, if you like."

"That would be nice," Clara replied, realizing it didn't matter to Victoria whether she accompanied them or not. Victoria's attachment to Sidney was without question. There they were, on their hands and knees, covered in dirt, happy as pigs in mud. Would it have been the same with Maze? Of course not. Paint maybe, but dirt never.

Clara would have liked to join them, but she hadn't heard from her parents and couldn't reach them on the telephone. "You go with Daddy, darling. I have to make sure Grandma and Grandpa are all right."

"If it were anything bad, you'd have heard," Sidney assured her as he continued to dig a trench for Victoria to drop in seedling potatoes. "We have to push them right down, luv." He showed Victoria what he meant. "We don't want the rabbits and the foxes to dig them up and eat them before we do."

"What will they eat then?"

"Whatever they can find, just like us."

"Why can't we have chickens? Mother Gould had chickens."

"She's not your mother," Clara yelled for the umpteenth time, trying to find a way to bring an end to Victoria's constant reference to Mother Gould. "And we don't live on a farm, and I have enough trouble feeding us, let alone chickens!"

"What about Gregory and Bonnie? They live here." Victoria kept on.

"Bonnie eats scraps, and Gregory's a hedgehog, and hedgehogs look after themselves; anyway, we haven't seen Gregory for weeks."

Victoria pulled herself up to her full height. "I have. He's in the shed under a blanket. I put him there myself, and Bonnie goes to visit him every day."

They finished the planting with ample time to get to the West End to see *Fantasia*. Sidney washed up. Clara scrubbed Victoria, who chose a pretty dress for her outing — another gift from Uncle Julius. Sidney might not have much respect for his brother, but Victoria loved him; he'd always brought her something from America. Not lately, though, since Julius wasn't making those trips any more.

Clara waved goodbye at the gate, and off they went.

"Got to move a bit faster," Sidney said, approaching the station, "I can hear the train coming."

Victoria hopped on one foot while Sidney bought the tickets, and on the train they went. Half an hour later, having changed at King's Cross Station, they got off at Piccadilly. Again, it was a rush. Sidney and Victoria ran up the escalator, dashed down Regent Street through one of the side alleys into the Haymarket. They arrived at the cinema as the music to introduce the picture began to play.

"Yea, we made it." Victoria sat on the edge of her seat, enchanted by the vivid characters and clever animation, the colors, the movement transporting her into a magical world.

Just as the "Danse Macabre" scene opened and the bones were getting up to walk around, the screen went black.

"What happened, where are they? Are they coming back?" Victoria couldn't wait for the screen to light up again. It didn't. Instead, the manager came to the front of the cinema with microphone in hand, "Sirens sounded. All out. We suggest you make for Piccadilly underground. Do not panic, and leave in an orderly manner."

"It's not fair, Daddy, the bones were just starting to walk."

"I know, sweetheart, but when the siren sounds we have to take cover."

Sidney lifted Victoria in his arms and followed the crowds to Piccadilly Underground Station. By the time they got there, it was jammed. Sidney made a decision and ran a half-mile farther down the road. He knew the back streets, and with Victoria in his arms it took him about ten minutes to Leicester Square Station. There they took the long escalator to the platform far below the ground and

waited until the Station Master announced the all clear had
sounded.

"Now we can go back to *Fantasia*, Daddy?"

"We'll try, can't make any promises."

They arrived back at the cinema to find a notice placed on the door:

NO MORE PERFORMANCES
UNTIL FURTHER NOTICE

"Now I'll never know what happened to the bones," Victoria cried.

It would be light for a few more hours, the trains were crowded
and there was no rush to go home. Julius had persuaded Sidney to see
if there'd been any damage done to the factory from the previous
night's raid. Sidney reluctantly agreed to go on Sunday morning, but
as he was halfway there, he thought he might as well go now.

"Tell you what, Victoria, we'll go to the factory. Need to have a
look around there, and then we'll meet Mummy up at Twenty-One,
okay?"

Victoria had her cross look on; she was prepared to wait outside
the *Fantasia* cinema "til further notice' came around. Sidney explained,
"Further notice doesn't have a date or a day, Victoria. It means sometime, and we don't know when sometime will be."

"All right then," Victoria answered, "but I'm going to see it SOME-
TIME, and I don't like that Hitler, cos' he stopped me seeing my very
bestest film."

"Nobody likes him, Victoria. When *Fantasia* comes back I promise you we'll see it."

ON THE DOUBLE-DECKER bus taking them to the East End, the conductor came up the stairs to where they sat in the front seats to take
their fares. "Best view you can get without having to drive yourself.
Now where you going, young lady?" he said, addressing his question
to Victoria

"To where my daddy works," she answered.

Sidney gave their destination, "Hessel Street, just off the Commercial Road."

The conductor took two tickets out of his leather pouch, punched
a hole in them and gave them to Victoria to hold. "Had a real go at it

last night, them Jerries. If they'd had a kitchen sink, they'd 'ave probably dropped that too! The 'ole place was lit up like a Christmas tree. Craters as big as what you expect to find on the moon. House next door to me got a pond in their garden now, wasn't there the day before." The conductor was on a roll; nothing stopped him. "My missus 'as made 'er 'ome at the bottom of 'olborn Station; says it's the deepest, not sure about that. I 'finks it 'ampstead, not arguin' anyway, it's miles away from us. Well, I said to 'er, if you wants to spend 'yer life in a bloomin' tunnel then so be it. Me? I'll take me chances where the sun still shines; I'll be underground long enough when me time comes!"

"I'm with you there." Sidney felt he had to say something.

"Might take a bit longer than usual gettin' to where you're goin'; don't know why we're still runnin' to tell you the trufe. Had 'free soldiers on the bus all afternoon, and they were only going a couple of stops, could have walked it faster. Yanks. You know what they say about them: oversexed, overpaid and bloody well over here. I don't mind 'em, really; if they weren't with us, gawd knows where we'd be."

"Not your usual route." Sidney wondered why they were turning onto a side street.

"No, there ain't a usual route no more. Detours, always perishin' detours. Still working the buses; makes me feel like I'm doin' my bit — too old for the army, so when they called me back to do this, I didn't object. Better to have some'fing to do. Can't sit about all day watchin' the bombs fall out of the sky, can you now?" The conductor turned to leave. "Don't worry, we'll get you there eventually."

The driver made an effort to take the scheduled route; he turned down streets he'd taken the day before and found himself in dead ends. He maneuvered his vehicle up alleyways never meant for buses. At one stage he stopped altogether and got out to have a word with his conductor. Sidney could hear them chatting.

"What you think, George?"

"Got passengers, 'arry."

"I mean, what you 'fink as to which way we go?"

"Don't know, George."

"Where they 'eading?"

"Commercial Road."

"St. Paul's shut 'orf."

"'Ave to wind yer way around, George."

"Right, 'arry. I'll get to Bishopsgate some'ow. Pray that Leadenhall ain't blocked, then we'll see where we are from there."

"Good on yer, George."

"We got a job to do, 'arry; won't let them German bastards get us down."

"Wot you need is a bleedin' tank, George."

"You're right there. Want a cig?"

"'Fanks. Better get on our way. Knock on the glass if yer needs me."

"You do the same, 'arry."

As they drew closer to the East End, the damage became steadily worse; buildings began to resemble ancient ruins with only a couple of walls standing. There were large open spaces where shops stood the day before, pedestrians standing, trying to find their bearings when so many of their markers had disappeared.

Sidney knew there'd be damage, but hadn't expected anything like this. He wouldn't have brought Victoria with him had he'd known. If they got off the bus now, they'd have to find some other transport to get them home, and that wouldn't be easy. They'd come this far, they might as well complete the journey. They weren't that far from Twenty-One; if the worse came to the worst, they could always go up there, assuming Twenty-One was still intact. The news on the wireless had said the raid had caused considerable damage; but this, this was total. He wondered if Clara had made it. There was no way to find out. He just had to plod on and hope for the best.

They came to a halt at St. Paul's but couldn't get around it. Police and fireman surrounded the church. The dome was intact, and apart from being blackened and soaked, the outside looked all right. The driver climbed out of the bus again to have a word with one of the policeman, didn't take long, looked like they were giving him instructions, and soon they were on their way again, a few of the firemen having climbed on the bus with them.

"Never thought we'd see a bus coming down the road after all this," one of them said.

"England expects — " the conductor began to quote Nelson.

" — every man to do his duty," the fireman chorused.

Upstairs on the bus Victoria was holding Sidney's hand tightly. "I want to go home, let's go home, Daddy."

"Just a few more stops, then we'll take a look at Uncle Julius' building and go up to Grandma and Grandpa."

The structure of the Simon Fur Company looked intact, a bit sooty, nothing changed there. But then all the red brick buildings in the city had lost their original color, blackened through the years. The windows were broken, they'd have to be shuttered or replaced, otherwise not too bad. Sidney took the keys from his pocket, chose one and unlocked the grid over the front door. Julius insisted on the grid; furs were too valuable and had to be protected. With another key he unlocked the door that caused the alarm to go off.

"Another air raid," Victoria announced as if it was the most natural thing in the world.

"No, darling, just the burglar alarm."

"Oh, that's all right then. I can't see any burglars, can you?"

"That's why we have an alarm, luv, it frightens them away." Sidney found the box and turned it off. That was a good sign; it was still working.

"Got a few stairs to climb. You ready?"

"Ready."

Up the stone staircase they climbed, passing Feingold's Fashion Factory on the first floor and Shapiro-the-Tailor on the second, finally getting to Sidney's place of work at the top. Again Julius, in his paranoia, had installed another deterrent, this time a heavy iron door.

"It's a good thing you've got lots of keys, Daddy."

The door felt hot. Must mean an incendiary dropped somewhere inside. The key wouldn't turn. He took out his handkerchief and covered the key before placing it back in the lock. Still it wouldn't budge.

"Maybe you've got the wrong key, Daddy."

"I don't think so, Victoria. I've opened this door a thousand times, I know which of the keys fit, it's just got a bit stiff. Not to worry, it's easing in a bit. I'll get it to work." Finally the key turned, and Sidney pulled open the door.

"See, I did it. A lesson taught is a lesson learned. That's what Grandma Nelly always says," and just as he turned to walk into the factory, Victoria let out a horrified scream and grabbed his coat and held on as tightly as she could. "Daddy, Daddy, look, you can see right down to the bottom; there's no floor, there's nothing there!"

Sidney stepped back, stunned, feeling sick, unable to speak, staring down into a gaping hole. The entire floor of the factory had disappeared into a pile of rubble three floors down. Everything was gone. If it hadn't been for Victoria's scream they would have gone with it. He picked up Victoria and, holding her close, ran as fast as his legs would take him down the stone steps to the street. There, in a state of complete shock, he sat on the curb, hugging Victoria, speechless.

"It's all right, Daddy; it's not your fault. Uncle Julius will get a new factory."

Out of the mouths of babes, Sidney thought. "I don't care about the factory, luv. It's just a good thing you came with me." He took out his handkerchief and blew his nose hard.

"Can we still see *Fantasia* next Saturday?" Victoria said in an offhand way, as if sitting on a curb and having saved her dad's life was something she did every day.

"Of course." Sidney stood up. "Want to go up to Grandma Nelly's place?"

"Yes. Mummy will be there — then we can all go home together." Sidney lifted Victoria onto his shoulders.

"You didn't lock the doors, Daddy."

"Might as well throw the keys away, luv. No use to anyone now."

Victoria never did get to see *Fantasia*.

1941

CHAPTER 39

Goodbye Twenty-One

CLARA HURRIED FROM her seat, ready to get off the train at Aldgate Station, when the train came to a screeching halt and threw her against the door. At the same time the carriage lights failed. Suddenly it was pitch black, except for the glow of a smoker's cigarette. Someone lit a match, then another and another — flickering, short-lived flames doing little to light the darkness. Clara fumbled her way to a seat. Better to wait it out sitting than standing. Eventually a guard came through the carriage shining a torch.

"So, what's it this time?" the man sitting next to Clara asked.

"Tunnel's collapsed somewhere down the line. Driver's looking for alternative routes, but as of now we're stuck, can't go back and can't go forward. There are trains in front of us and trains behind us. We have a crew on the job, but it looks like it'll take a long time to clear. The transport authorities have ordered us to abandon this train. I'm in charge of your evacuation. We will walk along the sidetrack leading to Aldgate Station. Collect your belongings and follow me."

"That's the most ridiculous thing I've ever heard," someone said.

The guard moved his torch in the direction of the voice. "If you have a better solution, sir, I would like to hear it."

"You expect us to walk along electrified rails. Are you out of your mind?" a voice from the darkness complained.

"I told you. There is a sidetrack — and you may have noticed, there is no electricity; the rails are not live. We have given the matter careful consideration and have made our decision."

"So, in actual fact, we don't have a choice," another voice from the darkness said.

"That's right. Do as I told you."

Several torches were provided to designated leaders. A young man in uniform was one of them; he helped Clara down from the train to the sidetrack, and she joined the line of reluctant passengers snaking their way in single file through the maze of tunnels.

Eventually the guard appeared with a paraffin lamp held high, throwing shadows on the tunnel's damp walls. Water dripped from above, making the pathway even more hazardous.

The woman directly behind Clara slipped. "My one pair of stockings, ruined." Her voice echoed through the tunnel.

Many were coughing; the stench was unbearable. Clara held a handkerchief to her nose and labored on.

"Sorry, need to stop for a minute," the guard with the lamp apologized. "We've reached a two way — rails going off in different directions — got to work out which one to take."

"Flip a coin, mate," an unknown voice suggested.

"Have to admit it's a bit of a toss up, but I think if we take the left route we'll land up somewhere, not promising it'll be Aldgate, but it will be a station with a platform."

It took this slow-moving line over an hour to emerge from the tunnel. One by one they climbed onto the platform, having no clue where they were, all signs having been removed.

"Looks like Liverpool Street to me," a fellow traveler said.

"That's a hell of a way from Aldgate — we should have gone the other way," a bowler-hatted businessman complained. "And someone stole my briefcase."

"Oh, shut up, you old fart. You should be thanking the guard, not criticizing," a thankful passenger angrily told him.

"'Ere, I found it." A young lad handed it over. "I just stumbled over it as I came out of the tunnel."

The businessman softened. "Well, that's very good of you," he said, and he gave the lad a half a crown.

Clara had started out in a crisp white blouse and a striped green skirt. Both were covered in soot. The heel of one of her shoes had come off. Her hair dripped trickles of grimy slime, and she resembled a chimney sweep's apprentice.

A woman handed Clara a clean hanky. "Might get a bit of it off, luv. Still, we made it, and a bit of dirt never really hurt anyone."

The guard gathered his flock around him. "I'm told it's all quiet outside. There are two buses waiting; they will take you in the same direction the train was heading. Neither the escalators nor the lifts are working. If you need help climbing the stairs, we have men on duty to assist you. Trains won't be running for a while; buses are scheduled to take over. We apologize for the inconvenience. You've all been most cooperative, and I thank you — and London Transport thanks you."

"Where do we send the laundry bill?" the young lad asked smartly.

The guard, who'd been politeness itself up to that moment, replied, "Adolf bloody Hitler — Number One, Fucking, Germany!"

CLARA ARRIVED AT Twenty-One six hours after leaving home. Unlike most of the shops and buildings around it, Twenty-One remained standing. A pathway had been cleared to the entrance in Half Moon Passage, and the door to her parent's home was ajar. She walked over the front step and saw it was pitted by bits of shrapnel. Inside the stairway carpet was ripped. She climbed the stairs to Nelly's parlor, fearful of what she might find. Twenty-One, the once inviting, loving home she knew had become a sad and badly damaged replica of what it once was.

She called out, "Mum, Dad, are you here?"

Nelly came out of the front room, a blanket draped around her shoulders, her hair in disarray.

"Thank God, you're alive," Clara cried, hugging Nelly. "Where's Dad?"

"Right behind me . . . "

Henry took one look at his daughter and burst out laughing. "You got yerself a job down the mines?"

"It's a long story, but, well, we had to get out of the train and walk the tunnel. Landed up at Liverpool Street and got a bus from there. I'm all right, but I've been worried sick about you. Your phone's gone dead. I tried it before I left home."

"Not surprised. We had a bad night, bombarded us for hours. We got to St. Botolph's and spent the night there. 'Orrible it was — not doin' that again."

"Hadn't much choice." Henry sat down next to Nelly, holding

her hand. "It started the moment the warning faded. Wardens ordered us out. Like a bloomin' firework show it was. And when it was over and we made our way back, we found the record shop next to Alf's pub got a direct hit, Alf's place finished and lots of casualties; we're lucky to be alive."

"You can't walk around like that, Clara. Take off that dress," Nelly admonished.

"Leave it, Mum. I don't care what I look like."

"I'll wash it. Henry get your dressing gown — give it to Clara."

"Can't get upstairs, Nelly," Henry reminded her. "And there's no running water."

"Oh, right, I forgot." Nelly seemed confused. "Not sure what to do for the moment. Still, when the air clears, I'll clean up, and we'll be fine."

"No, Mum. You can't go on living like this; you have to leave. There was a condemned notice on your door; that means you haven't a choice. Just about every building on this street has a condemned sticker on it. Alf's pub has one, too."

"Mum took it off," Henry said. "Alf's gone to his sister."

"I did not. It fell off." Nelly sat stubbornly at the table. "Give me time. I'll clear it all up. Won't take long. Just need to catch me breath."

Clara realized her mum, a proud, determined women, who'd rarely given into anything, wasn't fully aware, or more like it, refused to be aware of the danger surrounding her. Henry wasn't having any luck convincing her, either. With someone like Nelly it was no use beating around the bush. Clara had to face her full on.

"Listen, Mum, you want to be forced out and make a spectacle of yourself? It won't be very pleasant, and you'll have no chance to pack anything."

Nelly sat, clenching her teeth, determined to beat the odds. "They have no right; they can't come into my home and make me move. I won't go."

"I'm telling you this for the last time, Mum. You've got three days. That's what's left on the sticker. By Tuesday everyone has to be out of here, and that includes you. No exceptions. We'll help you pack. Forget what's broken. Leave the furniture. Don't attempt to go upstairs; what's there will have to stay. I'll speak to Solly. He knows a bloke with a lorry."

"She's right, Nelly. We've got to go." Henry had done all he could to convince Nelly. It was Clara's turn to make her see some sense. He reached for his deck of cards — might as well play Patience; not much else he could do. It wasn't easy for him to leave Twenty-One either.

He understood Nelly's reluctance, but there came a time when stubbornness became stupidity. Cowering under a table or going to St. Botolph's every night might be all right for kids but not for two old codgers like them. Just this morning he had to help her up the church steps; her back hurt, his legs were stiff, both of them walking around like cripples. No running water; had to go to the public washhouse to have a bath. Soup kitchen down the road — Nelly wouldn't go there. Salvation Army knocking at the door. Wardens frightening the life out of them. What sort of life was that? Everything has its day, and Twenty-One was no exception.

He glanced at his daughter, filthy, never seen her like that; even as a kid she never got dirty. Traipsing through an underground tunnel, risking her life just to get to them. It wasn't right. He placed the black queen on the red king and dealt the last three cards. He'd come to the end of the pack, the end of the game. Finished!

Clara could see Nelly might be weakening. "Who do you think you're holding out against, Mum? The wardens who want to help you or the Germans intent on destroying you?" Clara asked, not waiting for an answer. "Can't you see the enemy has the upper hand, at least for now, and your staying here won't change it? They know what they're doing; the fire from the incendiaries show them exactly where to aim and what to hit, and now they've got heavier bombs — and they don't just burn, they obliterate."

Tears ran down Nelly's face. "No need to go on, luv. I know it's useless. I know they don't care if civilians get killed; I know they know where we Jews live, and they can get two for the price of one. They got my sister; I made a vow they wouldn't get me. It's just — it's just — I hate to give in to them."

"You're not. If you stay and become a target, you will be. You don't want to be the last to leave the East End. There's no glory in that, Mum."

Nelly stood up, walked around the table, straightened a picture on the wall and made her way back to the front room. She pulled the piano bench over and sat at her window. A slight breeze blew the torn lace curtains over her head. The street was quiet. The tramlines had buckled, catching a standing tram like a rat in a trap. No stalls. No open shops.

Just a few weeks ago it was a bustling and crowded scene. Today silence — just a street in mourning. Tomorrow would be the same. The Germans had destroyed the buildings, the people and their homes. Clara was right; there weren't any medals given for the last ones to leave. There was nothing to stay for. She and Henry would have to go. Maybe one day they could come back, but it wouldn't be to Twenty-One. Twenty-One had had its day.

It was time to say goodbye.

She pushed the piano bench back and spoke to it. "You two belong together; we'll find a way to take you with us. We'll back up a lorry, horse and cart, if necessary. Don't know where you'll land up, but it don't matter; you're like Henry and me — where he goes I go. Where the piano goes, the bench goes."

Clara came in. "Who you talking to, Mum?"

"The piano." She had said this as if it might be the most natural conversation to have.

"Oh. Did you get an answer?"

"As a matter of fact I did."

"What did it say?"

Nelly hesitated for a moment. "You'll think I'm losing my mind."

"No, I won't. Everything has some sort of voice, Mum."

"It said music can't be destroyed. You hear it, don't have to touch it, don't matter how many bombs drop, memories stay and words stay and — " Nelly broke down, sobbing.

"It's all right, Mum. Things are only things. It's family that matters. We'll get as much out of here as we can. Sidney will help, and I'll get Bernie and Mannie. You've stayed as long as you possibly can. It is time to leave."

"I wrote a little song the other night, practiced it when Henry was down talking to Alf. Want to hear it?"

Nelly sat at the piano and began playing an unfamiliar melody.

"You wrote that, Nelly, that music? Never thought you had it in yer," Henry said, surprised.

"Just shows you, Henry, after all these years, I can still be a bit of a mystery."

Nelly played on, accompanying herself as she sang:

Goodbye to Twenty-One
and all of our years
so little left, only our tears.
Tears of the joy we had,
A few for the pain.
All of it dis-appeared
Won't be the same.

Don't want to go,
Ain't got the will,
Got to get on with it,
Life don't stand still . . .

Nelly put her head down, overcome with sadness, she'd run out of words, sung what was in her heart.

Clara and Henry sat down on the bench beside Nelly, putting their arms around each other, tears falling. Nelly's song summed it up; she'd realized all along it was time to go.

Twenty-One was never just a number, it was their home. A home where Clara and her sisters were born, their landmark, their anchor, where Mum and Dad lived, where they all once lived, where they grew up, their roots, their family. It had stood as a reminder of who she was and where she came from, and though she tried not to show it, she felt a piece of who she was, who they were, had been taken away from her.

It was an old building with a long history, and it would not be rebuilt. Nelly was right; the enemy could destroy bricks and mortar, they could kill innocent people, but those who escaped could take their memories with them and pass their stories on to their children. This was what history was about, recording what happened, how it happened and perhaps why it happened. The Levy family had a collective memory, and whether Twenty-One continued to stand or had to be demolished, the warmth and love it harbored in their hearts and minds would outlive the Mosleys and the Hitlers, and anyone else who tried and eventually managed to destroy it.

THE FOLLOWING TUESDAY Mannie, driving a lorry somehow located by Solly Tenser — no questions asked — and with Henry and Nelly in a hired taxi not far behind, were transported with just a few of their belongings away from their home of forty-five years to a house in the suburbs, or as Nelly called it, "My nightmare!"

They took with them the gramophone and their records, the piano and the piano bench filled with sheet music, a box of photos, blankets and linens, and Boadicea. Oh, and one more thing, the red chenille table cloth that enhanced the parlor table when meals were finished and dishes put away, "For," as Nelly said, as they turned off the Whitechapel Road into Bishopsgate, "where we ate is where we lived, and if we can't move the table, at least I can take the cloth that covered it."

The Jewish East End had disintegrated into a pile of rubble and would never be reborn as it had been — once upon a time.

CHAPTER 40

Suburbia

Sula's brother-in-law Harold, a bachelor by default rather than design, purchased a house in the suburbs of Woodside Park with a definite plan in mind. He was convinced that being a man of property would precipitate his chances in the marriage market. His timing couldn't have been worse. The very day he signed the deed he received his calling up papers. Harold was headed to North Africa and leaving Woodside Park far, far behind.

Clara asked Sula to prevail upon Harold to rent his house to Henry and Nelly, and, after much coaxing, Harold reluctantly obliged. Clara took on the task of persuading her parents to accept. Henry gave in easily. Nelly wasn't convinced.

"The alternative, Mum, is for you and Dad to move way out of London, say a village in Devon or Cornwall, where no Jew has ever set foot, and I don't think you'd find that to your liking."

That got Nelly's attention. "Not much of a choice then." Nelly hated the idea of moving to that abhorrent place known as the suburbs. "All right. I'll take the house 'til Twenty-One's back in shape," she relented.

Clara knew Nelly's dream of moving back to Aldgate would never happen, but this was not the time to set her right.

Every weekday morning Henry took the train to the city to work his stall in Leather Lane. Nelly found herself alone in a large house where, instead of a parlor there was a kitchen and a front room that looked out on a silent street and a back garden that stretched to eternity. She couldn't tell a weed from a petunia; the grass grew quicker than Sidney could cut it; the neighbors were snooty; and, beside it being all too green, too quiet, too secluded and too darn posh, she had no one to talk to — except that perishing parrot.

Tired of Nelly's complaints, Clara told her mother how lucky she was to be in beautiful surroundings. "You even have a fish pond in the back garden. How many of your friends have one of those?"

"The only fish I'm interested in are dead and sliced on a fishmongers slab in Petticoat Lane," Nelly replied, "and at my age I ain't about to have to catch me own!"

Nelly, accustomed to open air markets, now had to queue up with ration books outside real shops. She queued for bread at the baker, meat at the butcher shop and groceries at Hayes. She despised the woman serving at the sweet shop who had equal disdain for her. "You'd think she was sent there by God!" Nelly exploded. "I'm not putting up with it. She can take her two ounces of chocolate and shove it!"

Henry saw the fire in Nelly's eyes. It was one thing shouting at a vendor in the market, and it was another letting loose on a lady serving in a suburban sweet shop. "That's enough, Nelly. I'll buy the sweets from now on."

NELLY ESCAPED TO the East End whenever no one was looking. Up at Twenty-One she'd sit on a broken chair beside the cold stove, recalling the years she and Henry had spent there. Sounds from the past filled the room, children's voices, friends, music; she heard it, felt it. On one of her forbidden visits she saw a boot sticking out from the cupboard in the parlor and went to pick it up. It was attached to the leg of a man. "Oh, my gawd!" she screamed, waiting to be attacked.

"I'm sorry, lady, never thought anyone would find me 'ere." He was an old man, a tramp. He shuffled out on his backside, as frightened as she was. He got up to leave.

Nelly, realizing he was harmless, stopped him. "No," she said. "Stay. I'll find something to cover you; might as well have a roof over your 'ead. Sorry I can't offer you a cup of tea, got nothing here. I mean it, stay. Won't make any difference to me. Gives me a good feeling, knowing Twenty-One still has its uses."

"That's kind of you, lady, but I 'fink I gotta move on."

Her visits stopped the day a constable followed her to Half Moon Passage. "Can't go there, luv, it's condemned."

"I'm not doing anyone any harm, officer, that's my home. Just want to spend a little time in it, won't be long."

"Sorry, deary, one day the floor's going to give in, and you don't want to be there when it happens. It just ain't safe."

CLARA SPENT MANY a night in the cupboard under the stairs with Victoria, and this night was no different. She'd been humming Brahms' "Lullaby" for well over an hour, trying to get Victoria to sleep and had just about succeeded when the siren went off and an enormous thud shook the very foundations of the house. Victoria sat up. There would be no more lullabies. Clara knew it wasn't incendiaries; they didn't make that sound. It had to be something bigger.

Sidney, on air raid duty that night, had come in for a cup of tea. It was while he was putting the kettle on that he heard a strange whistling sound followed by the thud. He threw himself to the kitchen floor, and, keeping his head down, crawled to the cupboard to make sure Clara and Victoria were all right. "Stay where you are. I'll go see what it is." He opened the door and walked down the path to where his little wooden gate had been. The house opposite was gone — just a pile of bricks. Farther down, three other houses had a direct hit, and there was a crater the size of a small swimming pool in the road. He looked back at his house, the windows were shattered, most of the tiles on his roof knocked off, and his front garden had all but disappeared under debris. He ran over to where the wardens were looking down into the crater.

"Must have been a bloody big one," one of them said. "Better get the family out of there."

Sidney rushed back. He opened the door of the cupboard where Clara and Victoria were still huddled together. "Come, be careful, there's broken glass everywhere — we have to leave."

One of the wardens had followed him in. "I've just been informed the bomb outside your door is a UXB."

"What's a UXB?" Victoria asked.

"Oh, my God!" Clara held on to Victoria. "It's a time bomb."

"We can't do anything about it right now. The bloody thing is ticking away — likely to go off at any time. This isn't an incendiary; we can't put it out with a stirrup pump. You have to leave immediately, and you won't be able to come back until we have either removed or defused it."

"But — "

"There ain't no buts, lady." He looked at his watch. "Collect your valuables and get out."

Clara threw a few things into a suitcase. Sidney wrapped Victoria in a blanket and gave her to Clara. "I can't leave. I'll join you later; go to your mum and dad, and I'll join you when I can." He ran off to man his hydrant.

Clara carried Victoria past the ticking time bomb, past a policeman arguing with a lady who wanted to know why she had to run from a house she had only moved into the day before, passed a chain of men passing buckets of sand to wardens attempting to put out fires. She declined a ride in an army vehicle; there were others whose need was greater than hers. She was fortunate — had somewhere to go — and it was only a fifteen-minute walk to Nelly's unappreciated cul-de-sac.

"Who digged that big hole outside my house?" Victoria asked.

"Hitler, Hitler — made that hole! We'll be at Grandma and Grandpa's very soon. Close you eyes." Clara covered Victoria's head with the blanket. The child had seen enough.

"Grandma told me she doesn't like her new house."

"She'll have to get used to it." Clara was in no mood to worry about Nelly's likes and dislikes.

"Grandma hasn't got any friends."

"She will now. She'll have more friends than she'll know what to do with."

HENRY HAD BEEN up all night listening to the radio, going outside every now and then to look up at the sky, watching the planes overhead. He was there, sitting on a stool, when Clara and Victoria arrived. "What you doin' 'ere in the middle of the night?"

"There's a bomb outside our house, Grandpa. I heard it ticking!" Victoria informed him.

"Nelly, we got visitors!" Henry shouted as if it were a normal occurrence.

Nelly came running out, pulling on her dressing gown. She took one look at Clara and Victoria, and ordered them inside. She didn't ask what happened; she took it for granted they wouldn't be there if it weren't serious. She released Victoria from Clara's arms. "Tea and porridge, that's what you need. Henry, stop staring into space, come in and stoke the boiler."

"It's the middle of summer, Nelly; we don't need no fire."

"We need warmth, Henry. A one bar electric heater won't do it."

THEY'D BEEN AT Nelly's for a week when the Civil Defense strongly advised all parents to consider sending children away from London. It wasn't that Clara didn't realize the seriousness of the situation; she still had the vision of Mrs. Gould on her mind, and she wasn't about to repeat that experience. Victoria's friends were being sent overseas to Canada, America and even as far as New Zealand and Australia. Clara was bound and determined to find a safer place somewhere in Britain, hopefully with a reliable family. It was then she thought of Paul Maze. Without telling anyone Clara decided to go see him.

On arriving, she found it wasn't the Chelsea she'd once known. Houses were boarded up. Yachts with white sails weren't gliding down the river, not a single pleasure craft in sight, and no nannies. In their place were tankers and battleships making their way down to the open sea, merchant ships and Coast Guard vessels proudly flying the Union Jack.

The street signs had been removed, and had she not known exactly where she was going, she wouldn't have found her way. She arrived at Cheyne Walk and stood on the embankment looking across at the Maze residence. Was it the right thing to do? What sort of reception would she get? She reminded herself she was there for a specific reason — the safety of her daughter. Determined, she crossed the road. She rang the bell, and moments later Rogers opened the door.

"Mrs. Simon, the last person I'd expect to see. What a surprise! Do come in." There were boxes everywhere and sheets over furniture. The walls were bare, paintings were stacked, waiting to be packed, and no sign of Maze. "Excuse the mess, Mr. Maze has moved out for the duration. I had to push him a bit. He's not a man to run away, as you well know. What with the river noise and the planes coming over every few minutes, he had to agree it was becoming unbearable."

"Where is he?"

"He's rented a cottage in Petersfield; it's not that far away — safer too. It's a charming little place where he realized he can paint as easily as he does here. He's attached to an army unit in nearby Hampshire; got quite a high up position with the Home Guard."

"You're not joining him?"

"No, but Maggie's there with him. Couldn't see myself sitting on a bench in the country doing nothing. I do my bit with the Auxiliary Fire Service; been a bit rough where I live, but they'll take anyone they can get their hands on, even old codgers like me."

"And Mr. Luftmann? Is he with Mr. Maze?"

"No. I understand he's got a room in town. Haven't heard a word from him. Come, let's have a cup of tea. Have to make it myself. Cook's retired."

They walked the servant stairs to a deserted kitchen. Rogers put the kettle on. Clara found a couple of cups. They sat chatting about old times. "He really missed you, Mrs. Simon," Rogers informed her thoughtfully.

"Call me Clara, please."

"After you left he wasn't himself. Morose, he was. If not for Maggie, well, I don't know what he'd have done." Rogers got up from the table and walked over to his old desk in the kitchen. "I have his address somewhere." He shuffled through some papers and found it. "Keep it in a safe place, don't suppose any of us will be back here for some time."

They chatted over tea until Clara realized it was getting late, and she had to leave. "Thank you, Rogers. It's been good spending time with you. Thanks for the address; I'll write to him."

From Waterloo Station Clara took the underground back home to Woodside Park. At each stop people of all ages with sleeping bags and blankets were preparing to settle down for the night. The platforms had become dormitories, and tube stations were now being used as shelters. Not something she could ever do, sleeping alongside someone you didn't know and probably wouldn't want to know.

SUMMER BRINGS LONG hours of daylight to England. Since neither Henry nor Nelly had a clue about gardening, Sidney had taken it over, and it really was a lovely setting. Flowering bushes alongside the fence, pottery gnomes peeping out of a rockery; he could do without them, though he had to admit they were colorful. If only he hadn't been talked into that awful Anderson Shelter, useless bloody thing, always filling with water; nobody used it, and it took up more room than it was worth. He glanced over the fence to the neighbor's garden; they had an Anderson, covered it in grass, made it look like a hill and even had a few buttercups and daisies popping their heads through. He could do that, but it was a waste of time even thinking about it now. No idea when they'd be allowed back home, they'd already been away a fortnight.

Clara stood at the edge of the pond watching Victoria try to catch a fish with a tea strainer. Sidney joined them. Earlier that day Clara had snuck back home to find clean clothes; she was tired of washing out the same old underwear and shirts every night. While there, the postman delivered a letter. It was from Paul Maze, in answer to the letter she had written him at the address Rogers had given her.

Dearest Clara,

Of course you must bring your daughter to us in Petersfield. I can't wait to see you and meet Victoria. It has been far too long. Just let me know when you are coming. We will be waiting for you at the station.

Touts mes amit´e,
Paul

She'd read the letter over and over, short and to the point. The "we" sort of concerned her, but then Rogers had told her Maggie was there. It was time to broach the subject with Sidney. Might as well do it with Mum and Dad around — get it over, she thought.

"I've been thinking," she began. "We can't sit here and wait for the next bomb to hit. We have to get Victoria out of London."

"You were the one who insisted on dragging her back," Nelly noted.

Victoria had caught a little fish and brought it to show Henry and Nelly. "Well done, now put him back," Henry told her. "See if you can catch him again."

"Okay, Grandpa." And off she ran.

"That was then, Mum. This is now. Look how we're living. Her school is closed, her friends have gone, she's bored, and we're being selfish. Even if we're allowed back to our house tomorrow, who's to say we won't be hit again? We're too close to Hendon Airport; the army's taken over the school. It's not as bad as the East End, I'll give you that, but there's nothing left to destroy there. It's us now and — how long can our luck hold out?"

No one ventured an answer to Clara's question. She went on. "I made inquiries, and I found Mr. Maze. He's moved to Petersfield. I wrote to him, and he wrote back."

Sidney literally dropped his cup into its saucer.

Clara couldn't let the momentum slow. "I realize you don't approve, but he's willing to look after Victoria, and, under the circumstances, we have to put our personal feelings aside. She'll be going to a decent home, Sidney, to someone we know."

"Know? Clara, he's someone *you* know. We're getting a Morrison any day now; she'll be safe in that." Sidney fought back.

"So, we get a Morrison Shelter, and the house comes down on top of us, and we're trapped. It didn't save the Landaus; they had one. So far we've been lucky; luck doesn't hold out forever."

"Then we're right back where we started!" Sidney was furious.

"You're nursing old wounds, Sidney. I'm asking you to think of Victoria."

"Then send her back to Mrs. Gould. She loved it there."

"Never. Mrs. Gould gives me nightmares!"

"Stop being dramatic, Clara. She wasn't that bad."

Nelly pulled herself up from the lawn deck chair. "Come, Henry, they better work this one out between them. These canvas things are a bugger to get out of; give me an old kitchen chair any day. Victoria, you come with us. We're going inside the house now — just the three of us."

Sidney and Clara continued arguing. He told her he'd rather send Victoria to Australia than have her live with a man he didn't know and didn't trust. Clara would not budge. The nightly raids were becoming more intense. The city of London was on fire, and the suburbs, though not as dangerous as the city, were being attacked. Incendiaries, basket bombs and now time bombs fell every night, and no one could tell where they'd land next. Civilians were equally vulnerable. Clara was determined to take Victoria to Petersfield.

"And there's something I haven't shared with you, Sidney. I tried to find another school for Victoria. I tried the convent, St. Michael's, the school at the top of Nether Street. I spoke with the Mother Superior; she was quite willing to take Victoria. In passing, she asked if we were Catholic. I informed her we were Jews. 'Not a problem,' she said. 'We'll baptize her, and she'll be one of us.' Is that what you want, Sidney — Jesus looking after our Jewish child with nuns who rely on their Lord to save them?"

Clara's remark hit Sidney like a ton of bricks. He got up and walked toward the pond.

"That's our alternative as far as schooling is concerned," Clara shouted after him.

"That's ridiculous!" he shouted back at Clara. "Why can't you teach her?"

"I could, but she'd still be in London." She got up and followed along with him. "Think of what we're facing. The German intent is not to wipe out our villages or our countryside. Their plan is to destroy our cities, our factories, all the industrial areas, and they're succeeding. Don't think for one moment they're done with us. If the threatened invasion actually comes about, the outer counties are where they'll regroup. This is not random, Sidney. They know what they're doing. It's psychological warfare. Why do you think they haven't bombed Paris? It's where the Gestapo has its headquarters; they're living like kings in a beautiful city, and they know we won't bomb it, since France is our ally. The Germans walked into Paris. Not much resistance there; the French just about handed it to them. They could walk in here, too. Destroy first, rebuild later. And one other thing, in case it's slipped your mind, as it appeared not to slip the Mother Superior's understanding. We're Jews, and we'll be first on their slaughter list."

"So they'll get us either way." Sidney turned and walked back to face Clara.

"Maybe. Maybe not. But while we're still in charge of where we are, I'm determined to take Victoria out of harm's way. Maze is an old soldier. He won't let anything happen to Victoria. I trust him and the people he knows, people like Churchill and Montgomery, probably Roosevelt, too. Would you still prefer her to be with Mrs. perishing Gould and her pigs?"

It still took Clara a week to convince Sidney. He'd fought to the last to keep Victoria at home until reason won out. He feared for his daughter, and now he once again feared for his marriage. He was close to tears.

Victoria sensed his sadness. "That's all right, Daddy. Mummy says Mr. Maze is a very nice man."

"I'm sure he is. Mummy's right, London's too dangerous, and they don't have air raids in Petersfield. You won't have to go under the stairs or in the Morrison."

"Then you should come, too." Victoria patted her father's cheek.

"The government won't let me. I'll visit, and when this very bad war is over, you'll come home, and we'll carry on with all the things we like to do together."

"Like planting vegetables in the garden?" Victoria added, as if trying to brighten the future.

"Right. Except we won't need to dig for victory after the war; we'll grow beautiful flowers instead."

And so, once again they were at a busy railway station; Clara's life had become a series of train stations. Going from one to the next and back again, and now they were at Waterloo with Sidney talking to Victoria, father and daughter, so much to say, so much to share. He held on to her — not wanting to let her go until the last minute.

Clara kissed Sidney goodbye and got on to the train with Victoria. They stood at their compartment window; Victoria leaned out and held Sidney's hand until the guard blew his whistle, and the train chugged slowly out of the station. Sidney had lost the battle to keep his family together.

A few days later Chancery Lane Station was bombed, Henry's stall and the chemist's were destroyed on Leather Lane. Henry could no longer pretend he was a man of property. He was a man without a job in a house where he couldn't pay the rent and with a wife who couldn't, or more like it wouldn't, adapt to where she lived. Dignity gone down the drain. He'd have plenty of time to stare up in the sky. Too old for war work and not ready to retire. And now that Clara had taken Victoria to Petersfield, he didn't even have a little girl to tell stories to. He was left to look after Bonnie, the little dog he and Victoria had chosen together — that is, until Nelly told him Bonnie was needed to run messages in France. "Bonnie's been called up," she told him.

"What are you talking about, woman?"

"To run messages in France!"

"Really? That's impressive. Have to write to Victoria and tell her."

Animals in war time took second place to family and friends, many of whom took refuge with Nelly and Henry — for they, like so many others escaping from the East End, had no where else to go.

Nelly was back as if in the early days of Twenty-One, except it wasn't Twenty-One, just a new house on a cul-de-sac in a suburb with a bunch of East Enders who were used to shouting at each other. Like Nelly, they couldn't get used to the silence; they'd been brought up having to make themselves heard above the city din.

After the time bomb was defused and the crater filled in, Sidney went back to the house. Julius phoned to tell him the war office could provide a factory in Camden Town as long as he agreed to continue to make fur coats for Russian soldiers. The government provided the skins. Sidney did the work. Julius, with no selling to keep him occupied, sat on his backside and reaped the profits.

Henry believed Nelly's white lie about Bonnie. He believed it until the day peace was declared. It was then he found out that Bonnie had been sent away, put down would be more to the point. Nelly couldn't find enough food to feed all her friends and animals, though she kept a couple of cats. They could live on field mice.

And Boadicea?

She disappeared when someone, probably Nelly, left the cage door open.

CHAPTER 41

Petersfield

THE TRAIN DREW into Haselmere, the nearest stop for Petersfield. Clara had come to seek safety for Victoria, ironically choosing the one person she'd reluctantly dismissed from her life for the very reason she now returned to him.

Trying hard to conceal her nervousness, Clara stood up to take the cases from the rack above their seats. "We're here, darling."

Victoria, clutching Cuddles, jumped up. "I'll carry my bag, Mummy."

"There's a high step down, be careful." Clara glanced along the platform hoping to see Maze, but it was Rogers who'd come to meet them. "I thought you were staying in London," she said as he greeted her with a big smile.

"Long story. We'll talk about it later — and this is?" Rogers asked, bending to Victoria's level.

"I'm Victoria," Victoria answered, somewhat in awe of Rogers, who was much taller and sturdier than her daddy.

"I'll carry the case, Mrs. Simon, and, Victoria, yours too. We have a short walk to the car."

"All right, but Cuddles stays with me." Victoria wasn't going to let her one and only doll get into the hands of a stranger.

Chattering along the way, they soon reached Maze's old car, the one they'd travelled in together in France. "Yes, the old girl still runs, much to Mr. Maze's amazement, and just as well — couldn't get a new one if he wanted to," Rogers remarked as he packed their luggage in the boot of the car. "You want to sit with me in front — Victoria?"

"No, thank you," Victoria said firmly.

"She'll sit with me at the back, Rogers. She'll need a little time to get to know you and her new surroundings, and when she does you'll never get rid of her."

As Victoria and her mother climbed into the car, Victoria asked, "Who's that man?"

"Mr. Rogers. He's Mr. Maze's right hand man," Clara told Victoria.

"What about his other one?" Victoria whispered to her mother.

"It's just an expression."

Rogers drove them through the beautiful Hampshire countryside. The sun was shining, the hedgerows of hawthorn were in full bloom, and the air was filled with a sweet fragrance. "I like it here," Victoria announced. "It's even better than Mrs. Gould!"

Clara was delighted; the demon of Derbyshire had at last been exorcised.

"We hear about the bombing on the wireless, must be awful," Rogers allowed somewhat grimly. "Wish I could get my wife to move, but she won't — says her work in the factory makes her feel she's doing her bit; can't argue with that."

"And Mr. Maze?" Clara asked.

"He's up to his neck in it, too. Works every day with government and army representatives and travels to London quite often; not one to sit back and have others win a war for him." Rogers made a sharp turn to avoid a squirrel.

"Ooops!" Victoria exclaimed. "That was a very lucky squirrel, Mr. Rogers."

"He certainly was, Victoria."

They drove on in silence, apart from the occasional squeals of joy from Victoria. Clara's apprehension lessened, knowing she'd made the right decision. Victoria would be safe here. It was all quite beautiful, even serene, with haystacks, wheat fields and sheep in the meadow — the total opposite from where, just that morning, they had been.

Half an hour after leaving Haselmere they arrived at their destination. As Clara stepped out of the car, she had the strange sensation of entering a Maze painting. There was Maggie in the garden picking ripe tomatoes, placing them one by one in her basket, and Maze, wearing the same old floppy hat, sitting, as he had always done, on his rickety old stool in front of his easel — painting. Every emotion she had once felt for him came back with an urgency she'd tried hard to retract.

"It's boooootiful, Mummy!" Victoria couldn't contain her excitement. "Can we stay, please, please?"

Rogers jumped out of the car and opened the back door for them.

Paul looked up as they approached. He put aside his brush, wiped his hands and rushed over to greet them. "Clara, welcome." He held her at arm's length, studying her, then kissed her on each cheek before he knelt to introduce himself to Victoria. "I'm your Uncle Paul. And that lady over there is Maggie. You can call her Aunt Maggie or just Maggie, which ever you wish."

Victoria thought for a moment. "I already have two aunties, Uncle Paul, don't know if I'm allowed three."

"You can have as many aunties as you like. So, what will it be?"

Victoria thought for a moment, looked at Clara, looked at Maggie then made her decision. "She's Aunt Maggie."

"Then, no uncles?" Paul enquired.

"Yes, they are married-in uncles, and that means Grandpa and Grandma didn't born them, and that makes a difference."

Impressed with Victoria, Paul called over to Maggie. "You remember Mrs. Simon, Maggie?"

"Of course," Maggie wiped her hands on her apron and came over to warmly embrace Clara. "And what is your name?" she asked of Victoria.

"Victoria, and this is Cuddles."

"We have a wee room ready for you both. Come, let's get you settled in."

"And, if you like, Victoria, you stay with me," Paul suggested, looking at her intently, "and we'll get to know each other while Maggie and your mother are busy unpacking."

"Goody. Can I play in the garden?"

"Of course, you can," and off they went, hand in hand.

"She's 'no a shy one, I can see." Maggie gave Clara a knowing wink as she led her into the cottage.

Clara noted Maggie and Paul were on a first name basis — very different to their Chelsea days. Maggie was obviously more than the parlor maid now.

Clara had to admit she felt a tinge of envy. She'd have to get over it; she had had her chance. Had she made the right choice? Of course she had. Still, this lovely cottage, far from harm's way, it could have been hers . . .

"Will you be staying long?" Maggie asked.

"Just time enough to get Victoria settled in," Clara replied, still mulling over how different her life might have been.

"Never thought he'd be good with children," Maggie observed, "but I was wrong; the wee ones in the village adore him."

"Just being away from London puts my mind at ease, Maggie."

"She'll do well here, I can promise you that," Maggie assured Clara. "Now I'll show you around our home, not nearly as grand as Chelsea, but what does that matter — it's a lot easier for me to take care of and that's a blessing in itself!"

"THAT'S A PRETTY picture, Uncle Paul." Victoria pointed to Paul's easel.

"I'm glad you like it. When I heard you were coming to stay with us, I bought a box of paints for you — here, they're yours. And this is a sketch pad and pencil, and that's also yours."

"Thank you. I'm not very good at drawing."

"I'll teach you. We'll paint together. Look for something you like — a flower, or a tree, a person, anything, then choose your colors."

Victoria glanced around. Her eyes settled on a patch of tall sunflowers. "Those, Uncle Paul, what are they?"

"Sunflowers."

"They're even bigger than me. I think I want to make a sunflower."

"I'll tell you a little story about sunflowers. Every morning when the sun comes up, the sunflower looks up in the sky to see where the sun is. Then all day long her big yellow head follows the sun wherever it goes. And at night she puts her head down and goes to sleep again. The next day she does the same thing all over again; she follows the progress of the sun."

"Tell me again, Uncle Paul."

"Tomorrow. Today we have to paint. Look at the colors in your paint box. Do you see a bright yellow?"

"Yes — it's the same color as the sunflower."

"See the little brush? Take it out and wet it in this jar of water, and you're ready to be a painter just like me!"

"I choose . . . " Paul watched as Victoria determined which colors she wanted. "I'm going to use yellow, brown and green, and maybe blue for the sky."

"Excellent," he congratulated her. Having Victoria at his side made him think back to when his children were young. It was good to have a child in his life again.

While Paul and Victoria worked together, his mind strayed to the day Clara came into his life on Cheyne Walk. He'd expected someone older. She was a pretty young thing, a little nervous at first, neither of them knowing quite what to say, he wanting someone who could help him write, she needing a job, unsure if she could fulfill his needs. Clara had been everything Ronan said she was — intelligent, competent and good company. He'd never met anyone quite like her; she'd added another dimension to his life. Two strangers who came together to write a book about a dreadful war. As swiftly as she had entered his life, she was too soon gone. And now another war, the same adversaries fighting each other, yet because of it, she was back with him again, bizarre, serendipitous. He recalled the interest Clara had taken in his tin soldier collection, now safely stored away except for the one he kept in his pocket as a talisman; actually he'd kept two, one stood on his bedside table — wasn't so silly, really. Others wore religious symbols; Paul had his little tin soldiers to keep him safe.

Victoria finished her sunflower and showed it to Paul.

"That's very good, really, very good indeed." He reached into his pocket and gave her the little soldier. "It's for you. I have another one in the cottage, so we'll each have one."

"I love him, thank you, Uncle Paul. I like his uniform, pretty colors. Tomorrow I'll make a picture of him."

"A good idea."

"Where'd you get him, Uncle Paul?"

"He belonged to my father; he gave him to me."

"Where's your father now?"

"In heaven with a lot of other soldiers — ah, here comes your mama. Go show your art to her. She'll be proud of you."

"The soldier, too?"

He smiled, delighted by her. "Of course, my dear. She may even remember your little soldier."

IT WAS A relief for Clara to be away from the air raids. In Petersfield she awoke to the sun shining through her window and little birds singing in the trees; it seemed like another world, yet it was less than fifty miles from London. Victoria had settled in completely; she played with children from the village, danced around the maypole and helped Maggie in the garden.

"We have a garden in London, Aunt Maggie; it's my daddy's garden. He doesn't grow flowers anymore, only vegetables. He says we'll have flowers when the war ends."

Meanwhile, Maze made time to be with Clara and Victoria, even though his Home Guard roster took up much of his day. He'd just received another assignment . . . to map the placing of land mines along England's southeast coast, which he soon found was not a one-man job. He'd spoken to Rogers about it, and it was Rogers who suggested Clara.

"She's the one you need," Rogers said. "Someone you can trust. If I were you, I wouldn't look any further."

Later that afternoon Paul and Clara sat in the garden, filling in the years they'd been separated. Clara spoke about her house in the suburbs, her parents bombed out of their home, how difficult it was for them and how helpless she felt. He told her about his escape from France, how he and Maggie had to commandeer a boat to get them back to England. He made light of it, but she knew him well enough to know it must have been an ordeal.

"Life in the country must be quite dull after all that," Clara observed.

"It would be if I weren't involved with the Home Guard and doing highly secretive work." He hesitated a few moments. "I would like it — if you could help me."

Clara's interest perked.

"There's something about you, Clara, you have a unique ability to arrive in my life just at the right time."

"Serendipity, it's called, serendipity, Paul."

"I told my Commanding Officer about you."

"Not everything, I hope — "

"Of course not — about our book, our German escapade. He was impressed, said he could arrange clearance for you."

"I've been here less than five hours, and you've got me employed? What do you want me to do?"

"Help me map and strategically position mines to be set along our southeast coast line; I've been given quite a long section of the coast. The Germans are only seventeen miles away in the Channel Islands. We hope to stop them before they get to our shores, but should some get through, we will have the whole of the British coast to defend. We have to know exactly where we've placed the mines so that they can be removed at the end of the war. I need someone I can trust, Clara, and that someone is you."

Clara considered her options. She could stay in London and do nothing to help the war effort or work again with Paul on a worthy assignment. She'd have to persuade Sidney. He'd be jealous as all get out and envious of her being with Victoria. Oh, God, she was back in an impossible situation again.

The last thing on Clara's mind when she'd come to Petersfield was working with Paul again. His request had come as a complete surprise. Sidney would never believe her, and how could she explain it and make it sound plausible? Paul had made it quite clear. It wasn't about him and her anymore. He was no longer a threat to her marriage; she'd moved on and so had he. Maggie had taken her place. She could see they were partners, and they were happy together.

"Say yes — please, there is very little time. Germany has plans to invade, and we know that for a fact."

Clara had been a stay-at-home wife and mother for nearly four years. With Victoria safe, Sidney stuck in London and Paul needing her, she didn't have the right to say no. The war took precedence over old hurt feelings. Whatever Sidney's reaction, she could not — would not — turn Paul down.

At breakfast the next morning Clara accepted Paul's offer. "When would you like me to start?"

He stood up and gave her a hug, saying, "Rogers said you wouldn't let me down."

"Rogers is never wrong," Clara joked. "I will travel back to London next week on the night train, gather my things and come back the next day. I understand the urgency, and I will do my best to explain it to my husband."

"This is highly secretive work, Clara; do not give any details. Just say you will be working with the British defense force."

"I understand."

Victoria, having fed Floppy, her new pet rabbit, ran in to sit beside Clara at the table. "First I have to finish my breakfast and then Aunt Maggie says she has shopping to do in the village, and I can go with her," Victoria said, as she spooned globs of porridge into her ever open mouth, "You and Uncle Paul can keep talking; Aunt Maggie says that's what grown-ups do when they haven't seen each other for a long time."

After Maggie and Victoria departed, Paul and Clara took a long walk across a nearby field. It was a lovely summer day; there were few people around, and secrets were safe. There was so much to say, so much catching up to do. They were completely at ease with one another, as if not a day had passed since they were in Amiens, walking in the footprint of a previous war.

"I like to stay off the road, if I can. On the other hand, if I still had my motorbike, I'd — "

"Safer by foot, Paul."

"You've been listening to Rogers!"

By noon they'd arrived at a pub that had just opened. They sat at a wooden table under a cherry tree, its buds a touch of pink. "We'll be their first customers. What will you have?"

"A shandy, please," said Clara and relished a long sweet breath of clean country air.

Paul returned balancing two overfilled glasses and set them down carefully.

Smiling, Clara observed, "You do manage to find the loveliest of places."

"I'm used to the city, but I think I'm beginning to like the country better, though I miss my old friends. Occasionally I get a chance to have a brandy with Winston, and I do stay in touch with Heinrich."

On mention of Heinrich, Clara's memories of their awful time in Munich came rushing back. "How is he?"

"He's fine; employed at the Bruton Gallery in Bond Street." Paul looked around to make sure no one was in earshot. "The gallery acts as a front for the French Resistance Movement. It carries on business in the usual way. Only a carefully selected few know of its other involvement."

She nodded and moved on; it was best not to know too much about other people's business, so she turned to her own future. "How long do you think it will take to complete the mine survey?"

"I would think maybe a month, six weeks. I cannot say for sure. "

They sat for a while, watching the squirrels in the trees, listening to the sound of a running brook close by. All was peaceful. Paul broke their silence, saying, "It may be too early for you to think about now, Clara, but when the mapping of the mines is completed, I would like you to work at the gallery alongside Heinrich. Agents come in various disguises, usually carrying art. You and I have done this before, and it worked. So, I have used the idea again."

"One job at a time — please," Clara replied.

"Keep it in mind. You're needed."

CHAPTER 42

Woodside Park

ROGERS REVVED THE engine of Maze's old car. "We need to get on our way if you're going to catch the nine-forty train," he reminded Clara.

Clara, teary eyed, gave Victoria one last hug and got in beside Rogers. "See you very soon, darling, don't worry. I'll be back as fast as I can."

Victoria, not in the least concerned, waved. "Bye, Mummy, me and Uncle Paul have painting to do, and Aunt Maggie says the raspberries are ready for picking," and off she ran into the arms of Maggie.

"It's like she's known them all her life," Rogers noted as they drove off to the station.

Clara had stayed in Petersfield for the week. The village school was adequate, the teachers sweet. She'd made a difficult decision, and nothing would tempt her to go back on her word. She wasn't jealous of Maggie; Paul was the type of man who needed a woman by his side. Sweet, lovely Maggie, as pretty as a picture, quiet and unassuming — she calmed him, she loved him, they were happy together. They hadn't discussed his wife or Sidney — no more emotional attachment for them, though a flicker of the old flame was still there. She felt it; she wondered if he felt it too. Just a feeling, nothing else, and she promised herself she wouldn't let it get in her way.

Later, seated in a crowded compartment on her way back to London, Clara mulled over the outburst she expected when she would tell Sidney she'd be working with Maze again. She couldn't reveal any details; she was sworn to secrecy. The only hint she could give was to say it had something to do with civil defense; he'd understand that better. British Defense sounded a bit too highfalutin'. He'd ask why it meant staying in Petersfield. Obviously he'd think there was an ulterior motive. Memories of his resentment of the French and German trips with Maze came flooding back. She hadn't convinced Sidney and the family then; it would be much harder to convince them now.

THE GRIME AND the smell of a smoldering city hit her as she stepped off the train. In the one week she'd been away there'd been no let up in the bombing. London, as she knew it, was quickly becoming a mass of broken buildings, leaving landmarks unrecognizable and many people homeless. Petersfield was paradise compared to this. How she wished she could shift her parents out of London completely, but it was hopeless even to try. Hard enough getting them to the suburbs; she'd never get them to move again. Nelly was doing better now that she had people staying with her. Funny thing about her, for years she would yell, "You never give me a moment's rest; all I want is a bit of peace and quiet," and when she had it, she hated it.

Clara phoned Sidney at work from the station. "I'm back. Come to the house, I'll meet you there before we go to Mum."

The walk from the station at Woodside Park took longer than usual. The cut through the park had been closed, and more houses had been hit in the previous night's raid. A warden kept guard beside the cordoned off area outside her home. The crater had been roughly filled in with bricks taken from the bombsite opposite. "We've defused the bomb," he said. "Still we keep a careful watch, just in case."

The two houses that had been hit stood out in the early evening light, sad and crumbled shells, streets lights twisted, no one around. "Anyone living here?" she asked.

"Not on this end. There's a few holding out at the other end. Looks a bit dodgy to me, but we can't move them unless their roof falls in!"

The paint on her front door was blistered. One hundred and eleven, three ones, their street number, once attached to the wall, lay like fallen soldiers on the ground. It didn't bode well for what she might find inside. She turned the key gingerly and pushed open the door. The mirror in the hall was shattered, the net curtains in the front room, once pristine, had ragged holes, the Morrison Shelter in the dining room was covered in an inch thick residue, and the cups and plates on the kitchen table, set for breakfast before they were forced to evacuate, were cracked and broken. There were dishes in the kitchen sink and some powdered milk and corn flakes in the larder. She wondered whether Sidney was using his ration book. It didn't look like it. He'd probably given it to Nelly; she'd suggested he eat his evening meals with the family.

She ventured up the stairs inside the house. Someone had put a piece of tarpaulin over the ceiling in Victoria's room; the carpet was scorched, the centre light fixture had a crack in it, and when she looked around she discovered most of the walls had cracks too. Her bedroom furniture was piled up in a corner of the front room away from the window. Apparently Sidney had given up on the house, probably been more concerned about his garden.

She heard the key turn in the front door. Sidney was home. She ran down the stairs to greet him. He gave her a peck on the cheek, not the most loving of greetings. He seemed dejected, lost. She took his jacket from him, put it on the back of a chair and together they sat down at the kitchen table.

"Sorry about the mess, didn't know where to begin; we're not supposed to be here anyway. Is the gas working? It wasn't yesterday." He took a box of matches out of his pocket. "Here, try it."

She got up and struck a match. The gas gave a faint glimmer.

"Enough to make a cup of tea?"

"I think so." Clara opened the pantry and found the tea caddy. She put the kettle on.

"How's Victoria? Is she happy?" he asked.

"Very. Says it's even better than at Mrs. Gould's, and that coming from Victoria is high praise indeed. It is really very nice."

"I'm sure it is. Nothing like this perishin' mess, I suppose," Sidney added with a degree of irony.

"They haven't been bombed; it's safe there."

"Well, aren't they the lucky ones."

Clara ignored Sidney's jibe and said, "Get out of your work clothes, we'll have our tea in the garden."

Clara washed the dishes and tidied up the kitchen while Sidney freshened up. She took a couple of deck chairs from the garage and put them on the patio. The garden was in better shape than the house. The grass he'd put in when they first moved there was lush and green. He'd even managed to encourage flowers to grow on the Anderson Shelter. The fruit trees they'd planted together were beginning to blossom, and he'd kept up Victoria's little garden. If anyone was digging for victory, Sidney was.

The kettle boiled, she warmed the pot, put a couple of spoonfuls of tea in, then filled it with boiling water.

Clara served the tea and joined Sidney at the table. For want of anything better to say, she asked him, "Work looking up?"

"It's all right. Julius dumped a sack of skins in front of me this morning, gave me a pattern and told me to get on with it. We've only got five machinists; we had ten. They get better pay in munitions factories. Julius feels put upon. Even if we double our output, he won't make the kind of profit he made before the war."

"Well, you should be proud of what you're doing. Without the coats you're making, the Russians would freeze to death."

"Proud? I'm a laughing stock. I've stopped telling people what I do. Its slave labor, that's what it is; nothing creative about it, same thing day in and day out. I don't know why they can't make their own perishing coats."

Clara needed to get off the subject of Julius and his factory. She'd heard it all before. War or peace, Sidney grumbled. "We've a lot to be thankful for," she said. "All you have to do is look across the road; it could have been us."

"It's not over, Clara. It could still be us."

"Change your attitude, Sidney. Stop feeling sorry for yourself." Clara had enough of his complaints and decided to unload what she had to say then and there. No time would be right to say what she had to tell him, so why not now? "While I was in Petersfield, Maze asked me to work with him."

"Here we go again. I knew it. No wonder you were so keen to take Victoria there!"

"Stop it. I had no idea; it came as a complete surprise. He's with the Home Guard, has an assignment to complete, needs an assistant and asked me. It's war work. I give you my word — there is nothing personal. I cannot turn down this job. I'll be with Victoria in the evenings. When we've completed the task I'll come home, and if it's quieter here and the house is livable again, I'll bring Victoria home."

"There's always something not quite kosher when you're with him. How come he didn't contact you before this? The war's been on for two years."

"I went to him, if you remember. The work he's been assigned has only just been approved and has to be carried out immediately. I turned up at the right time. He was looking for someone he could trust."

"Come off it. I wasn't born yesterday." His words were heating up.

"I believe you're doing what you can for the war effort. I want to do my bit, too, and it happens to be with Maze. If it was with anyone else you wouldn't question it. More than half the country has a husband or a wife away; don't know whether they will ever see each other again. I'll be gone for six weeks. I don't think it's too much to ask."

Sidney rose from the table. Obviously he'd heard enough. "I may not be here when you get back."

Clara wasn't sure she was hearing right. "What did you say?"

"You heard. I'm not sticking out this war in a fur factory surrounded by rabbit skins." Sidney stood up and walked over to the shed to get the lawn mower; there were still a couple of daylight saving hours left. How could he know if what she was doing was genuine? Top secret? What a load of ballyhoo. Up to her old tricks again? Well, Victoria would be with her — safety valve — maybe. No use arguing. Once Clara made up her mind there was no changing it — he'd been there before — grass needed seeing to, better get it done. Six weeks wasn't a lifetime.

Later, after Sidney had gotten his garden in good shape and Clara had cleared up what she could, in a mild truce they left the house and walked down the hill to Nelly and Henry. As they reached the shops, Sidney noticed the off license was still open. "I'll pop in and get Nelly a couple of Guinness. Want anything?"

"Packet of crisps, if they have them."

Waiting for Sidney, Clara looked around. A couple of houses hit, front rooms ripped open for all to see. A tarpaulin hung over what was once a sitting room. The roof of another had caved in. The clothes cleaner on the corner had gone up in flames, bits of it still smoldering — must have been the solvents they used. A notice in Kirby's Green Grocer read: Expecting Cabbages on Tuesday.

Just a few months ago they lived in a beautiful, well-kept garden suburb where children played hopscotch on the pavements, where mothers wheeled prams in the park and where fathers played cricket on the green. None of that now — pavements were cracked, and the cricket green had been converted into allotments. The children who stayed collected shrapnel and played hide and seek in sand containers. Mothers left their babies with neighbors and queued for food, not knowing whether there would be anything left when it came their turn.

"Got you a Ginger Beer to wash down the crisps," Sidney said and sat down beside her on a piece of broken wall. Clara opened her bag of crisps, undid the little blue packet of salt and sprinkled it over them. "Want one?"

Sidney shook his head. He wasn't sure how to say what was on his mind.

Clara, realizing his hesitation prompted him, telling him, "Just say it, Sidney."

"You will come back to me when all this is over? I don't know what I'd do if you left me."

Clara reached out and took his hand. "I'll never leave you, Sidney. We're like a pair of old shoes, a bit scuffed but still got lots of wear and a bit of tear left in us."

"I'll have one of those crisps now, Clara."

It was getting dark, near to the time of raids. "Better get moving, don't want to be caught in the crossfire."

"Isn't that your dad over there, the other side of the street?" Sidney asked.

Clara looked up, "Yes . . . What's he doing out this time of night?" They walked over to where Henry was, looking up in the sky, doing his nightly watch while walking in the wrong direction.

"Turn around, Dad, you're going the wrong way." A couple of Spitfires roared over head.

"Be a warning in a few minutes," Henry announced nonchalantly. He was right; the siren began just as he predicted.

"Got to get back, Dad." Clara took Henry's arm and led him homeward.

"Thank God, you found him." Nelly met them as they turned into her street. "He's been missing for over an hour!"

"There's a shelter in the park, you know the one we cut through to get to the train station? Thought I'd have a gander at it." Henry seemed to have lost all recollection of time.

"Knock it off, Henry. In the future don't go running off without telling me," Nelly warned.

Clara came to Henry's defense, "Don't be too harsh on him, Mum. He's just trying to find his way; no different than the rest of us."

Henry's stall in Leather Lane had been destroyed in the worst night of the blitz, and so far he hadn't replaced it or gone back to work. He was bored out of his mind. He tried gardening; everything he touched withered. When Nelly sent him shopping, he'd forget what he'd gone to get. He took what he called his constitutionals, announcing, "Be back in ten minutes," and got lost every time he left the house.

NELLY, ACCEPTING HER predicament, had created a suburban version of the Whitechapel establishment in a borrowed home on a dead end street few people could find. It was cleaner, newer, and posher than Twenty-One, with a family room, four bedrooms, a bathroom and a separate toilet. Sula moved in without Mannie. She now walked with the aid of two sticks, her condition having deteriorated considerably over the last couple of months. Mannie had a job at one of the Aldgate Casualty Clearing Stations and came out to be with Sula on the weekends. Sidney took his evening meal with the family most nights. Anna and Bernie completed the ménage, and Henry's war effort consisted of gazing at the sky, searching for enemy planes.

Nelly's acquiescence began with the spreading of her red chenille cloth over a very expensive antique table. Clara said it was a crime to cover up such a beautiful piece of craftsmanship.

Nelly wasn't having it! "If you think I'm going to spend my days polishing that monstrosity, you're very much mistaken. I don't care if it's got Queen Anne or Queen of Sheba's legs, it's not for me." She covered the shiny, mahogany surface with a blanket, spread a sheet over the blanket, then the red chenille tablecloth over the sheet — to bring a bit of color into the place. Out went the matching mahogany breakfront to the garage and in came her somewhat battered sideboard together with the gramophone, a bit scratched but still in working order. On a final search though Twenty-One they'd found more gramophone records. A box of them had actually melted, another looked all right.

"One more trip like that and me hernia will not only double it will quadruple; none of me private parts will be any use." Solly puffed and sweated as he placed the last of the rescued furniture from Twenty-One.

Nelly took charge of the ration books. With their combined coupons she scraped up a meager amount of meat once a week, the occasional chicken and fish when she could get it. Eggs were scarce. They were lucky if they got one a week. Solly Tenser came to the rescue once again. A friend of his had a farm in the Lake District, and once a month he arrived with a parcel marked: Handle with Care — Billiard Balls. The dustman, when he picked up the rubbish, wanted to know if she was running a billiard hall.

Clara slipped off her jacket and sat beside Sidney while Nelly set the tea on the familiar red cloth.

"Enough of Dad and his wanderings, tell us about Victoria," Sula wanted to know.

"Victoria has settled in well. Maggie, the Scottish lass from the big house in Chelsea, is in Petersfield with Mr. Maze, and Victoria and Maggie get on like a house on fire!"

"Is that the best analogy you can think of?" Sula joked.

"You know what I mean," Clara replied. "Having Maggie there puts my mind at rest."

"Miss having my little girl around," Henry said as he laid out his cards to play Patience.

Nelly picked up a Queen and put it over the King.

"This is Patience, Nelly. That means you play the game on your own."

Nelly ignored him and turned over another card.

"Am I not allowed to play me own game with me own pack of cards?" he demanded.

"All right, be like that." Nelly stood up from the table and headed for the garden. Clara walked out with her.

It was a clear, beautiful night. In the distance they heard the ack-ack guns. Searchlights swept the sky and somewhere, not far away, there was a red glow, a fire, an incendiary dropped indiscriminately on some innocent family or hopefully in a field. At least here they had a chance. It wasn't densely populated like the East End. It wasn't old and built of dried-out timbers. Even Nelly had to agree it was safer.

"So it's not so bad, is it, Mum? I mean — living here?"

"No, luv, not bad. It's a bit dull, boring. Still, with all of them staying here, I'm kept busy. I've made a few friends. The lady next door, Mrs. Karpel, her mum was killed two weeks ago; she'd gone to the Elephant and Castle to see her sister, rotten luck. I've done my best to comfort her. She comes in for a cup of tea every now and then. The thing is we all feel a bit guilty. I mean, why should we be safe and they're not? Mrs. Costello at the end of the road, her brother got caught in that tube disaster in Bethnal Green, on the escalator stairs, he was. All I can say is if it's your time to go, there's nothing going to stop it."

"I sleep better knowing you and Dad are out of there," Clara said quietly.

They listened to the evening sounds. An owl hooted off in the distance, the guns kept up a steady barrage. Nature and War, War and Nature, neither took precedent over the other.

"I'm going back to Petersfield in a couple of days, Mum, to work with Mr. Maze. He's with the Civil Defense, has quite an important position. One of the generals requested his help. They didn't have to ask more than once, told him to find a trustworthy assistant, and he asked me. I couldn't refuse."

"For gawd's sake, don't get involved with him again," Nelly cautioned.

"No intention to, Mum. He has Maggie. I told you about her."

"Not a patch on you, though."

"She's a caring young woman, not attached to anyone; she's what he needs."

"And Sidney? What's he got to say about it? Can't imagine he's too pleased."

"Hasn't taken it too well, couldn't tell him much. All I'm allowed to say is it has to do with the war; I'm sworn to secrecy. As long as he can come 'round here to the family and not be entirely alone, he'll be all right. In any case it's only about a six-week stay in Petersfield — and then I'll be back. If I think it's safe to bring Victoria home, I will; until then, I think it's best to leave her there."

Nelly couldn't help wondering how long it would be before Clara got involved with Maze again. "Just be careful, luv. Those feelings never disappear completely. You might think they do, but they don't. You have a job to do — do it. No more flings. Sidney's a good man; don't break his heart again."

"I won't," Clara promised. "I'm lucky to have a mum like you. Don't have to dot all the i's and cross my t's."

Nelly shrugged off the compliment. "You know what I miss here the most of all, Clara? City clatter. We can do without it inside, but there sure ain't much of it on the outside. Remember how the trams used to rattle their way along the tracks? And the clip-clopping of horses pulling wagons, carts, anything on wheels? I'd say good evening to the lamplighter and good night to the copper going off duty. There's none of that here. Can't really pop in anywhere, either; everything has to be planned, even shopping. Monday you do this, Tuesday you do that — not what I'm used to. I feel it all closing in around me like I'm wrapped up in a ball of wool and can't get out."

"I felt the same when we first moved here. You get used to it."

"I won't. It'll do for the time being because it has to. When you get to my age you get set in your ways, you know where you are. You can find your way blindfolded along alleys and side streets where you were born and brought up. It's not easy to adapt to the newness of all this. The East End had a real history, a spirit; it had a flavor, and we were part and parcel of it. This, this is sterile — hasn't been around long enough."

The all clear sounded. They went back into the house. Sidney was reading the paper, Henry, Sula and two people she had never seen before were playing cards, and apart from the lack of traffic and voices outside, they could all have been back at Twenty-One.

CHAPTER 43

Petersfield — Clara and Maze

CLARA RETURNED TO Petersfield on the night train. She left home with the reluctant approval of her family — Nelly cautioning her, while Sidney refused to talk about it.

Back in their Chelsea days she'd helped Paul Maze relive the First World War. This time, instead of writing about war, she was living it with him, and it was taking place on her turf in Britain's green and once pleasant land.

The Germans had marched into France and occupied the Channel Islands. It was from one of those islands — Jersey — that they planned to invade England. Now the Corps of Engineers was placing mines along the English coastline from Portsmouth to Dover, a distance of about eighty miles. This was the region where Maze was to map mine positions and for which he needed Clara to record each placement.

With the help of Victoria, Maggie made supper every evening, and after washing up the dishes, Clara, Paul and Victoria took walks along the country lanes. "I know I keep repeating myself," Clara said as she watched Victoria skipping along, "but being here, it's hard to imagine we're a country at war and our cities are being bombed every night."

"Enjoy it while you can, Clara," Maze cautioned. "If the Germans make it, this is where they will land; our mines will deter, but it won't stop them."

"Wish you hadn't said that."

"May as well face up to it; they're better prepared than we are. Should have listened to Winston; he kept warning us."

"Such stupidity, when I think of — "

369

"Water under the bridge." He glanced at his watch. "Ten more minutes and we have to get back. I have an appointment with Lieutenant Saunders of the Royal Engineers; can't leave him alone with Maggie — he's far too handsome!"

"And Aunt Maggie said if I want her to read me a story I have to have a bath and be in my nightie by seven o'clock," Victoria put in.

Paul, using his soldier-voice, commanded, "About turn, at the ready, advance!"

Victoria, giggled, saluted and the three of them marched home.

Tomorrow their work would begin in earnest.

MOST ROADS ALONG the coastline were closed off to traffic. Barbed wire lined the beaches leaving the occasional opening for the engineers. The Lieutenant and Maze trudged ahead of Clara, both taking long strides, while she, carrying the maps, a tape measure and her notebook, tried to keep up with them.

"Hey, you two, slow down a bit," Clara pleaded.

"Sorry," they called back and allowed her to catch up, but as soon as she had, they took off at the same pace as before.

"These," Saunders said, pointing to mines being immersed, "these are delicate machines, dangerous weapons, really. Make a wrong move, they go up and you go with them — which is why we must know exactly where they are located. We lost a lot of men in the First World War because of them. The French were still digging up unexploded mines when this war started. Residents around here are strongly against them, saying they keep getting washed up on the beaches, and they don't see why they should be put in mortal danger every day." Despite Saunders remarks, he didn't seem to be particularly interested in their complaints. "I try to ignore them most of the time. If they think they can laze on a beach having a picnic when an army of Jerries decide to launch an attack on us, they're living in Never, Never Land." He took a sheet of paper from a file he carried. "Here, read this. I had it sent 'round to everyone in the vicinity. Much good that did, they probably used it as toilet paper!" He handed it to Clara.

Clara read it out loud to Paul: "Beach sitting and beach strolling are off limits until the end of the war. Beach property is no longer your property until the end of the War. Your alternative is to move out until the end of the war!"

"And have they moved out?" Paul asked Saunders.

"Of course not, they're too bloody obstinate. Some of them have never been in a real city, and they only hear about the war — haven't experienced it, well, not yet, anyway. They're not about to give up a few short months of summer sunshine. If they had to share their beaches with mines, then so be it. They stack their deck chairs behind the barbed wire and hope the tide will flow through the barbed wire and bring in sufficient seawater to cool them down."

"I always said the English were peculiar," Paul observed.

"Some of us, maybe, not all of us, I'll have you know." Clara stood up for her countrymen.

"I can prove it," Paul insisted. "I met a man on his way to the beach the other day. He wore a bathing suit, which had to be left over from the early twenties, and 'round his neck hung what could only be described as ancient diver's goggles. I asked him if he was with the navy. He looked at me as if I might be crazy. 'I'm eighty years old,' he said. 'What would the navy want with an old codger like me?'"

"I trust you warned him he might as well shoot himself in the head if he was determined to commit suicide swimming in the sea," Saunders said.

"Didn't have the chance. He told me I had no right to question him; it was his bloody English Channel, and until it becomes the German's bloody Channel, he was going to swim where he bloody well liked."

They all had a good laugh.

Saunders said he'd had a similar experience. "I have to admit we're a weird lot. Last week a woman stopped to ask if I was a spy. I told her if I was I wouldn't own up to it, would I?"

"Did that stop her worrying?" Clara asked.

"On the contrary. She said, 'Prove it.' I assured her I was no more a spy than she, told her we were army engineers defending the coastline against the Germans. She drew herself up to her full five foot two stature and proclaimed, 'England hasn't been invaded since William the Conqueror, and if you think that little runt of a Hitler could do what hasn't been done to us for nearly nine hundred years, you better think again,' and she went on her way, waving her hand in the air and shouting, 'We will prevail!'"

Paul, amused by Saunders' anecdote, countered, "She put you in your place, that's for sure."

"That's the spirit of us Brits," Clara boasted.

"However," Saunders continued, "what I refrained from telling her was — she was right, there are spies, everywhere. She could have been one herself; the more perfect their English, the more likely they are to be impostors. Careless Talk Cost Lives. It's not just a slogan, it's a fact. This only amounts to passive defense, that's all it is." Then Saunders reminded Clara, "On the more remote beaches, the combination of wire and mines is all that stands between us and the enemy."

THE ENGINEERS PLACED antitank and antipersonnel mines on and behind the beaches, and Paul and Clara recorded their locations. They worked seven days, until Paul, exhausted and frustrated, called a halt. "I'm not a religious man," Paul admitted, "but in this case I want to believe what the Bible says."

"And on the seventh day they rested," Clara recited.

"Exactly. The young army boys can work Sundays; you and I are taking it off."

Sunday wasn't exactly a day of rest. Victoria demanded their attention. She pulled Clara out of bed and down for breakfast when all Clara wanted to do was sleep. Roy, the gardener, Victoria's latest conquest, built a tree house for her in an old oak tree; she demanded Clara and Paul join her up in the tree for tea. Clara wanted to run a mile. Paul considered the request and declined.

"I can't climb up there," Clara shouted as she saw where Victoria was literally hanging from one of the tree's limbs.

"Yes, you can; there's a ladder on the other side."

"No, Victoria, you come down here and we'll have tea at the bottom of the tree."

"Oh, all right, scaredy cats."

They waited for Victoria to disentangle herself from the branches.

"She's so much like you, Clara," Paul observed. "I imagine you did the same when you were a girl."

"Unlikely, Paul; there weren't too many trees around when I was a girl. I had thought of swinging from Tower Bridge, but my sister refused to do it with me."

"A wise decision," Paul remarked, catching Victoria as she jumped down from her tree house.

Watching them together, Clara couldn't help noticing a resemblance. Was it her imagination? And even if the subject of paternity ever came up, what difference would it make? Sidney was Victoria's father in every sense of the word. Paul could never take his place. To Victoria, Paul was her uncle, and an uncle he would remain. Clara promised herself again she would take the quandary with her to her grave. No one would ever know.

They sat on the ground underneath the tree and drank tea out of a toy tea service. Maggie brought scones hot from the oven and joined them.

"Oh, I forgot, Cuddles," Victoria remembered. "I left her in the treehouse; she has to have tea, too!" And back up the tree she went.

"You think this will be another book when the war's over?" Clara asked as they sat waiting for Victoria to swing like Tarzan from the branches above.

Paul thought, then said, "I don't think so. When this is over I'll be a painter again. One war is much the same as another, and I think I've said all I have to say. This one is only an extension of the last one. We made so many mistakes; the Treaty of Versailles I absolutely believe is what caused this one. We created an untenable situation for Germany, ripe for Hitler and his Nazis to convince the Germans to blame the Jews — and anyone else who refused to follow their regime, *Deutschland Über Alles* — to give them back their pride. Tell me, have you heard anything from your aunt in Munich?"

"No. She just disappeared. We haven't been able to trace her," Clara sadly remembered.

Victoria had made it safely down from the tree. "Okay, if you won't come up to my tree house," she advised them, "then we must go blackberry picking after our tea. Maggie and me found lots, and she says she needs more to make a pie."

"Maggie and I," Clara corrected her.

"No, Mummy, you didn't come with us. It was just Maggie and me."

Paul smiled. "Now your mama is correcting you; usually she

corrects me. Go get a basket, get three if you can find them, and ask
Maggie if she wants to join us."

"Nope, Aunt Maggie wants to rest," Victoria adamantly responded.

"I'd like to rest too." Clara groaned.

"Well, you can't; you have to come with me, and when you write to
Daddy I want to sign my name at the bottom of the letter. Don't forget."

"She's becoming a tyrant," Clara said.

"What's a tyrant?" Victoria heard what she wasn't supposed to hear.

"A bloomin' nuisance just like you," Clara replied. "Now get those
baskets and let's get this over with."

Petersfield August 1942

Dear Sidney,

 *Do you remember the letter you wrote when I was in the
hospital? After Victoria was born? I shall never forget it because I
don't think the realization of your being a father had actually hit
you. You told me you were pleased I had a daughter. That you
were going to see Arsenal play some team or other (they were
always the same to me) and you signed it, Yours faithfully, Sidney
Simon. I had a good laugh over it at the time. Anyway, your
daughter is very happy here; she has friends, and Paul is teaching
her how to draw and some of the techniques of painting. I don't
think she is going to make a great artist, but she enjoys it, and
that is all that matters.*

 *We work every day, and it is grueling at times, especially
walking the beaches as the tide is coming in. No, we don't walk
for pleasure, it is all part of the defense scheme assignment.
Sometimes I think I would be better off being a Land Army Girl;
at least they have a cute uniform, whereas my clothes continue to
get spattered in mud and wet sand. You would be surprised to
know that every village and hamlet in England is prepared
against invasion. The Jerries would have a very thin time of it if
they tried it on. It looks like England is a bristling arsenal from
end to end, and it need be with the news as it is.*

 Things look very black right now, don't they?

 *I recently realized that we are closer to the enemy here than
we are in London, seventeen miles to be precise, and with an*

expected invasion I'm seriously thinking of bringing Victoria back with me when my work here is finished. Fifty miles from London and seventeen from Jersey — it seems incredible. I suppose the one good thing about being here is that we avoid the bombs. I don't know what's worse — hovering on the brink of invasion at the coast or taking to the shelters every night.

I hope you are going 'round to Mummy for your evening meal. She expects you and would be disappointed if you don't turn up.

If you were here, you would love all the wild flowers. The countryside is quite beautiful this time of the year, what else can I say?

I read the papers and listen to the wireless so I know how awful it must be in London.

Stay well, we will be back soon.

Fondest love,
Clara and Victoria

Further requests from the Corps of Engineers were added daily to their already heavy load. It took close to three months to finish the work Paul had been asked to do. The placing of mines on the beaches completed and recorded, he and Clara were then instructed to make sure the small towns close to the coast were prepared for invasion. Their territory was increased to include Sussex, Hampshire, Dorset, parts of Somerset and down through Devon. Long tedious days and catching up with paper work at night. All road signs and names had been removed, and if it wasn't for Rogers' uncanny sense of direction, they would never have found their destinations.

On arrival they were instructed to advise town and village officials to report any suspicious incidents and to itemize damage to property, not to repair it. Arrangements were made for important items to be hidden or sent away for protection. Churches, town halls, all public and historic buildings were to be guarded. Identification cards, ration books, etc., were to be kept on persons at all times. There were very few Jews in their jurisdiction; if Clara recognized a name or a house with a *mezuzah* on the door, the owners were advised to remove the identification. She had seen too much in Germany not to realize Jews would be the first to be rounded up come the invasion.

Clara and Paul, together with Rogers, were an efficient team. Paul, thankful to lend his expertise, and Rogers, grateful for employment and feeling he was doing his bit. It was one thing doing research in peace time and quite another working in an actual war situation. There was little time for socializing — time was not on their side. Much of Europe was occupied; England was next on the list.

Meanwhile, Clara managed an occasional Sunday at home in London. She'd take Victoria with her. They'd leave Petersfield early in the morning, be met at Waterloo by Sidney, go directly to Nelly's, spend a little time with the family, and leave to catch the late train back. It was a rushed eight hours, so much had to be crammed in.

The family accepted her absence; their friends, ever present and inquisitive, wanted to know what she was doing in Petersfield. All she could tell them was defense work, top secret. They looked at each other as if to say, "Tell me another one!"

On a quick pop into their own home Victoria found her pet tortoise in the shed where she'd left him, but she couldn't find Bonnie, who'd been left with Nelly.

"What happened to Bonnie, Grandma?"

Nelly knew the question would come up and had prepared an answer. She walked over to a drawer in the kitchen and took out a brown envelope, addressed to Mrs. N. Levy.

"Bonnie was called up, sweetheart; he's over in France, Normandy, I think, sniffing out bad things. I had this letter just the other day from his commanding officer. I'll read it to you."

"I can read it myself, Grandma."

Nelly handed it over.

Aloud, Victoria labored through the letter:

Dear Mrs. Levy,

> *I want to let you know Bonnie is a very brave dog and a great sniffer. She is very happy here and may not want to come back after the war is over. Thank you for letting us have her, she will always be a very special dog.*

Signed
Herbert Wuffer

"My Bonnie's joined the army, Mummy. Isn't that wonderful?"

Clara gave Nelly a piercing look. Even Clara couldn't have thought up this one. Nelly took the letter from Victoria and put it back in the drawer. "See, Victoria, everyone has to do their bit."

Henry continued questioning Clara. "Why'd you have to leave London to work? What you doing with them bumpkins?"

Like most Londoners, Henry considered anything outside London, except Kent, where he once went to pick hops, wasn't worth a toss. "What you doing down there, counting the cows, saving the apple trees?"

Victoria answered for Clara. "No, Grandpa, Mummy works very hard. She sometimes comes back with wet shoes."

"Wet shoes? What she do? Swim under the sea looking for the enemy?" Henry ran his fingers through his sparse hair, trying to fathom why Clara needed to work in Hampshire. If you asked him where it was, he wouldn't have a clue.

"Now you've mussed it up, Grandpa."

"Don't matter, darling," Nelly said, straightening what was left of Henry's gray mane. "Not much left up there to worry about."

Sidney was only interested in his daughter's welfare. Whatever his wife was up to she couldn't say, or maybe she chose not to say. He wasn't happy with the situation, six weeks had long past, and she hadn't said anything about coming back. He had no choice; he had to trust her.

After tea and a bit of family gossip Sidney walked Clara and Victoria back to the station. Sidney stood dejectedly on the platform as the train pulled out — wouldn't leave until it was completely out of sight.

"Did they get off all right, Sidney?" Nelly asked when he came back to her place.

"Trains don't give you any time for goodbyes," he answered dejectedly. "All I got was a quick kiss; they got on, the doors closed, and the train left. It's not supposed to be like that. I'm the one who should be leaving, not her. Instead I'm the bloke left on the platform with tears in my eyes. Clara should be at home worrying about me."

CHAPTER 44

Mannie

THROUGH THE KITCHEN window, Rogers watched a telegram delivery boy ride his red bike up the garden path. Rogers wiped his hands on a dish towel and ran out to meet him halfway. The boy handed him a brown envelope, addressed:

Mrs. Clara Simon, On His Majesty's Service.

Rogers tipped the young lad a shilling and called out for Maggie. Maggie came running. "Don't like the look of this," he said, showing the envelope to her.

"They won't be back for an hour or so. I'll see that Victoria's in bed before then." Maggie took the telegram from Rogers and placed it on the sideboard.

Maze and Clara, tired and sunburned from the days work on the beach, came in as expected, ready to flop down on the nearest chair. "I'll just pop up to say good night to Victoria," Clara said.

"She's waiting for you," Maggie replied, making sure the telegram was still on the sideboard where she'd left it.

"Anything of interest happen today?" Maze inquired of Rogers.

"Well, yes, sir, a telegram arrived for Mrs. Simon. I suggest we let Maggie give it to her when she comes downstairs."

"Never good news in telegrams these days," Maze noted. "We'll have to see what it says before we make further plans."

"Quite right, sir."

They waited for Clara, Rogers not knowing where to put himself, Maggie pottering and Maze pacing.

Clara was smiling as she walked in "That child of mine has one yarn after another to tell; anything to delay going to sleep. Sorry if I've held up dinner."

"Not a problem, Clara," Maze assured her.

"You all look so glum. What's the matter?"

Maggie handed the telegram to Clara. She looked at it and saw her name. "Oh, God, it's for me?" She opened it with a trembling hand, read it and gasped in disbelief.

She handed it over to Maze. Maggie came to sit beside him, reading over his shoulder.

Mannie killed in rescue attempt in Stamford Hill. Please come home.
Sidney

"I'm so sorry. I don't know what else to say. What a terrible shock for you." Maggie helped Clara to a chair.

"Can I get you something to drink?" Rogers asked.

"Please, a cup of tea, yes, just a cup of tea."

Paul put the telegram down and looked at his watch. "It's just after six, there's a train to London at eight-thirty, gets in about ten. Is there someone to pick you up at the other end? Wait. I'll phone Luftmann; he'll meet the train and see you get your next connection. I'd suggest Rogers drive you all the way, but we have so little petrol."

"The train is fine. It will give me time to compose myself. I'll try to get hold of Sidney; he can meet me at our local station. I'm not sure the trains run that late. If not, I'll get a taxi," she rambled on. "Yes, that's what I'll do . . . "

"You sure you'll be all right?" Paul insisted. "Would it help if I came with you?"

"No, I have to go home to my family, Paul. They must be in a terrible state."

"It's a terrible war, this. We're not safe anywhere," Maggie said, holding Clara's hand.

Paul came over and put his arms around her. How many times in the past had he been the bearer of bad news to families of soldiers killed in battle? He'd thought those days were over. Obviously they weren't. He could do nothing other than comfort her. He'd offered to go with her, but he understood this was a family affair. He'd only heard of Mannie, never met him, but it didn't matter that Clara kept her family quite separate. He remembered the one line that struck him when they were in the restaurant in France: "Where I live nannies don't push babies in beautiful coach prams. Crates and boxes on wheels, that's what they have; they call them prams. It's very different to where you live." And he had understood then, and he understood now.

"It wasn't enough Mannie was wounded in the last war, did he have to be killed in this one?" Clara cried.

Rogers gave her his whiter than white handkerchief, the one he always kept in his jacket top pocket.

"My sister, my poor sister, they were so good together. She needed him; he needed her — an equal partnership. She'll be devastated."

"From what little you have told me he was a very fine man," Paul said.

"Mannie was one of a kind. Never let his injuries hinder him, made Sula face up to her disability and accept it. I don't understand what he was doing — he told us he worked inside, some sort of civil defense desk job."

"You won't know anything for sure until you get to London. I suggest we have dinner and then help you get ready, won't have you leaving with an empty stomach," Maze insisted.

"Haven't much of an appetite, Paul. Still, I suppose you're right. I'll need all the strength I can muster, they may need me to stay."

"Don't worry about the work here. It is nearly complete."

"I'm letting you down."

"Not at all. You will work with me in the gallery in London. When you feel up to it join me there."

"And Victoria, what about Victoria? I can't just leave her. Should I wake her, take her with me? I can't think straight, don't know what to do for the best."

"Better for Victoria if she stays in Petersfield with us," Maggie suggested. "London is too dangerous. You know I'll look after her, and we get on well together."

"Thank you, Maggie. What would I do without you?" Clara's mind was racing, images jumping in and out of her head. "What if there's an invasion and the Germans land here?"

"Be still, Clara, she'll be fine with me. Put silly thoughts out of your head," Maggie tried to reassure her.

"An invasion isn't dangerous?" Clara cried out.

"Of course it is," Paul stepped in. "We'll know soon enough if that's going to happen. We'll leave ahead of it. And anyway I doubt whether the Germans have sufficient troops to attempt an invasion; they're fighting on too many fronts. We might not be safe from the air, but you know our shores are well guarded."

"I won't wake Victoria then. Just tell her I had to go home. I think it better not to say anything about Mannie, not just yet."

"Was she close to her uncle?" Maggie had to know how to approach Clara's hasty disappearance.

"Not really. She's very close to his wife, my sister, Sula. Mannie wasn't around all that much, always involved in some political thing, on a soap box, in a fight, standing up for the rights of the people."

"Then, perhaps we won't say anything *forrr* now — no need to frighten the wee thing. There's time enough *forrr* bad news."

THE TRAIN WAS over an hour late arriving in London, held up along the way by signals and debris on the tracks. The last time she'd been with Heinrich he was recovering from the wounds inflicted by the Gestapo and wrapped in bandages; she wondered if she would recognize him. Better to wait for him to come up to her.

An American soldier sitting beside her lifted her case off the overhead rack. Clara thanked him. "It was good talking to you, made the journey a little easier."

"My condolences on the loss of your brother-in-law; he sounds like a fine fellow."

"He was. He'll be greatly missed, had quite a following — spoke up for the old soldiers and the unemployed. He had their respect, and they loved him."

"Better to go off in glory than in dishonor, my granny always said. I'll remember you and your countrymen when I get back to the States. Been a privilege."

"Thanks, and thanks to all of you for being over here."

"It's our duty and our pleasure. Here, let me take those for you." The American carried Clara's luggage onto the platform.

"Where you off to now?"

"A bit of R and R in old London town. Always wanted to travel —

not sure this is the best way, though, but still going to make the most of
it while I can."

"Not much left of my London, I'm afraid. Good luck to you."

The soldier waved goodbye and went on his way. Clara stood
there, hoping Heinrich would recognize her.

Heinrich, standing on a porter's trolley, finally spotted her; she
was one of the last people left on the platform. He got down, collected his bicycle and pushed it to where she was standing.

"It is so good to see you again," he said and gave her a warm hug.
"So sorry. Paul told me about your brother-in-law."

"Hard to believe he's gone — that he won't be there when I get
back. It's going to take me a while to get used to it, Heinrich."

They walked from the station together. "You are so kind to meet
me, Heinrich. To say I'm feeling a bit lost is putting it mildly."

The asphalt on the ground at Waterloo was soft and spongy from
the heat of the fires in some of the vaults underneath the platforms.
The station had been hit. It was a strange sensation — like walking on
a beach, the sensation of sinking a little more each step they took.

Heinrich kept up the conversation. "There was a terrible raid last
night, many civilians killed and, well, you'll see for yourself. It seemed
to go on for hours. The planes came over in droves — one wave after
the other — it didn't let up for hours. There are very few buses running. I came by bicycle. I have a carrier on the back, and you can sit
on the cross bar. It won't be very comfortable, but it will get us to
where I live. Better than sleeping in a shelter, I think."

"Is there a taxi?" Clara asked hopefully, thinking she could get
back to the suburbs and be with the family.

"No taxis. I have not seen a bus, and I don't think the underground trains are running."

Clara asked a policeman standing at a broken traffic light if there
were any transport available.

"Listen, lady, if I were you, I'd find somewhere to doss down for
the night. Nothing's running now; should be up by the morning,
even if it's only a horse and cart. Bicycle is your best bet, and I see
you're lucky to have one."

"So you must stay with me," Heinrich injected. "I will make sure
you get home early tomorrow."

Heinrich took Clara's luggage and placed it on the carrier at the back of his bike, strapping it on tightly with his trouser belt. He took off his jacket and made a cushion of it for Clara to sit on.

With Heinrich on the seat, and Clara on the crossbars, they cycled through the bomb damaged streets of central London. He maneuvered his way through massive blocks of broken concrete, bricks, wooden beams, paper, clothing, machinery and people searching for belongings. Street after street, the same scene.

They cycled past firemen hosing down still-burning buildings, wardens directing the now homeless to shelters, canteens set up on street corners, and tea ladies offering cups of tea to workers and the wounded waiting for medical attention. They saw ambulances lined up outside St. Thomas's Hospital; it too had been hit. Patients on stretchers waited to be moved to other hospitals, the Salvation Army in attendance. Bomb damage everywhere — Westminster Abbey, Houses of Parliament, Hungerford Bridge, every one of them hit.

They had to walk from the Imperial Hotel on Southampton Row to Russell Square, where Heinrich lived. There was no other way to get through. They pushed Heinrich's bike, and when the suitcase fell off, he carried it. They reached Heinrich's building 'round about midnight, one of the few left standing.

Heinrich lived in a one room flat with very little furniture; nothing like the large atelier space he had in Munich — just the bare essentials: a bed, a sofa, a table, an armchair and a gas ring for cooking. Books were piled up in a corner. Obviously missing were his paintings.

"Please excuse the accommodation. I have tried to make it as comfortable as I can. I have a telephone, please use it."

Clara picked up the phone. There was no sound; the line was dead. She put the receiver down, resigned to wait 'til morning.

A bottle of brandy was on the table. "A friend got it for me; I accepted with no question. Would you like to join me in a little schnapps?"

Clara did not hesitate. "Please, but not too much. I'm not used to alcohol."

Heinrich took two glasses from the cupboard. "Back at home I had brandy glasses; here I have only these. Please excuse."

"I wouldn't care if it was in a jam jar, Heinrich. I'm grateful just to be here with you."

It didn't take long for a couple of sips of brandy to take effect. Clara found herself talking — so much to say . . . "You should have seen Paul trying to convince the villagers an invasion could happen any moment." She giggled. "From the look on their faces they must have thought, What is that crazy Frenchman talking about?"

Heinrich smiled. "The English, how do you say, ah, stiff upper lip; they prefer to hide like an ostrich. Many in Germany did the same."

"I assured Paul those villagers would be on the beaches throwing stones if they had to."

Heinrich swilled his brandy in his glass. "I wish I could see a reason for Hitler to stop at France; I don't. The French are cowards. Germans walked right in, and they say, 'Here, take it, and we'll make you coffee.' I am sure he's intent on taking Britain; he's so close. We, I mean, you are the last stronghold!'

"Britain, Heinrich, will fight to the last man standing, and that includes the villagers in Hampshire."

They were both tired. Clara yawned, and Heinrich had trouble keeping his eyes open.

"Perhaps I can get a little sleep before dawn." Clara said, more than ready to lie down.

"Of course, please. I hope you don't mind sharing a bathroom with the other people on this floor. I will give you a towel and soap, and then you must take my bed and get a good night's sleep. I will sleep on the sofa."

Clara was too tired to argue. The siren sounded when she finally put her head down on the pillow.

"There is a shelter downstairs," Heinrich called out as he pulled a blanket over him. "I don't believe in shelters. I believe in fate. If it is my time to go, then there is nothing I can do about it."

"I have the same belief, Heinrich."

"I have to believe it was Trude's time and not mine. Yet, it was me who put her in danger. I will never be able to forgive myself."

"The Nazis would have found her just as surely as they found my aunt Lizzie," Clara answered sleepily. "Both were Jews; neither would have escaped. Go to sleep, Heinrich. We can't bring them back, and you must not take the blame."

They could hear the planes overhead. "We still can go to the shelter if you like."

"I'm not moving," Clara answered in a quiet, going-off-to-sleep voice.

"The Luftwaffe have done all the damage they need to do on this side of London; perhaps they will attack somewhere else tonight. Good night, Clara."

"Good night, Heinrich. And thank you for listening to me. You are a kind man."

The remainder of that night Clara and Heinrich slept while London burned.

CHAPTER 45

Shiva

HEINRICH WOKE CLARA from a deep sleep. She sat up, not quite knowing where she was — to see him standing at the bedside, offering her a cup of chicory coffee and a slice of toast. "It's the best I could come up with," he said apologetically.

"I didn't expect you to make me breakfast, Heinrich. Thank you."

"I have to get to the gallery now. Stay as long as you wish, and when you are ready, let yourself out. I hope to see you again soon."

"You will. We'll be working together, and I'm looking forward to that. Thank you again for meeting me and giving me your bed." Taking a sip of her coffee and coming to her senses, she asked, "Would you mind if I leave the suitcase? I'll come back with my husband to collect it at the weekend."

"Not at all. I meant to suggest that. It is far too heavy for you to carry."

It took Clara less than fifteen minutes to freshen up, and soon she was on her way to Holborn Station.

The streets had been partially cleared of the debris caused by the previous night's raid; one or two buses were getting through, and the trains were running. Women from the WVS who'd worked through the night continued to dish out tea and biscuits, feeding weary wardens and bombed out victims needing a few stolen moments of comfort. The wardens reconnecting telephone wires swung like monkeys from the top of leaning poles while civil defense units attempted to divert water from gushing mains. Though Clara was well aware of the cussing and swearing all around her, laborers resting on shovels still managed an appreciative whistle as she passed by.

A postman attempted to deliver the morning post, a near impossible task since so many of the addresses no longer existed. He scratched his head as he faced an empty space where a numbered building once stood. "Well," he said, "can't stick a letter in a bit of rubble. Better to shove it in me bag and take it back to the post office," and he walked onward to the next hole in the ground.

It was late afternoon when Clara eventually arrived at her parent's home in Woodside Park. Mrs. Karpel, the neighbor from next door, was making tea in the kitchen.

"They're waiting for you," she said. "I offered to help out, not much else I could do. Sad to come home to this. Here — give me your coat. Sula's in the front room with the family."

Clara bent down to kiss Sula, who sat dressed in her everyday clothes on the low traditional mourning chair. "I refused to wear black," Sula whispered. "Why I'm doing this, Lord alone knows. Mannie wouldn't want it. It's Mum; she says I have to because of his parents — it's the right thing to do."

"I can't get it into my head Mannie's gone," Clara said, holding Sula's hand.

"Neither can I; it's as if he's just left for a few days, and he'll be back soon. Dad's in a terrible state, so is Mum, and I'm, numb; it's the only way I can describe it — numb."

Nelly and Henry sat with the older family members. Henry broke into tears when he saw Clara; Nelly twisted her handkerchief ever tighter as she spoke to friends coming up to her. Clara spent a little time with each of the mourners and wished them long life, a Jewish tradition spoken at the time of a death. There was little she could say to comfort Mannie's parents, other than praise their son and tell them how much she admired him. His mother dressed completely in black — tears running down her face — repeated Mannie's name over and over again. His father stood, mumbling in Hebrew, reading from an old prayer book.

Back with Sula, Clara asked what had happened.

"From what I can gather, Mannie left his station to be with the wardens after the all clear sounded. It had been a really bad raid, and they were searching in the bombed buildings for survivors. Mannie was instructed to stay outside, call for extra help if they found or heard anyone. You know Mannie, never one to stand and wait. He went in, too. The warden said he slipped, and as he fell, a wooden beam came down — he couldn't get out of the way in time. They tell me he was killed instantly."

More people were arriving as Sula spoke. Clara didn't recognize the rabbi coming over to where they were sitting. "I wish you long life, Sula. Mannie, I know, wasn't a religious man, but at times like these we look to God for answers. We don't always get them; still, we should never stop looking or believing."

"So, what do we get, Rabbi?"

"We find solace in the psalms and in the scriptures."

Clara waited until the rabbi went over to the others sitting shiva.

"He's a nice enough man," Sula said, "but I don't find him comforting. Biblical quotes don't help me. He's Mannie's parents' rabbi, here to conduct the service, nothing more. He must look on us as a bunch of heretics."

"Probably does," Clara concluded.

"Sidney made arrangements for the funeral; for once his orthodox background came in handy. I begged the Rabbi to wait for you, Clara; he wouldn't give me the time of day. 'Jews,' he said, 'have to be buried within twenty-four hours.' Well, if we lived in a hundred degree desert like they did when those laws were made, I could understand. I argued with him. I said, 'But we're here in England, where the temperature rarely goes above seventy, and that's if we're having a heat wave . . . ' 'We answer to God,' he told me, 'not you.' These religious men, they won't give an inch. They're stuck in the dark ages. Everything is by the book."

"And they have as much respect for their women as they have for their camels."

"More for their camels, Clara." Sula was angry. "Here I am pretending, doing what they want me to do, when Mannie couldn't care less for prayers and eulogies. He wanted to be cremated. They took over, and I've betrayed him."

"Tradition betrayed him." Clara reminded her.

"When my time comes, Clara, you make sure they don't put me under a slab in the ground."

CLARA HAD HER differences with Mannie over the years. He was a Communist, she a liberal. He was a man of strong opinions, she no shrinking violet. He had definite beliefs and rarely listened to others; she refused to give in to him. He stood up for what he believed, and so did she. The one thing they had in common was their belief in social justice. And now those days of baiting without switching were over. Clara had to own up — she would miss them.

The atmosphere in the house was stifling. She had to get outside. Clara handed Sula her sticks and helped her up. "We're going to take a walk in the garden," she announced to no one in particular. "We'll be on the bench near the pond."

"Be back in time for the rabbi," Nelly shouted across the room. "And be careful near that pond."

In truth, the pond was no more than three feet deep and covered in water lilies. It was tranquil and quite beautiful. Sula was right. Why did she have to sit inside and listen to professional mourners, friends of Mannie's parents, who made a shiva an outing for the day? How they loved a good funeral, especially the food, not as good as it was before the war, better than they'd get at home. Everyone brought something — a plaver cake, egg salad, chopped herring and liver, anything to spread on a bridge roll. They'd sit for hours talking about what happened twenty, thirty years ago, never in the present. Perhaps they couldn't face the present. All of them displaced, living where they didn't want to be, hoping to go back to where they'd come from, knowing what they once had probably wasn't there anymore.

The sun came out to welcome Sula and Clara — time for the clouds to disappear. They were due for a bit of warmth. It had rained heavily the night before; the grass was wet.

Clara helped Sula to a garden bench, surrounded by gnomes. Gnomes in gardens, the latest craze, peeping out from bushes and sitting on doorsteps, must have something to do with *Snow White*, the latest Disney film. A concrete cherub sat on the side of the pond. Henry called it "Our Lady of the Lily Patch."

Sidney refused to buy ornaments for his garden, although he did give in to a birdbath. Mannie wanted to bury the gnomes, smash them on the head with a hammer. He suggested taking them up to the army barracks near Sidney's place to use them as target practice. It was one of the few things Mannie and Sidney agreed on. Gnomes belonged in Hansel and Gretel forests, not in suburban gardens.

"I'm glad I'm not in Aldgate," Sula said as she sat arm-in-arm with Clara. "Here I can think, haven't wanted to go back. Anyway, I couldn't bear to now."

"Nothing much left there. Just between you and me I think the Germans did us a favor; the East End needed a good clean out. Awful about the number of casualties, though, and a pity the historic buildings are gone, but the tenements are no great loss. They were a disgrace, owned by landlords making money off immigrants, taking advantage of them. My old boss Abbott was probably one of the worst. He had a couple of run down doss houses. They're rubble now. Good job, too."

Sula made herself comfortable, laid her sticks down beside the bench. "We were together a long time, me and Mannie. He wasn't the easiest of men. Had his idiosyncrasies, don't we all? Bolshie as all get out, and it got him killed in the end. He'd have these nightmares of being back in the trenches, wake up in the middle of the night in a cold sweat, sobbing. I'd hold him, and he'd eventually go back to sleep."

"When this war started," Sula went on, "he was frustrated, wanted to do something, anything, just to be involved. He hated being on the outside looking in. We'd talk about it. I'd say to him, 'You've done your bit,' and he'd answer me, 'No, I haven't; I was wounded, and they sent me home and wouldn't let me back.' He wasn't allowed to see it through to the end. Seems to me he chose his own end. He's gone to be with the boys who died on the battlefields — I have to think of it that way. Mannie had a purpose, and he was willing to give everything to that purpose. He was a hero in many ways, mine and theirs."

Nelly came out to join them. "Wanted to spend a bit of time with my girls, had enough of them in there. I'm worried about your dad, can't seem to hold back his tears. Why do we have to dwell on miseries? Oh, I know this is a sad time, but, well, there has to be a silver lining somewhere. And Mannie, Mannie courted death, did it daily, and it finally caught up with him. I can't help feeling he's in a better place now."

They spoke about the years they lived up at Twenty-One.

Clara remembered Nelly's wait-and-see dinners.

"So do I," Sula recalled "Whenever we asked, 'What's for dinner?' you answered, 'Wait and see.'"

"It wasn't the Ritz, you know." Nelly tried to defend herself. "You weren't expecting me to place a menu on the table and stand there while you made a choice, did you?" She sat down beside Sula, not waiting for an answer. "To tell you the truth, much of the time I hadn't got the faintest idea what we were going to have. It depended on what the fishmonger had on sale or whether the chicken plucker had a chicken left over from his day's work. One thing I do know: you never went hungry."

"That's true. You always managed something, Mum. Like your other famous dishes — Kipper on Horseback, Airpie and Windy Pudding." Sula smiled. "We kept on at you, asking what they were, when they'd be ready, and you never gave a definite answer."

"I did. I said, 'Octember the Swift' or 'Quarter to From,' and that kept you quiet."

"And what, may I ask, is Roast Merkin, Mum? We never got it. You just threatened us with it," Clara asked and looked her mother straight in the eye.

"Roast Merkin? Haven't a clue," Nelly answered, as if it was the first time she'd ever heard of it.

"I looked it up in the dictionary. Merkin wasn't there, so you did make it up. There is no such thing, right?" Clara challenged.

"Me? Never! They were all just nonsense sayings, as old as the hills, handed down through the years; kept us quiet when we were kids — worked on you, too. All I know is there was always something simmering in the pot or baking in the oven."

"And carrot sticks and bread on the table," Sula reminded her.

"Kept the wolf from the door, that's all that mattered. I fed my children, their friends and anyone else who happened to be around, and there were no complaints. What's more, I seem to be doing the same thing here."

They sat together in the garden, recollections, memories, some Clara and Sula hadn't heard before, others they'd heard over and over again — never tired of them.

Sula brought the conversation back to Mannie. "How we looked forward to having our own place. I know you wanted us to stay with you, Mum, but a young couple like us needed to be independent, and for a short time we were. It all seems so unfair."

"Life isn't fair, Sula; when you get to my age you'll realize that. It's not fair you have to walk with sticks. It's not fair young men get killed in outrageous wars. It's not fair we've lost our home. Nothing's fair — never has been and never will be. Somewhere there's a plan, don't know if it's God's plan or just something I've dreamed up, but as each day passes I believe it more. We're loaned to each other for a certain amount of time, and then the loan is called in. Some of us are luckier than others. Don't ask me why; I haven't got the answer. We all loved Mannie, and he loved you." Nelly's voice wavered. "You'll be back with us now, and I'll make Wait and See and Roast Merkin, and you'll be strong and healthy again. You think you need us? Let me tell you, it's the other way around. We need you, my darling, and I may complain about all the people who turn up on our doorstep, but they keep me busy and make me feel useful, and they'll do the same for you. This bad time will pass. It will." Nelly stood up. "And now I have to go back in that house and face that perishin' rabbi."

Sidney came home from work that evening and went directly to the shiva to take part in evening prayers. He wasn't staying there, the bomb outside their house had been dug up and carted away, and where the crater had been there was now a large circle of black tar. "You wouldn't know anything had happened." That's what he said.

Hours later, as they were walking home, Clara gave him the news he'd been waiting for. "We've finished our work in Petersfield. I'm home to stay."

"What about Victoria?"

"She's very happy in Petersfield, but, well, I've given it a lot of thought and, though it's dangerous here and maybe not the best solution, I want her to be with us as a family. If the worst happens, then it will happen to all of us, and that may be a selfish way of looking at it, but it's what I think is the right thing for all of us to do."

I'm glad; it's what I've wanted all along. She's my little girl, and I miss her more each day." Sidney couldn't help the emotion he felt. "Sula says the school has reopened, so Victoria will have her old friends with her."

"I'll be working at the gallery in the West End during the week, we've discussed it, and I don't want to hear any more about it. Victoria can go to Mummy for lunch during the week, and Sula will take care of her after school. When the shiva's done I'll go to Petersfield to get her. If you like you can come with me."

"No," Sidney was quick to answer. "I don't want anything to do with that side of your life, Clara. I've trusted you, but when this war is over I want your attachment to Maze over, too." Sidney, tentatively slipped his arm around his wife's shoulders.

"It's not an attachment, Sidney, it's a job." Clara reminded him.

They walked up the hill, Sidney and Clara holding hands. They passed a man walking his dog and a couple of wardens having a cigarette in a sheltered alcove.

"Not too bad tonight," one of the wardens remarked.

"So far, so good," said the other one.

Someone put a light on in an upstairs bedroom.

"Put that light out!" the wardens shouted. "It's bad enough they come over here, we don't have to light their bloody way!"

At eleven o'clock the siren sounded. Sidney and Clara quickened their pace and reached home as search lights swept the sky for enemy planes.

"We'll take our chances tonight," Clara said as she climbed the dark stairs to their room. "I want to be in my own bed in my own house and not sleep in that rat trap under the table. No excuses when Victoria's back, but while she's away, I'll indulge in the luxury of a real soft, feathery bed."

Sidney locked the front door and put up the shutters in the front room, heavy wooden things they were. He lit the Ascot burner so they would have hot water in the morning, then he too climbed the stairs to follow Clara into their bedroom. For the first time in many weeks, he would not have to sleep alone.

CHAPTER 46

French Resistance in London

THE ART GALLERY on Bond Street turned out to be an exclusive establishment with an upper crust clientele. It was also a front for the French Resistance Movement in London. Clara's time spent in Chelsea placed her in good stead.

Clara loved being surrounded by beautiful art work, not just Paul's work, but major artists too — Degas and Renoir, Lautrec and Braque — paintings she had only before seen in the National Gallery. The fact that she didn't have to go back to Aldgate every evening, as she did when she worked on Paul's book, was a blessing. The Resistance work continued unseen at the back of the gallery, while bombs kept falling from the sky.

Paul stayed in London during the week when he wasn't off on some secret mission in Europe. Rogers helped out by moving pictures around, hanging the shows, being a gallery butler instead of a Cheyne Walk one. He had plenty of time on his hands. His services were no longer required in Petersfield. His beloved car had been put to sleep for the duration — on blocks, in a barn back in Hampshire.

Rogers took Clara aside a few days after she arrived. "If the client asks your opinion on a painting and you're not sure what to say, tell them art is a very personal choice; buying for investment is one thing, buying because you love what you see is another."

And that had been a help. She had to bluff her way most of the time, except when Paul's patrons came in, some of whom she recognized. Then life was easier.

The gallery was an old established company founded by two of the most eminent dealers in French Impressionist and modern art in the United Kingdom. Paul's work was shown there, much of it Clara recognized, including the woman in the field of sunflowers — the one he said he never wanted to sell.

When Clara worked at the back of the gallery, she locked the front doors. Serious collectors made appointments; those passing by rang the bell if they saw a painting they liked. Secret documents, hidden in paintings sent from France, were delivered without question, and undercover agents visited daily. One particular agent, Lucien Detois, she came to know quite well.

It was late in the afternoon and the gallery was closed when Clara first set eyes on Detois. At the time she had no idea who was persistently pressing the bell of the gallery's locked door. She walked from the back of the gallery to find the bell ringer was holding a rolled up canvas. Clara, thinking he was just another artist trying to sell his work, refused to let him in.

"Come back tomorrow."

"I cannot come back tomorrow," he said in a strong French accent.

"Then I am sorry. It will have to be another time."

The young man persisted.

She'd been warned there would be many like him; every artist needed someone to represent them, and they couldn't just walk in and expect to be seen. Appointments had to be made. On the other hand, secrets had been known to be leaked, and precautions were necessary. As she was waving the fellow away, Paul came out from the back room and recognized Lucien through the window.

"*Ouvres la porte. Je le connais.* Let him in. He's an old friend of mine."

"How was I supposed to know?" Clara asked. Had she let in a burglar, Paul wouldn't be quite so affable.

"In war time, my dear Clara, you trust your instinct. A Frenchman with a painting might give you a clue."

"A Frenchman with a painting could be a Nazi for all I know."

"He's French, not German."

"And I'm to know the nationality of the person standing outside?"

Paul ignored Clara's outburst. "This is Lucien Detois. He is an important liaison with our contacts in Paris."

"I apologize, Monsieur Detois; your friend does not always tell me who he is expecting."

"We artists are absent minded — please forgive him," Detois joked.

"That is one thing I am made aware of daily," Clara replied. "Still, we manage to get things done despite his occasional lack of recall."

"*Touché*," Paul said, admitting his transgression.

That evening Paul, Clara, Heinrich and Lucien had drinks at a local pub. Lucien spoke about the Germans in Paris. "They are buying up art for ridiculous prices and often just stealing it, taking it from museums, hanging the priceless works of art in the apartments they appropriate."

"What about the Jews?" Clara asked.

"It's terrible for them. They are rounded up and herded away in lorries, jammed in cattle cars, going God knows where."

"And you can do nothing about it?" Clara was horrified.

"We try, hide as many as we can, but we have little help. The aristocracy is hand in glove with the Germans, and many of our women have become their whores. Paris may not be bombed, destroyed like London, but it has lost its dignity. Parisians have cowered to the enemy. We capitulated too easily. It is said we are lovers, not fighters; I'm afraid I see us as lovers of the enemy, and I am ashamed of my countrymen."

On the train coming home that night Clara couldn't get Lucien out of her mind; the scenario he painted of France could happen in England. What if they lost the war? What if the Germans invaded? What would happen to the Jews in Britain? Would the government protect them? Would their neighbors give them away? My family? Me?

Lucien's description of Paris frightened her. The Germans were entrenched twenty miles from Britain's shores. They'd walked into France; the government put up no resistance. Marshall Petain was a collaborator. England's William Joyce, whom they dubbed Lord Haw Haw, broadcast from Germany against the Allied Forces, and Tokyo Rose spoke to the Americans — all of them traitors, all of them with an ever increasing following. Paul reckoned Germany was spread too thin. Churchill? He'd go down in flames if he had to. Britain had to win; the alternative didn't bear thinking about.

Much of the City of London had been destroyed. The Germans were concentrating on other major British towns and cities now. If they succeeded in reaching England's southern beaches, they'd camp in the small Hampshire villages — and Petersfield was one of them.

Though Clara had told Sidney her decision was to keep the family together, her main reason for bringing Victoria home was the threat of invasion.

Nelly, when asked why she'd allowed her granddaughter to be brought back from safety, continued to give her stock answer. "Youngsters shouldn't be with people they hardly know. It isn't natural!" No use letting on that Victoria was as happy as a pig in mud in Petersfield.

Sula, pampered by the family, felt trapped and frustrated. "I lost my independence the day Mannie died," she told Clara. "I can't do anything here — Mum watches me like a hawk, Dad treats me like an invalid. You've got to tell them to stop it; they won't listen to me."

Clara had the answer. "Now that Victoria's back home, I want you to look after her while I'm at work. Mum's got a lot on her shoulders; you can help me out — just be there for Victoria." Sula perked up. Victoria was the closest she would ever come to having her own child, and every evening after school they spent time together.

"I'm very bad at sums, Auntie Sula, and very good at art; Uncle Paul taught me — he's my best uncle since Uncle Mannie died." Victoria looked puzzled. "Every time I get used to somewhere, Mummy takes me away. Mrs. Gould told me I had to leave because Mummy said there was no hot water and she couldn't find a plumber — isn't that silly? We did have hot water, it just didn't come out of a tap! And Uncle Paul was going to show me how to draw a rose, and Mummy took me away from there also. I'll never learn how to milk a cow or draw a rose."

"Can't help with the cow," Sula confessed. "But I can show you how to draw a rose."

"Oh, all right, but you're not a proper artist like Uncle Paul."

"I might be one day, you never know."

Nelly finally accepted where she lived, even gave it a name: "The Other Twenty-One." And if it had any advantage over the East End, it had to be the lack of punters on the street.

Henry, as a last resort, asked Alfred the road sweeper if he knew any bookies.

"Naah," Alfred replied. "The only 'orses I have to deal with are them what do their business on me streets. Mind you, its good stuff; got a special bag for it and give it to your Victoria for 'er little garden."

LEATHER LANE CAME back to life. What could be salvaged from the bombed out stores nearby found their way to the market stalls, and one of them was Henry's. He returned to the bustle of London proper. Be it tattered and torn and very forlorn, it was his and Nelly's salvation; it got him out of the house and gave her some breathing space.

Solly Tenser still supplied him with goods. Henry paid for what he received and eagerly looked forward to the next delivery. The chemist shop re-oponed and supplied him with whatever became available. Yardley and Imperial Leather soaps were big sellers, as was 4711 Cologne, even though it was German. Hairpins, shampoos and hair nets did well, too. Henry's loyal customers had preference over passersby.

Special Treatment for Special People, was Henry's slogan, or You Look After Me, and I'll Look After You, or Under the Counter — another name for black market items.

Henry was always up to date.

His greatest concern was bath salts, couldn't get enough of them. They sold the minute he put them out, and you didn't have to be a genius to know why. Bath salts made the hard London water fragrant and soft, and as you were only allowed to immerse yourself in five inches of water in the bathtub once a week, you'd better get out of it smelling and feeling fresher than when you went in.

"Thank Gawd for Leather Lane," Nelly admitted to Sula. "Your dad was beginning to drive me insane. Couldn't find this, couldn't find that . . . "

SIDNEY TOOK VICTORIA to the pictures and sometimes to the theatre on weekends. When they weren't in the West End, they went on long walks in the fields near their home. They dug up carrots from the garden and fed them to the horses in the Rest Home for Tired Horses. They picked wildflowers and brought posies home to Clara. The Germans had the artillery to demolish buildings, but the trees still stood tall, and the hedge groves remained untouched. They walked for miles, he and his daughter and other children they collected on their way. Their fathers were away fighting in the war; Sidney, saved by factory work from active duty, became the neighborhood's surrogate Dad.

Meanwhile, Sula went into remission. She could walk more easily and managed to get around a bit, though still with the aid of a stick. Clara suggested she visit the gallery and promised to take her to Fortnum and Mason for lunch where Clara's ration book was registered. "It will do you good. We'll have a cup of coffee-chocolate and a pastry; it'd be a special treat for both of us."

Henry offered to go with Sula as far as Oxford Circus. "You've been stuck in the suburbs too long; get out and enjoy a change of scenery," he said. "I won't go as far as the gallery; it'll be far too grand for a man with a stall in Leather Lane."

Henry was probably right on that score; with him anything could happen — a bit like taking Liza Doolittle's dad to Belgravia. Not the right place for him. He'd probably put his foot in it, say the wrong thing and embarrass Clara. They loved their dad, but out of his own environment, who knows what he'd come out with? It was bad enough in the hospital when he asked the doctor why his daughter was in a ward with a load of cripples.

Henry was an outside market man, not an inside market man. "I'll tell you what, get a taxi from Oxford Circus — I'll pay for it — and you'll arrive in style."

"A bit extravagant, Dad."

"You enjoy yourself, Sula. Does me heart good to see you back in the land of the living."

It was only a short ride to the gallery from the station, but it would have been a tiring walk for Sula.

Clara greeted her as she came into the gallery. "You're here! I'm so pleased. This is my sister, Sula," Clara introduced her to Paul, Heinrich and Lucien. "She's the artist in the family, should be working here instead of me. She knows a lot more about art than I do."

"We can always find a place for you," Paul said as he settled Sula in a chair. It wasn't difficult to see why Clara had fallen in love with Paul. He was a smashing looking bloke and a charmer. The German fellow was a looker too. No wonder Clara was eager to go to work every day. If I didn't need these rotten sticks, I'd take him up on it, Sula thought.

"A few more weeks of treatment, then maybe I can work again," Sula answered, "but it will have to be somewhere closer to home.

Don't think I'd manage the journey every day. Thanks, anyway."

"Coffee? Tea?" Paul asked.

"That would be nice. Tea, please."

"Rogers will get it for you."

Finally Sula would get to meet Rogers, the butler. She'd never seen a real live one before. She imagined him to be like Jeeves, the butler in the P. G. Wodehouse books, and she wasn't disappointed.

Clara and Sula had lunch in the very posh tea room at Fortnum and Mason's, bone china plates, linen serviettes on a whiter than white tablecloth. Sula ordered fish, lemon sole on a bed of spinach, Clara had breast of chicken.

"So this is how the other half lives!" Sula glowed with anticipation of the meal she'd soon have in front of her.

"Not bad, eh?"

"Can you see Mum and Dad here?" The mental picture gave them the giggles.

"Dad would order winkles!" Sula declared.

"And, Mum, now let me see . . . " Clara tried to come up with a plausible suggestion and failed. "What do you think?"

"Jellied eels."

And that set them off again.

Heinrich joined them for coffee. He said to Sula, "I came with the intention of taking you to the Royal Academy, just across the road. But unfortunately it is closed. May I have the pleasure of taking you there one day soon?"

"I would like that." Sula seemed pleased to have Heinrich take an interest in her.

Back at the gallery, Sula sat at the front desk while Clara had work to complete at the back. She'd heard them speaking French, never realizing Clara was so proficient in the language. It seemed strange, there were people coming in having not the slightest interest in art and asking for Lucien or Paul. There was more in this than met the eye. She knew Clara was involved in secret work, but what was it? It had to have something to do with France and the war. This wasn't the time to ask questions, she decided, but she promised herself that she'd know some day.

Heinrich came to where Sula was seated. They talked. He told her how much she reminded him of Trude.

"Who is Trude?" she asked.

"Was — was Trude. The Germans murdered her." He told her how it happened. Sula listened, horrified. And he could see in her a kindred soul. Before they parted, Heinrich asked if he could come to visit her at her home. Clara, putting on her jacket, heard Heinrich's request and realizing Sula's hesitation, jumped in, "Of course you can. We'd love you to meet our family."

On the train home the subject of Heinrich came up again. "What were you thinking?" asked Sula. "What are we going to do with Dad?" Sula looked at Clara as if she had completely lost her mind.

"I'll deal with him," Clara promised. "Heinrich's lonely; he needs company, and he's certainly taken a shine to you."

"Well, he's very nice." Sula admitted.

"You have a lot in common."

"It's a bit early to start pairing us off. Besides, he's a German."

"I realize that, Sula. So what? Not every German is guilty, especially if they escaped the way he did. I think he's smashing. I don't care where he comes from. Makes no difference to me, and it shouldn't make any to you."

Clara had it in mind for Sula to meet Heinrich when she first suggested Sula come to the gallery with her; now she'd have to convince her parents he wasn't the enemy.

Trying not to anticipate a disaster in the making, Clara asked Heinrich, Sula, Henry and Nelly over for tea at her home in Woodside Park the following Sunday afternoon. Sidney was all for it. The garden was in good shape and he'd mowed the lawn, front and back. His roses gave off a sweet scent, and if it weren't for the bombed-out houses opposite, it was a perfect setting. Out came the deck chairs and the little side tables.

"The worst that could happen is Henry gives the Hitler salute," said Sula.

"I've warned him," Nelly promised.

"And as for you, Mum, you really can't complain. You've collected all types in the past: the sailor who left the parrot, the child of the cleaning lady, the butcher's uncle who came for a week and stayed a year, Eddie's illegitimate child, Henry's out-of-work cohorts, and I could go on, but I've run out of breath."

Nelly's life story was a play with a long list of characters, and the latest to join the cast would be Heinrich Luftmann, a German who desperately needed a friend and a family.

CHAPTER 47

Clara, Sidney and Victoria

THE LUFTWAFFE ADDED daytime raids to their night raids on London. Victoria spent the first three weeks after her return from Petersfield in the classroom at Frith Manor Primary School and the remainder of the school year in an air raid shelter under the school building.

"I liked it better at Uncle Paul's," she told Clara. "It's dark and smelly and cold down there, Mummy, and we can't see to read or write in our exercise books, and all we do is sing silly songs."

"It's safer in the shelter, darling. That's why you're there."

"It's safer with Uncle Paul, Mummy. That's why I was there."

Clara couldn't argue that point; instead, she made an appointment to meet with Mr. Giles, the headmaster, to see for herself.

"She's right, it's pretty awful down there," said Mr. Giles. "We're hoping to get stronger lights put in. There's nothing we can do about the dampness; give your daughter a cardigan. I have to tell you it's no picnic for us, either. When the raids are over and we let them out, they behave like wild animals, climbing everything in sight and running around like whirling dervishes. One of our teachers actually told me she thought they'd be safer left in the classroom, they get so many injuries on the playground!"

The next day at school Mr. Giles put his foot down. The children were marched into the assembly hall, told to sit on the floor and listen. "You will leave the shelters in an orderly manner. The shelter is unpleasant, I agree; it does not, however, give you permission to act like hooligans when you're let out. Insubordination will not be tolerated."

The girl next to Victoria asked what the word meant.

403

"Don't know, have to ask my Auntie Sula," Victoria whispered.

"You will all respect your teachers. You will play like normal, well-behaved children in the playgrounds, and if I hear any further bad reports, you will all stay after school and write one hundred lines repeating, 'There is a war on, and I will behave.'"

Teachers were instructed to involve their pupils in some creative way in the war effort. Miss Francis gave them knitting needles and wool, and showed them how to make socks. Victoria's effort, like her mother's effort before her, was knitted so tightly her teacher couldn't get two fingers into whatever it was Victoria produced. It certainly wasn't a sock. She suggested she unravel it and start again. Mrs. Costello, whose husband was in the army and always had a very sad look on her face, suggested the children collect waste paper and any reusable discarded objects.

When Nelly found Victoria raiding her dustbin, she had a fit. "What are you doing, Victoria?"

"I am helping to win the war."

"Don't be ridiculous. Get your head out of that bin."

"No, Grandma, teacher says we have to rescue anything that can be used again like rags and bottles and tins and jam jars . . ." Victoria kept going.

Nelly wasn't having it. "You tell that teacher for me, the disease you pick up from that dustbin ain't worth the few bits and pieces you find."

"But the tins can be melted down and made into airplanes."

"Have you any idea how many tins it would take to make one airplane? I'm not interested. Come in here, wash your hands and have your lunch." Nelly was losing patience.

"I'm a salvage collector, Grandma."

"You're my granddaughter, and you need disinfecting. Pull your head out of the dustbin and get in here immediately!" So much for Victoria's war effort. Nelly had spoken.

In actual fact Mrs. Costello was sorry she ever made the suggestion. Every day a heap of rubbish was dumped on her desk, and try as she may to get the authorities to collect it, they said they had far better things to do, and she'd be better advised to put it back where it came from.

Alfred the road sweeper was called in to take it away. "Don't know what you got it 'ere for in the first place," he said as he wheeled his cart through the school's corridors.

"We're helping to win the war," Victoria told her friend Alfred.

"What you going to do with all the stuff we collected?"

"He's going to dump it back in the rubbish heap where it belongs," Mr. Giles said as he walked by, "and you, Victoria, should be in the playground with your friends."

"Don't be too hard on her, they're only trying to help," Alfred defended Victoria. "Me? I've been picking up rubbish for thirty years, through two world wars. It don't look to me like we actually won the last one, and I ain't looking to me like we're anywhere near winning this one, so every bit of encouragement we can get won't do no harm!"

Miss Francis thanked him for helping out and sent him on his way. She asked her class if there was anything else they could think of doing to help. One child suggested they send a letter to Hitler asking him to stop dropping bombs. Another said they could give back their gas masks; they had only worn them once in a drill and that was two years ago. And as they didn't have to carry them anymore, why not send them to the army?

Mrs. Costello thought that was a great idea; however, having had the experience of the rubbish collection, she didn't think she could dispose of twenty-five gas masks very easily and told them to keep their gas masks just in case they might have to use them one day.

Victoria was at a loss as to how to win the war. She'd seen the Land Girls up at the farm opposite her school and wanted to be one of them. "I don't want to go to school anymore; I want to join the Land Army," Victoria announced when Clara got back from work one evening. "I'm going to tell Mr. Giles."

"You have to be seventeen, and you're not yet six," Clara informed her.

"But, I know about animals, and I like the uniform, and — "

"Sorry, Mr. Churchill says little girls must stay in school, and that's that," Nelly said and put an end to Victoria's Land Army conversation.

Still Victoria had the last word, saying "I hope the war lasts long enough for me to be a Land Army girl," and followed it by, "So there!"

If Nelly had heard her she would probably have got a clip 'round the ear.

So, the war continued without the help of Victoria.

If it wasn't incendiaries dropping out the sky, it was time bombs exploding wherever they fell. When a raid happened on her way back to Nelly's for lunch, Victoria would jump in the closest sand bin and stay there with her friends Anthony and Geoffrey until the all clear sounded. After the raids, Alfred the road sweeper kept the best bits of shrapnel for Victoria. Her collection was the envy of all her classmates.

AT THE FACTORY Sidney was told the rabbit skins he made into coats for the Russian soldiers were useless against the cold; they needed a thicker and denser fur. Julius applied and was granted permission to travel to America to purchase lambskins. "It will give him something to do other than sitting in the office on his backside," Sidney told Clara over supper. "He's either doing that or standing over me complaining."

"Isn't lamb easier to work on?"

"Yes, any short fur skin is."

"Then, it will be better for you too."

"I suppose so," Sidney reluctantly agreed, still envious of Julius. "Why he gets the perks and I get the work, I don't know, and he started to sing, 'It's the rich that gets the gravy, it's the poor that gets the blame. It's the same the whole world over, ain't it all a bloody shame.'"

"Well, there you are, and there's not much you can do about it," Clara declared.

A few weeks later a large parcel came from America. Victoria wanted to open it immediately.

"We will wait for Daddy, and we'll open it together," Clara told Victoria, who watched the clock. Time couldn't pass quick enough for her. Finally it reached six o' clock. She ran out of the house and halfway down the hill to meet Sidney.

"Daddy, Daddy, we got a parcel from America. Uncle Julius sent us a parcel," Victoria announced as she grabbed Sidney's hand and urged him up the hill.

Clara had the parcel in the dining room, ready for the grand opening. Victoria jumped around as Sidney revealed the contents of the American package, one item at a time. Out came Hershey's chocolate, chicken in a tin, nylons for Clara, biscuits, coffee and chewing gum.

Clara grabbed the nylons. "Those are mine. Now let's see about the rest of it. We'll take the chicken and the chocolate to Grandma; we'll keep the biscuits here for when we have visitors; and, Victoria, you can have the chewing gum to share with your friends. Grandma and Grandpa won't need chewing gum."

"I know. You can't chew gum with teeth that come out at night!" was Victoria's response.

"How do you know that?" Clara asked, amazed at Victoria's knowledge.

"Because they keep their teeth in a glass in the bathroom when they go to bed." And she didn't stop there. "Tell me how'd they get a chicken in a tin? Why do we have to share the chocolate? Why can Uncle Julius go to America, and we have to stay here?"

"Chatterbox, come here. We must share what we have; it's not right to keep it all to ourselves." Clara was being generous now.

"Oh, all right," Victoria begrudgingly agreed. "But you're keeping the stockings. Is that fair?"

Clara, stymied by the question, waited a few moments to answer. "Because Grandpa doesn't wear them, Grandma won't wear them and Auntie Sula can't wear them. Therefore, they're mine."

VICTORIA WAS ONE of just a few children whose father wasn't in the forces, and though she adored her dad, she felt a bit ashamed he stayed home while other dads were away in Europe fighting the war. She wanted Sidney to be a hero like Stewart's dad, who got a medal for being killed in action, and Ronnie's dad, who lost a leg. Not that she wanted him dead or amputated, it was just that when he told her he was making fur coats for Russian soldiers, it didn't sound very brave — in fact, it sounded stupid. And being number one stirrup pump wasn't exactly a title to be proud of.

Every morning when they said the Lord's Prayer in school, she prayed that her father, not the one in heaven, her father in Woodside Park, could be brave like other children's dads. She wanted him to do something very special to help win the war, and one day he did. He rescued Mrs. Jeynes from her burning house with his stirrup pump and the help of a lot of firemen. In Victoria's eyes, it was her brave dad who saved Mrs. Jeynes — and not only her, but Misty, Mrs. Jeynes' cat.

The entire neighborhood came out to watch the rescue. They didn't care there was an air raid in progress. They didn't mind the street was soaked and so were they. They all saw Victoria's dad lead Mrs. Jeynes and a singed Misty out of a burning house.

The next morning Victoria's dad was declared a hero, and it didn't matter he wasn't in Europe fighting the Germans; he was in London saving the English. Someone had to do it, and her dad had proved that he was that someone.

Epilogue

Epilogue

AFTER THE INCENDIARIES and the time bombs, Germany launched unmanned V1 and V2 rockets that approached in silence and were near impossible to intercept. It was yet another attempt to scare the living daylights out of the Brits.

"What will they think of next?" Nelly said as she wiped up the dishes from the previous night's supper.

"Haven't sent the kitchen sink, yet," Henry said, not bothering to look up from gluing one of the many pieces of china that had cracked on the journey from Aldgate to Woodside Park.

Nelly turned to Clara. "How much longer you suppose your job will last, Clara? I can't see an art gallery doing much in the way of sales under these conditions, and what's more you're putting yourself in unnecessary danger every day. Give it up before it gives you up."

Clara agreed that sales at the gallery were not good. On the other hand she could not let on to her family why she had to be there. Sales were of secondary importance to work being carried out in back by Heinrich and Paul. Still, few could get one over on Nelly. She was right; purchasing art was not a priority for anyone in wartime London.

"Look, Mum, I could be killed crossing the street or from something falling out of the sky — it's not a matter of where you are, it's more . . . "

"I know, it's more of when your number's up — but what if your guv's number's up, and yours isn't?"

"I'm not giving up my job, Mum."

Nelly's demands came to an abrupt end the day a V2 landed in the London suburb of Southgate, less than three miles from where she now lived. "What's the use of us being stuck out here?" she demanded of Sula. "There ain't a safe haven left in the whole of the British Isles; we might as well find lodgings back in the East End. They've done with bombing there!"

"That's because there isn't anything left to bomb, Mum, nothing, not Twenty-One, not the High Street. It's all gone, flattened and unlivable. Put it out of your mind — the East End, as you knew it, is finished.

"It'll come back. You mark my words."

(It did come back — but not the way Nelly foresaw it would.)

CLARA KEPT HER job at the gallery despite Nelly's pleadings, acting as Paul's liaison when he made his frequent undercover trips to Europe. At the same time he was involved in the Resistance Movement and in the British Home Guard. Once lovers, Clara and Paul were now friends who knew instinctively they could depend on each other in one of the most difficult times in London's long history.

Clara missed the challenge of Chelsea. The Bond Street gallery, a wide open, inviting space displaying irresistible art, couldn't be compared to the intimacy of Paul's studio at Cheyne Walk. She'd tried to leave the emotional pull of the Chelsea years behind, but they were still there. They were there when she compared his sophistication to her family's working class background, and they were there when she said good night to Victoria and recognized her strong resemblance to Paul, and they were still there when she sat working side by side with him in the gallery.

Paul's extraordinary effect would last throughout her life and remain forever in her heart. He'd helped her become the woman she saw in the mirror everyday, the rough edges once needed to survive in Whitechapel had vanished. Though she never denied her background, Clara no longer fit in; she'd gained worldliness and poise.

The young girl who gingerly walked into the posh house in Cheyne Walk just a few years before was now a woman of consequence, innocence replaced by worldly understanding. Paul was her mentor and her lover — a man who despised war yet would never renege on his duty to his adopted land. He'd written about war as passionately as did the poets of his time — Rupert Brook, Wilfred Owen, Siegfried

Sassoon; and, like them, he needed to lay bare in his own way the horrors and futility of war.

Together she and Paul had completed *A Frenchman in Khaki,* in which Churchill had written in his preface, "It should be acceptable to the artists and the soldiers of the two great nations whose cause of freedom its author so ardently espoused."

Everyone who read it recognized the insanity of war, and yet here they were in the middle of another one. Winston Churchill had warned the earlier Baldwin government and then Chamberlain's over and over again to sit up and take notice of German rearmament. Now at the helm as Prime Minister, Winston was taking charge of a situation that might have been avoided if they'd listened to him. Eventually they did; only by then it was too late, and, ironically, because of their delinquency Clara was back working with Paul again.

Paul's friends were frequent visitors to the gallery. Too old to serve in the armed forces, some of them were offered positions at the War Ministry. During lunch hour they'd pop in to have a chat. Even Eleanor, the woman who'd praised the Nazis at that party Clara would never forget, turned up asking for Mr. Maze.

Clara despised her. She looked upon her as a turncoat, not to be trusted. From entertaining Nazis at her soirees, Eleanor had become an avid Churchill supporter and even found an American Army Captain to marry.

"When this war's over she'll take on New York and leave us and London far behind," Paul predicted.

Clara divided her working day between the front of the gallery and the operations taking place at the back, a confusion of artistic creations and destructive war, only this time the war was on her doorstep. Having written so much about conflict, she had a real understanding of it. Certainly the war they were fighting now was very different from the first one — soldiers weren't just cannon fodder fighting in mud filled trenches.

Meanwhile, thinking about days long gone as she sometimes did, she nodded and told herself that leaving Abbott had been the right decision, even if the family, at the time, thought she was wrong. She'd stood up for his Jewish clients, just as Mannie stood up to Oswald Mosley. Nothing for the dumb, Nelly always said, and with that in mind she spoke out. Clara believed her reward was finding Paul. Leaving Paul could hardly be compared; it was the most difficult decision of her young life, an emotional struggle and a choice she knew she must make. Phases, they were phases in her ongoing search, serendipity, something that happens along the way. Life hands out its gifts and punishments in mysterious ways.

PAUL, RARELY ALONE with Clara, nevertheless often returned mentally to the days when they were rarely apart. No one could ever replace Clara. She was his unexpected love at a time when love was absent from his life and his marriage crumbling. Clara brought joy and wit and warmth into his life. A short but memorable encounter, and one he would not forget. Now he had Maggie, the pretty lass sent down from Scotland to join the Cheyne Walk staff. She loved him, she looked after him; Maggie was all he needed now.

On school holidays Clara's special treat was to take Victoria to the gallery. Paul, only too pleased to have an excuse, took time off to play with her. Together they'd go to the park, watch the horses ride on Rotten Row and dip their toes in the Serpentine. If it were one of those days when Mr. Hitler decided to attack, they'd run for shelter to the nearest tube station. Best of all he'd buy her chocolate with his sweet coupons, and that, perhaps, was the greatest gift anyone could ever give to any child in wartime London.

"I wish I could draw like you," Victoria said to Paul when he took her around the gallery explaining the paintings.

"Ah, but I think it would be much better if one day you could write like your mother," he suggested.

"I can't write very well yet."

"You will."

"Remember the toy soldier you gave me, Uncle Paul? I pretend he's in the army and does very brave things. He comes with me every night into the Morrison Shelter, and he looks after me."

"That's what soldiers are supposed to do. Some go over to fight in other countries, and some stay here to look after us."

"My daddy's not a soldier, but he's also a very brave man."

"I know, your Mother told me about him. You are a very lucky girl to be his daughter."

There were times Paul sensed he might have fathered Victoria, though neither he nor she would ever know. For Victoria he was the uncle who spoiled her in Petersfield, taught her to fish in the stream and walked with her in the country lanes of Hampshire.

WHEN THE WAR was finally over and victory declared, Clara gave up her job at the gallery, and she and Paul went their separate ways. Paul, with Maggie by his side and a paintbrush in his hand, continued to be the bon vivant, the raconteur and a friend to all who loved to be in his company.

Clara put aside her ambition, but never her curiosity, and found her way back to Sidney.

SHORTLY AFTER THE war, Henry died, not knowing whether the horse he backed in the Derby won or lost, and Nelly carried on, away from the surroundings she'd loved so well, in a little house she shared with Sula in the suburbs. Never quite the same, Nelly did what she could to recreate the warmth and love that emanated from Twenty-One, though it hadn't the flavor or the character of that old place. It was too new, not steeped in history like Twenty-One, no wooden stairs that led up to her parlor, the parlor where Boadicea mimicked words no decent human being should be forced to hear, where Solly Tenser brought in suspect merchandise, where Henry did his football pools and where Mannie never gave up his Communist manifesto and foisted it upon all who entered. But it was Nelly's special window at Twenty-One Aldgate that looked out on the ever crowded High Street she missed the most.

AS FOR SIDNEY, at the end of his life, wrapped in a blanket, seated in his bedside chair, Sidney looked out on the magnolia tree he'd planted from a seedling, now in full blossom, its perfume wafting into his room by a gentle breeze. He recalled all the flowers he'd planted over the years, flowers he had grown for Clara — they were all for her. He couldn't remember if he'd told her that. He hoped he had. His garden and his wife had been his life — there was the Arsenal Football Club, too; they'd won their last match, they were doing all right.

Peter, Victoria's son, came into his room, "How you feeling, Grandpa?" He was a handsome lad. Thoughtful too.

"A little tired, going to rest my eyes. Why don't you take your grandma for a walk in the garden later on when she has the time; it's such a lovely day — pity to waste the sunshine."

Peter was gone just a few moments when Sidney called out for Victoria.

"What is it, Dad?"

"There's money in my black shoes at the back of the wardrobe and a few hundred pounds under the mattress. Everything else is in order; your mother will want for nothing." The blanket was falling off his shoulders.

Victoria came in and put the blanket back where it belonged. She felt his hands — they were icy cold. "I'll get you a hot water bottle."

"No, won't need one, not now. Just promise, promise me you will take care of your mother. She's been my love and my life for sixty-five years, and . . ."

Sidney's hand dropped to his side, his eyes closed. The last words on his lips were those of concern for Clara. Never an ambitious man, he was who he'd always been, a man whose love affair with his wife lasted until the day he died.

About the Author

Author/Screenwriter Patricia Friedberg was born in London, attended Henrietta Barnett School and The London School of Journalism. She married a South African doctor, and together they left for Johannesburg where they stayed for a short time before settling in both Northern and Southern Rhodesia, known now as Zambia and Zimbabwe. They first resided in Hwange, a mining town in Southern Rhodesia. With no legal experience, she was employed there as Clerk of the Court, dealing with tribal and European law. After two years, they moved to Salisbury (Harare).

Her government connections in Hwange allowed her to travel freely into the rural/bush accompanied by a photographer. Her articles were published and produced as *Tribal Documentaries* by the newly formed Rhodesian TV. In addition to her talent as a writer, Patricia wrote and produced a ballet, titled *The Return*, which was performed in Harare and later in Durban, South Africa. In the 1960s, political unrest continued in Rhodesia. For the safety of their children the family reluctantly left Africa to settle in the United States, first in Baltimore and then in Milwaukee. In Milwaukee she was commissioned to write two docudramas, *Dwellings* and *Babble* for Public Television.

Patricia attended a playwriting course at Marquette University where her first play *Masquerade* won the Marquette University Play Writer's Award. She established a Children's Theatre Arts Program, designed to encourage youngsters to write and perform in their own creative works. She enrolled her own four children in the program. She produced and directed two works of her own, *Is Today Tomorrow* and *Hamba Wena*, an African piece about a child trying to find his way in a foreign land. Further plays, *Tenement Torment* and *Through the Eye of the Little Green Buddha*, were both performed by a local theatre group.

Patricia wrote for the *Milwaukee Jewish Chronicle* and was moderator of "People of the Book" on WTMJ -TV (NBC affiliate) Milwaukee. She interviewed major celebrities, politicians and well-known personalities in the art and music world.

In Florida she wrote a weekly column, "From Land's End to Land's End," for the *Longboat Observer*.

She wrote a series of children's books, titled *The Alfred Stories*, which were reminiscences of her own childhood in London during World War II, a theme Patricia returns to in the novel *21 Aldgate*.

Studying scriptwriting independently, she wrote the screenplay *Journey from the Jacarandas*, a feature film which began filming in Zimbabwe in 1997–98 and was interrupted due to government sanctions.

Children's books, titled *Dear Sammie* and *Dear Jake . . . a letter from a grandparent to a child of divorcing parents*, were co-authored with her daughter Adrienne Meloni and published in 2008. Her screenplay based on the book *21 Aldgate* is to become a major Feature Film. Patricia is currently working on her second novel, *Rhodesia – A Distant Land* (working title).

The author can be scheduled for appearances (including SKYPE) by emailing legaciesliterary@gmail.com.

Visit her blog at http://21aldgate.blogspot.com.

Discussion Points

- What did you think *21 Aldgate* was about?

- What did you enjoy most about the book?

- How does this book compare to other books in the same genre?

- Which part of the story held your interest the most?

- Which of the characters would you like to meet? Why?

- With which (if any) of the characters did you identify?

- Some of the characters had to make a choice that had moral implications, would you have made the same decision? Why? Why not?

- How does the setting figure into the book? Did you feel you were experiencing the time and place in which the book was set?

- What are some of the book's themes? How important are they?

- How are the book's images symbolically significant? Do the images help to develop the plot and help to define characters?

- Did the book end the way you expected?

CPSIA information can be obtained at www.ICGtesting.com
Printed in the USA.
LVOW101520200912

299637LV00012B/43/P